SandStarr Publications
A division of SandStarr Entertainment
2500 Sheridan Rd., PMB 402
Zion, IL 60099
www.sandstarrpublications.com

This is a work of fiction. Names, characters, places, and events either are the product of the author's imagination or are used fictitiously.

Open Book
ISBN 10: 0-9826-6971-2
ISBN 13: 978-0-982-66971-6

Front cover design by Philip H. Kingsley (a.k.a. 5th Realm)
Back cover design by Skye Sanders

Open Book

By Skye Sanders

For Jacob

Open Book

Prologue

[Dear Diary],

    Somewhere along the line, adults forget what it's like to be in high school. Let me remind you. What you wear matters, how you wear it matters, how you wear your hair matters, who you date (or don't *date) matters-to make a long story short, and so we're not here all year, everything superficial you can think of matters. Everything worth a damn doesn't. There are those intelligent few who realize that most superficial elements have short life spans, but knowing this information in your adolescent years does nothing to help you then. It doesn't relieve you of feeling humiliation ever again, doesn't stop childish idiots from hurling spitballs at you.*

    In high school I didn't dress up in stylish clothes. My family didn't have the money to support a stylish wardrobe, fancy car, or extravagant parties. I wasn't popular, wasn't a part of what was considered to be the "in crowd," and maybe that would have been all right if I'd been a brainiac, or even the least *bit interested in my studies. I hadn't been.*

    I didn't fit in with the brain dead cheerleaders or *the geniuses. I was truly alone in my adolescent years. I had no friends to invade the mall with and no boyfriend to get caught making out with in the dingy den of my family's one-story house. Instead, I spent my personal time babysitting the neighbors' kids and writing anything from journals to poems to short stories.*

    That was my life: going to school, nearly flunking out of it, and babysitting tiny terrors. There were nights I'd sit on my windowsill and naïvely wish for better, or at least the chance to be happy. At times I'd cry because I felt I wasn't pretty enough or smart enough or interesting enough for anyone to like me. As time went on, I came to accept the morbid fact that some people were destined to be happy and some were destined to be miserable. I figured I was doomed to be thrown into the batch of miserables.

There was a day, and I remember it well, when I vowed I would do something with my life. I was sitting at my desk in health class (fifth period) and I was writing a poem about the health teacher, Mr. Carson.

Ethan Carson was tall and lean, well-built beneath the button-down shirts and slacks that he often wore. There weren't many females encased in the walls of Beach Park High who didn't have a crush on this man, students and faculty alike. He was fresh out of college, twenty-four years old, and 6'5" with dark brown hair that he kept short. Sapphire blue eyes blazed from beneath frothy lashes. He taught health, coached our school's varsity basketball team, and still had time to spare for individual students who had issues they needed to talk about.

I was so engrossed in the poem I was writing about this man that I barely felt the spitballs littering my hair, the top of my head, and back of my neck. It wasn't an uncommon occurrence to have objects thrown at me in the classroom, so maybe I'd just grown used to it. I didn't even realize spitballs were caught in my hair and the collar of my lavender polo shirt until the entire classroom (with the minor exception of Mr. Carson) erupted in laughter.

In that health classroom, I was dangerously close to having a nervous breakdown. Something in me snapped. The laughing around me faded and my vision blurred. I fumbled underneath my seat for my backpack; once my hand found it, I rose from my desk. I walked down the aisle of desks, paused in front of Mr. Carson, and gave him an apologetic look before calmly walking to the classroom door. I opened the door, stepped through it, and proceeded to slam the door shut. I slammed that door with all my might. I poured all of the pain and humiliation I'd ever felt in my entire life into that single motion. I slammed the door so hard that it strained against its hinges, the heavy thrumming sound reverberating through the desolate, second-floor hallway.

There were "oohs" and shocked gasps on the other side of that door. I can't honestly say I remember what I was thinking at that exact point in time. I stood in front of that door in the empty hallway and dropped my backpack to the floor. I lifted my hands to my hair and carefully removed the scattered spitballs, one by one. Then, leaving my books and backpack behind in a cloud of dust, I ran.

A minute or so later I was sobbing against a narrow, beige locker when I heard running footsteps approaching me. I could barely see through the veil of tears clouding my eyes, but after wiping the tears away I could see it was Mr. Carson. I opened my mouth to speak, to explain myself or apologize for disrupting his class, but before I could speak, he did.

"Are you all right?" he asked, lines of worry masking his face.

The first words out of his mouth had been an expression of concern for my well-being. I thought he had hunted me down to verbally abuse me for nearly obliterating his classroom door into a bunch of splinters. Instead, he'd left his classroom full of students to check on me and make sure that I was okay.

To this day, ten years later, I still don't know why I opened up to him the way that I did. I nearly told him my life story, how I was an outcast and how high school was hell for me.

Even now I can picture him, leaning against the lockers and listening intently to every word I had to say. Dark hair ruffled, crimson button-down shirt untucked, deep blue eyes understanding and sympathetic.

When I stopped talking what seemed like hours later, I pursed my lips, all of a sudden feeling like an idiot. He continued watching me for a few more seconds and then said, "You're young. You have your entire life ahead of you. What happens to you in high school, does it matter? Yeah, it matters-while you're in high school. You're going to leave this school and become something great." He added, "You write your stories and poems in my class all the time."

I froze, because I hadn't known that he was aware of my writing.

"I'm not lecturing you about it. Writing is what you do. True artists-their craft is their poison and their antidote. By that, I mean it's like an addiction. It's what drives an artist and motivates him or her. They go to sleep thinking about their craft and wake up thinking about their craft. It controls them, you know? That's the poison aspect of it. The antidote aspect of it is that while their passion rules them, the end product is usually worth all of that, because they've created a piece of art.

"Let me ask you this," he said. "If you weren't treated as badly as you are and didn't feel the way you do about life...would you even write as much as you do, if you wrote at all? No. If you were accepted by the 'in' crowd, you'd be laughing it up with them day in and day out. You'd be misbehaving in my classroom the way they do. You wouldn't be-"

The bell signaling the end of the period cut his sentence short. He turned his head and I remember thinking, I wouldn't be what, wouldn't be what? Please finish the sentence, I need you to.

Kids flooded out of the classrooms and Mr. Carson turned back to face me. A small smile curved his lips and he leaned forward a bit to whisper, "You wouldn't be as special as you are. Get your grades up, stop cutting classes, and I guarantee you'll be somebody when you leave here. If I didn't think so, I would *have gotten on your case about writing stories in my class. Chances are those kids who harass you will be nobodies. I hate to say that about students of mine, but it's true. Don't let them get you down like this. Let it inspire you to create something magical."*

Those were the wisest words I'd ever heard. You know what? I followed his advice. I wrote about everything I could, and buckle up your seatbelt, Diary. Because this is the diary of Paige Turner.

✍

Paige Turner was having a bad day. It started with not being able to find a pair of black silk panties that seemed to have been swallowed by her bed. It continued when she returned from the master bathroom to her bedroom to find her current boyfriend (also famed soap star actor and self-proclaimed wanton sex god), reading her diary with an expression on his face that she mistook for awed contemplation. Her heart shot into her throat and she couldn't seem to get across the bed fast enough. She seized the diary in a death grip and yanked it to her chest. "What the hell do you think you're doing?" she demanded vehemently, one hand gripping her fuzzy pink towel and the other hand clutched around the diary. She rolled off the bed and placed the diary in the top drawer of a cherry wood bureau.

Brandon Davies looked up at her with a slight wrinkle to his nose. He dragged a manicured hand through his ear-length dirty blonde hair. "It-it-it-" he stammered, aimlessly gesturing with his hand as he spoke. He rubbed his chin and narrowed his eyes thoughtfully. "All of that didn't really happen," he finally said. He turned incredulous eyes on the brunette standing near the four-poster bed dressing. "This is one of your books or something, right?"

She let the towel fall to the floor and moved around the room while collecting articles of clothing. After snapping a bra around her breasts and torso, she pulled an olive green turtleneck sweater from a bureau drawer and brought it down over her head. She tentatively peeked at him through the neck hole in the sweater. Her cinnamon-colored, elbow-length hair was pulled up in a topknot and bounced as she moved around the bedroom dressing. "No, everything in that really happened," she insisted. "Actually, I'm thinking about publishing that. Most of that is typed up and saved on disk. I was thinking that if I published it, it might help someone who was in the same situation I was in back in high school."

"You're thinking of publishing *that*?" He laughed and sat up straighter in bed, shirtless with cream-colored sheets bunched around his waist. "Now you're just being ridiculous."

She stood at the foot of the bed, folding her arms across her chest. "I'm being ridiculous? Elaborate, Bran."

"You're Paige Turner, famed romance novelist. No one reads biographies-and if they did, they wouldn't want to read one about some..." He let the sentence trail off as he shook his head, looking for the right word.

"About some what?" she pressed, her voice growing tight and her expression growing stony.

"Some nerd!" he said exasperatedly. "If you're going to publish that, you don't have to publish all three hundred and some odd pages of it. You could publish seven words on one page of paper. 'I was a nerd in high school.' You could make it a flyer, it'd cost a lot less."

He thought for a few moments and added, "Actually you still have to *be* a nerd to be writing a diary. You're twenty-seven."

"And?"

"Twenty-seven year olds don't write diaries. They *live* life. They don't spend hours on end *writing* about their lives. Paige," he said and swiveled around to drop his legs over the side of the bed. He pulled one of her hands into his and pulled her closer to him. "Don't publish that. You'll make a fool of yourself. You'll ruin this awesome career you've made for yourself. You don't want to *do* that. This would completely and totally *ruin* you. I mean...okay, fine, so you write a journal. You know, a journal is something to be kept private. If no one knows about it, I guess you're not *that* much of a nerd."

She released her hair from its topknot and said, "Well while you're thinking on that, I'm going to make breakfast."

"No need, babe. I've been thinking."

A worried look took over her features and she moved to stand beside him. "You didn't hurt yourself, did you? Are you all right?"

Not catching the sarcastic tone in her voice, his brows furrowed and he shook his head. "No, I'm fine. But maybe we should see other people, you know? We *have* been dating for three months now. And..."

She stared down at him in disbelief. "You're dumping me because of my *diary*, Bran?"

He stood up from the bed, firmly holding the sheets to his body. "No, no it's not that."

"You're not worried about me publishing this and ruining my career," she continued, her eyes narrowing with suspicion. "You're worried about shit hitting the fan and the *Enquirer* running stories that you date someone who used to be a geek."

He stood completely still, looking down at her. His Adam's apple bounced a few times, and he finally laughed. "Look, I have to think about my reputation, all right? My public is fickle. Something like this comes out and they're back to obsessing over Brad Pitt or Tom Cruise. You understand, don't you Paigie?"

"*Don't* call me Paigie," she said in a voice so cold that the temperature in the room was knocked down a few degrees. She stepped up close to him and snatched the sheets from his hands. Her gaze drifted down south of his waist and she sneered nastily. "Your public finds out about *that* and how clumsy you are with it and they're back to obsessing over Brad Pitt. Get the fuck out of my house."

She watched him collect his clothes with his face flushed red and nostrils flaring. A few times he hesitated and looked at her, obviously wanting to say something. Her steely gaze didn't allow room for comment. She stood on tiptoe to peer out the window of her front door and watched him shuffle to his car. As he drove off, she pressed her back against the door and cried.

"You're not crying over losing Brandon," Marissa Montana told her later while leaning towards the vanity mirror and applying eyeliner to her eyelids. She was a tall, leggy woman with deep bronze skin attributed to having a Venezuelan mother and African-American father. Her eyes were hazel, contrasting marvelously with her complexion. Her hair was thick, curly and wild. She was dressed in a skin-tight blue halter-top and a black knee-length skirt. The heels encasing her feet matched the top she was wearing. On more than one occasion, Paige had wished to possess her best friend's keen fashion sense. "You're crying more over the fact that he rejected you after finding out a very personal side of you."

"Could be," Paige allowed. She paced around her bedroom with her arms folded across her chest. After reconsidering her best friend's words, she added, "More than 'Could be,' you're probably right. Any advice on what I should do?"

Marissa sighed and looked at Paige for a few moments. "Normally, I would prescribe for you to come to the club with me tonight so you can meet a handsome stranger and let him turn you inside out," she said, managing to sound very serious, "but you've had nothing but mind-blowing sex for the past three months, so that's not what's going to cure you. The only thing that will cure you is a *real* romance with someone. You need to find a good man who'll take care of you and care about your feelings. You know, all that shit."

Paige arched an eyebrow, swallowing the urge to laugh. She wouldn't quite call Brandon's lovemaking *mind-blowing*. "*That's* your prescription?"

"Hell, Paige, I don't know," Marissa said, shrugging and scoping out her reflection in the mirror. "You're supposed to be the pro at this. You write romance novels for Christ's sake. You asking for advice on cures for the heart is like Michael Jackson asking for advice on dance moves."

Paige walked over to the bed and collapsed on it, resting her chin on her arms and trying to forget what she and Brandon had been doing on this bed the previous night. "You're *right*. I *should* know what to do. I'm a romance novelist who's never been in love. That's...that's *pathetic*."

Marissa didn't say anything.

"They have a saying. 'Write what you know.' I've spent my career writing about something I don't know," Paige went on.

"Maybe you should go on hiatus," Marissa suggested. "Do some intense research for the next book you come out with, you know? Go on some orgasmic vacation, get *inspired.*"

If only, Paige thought, lying on her back and staring up at the ceiling. A vacation was exactly what she needed. She was tense and stressed out, and at the moment all she wanted to do was take a trip to some secluded island and hole herself up in a hotel room with a substantially large stack of movies to watch at her leisure. She wasn't even sure if she would want to bring her laptop with her. She wanted a vacation from writing as well. She wanted a break from writing and deadlines, ex-boyfriends, being dumped...she wanted a vacation from herself.

Marissa had been talking and turned to look down at her friend. She clucked her tongue sympathetically and sat down on the bed next to Paige. "It's going to be all right. Brandon was *nothing.* I know you're not depressed over him."

"I don't know why I'm depressed, but I am," Paige said without taking her eyes off of the ceiling. "I should be *happy.* I'm a writer, something I've always wanted to be. I have awesome friends, an awesome career. My romance life is non-existent, always has been if you want to get technical. Brandon wasn't romantic. No man I dated before him was romantic. No one I've dated completely swept me off of my feet and made me ecstatically happy. I don't know how it feels to be that happy. I probably never *will* know how it feels to be that happy."

Marissa's eyes widened dramatically. "Now you're depressing *me,* Paige."

"I do need a vacation, I do."

"So take one," Marissa urged, nudging her friend's shoulder.

"Shane wouldn't hear of it, 'Rissa. He's always preaching on and on about how my career hangs in the balance and how I need to stay focused. I have two novels I'm supposed to be shelling out, and they have to carry the Shane seal of approval before I can even *consider* any sort of vacation."

Shane Luciani was her agent, more critical when it came to Paige's work than her editor was. He was brutally honest about everything, always having an opinion on something, an egotistical Italian who thought he was God's gift to women. He was chauvinistic, arrogant, and vulgar, with a severe case of commitment-phobia. While he lacked tact and discretion, it was refreshing to hear a man express honesty when it came to his intentions, and Shane did just that. He had no qualms whatsoever with approaching a woman and leaning over to whisper in her ear, "Here's what I want: you underneath me tonight, and possibly tomorrow morning, no strings, no guaranteed phone calls the next day, no guarantees you'll even ever see me again."

Marissa and Shane flirted mercilessly with each other, but whenever he was out of earshot, Marissa would tell Paige, "If he and I ever hooked up, I'd have him wear, like, five condoms. I don't know where his dick has been."

Now, Marissa was glancing at her watch and twisting it around her wrist anxiously. "I have to get going, girlie," she announced. "You're sure you don't want to come to the club with me?"

"I'm too old to be going to clubs."

"Hey, hey, now if you're too old to go to clubs, so am I and I won't be hearing that," Marissa admonished.

Paige sighed and shook her head.

"I'll give you a call later, okay?" Marissa asked, looking concerned. "Make sure you haven't jumped off of any roofs or anything."

[Dear Diary],

As of today, Brandon and I are over. He dumped me because he didn't want his fans to find out that he was dating a (former) nerd. Maybe I still am a nerd, I don't know. The only thing I do *know is that I shouldn't have been with Brandon Davies in the first place. We're nothing alike, we have nothing in common, and contrary to Marissa's assumption, he's not good in bed. God, when I lay everything out on the table like that, I have to stop and ask myself,* Why was I with him? *Was he just something to do, a way for me to pass the time?*

Marissa's advice is to go out and have a real romance, but nowadays I'd rather chew off my own arm than re-emerge into the singles' scene. We did *have a revelation, though, while she was misdiagnosing me. I'm a romance novelist who's never been in love. How pathetic is that?*

Well...hold on a minute, that isn't necessarily true. I have been in love before, but it was years ago. It was probably more along the lines of puppy love, because I was only seventeen. The teacher I caught Brandon reading about, Mr. Carson...

Honestly, I don't know if I ever got over whatever feelings I might have had for him. I still think about him, wonder what he's doing at any given minute...I even compare the men I date to him. Mr. Carson was my ideal man. He had all of the qualities I was and still am looking for, but he was my teacher so enough of that daydreaming

Back then, nothing could ever happen between him and I. By now, he's probably married anyway with a truckload of adorable kids. Which...would be good, because then it would be safe to assume that he was leading a happy life. I definitely want him to be happy. I'm happy *he's happy. Then again, I'd probably be* happier *if he were happy with me. God, Diary, would you help me out?*

Chapter One

The next day was a frosty February Friday. Paige cracked her eyes open and regretted it instantly. Her stomach was growling at her in disapproval of the pint of Cherry Garcia ice cream she'd stuffed into it the night before in her bout of depression. The phone on her nightstand shrilled in her ears and her already-pounding head throbbed in protest. She grabbed the cordless phone and pushed the ON button. "Yes?" she croaked into the receiver.

"I hope you didn't forget about our lunch date," chirped a cheery voice.

"Of course not, Evie," Paige lied, glancing at the clock next to the phone base. It was eleven o' clock in the morning. "I'll see you guys there." She hung up the phone, tempted to drop back into bed and hibernate for the rest of the month.

Evelyn Roberts, a friend of Marissa's and Paige's since college, was the stereotypical blonde-haired, blue-eyed woman you love to hate and hate to like. In high school and college she'd been a cheerleader; now, she was a presumably happy housewife married to a man who was too rich for his own good. Her days were filled with whatever she wanted them to be filled with. She had the freedom to go to the gym, eat Bon-Bons, and watch soap operas for the vast majority of the day.

With this fortunate life she'd been blessed with, she still had the nerve to consider cheating on her husband, which Paige couldn't figure out for the life of her.

"Yes, he treats me good, yes, he's good in bed, and yes, he's like...the most perfect man I'll ever find probably," Evelyn would say, "but maybe for once I want something that *isn't* perfect."

Paige was supposed to be meeting Evelyn, Marissa, and another friend of theirs, Deana Wheaton, for lunch. They'd all attended college together and had been friends ever since. Marissa was wild and crazy, pushing her friends to do things they'd never have even considered hadn't she suggested it. Evelyn was feminine and self-absorbed; in her mind, everything revolved around her and her happiness. Deana had an aggressive personality and was known for taking no bullshit from anyone. Every other week she was bashing men and talking about what horrible creatures they were.

Despite their flaws or indulgences, they were Paige's friends and she wouldn't trade them for anything in the world.

The luncheon was held at a restaurant called Claire's in a western suburb of Chicago. As soon as Paige walked through the doors of the establishment, various mouth-watering scents attacked her nostrils. Deana, Marissa, and Evelyn were already seated at a table when Paige arrived, clad in bell-bottom jeans and a sky blue sweater. After dropping her oil-black leather jacket on the back of the vacant chair, she pulled the chair away from the table and dropped into it.

Deana arched a brow. "Look who decided to join us."

Paige rolled her eyes as she scooted her chair forward. "Give me a break, guys. I had a horrible day yesterday."

"Marissa told us," Evelyn said, her blue eyes wide and expressive. She was looking exceptionally gorgeous in a cotton candy pink short-sleeved turtleneck and black slacks. Her usually straight blonde hair was curled into spiraled ringlets. "You and Brandon are over? Because of your *diary*? He's such a prick."

Paige cut a look across the table to Marissa.

"You're shocked Marissa told us?" Deana asked. "You know she can't hold water, let alone juicy gossip."

Marissa's jaw dropped in shock.

"I see you guys ordered without me," Paige observed, glancing around the busy restaurant for a waiter.

"We got tired of waiting," Deana said, shrugging. Her dark brown hair was pulled back with a hair clip and her face was devoid of makeup. She was classically beautiful, with slender eyebrows that arched over dark, luminous eyes. The cerulean blue dress suit she wore suggested that she'd interrupted a work day to join them for the luncheon. "Before you came in, I was just telling Marissa that piling on all of that dressing and cheese defeats the purpose of her even ordering a salad."

Paige laughed. "Oh, there's lettuce somewhere underneath all of that cheese?"

Marissa dramatically rolled her eyes and speared a tomato with her fork. "I didn't order a salad to be health-conscious. I ordered it because I wanted it to taste good."

"So Paige, did you cry when Brandon dumped you?" Evelyn queried, leaning over her plate of ravioli. Her golden-blonde curls bounced as she shifted positions in her chair.

"Evie, have some tact," Deana said, shooting a disapproving look in Evelyn's direction.

"Yeah I cried, for all of five minutes," Paige replied. "And when I was crying, I wasn't even really crying because he dumped me. I was crying because I knew from the beginning that he was shallow and obsessed with himself, his appearance, and his reputation. I knew a relationship between him and I would go nowhere, but still I wasted my time with him."

Deana nodded. "Most men are shallow and self-centered."

"*My* husband isn't shallow or self-centered," Evelyn boasted, grinning from ear-to-ear. "He's always conscious of my feelings and respectful of my opinion."

"If he's so great then why are you thinking of cheating on him?" Deana retorted.

Marissa swatted Deana's shoulders. "Quit being in attack-mode, Deana. Evie didn't do anything."

Deana shrugged and pursed her lips.

Evelyn had her nose tilted in the air. "My husband *is* great," she said haughtily. "*I'm* the one with issues."

Before Deana could agree, Paige cut in, "You're fine, Evie. Just don't take what you have with Eric for granted."

Evelyn silently pushed the food around her plate with a fork, the corners of her mouth tugged down at the sides.

Marissa leaned forward and spoke in a hushed whisper. "What did you do, Evie?"

Evelyn met Marissa's questioning gaze. "My trainer is always hitting on me," she said, her voice defensive. "One day I just decided to call his bluff."

Paige smothered a gasp with both hands, just as a waiter approached their table with a menu for her. She accepted the menu and thanked the waiter. Shaking her head, she glanced over the menu.

"He's gorgeous, he was very considerate and very much the gentleman," Evelyn added. She looked around the table at her friends, saw the dread and disappointment etched in their faces. "I'm always bragging about how great Eric is, but he's *not*. He's always working. He never has any time for me. By the time he gets home, he's too tired to talk, too tired to have sex."

Deana raised a napkin to her lips and spit the contents of her mouth into the napkin. "There goes my appetite."

"Evie..." Paige said. "You *didn't*."

"We're married, Paige!" Evelyn cried, dropping her fork on the plate placed before her. "We're married and he barely acknowledges my presence. When we do talk, it's about *work*. We haven't made love in a month. Sometimes it's longer than that. It's like...he's not interested in me anymore. He and I have talked about this. I told him how I felt and he told me it would change. For a few weeks, it *did* change. He *did* make an effort to make time for me. But now...all that's gone to hell and everything is back to the way it was.

"I refuse to have a boring marriage," she concluded, tucking her hair behind her ears.

"You could have divorced him instead of cheating on him," Marissa pointed out. "You don't have any children to complicate the situation."

Evelyn snorted with laughter. "Yeah, but he *is* rich. If I left him, I'd have to *work.*"

"God forbid," Deana muttered.

"You're staying with Eric because of his money?" Paige asked Evelyn, her brows furrowed.

"I'm staying with him because he's able to support the lifestyle with which I've grown accustomed," Evelyn worded carefully. "The trainer is sexy and all, but I don't love him, and he doesn't even own his own house. He rents an apartment."

Paige was speechless. She went back to studying her menu.

Evelyn wouldn't let the subject die. "You all don't know what it's like to be married," she insisted. "You don't know what it consists of, how being married makes you *feel.* Things are complicated. You can't just get divorced all of a sudden."

"But you can cheat on your husband all of a sudden?" Marissa asked with an incredulous expression on her face.

Evelyn sat back in her chair. "That's not all."

Even Deana raised her gaze at these words, her spoon held in mid-air.

Evelyn fidgeted with the tablecloth and said in a voice almost too low to hear, "I think I might be pregnant."

"Holy shit," Deana muttered, setting her spoon down.

"Oh my god," Paige said, her eyes wide.

Marissa simply shook her head.

"Who would be the father?" Paige questioned.

"These things are complicated-"

"Who would be the father?" Paige persisted.

"And I haven't told Eric yet. I don't know how he'd take it-"

"Who would be the father?"

"I don't know, okay?" Evelyn shrieked finally, squeezing her eyes shut and raising her fingers to her temples. "I don't know."

Everyone at the table was silent, no one knowing what to think or say.

Tears started at the corners of Evelyn's eyes and she whispered, "I'm scared, you guys. If it's not Eric's-"

"Don't even say it out loud," Marissa interrupted.

Evelyn stopped speaking and nodded, twirling noodles around her fork and looking gloomy. All four women were quiet for a few moments. The only sounds audible were the bustling of the waiters catering to the clientele, the clinking of glasses, and murmured conversations held by patrons seated at nearby tables.

Marissa turned her attention to Paige, looking to change the subject. "Did you talk to Shane yesterday?"

"He didn't call last night," Paige replied, setting the menu down on the table. "The last time I talked to him, he was lecturing me about how I need to keep the name I've made for myself in the business. He gives me the same lecture once a week."

"Whatever you want to say about Shane, you've got to admit, he's the most honest man you'll ever come across," Deana commented.

"Not that bad-looking either," Marissa mused, smiling slightly.

Deana arched a gaze towards Marissa, who was seated to the left of her.

Marissa shrugged. "Do you think he'd let you take that vacation?" she asked Paige before wiping her mouth with her napkin and tossing the napkin on her plate.

"It'll probably depend on the work that I submit." Paige sighed and crossed one leg over the other. "He's going to rip me a new asshole when he reads this latest piece. I already know what he's going to say. He's going to tell me it's not as good as the first one I wrote, it's not the best I could do."

Marissa looked confused. "Why would you even turn it in, then?"

"Because I wasn't going to come up with anything better. If this isn't good enough, then fuck it."

Even Deana looked surprised by Paige's use of vulgar language. "You *do* need a vacation."

"We all need to go out one of these nights," Marissa said. "We never do that anymore."

"Yeah, we need to plan on that. I'm going to have to break out in a few minutes you guys." Deana glanced at her watch.

Paige's cell phone chirped and she twisted around in her seat to dig inside her coat pockets. She found the phone, flipped it open, and lifted it to her ear. "Hello?"

"Paigie, is that you?" The voice on the other end of the line sounded excited and unnaturally high-pitched. It was the voice of her mother, a petite lady at the tender age of fifty currently living her life as a mild-tempered housewife.

"Yeah, Mom, is everything all right?" Paige asked.

"Everything's fine. Are you still planning on coming up this weekend?"

Paige's brows furrowed and she struggled to remember if anything special was supposed to be happening on the weekend coming up. She drew a blank. "This weekend?" she repeated.

"Your father and I are renewing our vows," her mother enlightened. "We sent a formal invitation in the mail to you."

"Why didn't you just call me?"

"We expected you to get the invitation."

A million thoughts were racing through Paige's mind simultaneously. Attending her parents' vow renewal ceremony meant going back to Beach Park, Illinois, a small town that housed less than twenty-five thousand people. It was a town that stretched alongside Lake Michigan.

Worries tumbled over one another. Was the town still the same? Had it grown? Was it any less friendly? Entering the city limits, would she diminish into the same angst-ridden mess she'd been ten years ago?

She thought about the last time she'd been in Beach Park. She'd visited her parents during a summer away from college. There had been many familiar faces, many questions. Because Paige's roommate at the time, Marissa Montana, had introduced young Paige to makeup and a brush, people were having a hard time believing Paige was who she said she was. There had been a lot of, "*You're* Paige Turner? The Paige Turner I went to school with? Are you *sure*?" They always asked this question as if Paige could have somehow misplaced her identity and unassumingly snatched up someone else's.

While she was ecstatic that her parents were still happy and healthy together, still in love to the point of renewing their vows, she couldn't shake all of the worries she had. Excuses popped at the front of her mind, none of them a sufficient reason to miss your parents' vow renewal ceremony.

"Of course I'm coming," she said finally, closing her eyes.

Her mother squealed with delight, and as Paige sat numbly in her chair, her mother went through the details. She described what she'd be wearing as she walked down the aisle, what cuisine she wanted served, and how many people would be in attendance. She ended the conversation with, "I can't wait to see you, honey. It'll be great having you back in Beach Park."

Sure it will, Paige thought miserably. She told her mother that she loved her and that she also couldn't wait to be in Beach Park again. The latter sentiment was a flat-out lie and while she regretted lying to her mother, her mother's giddy reaction to the lie was a small consolation.

She pressed the End button on her cellular phone and re-pocketed it. She turned back to face three friends with imploring expressions on their faces. "My mom and dad are renewing their vows," she explained in a monotonous voice.

Marissa raised her brow. "Don't sound *too* excited," she said sarcastically.

"I'm happy for them, but I don't want to go back to Beach Park," Paige replied, defying all rules of table etiquette by placing her elbows on the table and leaning her forehead against open palms.

Evelyn, seated at Paige's left, gave Paige a sympathetic pat on the shoulder. "It's not going to be as bad as you think it will be," she prophesized.

Appetite lost and not caring to stick around the restaurant, Paige rose from her chair and collected her jacket from the back of the chair. Slipping her arms into the sleeves, she apologized profusely for leaving early. Her friends told her that they understood, that she didn't have to apologize and didn't have to worry about it, but Paige knew as soon as she left the table, they'd be whispering. They would wonder why it was such a big deal for her to go back to Beach Park? Why, in all the eight years they'd known her, had she never invited them back to her hometown? Was the town that bad? Was it a hick town, where everyone knew your business before you did? Did Paige not get along with her family? Wasn't Paige happy for her parents, happy that they were renewing their vows?

Deana would no doubt go into a long speech about how Paige should be happy that her parents were still together, since Deana's parents had divorced. *"They divorced when I was eight years old,"* Deana would say with a stony expression on her face. *"My dad cheated on my mom and she wasn't the type of woman who would just sit around and accept it, so she divorced him. For that, my mom's my hero, but a small part of me would have liked to go back in time and somehow prevented my parents from splitting. I think having my dad walk out on us has forever warped my perception of men."*

Paige drove home, drowning in her thoughts and worries. It was twelve-thirty on a Friday afternoon, and highway traffic came close to being as heavy as her heart was.

Her mind was so preoccupied with thoughts that by the time she reached her driveway, she wasn't even sure how she'd gotten home. She hadn't been focusing on the road; at some point in time, her subconscious must have taken the wheel.

She stumbled out of the navy blue Ford Explorer and closed the driver side door, walked up the short pathway to her porch, walked up the three steps, and turned around to survey the neighborhood she lived in.

She lived in a neighborhood where neighbors bought cars for the sole purpose of showing off their wealth. Soccer moms no longer drove minivans; they had to have the most recent SUV that Lexus or BMW had on the showroom floors, and if the latest model was sold out, then a Lincoln Navigator or Range Rover would suffice. The lawns were the perfect shade of green and in fact looked as if they may have been spray-painted the color of emeralds.

Her neighborhood was beautiful, as were her neighbors, but it lacked character (as did her neighbors). Everything was *too* perfect. Looking down the street, there wasn't one battered car parked up a sloping driveway and no fences needing a few new coats of paint. It felt like a movie set, not an actual neighborhood.

Without realizing it, she was comparing the neighborhood she currently lived in to the neighborhood she'd grown up in. Snapping out of her reverie, she turned on her heel and unlocked her front door. Glancing once more over her shoulder, she entered her house, walked down the short corridor, and turned into a large living room. She dropped onto a sand-colored L-shaped sofa and brought a hand over her eyes.

She'd spent her entire adulthood trying to forget who she'd been in high school, trying to be the opposite of who she'd been in high school. She'd tried to forget her adolescence, erase it from memory, but it insisted on sneaking up and biting her in the ass whenever she least expected it.

Now she was supposed to go back to her hometown where she would have to stomach hundreds of hugs from people she'd known ten years ago, people who hadn't given a damn about her in the past but would undoubtedly give a damn about her now that she was a published writer. She could almost hear them asking her to put their names in her next book so they could have their fifteen minutes of fame. She could already hear them commenting on how different she looked. The last time many people from Beach Park had seen her in person, she had been a frightful mess. Of course, they wouldn't blurt that out, no. As they told her how pretty she was now, they'd be drudging up an image of a seventeen year old Paige Turner with dull, auburn hair pulled back in a ponytail, eyebrow-length bangs blanketing her forehead, and those god-awful flower-print dresses she'd had to wear because her father had been laid off from work while she was attending high school in her sophomore year.

Maybe she was being melodramatic. Perhaps she'd end up only seeing a few people she'd known in the past. Maybe no one would remember what she used to look like, *if* they remembered her at all. She *had* been a wallflower, after all.

She drifted off to sleep assuring herself that the trip back to Beach Park wouldn't be as horrendous as she'd initially thought it would be. Maybe it would somehow manage to be relaxing, the vacation she was hoping for. Maybe it would feel good to be back in Beach Park, now that she was successful. Maybe...*maybe*...

Chapter Two

Crystalline snow blanketed every yard on Ford Avenue, sparkling like several million diamonds as Paige pulled her SUV into the gravel driveway set to the side of her parents' modest, single-story house. Numerous times, she had offered to buy her parents a new house, and numerous times, the offer was turned down. Her parents had lived in the same house for nearly twenty years and they didn't want to sell it. It held sentimental value for them.

Paige sat in her car staring at the house she'd grown up in. Everywhere she looked, there was a memory. The solid oak in the front yard was a tree she'd climbed as a youngster. The withered garden below what would be the living room window was where she'd helped her mother plant hyacinths and gardenias. The porch swing was where she'd sat with her father as he tried to explain to her what being laid off meant for their family.

Looking at the house now, she noticed that the screen door hung slightly off-hinge. That was probably just the tip of the iceberg; snow could be concealing about a half dozen other imperfections. She felt that her parents deserved more than this. She was tempted to make her parents another offer to buy them a house, but her mother would insist, *"We're not a flashy kind of people, Paige. We don't need a huge mansion or six cars to be happy."*

She pushed the car door open and slid out of the sports utility vehicle. Her boots crunched over day-old snow encrusted with ice. She was attacked by a brutally cold wind. Her loose black sweater, faux fur trench, and dark slacks were no match for the bitter temperature. With her hands submerged in deep pockets, she trudged up the walkway and climbed the few porch steps.

From the other side of the door came sounds of laughter and pounding footsteps. Her parents rarely locked the front door during daylight hours, so when Paige tried the doorknob, it turned easily in her hands. She barely got over the threshold before she was nearly mauled over by a dark-haired, pint-sized ball of energy.

"Sorry about that," claimed what had to be the pint-sized ball of energy's older sister. The resemblance between the two of them was uncanny.

Paige's gaze drifted from the small girl with huge, dark eyes and long, dark hair to the teenager with the same huge, dark eyes and glossy dark hair. She was certain that she was in the wrong house. She turned around and pulled the front door open, intent on checking the house and its address to make sure she'd entered the right residence.

"Are you looking for Auntie Lori?" the younger girl asked, tugging on Paige's pant leg.

Paige turned to face the two girls again. "That's my mom. I thought I was in the wrong house."

"You probably don't remember me," the older girl said disdainfully. A sky blue towel was draped across her right forearm and in her other arm, she held a paper plate topped with a sandwich sectioned into quarters and chips grouped in the center of the dissected sandwich. "I'm Samantha Waterford. From next door. You used to babysit me."

Realization dawned on Paige. "Oh my God, you're so..."

"Old?" the teenager finished, smiling. She looked to be about sixteen. Braces were affixed to her teeth, but those braces didn't hinder her smile at all. She was dressed in a pink, long-sleeved sweater, jeans, and sneakers with her dark shoulder-length hair pulled back from her face in a ponytail. "Let's go into the living room. I can't hold all of this anymore."

Paige followed Samantha into the living room with the little girl who'd attacked her upon entry keeping close at her heels.

"That's Olivia, my sister," Samantha stated as she set the tray down on the coffee table.

Paige didn't speak, but instead glanced around the living room. There was a long, dark oak coffee table that was positioned in the middle of the room, bulky and low to the floor. Around the coffee table were a long, overstuffed couch and an equally overstuffed armchair, both of them colored in dark orange, gold, and deep brown. The entire room had been decorated in autumn colors. Painted pictures of the countryside graced the walls and childhood pictures of Paige were strategically positioned on the mantle of the fireplace in the corner. Glancing around the living room felt like taking a trip back in time, because the room looked almost exactly as it had ten years ago. The furniture hadn't changed, the wall hangings hadn't changed, and the room's décor hadn't changed.

Olivia and Samantha were watching her silently as she inspected the room. "Not much has changed since I was a kid," Samantha said as if reading Paige's mind.

"I was just thinking that. The only thing in this room that seems to have aged is you." Paige turned her attention back to the teenager.

Samantha smiled, apparently taking Paige's remark as a compliment. "I'm in high school now, a sophomore at Beach Park High," she announced proudly.

Paige laughed and sank into the armchair. "I feel so old."

"You don't look old. You look great," Samantha told her emphatically.

Olivia had turned her attention to the lunch on her tray and was oblivious to the both of them, seated and looking as prim as any little girl who was sitting on the floor could look.

"Thank you. You look great also," Paige returned. She could hear the faint sounds of clattering pots and pans that must have been trailing down the hall from the kitchen.

"I'll go tell Lori you're here," Samantha said shortly before exiting the room.

Paige's gaze lowered and rested on the bent head of the little girl intensely focused on her plate of lunch. "How old are you?"

The little girl raised her head. For an instant, she looked surprised that Paige was speaking to her. Then she answered, "I'm eight."

"Samantha's your big sister?"

The little girl nodded.

"Do you come here a lot?"

"Auntie Lori likes having us around and we like being here," Olivia said, fidgeting with the sandwich pieces on her plate. "And my mom had to leave town for work. We're staying here while she's gone."

Paige sat back in her chair, watching the girl's small fingers clumsily handle the piece of sandwich. The girl was adorable: large eyes, button nose, and rosy mouth. If Paige's memory served her correctly, she looked a lot like what Samantha looked like ten years ago.

The cell phone in Paige's pocket rang, and she plucked it out of her pocket. Before she could even say "Hello," Shane was yelling in her ear.

"Where are you and what do you mean you're taking a vacation?" he shouted over what sounded like a car radio.

Paige rose from the chair and walked towards the living room window with the phone held against her ear. "You must have gotten my voicemail message," she said, not able to stop the smile that spread over her mouth. "I'm at my parents' house. They're renewing their vows."

"And that's all great and everything, but we have a deadline Paige."

"The novel's done."

He chuckled dryly. "Good, now all I need is the manuscript in my hands. Where is it?"

"At the house."

"'At the house,'" he repeated. "What good does it do if it's 'at the house'?"

She fidgeted with the thin, gold drapes hung over the large picture window. "You can let yourself in and get it."

"You leave your house unlocked?" he asked in amazement. "Are you nuts, Paige?"

"Not exactly. You'd have to let yourself in by the window next to the back door-"

"You want me performing *Mission Impossible*-type stunts to get your manuscript? What do I look like, Paige? I mean come on."

She huffed in frustration, glancing over her shoulder to see if Olivia was paying any attention to her conversation. The little girl wasn't. Turning back to face the window, Paige said through clenched teeth, "I can't really talk now."

On the other end of the line, Shane was silent a few moments. "Hold on, Paige, let me pull the car over."

With her free hand settled on one hip, she waited patiently while he must have been pulling over to the shoulder of the road.

There was a rustle of paper on the other end of the line and he asked her, "Do you know what I have in my hands right now? Tell me what I have in my hands right now."

She shrugged, even though he couldn't see the gesture. "I don't know what you have in your hands, Shane."

"The 'paper," he said, answering his own question. "And guess what's in the 'paper?"

An anxious rumbling started in her stomach. "What's in the 'paper?"

"A review of your last book." More rustling was audible on the other end. "Well I call it a book, but this critic basically calls it a piece of shit, but to each his own, right?"

"Just read it, Shane."

"'With a name like Paige Turner, you'd think that this up-and-coming novelist would be able to write a couple of page-turners. However her latest piece, *A Lifetime Apart*, is mediocre to say the least.'" At this point Shane paused and grunted. "I'm going to skip a lot of this bullshit, okay? The gist of what this critic is saying is that he would have rather watched grass grow than spend a night reading your book."

The anxious rumbling in Paige's stomach grew fiercer and she didn't know what to say.

He didn't speak for a few minutes. A song on the radio played in the background. "Paige, I love you, I really do. You're an amazing woman and I *know* you're a talented writer. The world knew you were a talented writer, too, with that first piece you came out with."

She didn't say anything.

"The first novel you wrote was golden," he continued. "The ones you've been writing recently, they're garbage. I'm sorry to say it, Paige, but I'm not telling you anything you didn't already know. Something happened either while you were writing the first novel or before you wrote the first novel. Something happened that inspired you and got you to create this wonderful piece of art, this engrossing love story.

"What I need you to do is find this awesome inspiration. I need you to find this inspiration and trap it."

She closed her eyes, summoning an image of what her inspiration had been. Tall, dark hair, eyes that tilted down ever so slightly at the corners...long legs, strong body, charming smile, compassionate demeanor. Not to mention taboo. She tried to absorb everything that her literary agent was telling her. "I don't know if that's possible," she told him finally.

"Anything's possible," he corrected her firmly. "Look, Paige. I was hoping I wouldn't even have to go there, but I obviously have to go there. This next piece you come out with, it has to be golden, all right? Your name is slipping off the map. You've made this awesome name for yourself in the industry, and all you have to do is keep it, do you hear me? I don't care *what* it takes, Paige. I don't *care*. I'm going to try to get an expansion on your deadline."

"You don't have to do that, it's already done."

"You're *sure*, Paige? Is it golden? Is it good?"

It's good enough, she thought to herself. "Yeah, it's good," she said finally, her voice breaking.

He sighed on the other end of the line. "Look, I'm going to do this *Mission Impossible* shit and I'll get the manuscript. I'll read through it, tell you what I think. Does that sound kosher?"

"Sure. It's not printed out yet, it's still on disk," she said apologetically, "but the disks are on the..." She visualized herself sitting at her desk. "They're on the right side of my computer monitor, in a disk container. There are two disk containers, so you have to remember that the disks you're looking for are in the disk container on the right hand side of my monitor, all right?"

He wished her a safe trip and told her that if she wasn't back in town by the time he was finished reading the manuscript, he'd call her on her cell phone and let her know whether or not what she'd written carried his seal of approval. Slipping the phone into her coat pocket, she turned to face Olivia.

Olivia had been hopping around on the couch while Paige was on the phone. She paused in mid-hop and asked, "Was that your boyfriend?"

Paige smiled and shook her head. "Oh *no*," she said emphatically. "Just a friend, someone I work with."

"I have a boyfriend," the little girl said, bouncing up and down on the overstuffed couch cushion.

Paige's brows shot up in surprise.

"He's not eight, he's nine. His name's Jeremy."

Resisting the urge to laugh, Paige nodded her head. "And he's your boyfriend?"

The little girl nodded. Her long ponytail bounced up and down as she hopped around on the sofa. "A boy in my class hit me and I fell on the ground and Jeremy came and helped me up and he went and told the teacher and now we hold hands during recess."

Paige reclaimed her seat in the armchair and folded her hands across her lap. She was trying to convince herself that it wasn't as pitiful as it seemed, a nine-year-old boy being a better boyfriend than the self-centered bastard she'd dated for several months.

Samantha returned with a short, fit lady trailing behind her and a smile immediately broke out on Paige's face. Lori Turner's dark hair was swept up and held fast by hairclips and the clear gloss shining on her lips was the only makeup applied to her face. She was a fifty year old woman who looked to be ten years her junior, the only telltale sign of her age being the streaks of gray darting through her hair. She was fully dressed in a knee-length dress bedecked with pastel-colored flowers, a lavender sweater, and flat-soled black dress shoes, but even the old-fashioned flower-print dresses that she wore couldn't hamper the beauty radiating from smooth, ivory skin, sparkling brown eyes, and a smile that could illuminate an entire room.

Paige rose from the chair and crossed the room, gathering her mother in a tight embrace. Both mother and daughter murmured in each other's ears, how long it had been since they'd last seen each other, how was the other doing, how much each loved the other. They pulled back from the hug to appraise each other and hugged each other again. Finally stepping back, Paige smiled. "You look so happy," she observed.

"I'm very happy," her mother insisted, gesturing to where Paige had been sitting and taking a seat herself on the couch that Olivia was still standing up on. "I'm about to relive one of the best days of my life and now my daughter's here with me. I couldn't ask for more."

"I'm glad things are working out for you," Paige said honestly, sitting in the armchair and shrugging her coat from her shoulders.

Lori set a hand on Olivia's shoulders to stop her from bouncing. The little girl lowered into a sitting position on the couch and the older woman lifted her gaze back to her daughter. "How are things going for you?"

"They're going," Paige replied stiffly, avoiding her mother's probing gaze.

Brows arching, Lori leaned forward. "Career problems or dating problems?"

"A little bit of both."

"The boy you were dating, the actor...no good?"

"He wasn't worth the time I invested in him." Paige shifted in the chair uncomfortably. "We'll talk about it later," she added, aware that Samantha was still standing in the doorway and Olivia was seated next to Lori, kicking her legs back and forth.

Samantha walked over to Olivia. She gripped her little sister's hand and collected the lunch tray with her free hand. "Let's give the grown-ups some time to talk."

Paige watched the pair leave the room.

"Adorable kids, aren't they?" Lori mused. "They look like they could be your younger sisters. I take them to the grocery store with me and everyone thinks I've had more children."

"The little one says their mother left town," Paige said, trailing her finger along the velvety surface of the chair's armrest and raising her eyes to meet her mother's gaze.

Her mother folded her hands in her lap. "She's a business executive-type, not at home a lot," she explained.

Paige's eyes widened. "Where's their dad?"

"Their father cheated on their mother years ago and isn't on speaking terms with her."

Paige shook her head, not knowing what to say. *Those poor children,* she thought to herself.

"You said you were having problems earlier," Lori prompted.

Without hesitation Paige blurted out, "Brandon and I are over and Shane just told me that I need to get my rear end in gear or else my career's pretty much over. I've had better times."

"So find another man and write a better book," her mother suggested simply.

Paige stared at her mother and burst out laughing. "It's more complicated than that," she insisted.

"There are plenty of good men out there, Paige. You just don't make yourself available to any of them because you're a homebody. As far as your book, well," Lori huffed. "I know you'll come out with something great, something special that everyone will remember. You can't let someone else dictate when your career's over, honey."

Paige turned her head to gaze out of the living room's picture window. Her mother hadn't been single since the

1960's. It was the twenty-first century, and the dating scene wasn't so cut-and-dry. There were men who were after only one thing, men who assumed women were after only one thing, men with standards as to what their girlfriend should look like, how she should dress, what she should weigh and how much money she should or shouldn't have. Paige highly doubted that there were as many *single*, good-looking, good-natured men wandering around the world as her mother would lead her to believe. She didn't voice her thoughts aloud. She merely sighed in frustration.

Lori watched her daughter and shook her head. "You have grown to be an intelligent, successful, and interesting young woman, Paige. Sometimes I wonder whether or not I've been a good enough mother to you.

"There were times when you had to do without trendy clothes, and times when you weren't able to join the few friends you *did* have when they were going to the mall or the movies."

"You were a great mother," Paige said. "Who I was back then contributed to who I am today."

"A romance novelist who barely ever visits her parents?" Lori countered. When her daughter didn't respond, she made a dismissive gesture with her hand. "You never seemed to resent your father or I for the fact that we weren't financially capable of giving you all of the fancy gadgets and clothes that your classmates had, but sometimes I wonder if that was a part of why you never had a desire to put any effort into your appearance."

Paige rolled her eyes dramatically. "Gee, thanks Mom."

"I'm not trying to be mean. I'm just being honest. And honestly, back in the days when you were a teenager, you never really cared to make your clothes look fancy. You never really styled your hair, not to my knowledge anyway. And all of that resulted in your classmates making fun of you day in and day out. Even though all of that happened years ago, I'm certain that it has affected your self-esteem and self-image." Lori's eyes narrowed in concentration. "It would explain why you never come to visit your father and I anymore. He and I always have to drive down to Farmington Heights if we want to see you, even for Christmas."

It was obvious that Paige was desperately attempting to keep the expression on her face neutral and devoid of emotion. That had never been one of her strengths; her emotions were always clearly visible in her face, as they were now.

Deciding to give her daughter a break, Lori concluded, "There's someone out there for you, someone who will treat you the way you should be treated."

"You have to tell me that because you're my mother," Paige muttered under her breath.

"I don't *have* to do anything. I raised you for eighteen years," Lori said haughtily, lifting her chin up a notch. "I tell you that because I believe it. If I didn't believe it, I wouldn't tell you that."

Paige turned to look at her mother. "I wish I could believe that."

"What, are you going to feel pity for yourself and feel sorry for yourself forever?" her mother demanded, rising from the couch. "Look at how beautiful you are, how smart you are. You write books and people read them. Never mind what Shane told you about your career being over," she added before her daughter could interject. "Never mind that you and your boyfriend are no longer together. You're too strong of a lady to let those two things drag you down like this. I hate to sound like I'm lecturing you, I do, but I don't like seeing you like this."

"I'll be all right, Mom," Paige said, sounding tired.

Lori leaned down and gave her daughter's knee a pat. "I know you will." She paused and glanced at the inexpensive watch circling her wrist. "Your father's going to be home any minute. I have errands that I have to take care of and I still need to get dinner on the stove. Keep Sam and Olivia company, will you? We'll have plenty of time to talk while you're here."

Paige nodded and tilted her head back, closing her eyes.

Not two minutes later, there was a small hand tugging on the sleeve of her sweater. "You don't look happy."

Paige cracked an eye open. "I'm fine."

"Are you lying?"

"Why would I lie about being okay?"

"Because grown-ups sometimes lie about being okay," Olivia responded. "They don't think kids can handle grown-ups being sad, but we can handle more than you think sometimes."

Paige cracked the other eye open and looked down at the dark-haired child. "I'm okay. I'm just going through a lot of things right now."

"Bad things?" Olivia pressed, turning away from Paige and climbing on the couch.

"Some bad things, yeah."

"Maybe I could give you some advice," Olivia offered.

Paige laughed and clasped her hands together, bracing her elbows on her knees. She leaned forward. "My boyfriend and I broke up and my career might be over."

Olivia dug an index finger in her cheek with her eyes squinted in contemplation. "What do you do?"

"I write books."

"What kind?"

"The grown-up kind."

Olivia thought for a few moments again. "There are a lot of boys in the world and there are a lot of jobs in the world," she said finally. "If you lose one boy or one job, get another one."

"I don't want another job," Paige explained.

"But you want another boy?"

"My boyfriend wasn't very nice to me."

"Then why were you with him?" Olivia asked with her brows furrowed in confusion.

Paige started to explain the situation, but then stopped herself. "When you're grown-up, it's complicated."

"Grown-ups say that a lot," Olivia said slowly, "but what can be that much more complicated than when you're a kid? Me and Jeremy wouldn't be holding hands at recess now if he hadn't helped me that one day. If a boy isn't nice to you, then he shouldn't be your boyfriend.

"The word boyfriend is made up of the word 'boy' and the word 'friend.' To be someone's friend, you have to be nice to them. If a boy's not nice to you, he's not your boyfriend, he's just…a *boy*," she concluded with a wrinkled nose.

Paige had to laugh in spite of herself. The girl had spoken in simplified terms to say the least, but what she'd said had made so much sense it was scary. "You're right," she told Olivia, settling back in her chair.

Olivia's eyes widened. "I am?"

"More grown-ups should listen to you," Paige said. "You're a very smart girl."

Olivia beamed and dimples deepened into her cheeks. "I try to tell everyone that, but they don't listen."

"Jeremy's a very lucky guy."

The little girl tilted her head to the side. "See I try to tell him that, but he doesn't listen," she said.

Chapter Three

Paige should have awakened to a stream of near-noon sunlight beaming upon her face. What she got instead were the sounds of clanging pots and pans traveling down the hall and into her sleeping quarters. She was roughly roused from sleep at the crack of dawn. She made several attempts to sink back into pleasant unconsciousness, but to no avail. She rolled over onto her back and stared at the ceiling before sitting up, wrestling with the sheets (and losing), and nearly falling out of bed.

With her eyes narrowed into a squint, she took in her surroundings. The guest room was sparsely decorated with a king-sized bed and a dark bureau standing beside the bedroom door. The drapes and bed adornments were the same pattern, a splash of crimson, navy blue and forest green. The carpet was crimson and sank beneath her feet. Saying that the room was small would have been an extreme understatement, but while it was the size of her master bathroom at home, it was comfortable and cozy.

The banging of pots and pans continued, and her first thought was that the noise was a result of her mother cooking breakfast. That was until she realized that the clanging was happening at intervals, to the beat of a Britney Spears song.

She stomped out of her room and down the short hall to the kitchen. Olivia sat on the floor dressed in bubble-gum pink pajamas with a pot in one hand and a pan in the other. She looked up just as Paige entered the room and broke out into a huge grin. "Morning!" she called in a singsong voice.

Paige resisted the urge to snatch the pot and pan from the girl's hands and throw them out of the kitchen window. *Calm down, don't scare the girl, it's the butt-crack of dawn and you're not thinking rationally,* she thought, plastering a smile on her face and kneeling down so that she was eye-level with Olivia. "It's really early," she said in a hushed voice. "People are trying to sleep."

Olivia blinked chocolate-brown eyes with her head tilted to one side. She clearly didn't understand Paige's point.

Paige pointed at the pot, then the pan. "That noise woke me up."

"Oh!" Olivia exclaimed in a shout, then looked around the kitchen and covered her mouth. Moving the hand away from her mouth, she whispered in a library voice, "Oh. I'm sorry, I never thought of that." She quietly set the pot and pan down on the floor.

After collecting the pot and pan in her hands, Paige located the cabinet they belonged in and replaced them. "Don't you have school in the morning or something?"

"No school today, parent-teacher conferences," Olivia said, grinning from ear to ear.

"Aren't there cartoons on or something?" Paige demanded. "Cartoon Network…ever heard of that?"

"They're on commercial."

"So naturally, you can't sit during the commercials. You have to come in the kitchen and wake up the neighborhood by playing 'Baby One More Time' using pots and pans as your instruments," Paige muttered, running a hand through hair that had run amuck about her head at some point the previous night.

"You could tell what song it was?" Olivia asked, and made a little gasping sound. "I must be better than I thought."

Paige led Olivia to what had been transformed into a makeshift bedroom for the two sisters. Two narrow beds had been placed a few feet apart; in one of the beds, Samantha still lie sleeping with rose-colored sheets pulled up to her chin. The other bed, which was obviously Olivia's, looked as if a cyclone had hit it. The sheets were bunched up at the foot of the bed and there were no pillows in sight. When Paige moved her gaze, she saw that the pillows had been placed on the floor in front of the inexpensive armoire set in the far corner of the room. The television housed in the armoire was set at a volume so low, she wouldn't have known it was on if she hadn't seen it.

Olivia bounded towards the two pillows set on the floor. "You gonna' watch cartoons with me?" she asked, casting Paige a glance over her shoulder.

"I'm going to catch up on some sleep," Paige said, unable to hold back a yawn. She returned to her room and collapsed on the bed, pulling the sheets over her head and groaning.

She fell into a peaceful sleep that was again interrupted, this time by the ringing of a cell phone. Cursing under her breath, she clapped a pillow around her head. When it failed to block out the sounds of ringing, she piled a second pillow on top of the first. Growling and briefly visualizing flushing the gadget down the toilet, she flung the pillows to the floor and groped for the compact cellular phone lying on the nightstand beside her bed. "It's a Friday morning," she croaked into the phone. "This had better be life-or-death."

"Most people work on Friday mornings. Since I'm up, I figured I'd make you miserable, too." It was Deana.

"It's got to be, like…six in the morning. Don't you usually get in at 9?"

"Some of my employees wanted overtime hours," Deana explained. "Being the director of the department, either I or one of the managers has to supervise. Both of the managers are off on vacation, so guess who's left with the dirty work."

"What does a director of a department do, exactly?" Paige mumbled.

"Classified information," Deana replied just as Paige ended the sentence. "Hey, listen. Evelyn took a trip to the gyno and it turns out she's not pregnant. She's wanting us all to get together to celebrate."

"I'm still in Beach Park," Paige said dismissively. "My parents are renewing their vows, remember?"

"We know," Deana said. "So we're coming up there."

Paige sat up straight, temporarily forgetting how early it was, how little sleep she'd had, and the fact that she wasn't a morning person. "You'll all be bored to death," she protested. "There's not much to do around here."

"There's the lake," Deana pointed out.

"It's February," Paige countered.

"Oh, right." Deana was silent a few moments. "Well, Marissa's set on joining you up there and you know how she gets when she's set on doing something. Maybe a peaceful trip to the countryside would do all of us some good."

The sound of clanging pans filled Paige's head as she remembered that morning's events. "A peaceful trip to the countryside, that's exactly how this feels," she muttered.

"Great, then it's settled," Deana said. "One of us will call you later for directions. I know what a late sleeper you are so I'm going to let you catch some Z's."

As Paige clicked the cell phone off, she thought, *Yeah, like that's going to happen.*

The Turner vow renewal ceremony was beautiful. The event was held on Saturday afternoon in the banquet hall of the largest hotel in town, before nearly one hundred spectators in a room overwhelmed with flowers. The decorating in the hall had been done modestly and mostly in pastel colors. The columns on either side of the makeshift altar were wrapped with multi-colored bands of silk.

Paige sat in the front row, dressed in a beige silk top and a knee-length taupe skirt. Samantha and Olivia were seated on her left. Deana, Marissa, Shane, and Evelyn had all shown up at her parents' house the night before, and they were seated somewhere near the back. The last time Paige had ventured a glance over her shoulder, an old man had nodded off to sleep and was drooling on Deana's shoulder, Marissa and Shane were engrossed in each other, and Evelyn was speaking in hushed tones with a muscular-looking, dark haired man seated next to her.

The ceremony went smoothly. Her mother looked as beautiful and elegant as ever, and her father looked as suave and gentlemanly as ever. She was relieved to see that her mother wasn't wearing another one of her famed floral-print dresses to the ceremony. Instead, she was dressed in a beautiful, shimmering peach-colored dress suit belted over a lace-collared blouse.

Her parents had managed to stay married for thirty-two years, a blissful and happily-spent thirty-two years to the best of Paige's knowledge. She'd heard her parents argue over trivial things, on what television show they should watch, on how to set the dinner table, on what they should have for dinner. She'd never seen them engaged in a serious argument.

As her parents walked down the aisle hand in hand, she wondered to herself if she'd ever have a moment in her life like this. She wondered if she'd ever be this happy, if she'd ever marry a man who could make her forget life's woes. Would she ever even marry? She felt selfish thinking of herself on her parents' special day, but she couldn't halt the images that popped in her head, images of herself as a sixty-year-old spinster living in a house full of a hundred mewling cats.

She didn't put it past herself to end up that way, an elderly bachelorette who sat in a high-backed rocking chair knitting things for no one in particular, holding animated conversations with her pets, doomed to a life of nothing but watching the years stroll by her at a leisurely gait.

After the ceremony, Paige rose from her seat, as did everyone else, in a loud smattering of applause for the couple that had just renewed their vows. Lori announced the reception that would be held in about fifteen minutes, which would give the hotel's staff enough time to clear the foldable chairs and makeshift altar from the room.

Paige moved forward and hugged both of her parents, congratulating them. She embraced first her mother and then her tall, lanky father, whose dark hair was brushed back to reveal the veins of gray starting at his temples. Merry, green eyes twinkled at his daughter as he nearly crushed her in an embrace.

Moving away from her parents, Paige headed towards her friends. The previous night, Paige had been surprised to see Marissa and Shane show up together. Deana had shown up dateless, as had Evelyn. Paige's glance fell on Evelyn now, whose arm was intertwined with that of the gentleman who had been seated next to her. Both Deana and Marissa cast each other awkward looks, and Paige's brows furrowed.

"I'm glad you guys could make it," Paige said pointedly with her gazed locked on Evelyn, who was giggling and downright flirting with the man standing beside her.

"It was a beautiful ceremony," Marissa offered, smiling. Her thick, curly hair was pulled back from her face and held fast with jeweled hairpins. She wore a black, ankle-length skirt with an elegant, long-sleeved cashmere blouse the color of raspberries.

Paige folded her arms across her chest with her head tilted to one side.

"Oh, you haven't been introduced?" Deana asked gaily, setting a hand on Paige's shoulder. The smug expression on her face told Paige more than words ever could. "This is Evie's personal trainer."

Evelyn, hearing her name being mentioned, lifted her chin and returned Paige's probing gaze. "He's my date to this event. Eric couldn't make it because of work."

Paige took a step closer to Evelyn, plastering a smile on her face for the sake of anyone passing by them. "You brought your sex toy to my parents' ceremony?"

Evelyn paled visibly, inching closer to the man standing beside her.

"You used this event to exploit the fact that you're cheating on your husband?" Paige hissed through clenched teeth, her eyes spitting fire. "Do you know how despicable and dirty that is?"

Marissa and Deana both took a step back, looking like they didn't know what to do or say to contribute to the situation.

Paige tore her gaze from Evelyn and focused on the man standing beside her. "What's your name?" she demanded.

"Chris," he said. His voice was deep and rich and he managed to look debonair in a dark suit and sky blue silk tie that Evelyn had probably bought him with her husband's money.

"You knew she was married?"

"What goes on between her and the hubby is none of my business," Chris said, apparently irked that Paige was dipping her nose into his private affairs.

"*She's* none of your business," Paige snapped at him.

Chris looked down at Paige with a smirk on his face. "I'll let her make that decision."

Evelyn moved in between Paige and Chris. "He didn't do anything wrong, Paige. I invited him."

"You're a married woman, bringing the man you're having an affair with to my parents' vow renewal ceremony," Paige said, pressing an index finger to each temple. "I-I-I can't even fathom... what would make you think that you could do something this sinister. It's like...I don't know, I always knew you were self-absorbed and selfish at times, but...bringing him here-" she cut off the sentence with a bitter laugh.

"I'm sorry," Evelyn whispered. "I didn't think you'd react like this."

"How did you think I'd react?" Paige demanded. "Did you think I'd welcome this asshole with open arms?"

"Hey-" Chris began to interject, but Paige stabbed him with an icy stare. He backed down and returned to glancing around nonchalantly.

Evelyn's face was flushed, and she pushed back her hair. "I wanted to enjoy myself and have fun. I told Eric about the ceremony, but he was too busy for me."

"That's no excuse, Evie, I'm sorry," Paige said, shaking her head. "I'm going to help set up the reception. I don't want to talk to you until this is over." She turned on her heel and submerged herself in the task of helping the hotel staff to move the chairs off of the floor.

Shane approached her with his hands in the pockets of his neatly-pressed dark slacks. "I ever tell you that you're sexy when you're mad?"

She rolled her eyes. "You're here on a date with Marissa. Show some decency and respect."

"I'm not decent. Both you and Marissa know that," he said, teasing her, dark brown eyes twinkling. "Were you surprised to see me on your doorstep last night?"

"Thought you were coming to tell me that my vacation was over because you read the piece and it blew chunks," she confessed as she folded up a chair and walked a short ways away to lean it against a wall.

He moved with an over-confident swagger as he followed her. "Are you all right? You pretty much put Evelyn in her place back there."

"She takes everything she has for granted," Paige grumbled, walking back to fold up a few more chairs. "And I'm tired of it. And what she did was...horrible. Her husband is making the money she's spending on this guy. It's sick. And to use this occasion to show him off is disgusting."

He observed her, not making a move to help. "I don't know...if a man isn't taking care of his business at home, then I could understand why a woman would want someone else to man-handle her."

"Of course you'd take her side. You're usually the man that unhappily married women end up running to," she spat out.

His brows shot up. His dark hair was slicked back and his sexy dark eyes were expressive. He was looking all but scrumptious in his black suit and black dress shirt, and there was a time in the past when his thick, New York accent sent her over the edge. Now, she found his sex appeal and that strong accent annoying as hell. "Hey, don't cut me off at the balls here. I'm just offering an opinion," he said, laughing at her spunk. "I've got another opinion to offer you, too," he told her, his mood turning serious.

For the first time since he'd approached her, she straightened and looked him in the face.

"The piece I had to pull stunts to get my hands on, the one you're so modest about, it's golden." He leaned against the wall she'd been stacking chairs up against.

Now it was Paige's turn to arch her brows. "What do you mean, 'It's golden'?" she asked him.

"I meant what I said," he said, brushing off one of the lapels on his suit jacket. "It's golden. It's art. I'm shocked you made this and you didn't tell me anything about it, but…I was blown away. I really was."

Her breath caught in her throat. She ran a hand through the loose waves that fell upon her shoulders, trying to collect her thoughts. The piece of work she'd left behind for him had been the typical historical romance: hero and heroine despise each other in the beginning, chaos arises and brings hero and heroine together, some sneaky secret separates hero and heroine, turns them against each other, they overcome sneaky secret, marry and have a tribe of children. In her opinion, there hadn't been anything that stood out about the novel; it was pretty traditional, plot-wise.

Shane was still talking. "I wouldn't figure for you to do anything like this, but it's a breakthrough. The critics will eat their hearts out." He scratched his chin in contemplation. "I don't think the title we talked about applies, though. I want to change it, with your permission."

She nodded, speechless. Finding her tongue, she said, "Yeah, you can change it. I'm just…I don't know. I'm shocked you like it."

"I'm shocked that *you're* shocked. You had to know you were going to blow people away with this."

She shrugged her shoulders. "You should get back to your date. There will be plenty of time to talk business."

He turned his back to her and faced Marissa, who stood beside Deana, Evelyn, and Evelyn's trainer. "Gorgeous, isn't she?" he mused, almost to himself. "Yeah, I should get back to her."

She couldn't help but think to herself that she'd never remembered Brandon looking at her the way Shane appraised Marissa. Mentally kicking herself in the ass for even thinking about Brandon, she directed all of her frustration into folding up chairs and clearing the floor.

Several people, relatives and friends to the family alike, approached her, people who remembered her as "Little Paige Turner," the quiet girl who'd mostly kept to herself, the girl who was almost always writing something.

"I heard you were in the big-time now, a major writer," a middle-aged lady with big hair, thin lips, and a low-cut dress told her.

"I never did get a chance to read one of your books," a lady who looked old enough to have played Bridge with God offered disdainfully.

"Are you married now? Have any kids? You're how old, now thirty? Thirty-one?" queried a brunette only a few years younger than Paige was.

"Put me in one of your books," a slightly buck-toothed, large-breasted blonde pleaded, tugging on her arm like a child would have.

Paige's mother announced the beginning of the reception and introduced the DJ. The lights in the hall dimmed and people of all ages gathered on the dance floor, pairing up and dancing, some comically and others quite skillfully. For most of the reception, Paige observed everyone. She leaned against the wall and remembered a time long ago, when the lights were just as dim…

And the music just as slow. A seventeen-year old girl leaned against the wall watching all of the other high school students in attendance dancing and whirling on the dance floor. Pink, red, and white streamers hung from the rafters, and balloons of the same color were anchored by small pieces of plastic shaped into red and pink hearts. Everyone looked to be thoroughly enjoying themselves, except the girl leaning against the wall, watching with tear-filled eyes.

[Dear Diary],

I knew I shouldn't have gone to the dance tonight. The only reason I went was because it was the last high school dance I'd see, the only Prom I'd get to experience, and everyone said that going alone wasn't as horrible as it seemed. They told me that a lot of people go alone.

As soon as I got to Prom, I knew that I'd made a mistake in going. They decorated the hotel's ballroom beautifully, and everyone else looked to be enjoying themselves. I didn't know what to do so I walked around a bit, sat at one of the tables, and watched everyone else. No one asked me to dance. I danced by myself for awhile and no one came up to dance with me. I felt like an idiot.

I started to walk off the dance floor, to collect my wits and walk out the building so I could walk home. I was going to leave, because I had no reason to be there. I was going to leave...but then I saw him, and he was walking up to me with the brightest smile that I've ever seen. He was smiling as if he were happy to see me.

"That dress is amazing," he told me as he approached me.

I blushed and looked down at my strapless crimson dress. I'd put effort into how I looked. I'd nearly burned the side of my face while curling my hair and I poked myself twice in the eye with an eyeliner pencil while applying makeup. The fact that he noticed that I'd made an effort gave birth to butterflies that started dancing in my stomach.

"Care to cut the rug with a shabby ole' dance chaperone?" he asked, extending a hand. "Back in my day, I had skills on the dance floor, you know."

We danced, and for those few dance numbers, I forgot that I was Paige Turner, Self-Proclaimed Outcast. I forgot about leaving the Prom because I didn't belong there, and I forgot about not feeling pretty and not feeling important. For those few dance numbers, I felt special. He always made me feel special, even when he wasn't trying to.

Dancing with him, I also forgot about my mother giving me a lecture about how most girls develop crushes on their teachers.

"To be a teacher, you have to be sensitive and understanding," my mother had told me a few weeks before.

"And girls, they'll date a few high school boys their age, and a lot of the time they'll realize that some boys are after one thing. So they set their attentions on finding someone who isn't only after that one thing, someone who will listen to their problems, and try to help solve them, someone who will care for them and love them as they are. A teacher already exhibits a lot of these qualities. And this particular teacher, well, he's a gorgeous man. It's no wonder you have a crush on him."

For more than a year now I'd convinced myself that what I felt for him was more than a crush, and had told my mother as such. She'd responded with telling me that even if what I'd felt was more than a crush, and whether or not he did feel the same way, he was a teacher. Teachers and students-and furthermore, adults and minors- weren't meant to express feelings of such a nature to one another. "There are laws against it. You wouldn't want him to get in trouble, would you?"

And of course I didn't. That was the last thing I would want. So I'd kept my distance from him, only greeted him in the hallways and at school football and basketball games. I let that be that. That was until Prom night when he'd asked if I'd care to dance, and I felt all of my feelings rush up to the surface again. In those minutes, everything I'd ever known or learned slipped from my mind, and I didn't know anything except for the fact that this was my one true love, no matter who tried to convince me it was just a silly crush. In those moments, I knew that this man and I were meant to be together.

Paige nearly laughed out loud at the memory she'd had. *I'd been such a pitiful child,* she thought to herself now. *I looked nerdy as hell, was extremely anti-social, and crushed on a high school teacher who was only helping me because I was such a pitiful case.*

Before she got caught up in the "What is Mr. Carson doing now/Does he still teach," line of thinking, she reminded herself that there was no purpose in thinking about him. She was no longer in high school. She was twenty-seven years old, and she was presently at a lovely vow renewal reception…probably looking like a glassy-eyed cocaine addict due to the memory she'd just had, but she was there nonetheless.

Marissa and Shane found her hiding spot and each of them grabbed one of her arms, pulling her towards the dance floor.

"I'm not tolerating any of this moping shit," Shane said as he steered her towards the dance floor with Marissa's assistance.

Paige relented and danced with Marissa, then with Shane, then in a circle with the two of them. Eventually, Deana joined their circle, and so did Evelyn, sans Chris. Samantha politely asked if she could dance with them, and Olivia popped into the middle of the circle, shaking what little hips she had.

Laughing and letting her cares slip away, Paige laughed and danced with her friends, her parents, and her aunts and uncles until the reception was over.

"Now where are we going?" Marissa asked, not looking the least bit tired. "I don't want this night to end. What's there do to around here, Paige?"

"Watching corn crops grow and having hoe downs," Deana replied jokingly.

Paige rolled her eyes. "It's not that dry, okay. There are bars, and there are… clubs. Or the closest thing we have to clubs, anyway."

Marissa looked doubtful. "Maybe we should just drive into Chicago, go to a club there, and drive back here."

"We all drink like fish. Who's going to want to drive back?" Deana demanded. "We'll go upstairs to our hotel rooms, change, meet up after we're done changing, and go to a club or bar nearby. It'll be a lesson in culture, if anything."

An hour later, Deana, Shane, Marissa, Evelyn, and Paige stood within the entrance doors of Harry's, one of the few bars located within the city limits of Beach Park. The lighting was dim, except for bright white spotlights that beamed down upon the gleaming dance floor centered in the middle of the bar. On the dance floor, an inebriated group of people swayed their hips to the slow rock music that blared from the speakers.

Marissa looked around the place in disbelief. Her mouth dropped open. "I've never seen so many beer bellies in my life," she muttered under her breath.

Deana turned to Paige. "This is a club?"

"We're not staying here, are we?" Evelyn asked nervously.

"I see, like…no attractive men in here," Marissa commented with a short laugh.

Shane wrapped his arms around Marissa's waist and nuzzled her neck. "I'm the only attractive man you're going to need for tonight," he growled into her ear.

"You two are making me nauseous. Get a room," Deana said, moving towards the bar.

Evelyn's disappointment was evident. "I guess we're staying."

Shane and Marissa followed Deana to the bar and Paige set out to find a booth that didn't have dirty beer glasses or half-filled baskets of nachos lying on the table.

Finding a booth and claiming one of the seats, Paige glanced over her shoulder at the couple in the neighboring booth. She couldn't see much of the male counterpart of the couple, but the woman sitting across from him and facing Paige had outrageous, fire-engine red hair piled on top of her head in an abundance of curls. She was dressed stylishly, wearing a dark knee-length skirt and sweater blouse. She looked ridiculously out of place.

"I'm sorry," Paige heard, and twisted around to face Evelyn, who'd slid into the seat across from her.

"Sorry for what?"

"I shouldn't have brought Chris to the ceremony today," Evelyn confessed, anxiously running fingers through her straight blonde hair.

Paige hated to admit to herself that she honestly didn't want to hear anything more about Evelyn's marriage problems. Maybe she was a bit naïve in her perception of what a marriage should be. She believed that two people who married each other should be head over heels in love, but nowadays it seemed like people didn't care about marrying for love. Marrying was now an act of convenience.

Paige didn't doubt that there had been a time when Evelyn had been in love with Eric. Before they'd gotten married, he was all she would ever talk about. That was a few years before he became the vice president of a large corporation, a career move that kept him in the office, at times, for fourteen hours a day. Evelyn tried to be the supportive wife, but Paige guessed that she could see how any woman would grow restless having an absentee husband. *That doesn't justify her cheating on him,* Paige thought, *but Evelyn never was one to think things through.*

"Deana called me, told me that you weren't pregnant and that you thought that was cause for celebration," Paige said slowly. "I thought that you'd realized what you were doing had consequences and I thought that you would stop."

Evelyn's hands fidgeted with each other and she stared down at them. Her lips trembled, a sign that she was going to start the waterworks any moment now. "I do need to stop," she confirmed to herself, sounding determined. "Chris just makes me feel special."

Paige didn't even attempt at concealing her disgust. "I only exchanged a few words with him, but on first impression, he's a complete asshole. He's definitely not worth ruining a marriage over."

A dainty tear trailed from the corner of Evelyn's eye to the bottom of her jaw, where it dropped onto the snow white sweater she was wearing. Paige slid from her seat and joined Evelyn on her side of the booth, letting her chin drop on Evelyn's shoulder.

"You need to talk to Eric. You know you do," Paige pressed. "He might not be paying as much attention to you as he used to, but it's because he's off working, working hard to keep you happy so that you don't have to work."

Evelyn nodded and opened her mouth to speak, but before she could reply, Marissa dumped two large pitchers on the table. Amber-colored liquid sloshed over the rims of both pitchers. Shane and Marissa seated themselves across from Evelyn and Paige, and Deana approached the table with two beer glasses towered in one hand and three beer glasses towered in the other.

"Oh, no, you're not going to make me sit with the lovebirds," Deana said, setting the glasses on the table. She walked away for a few moments and when she returned, she had a chair in her hands. She placed the chair at the end of the booth and sat down.

"You okay, Evie?" Marissa asked, pouring herself a glass of beer.

Evelyn nodded, swiping at the tears trailing down her cheeks.

Marissa clucked her tongue sympathetically and reached across the table to clasp one of Evelyn's hands in her own. "It'll be all right," she assured.

"How long are you staying in town?" Deana directed at Paige, pouring beer from one of the pitchers into a glass she'd claimed as her own.

"I don't know. I was only planning on staying for the weekend," Paige replied, dipping a finger into the beer in her glass and swirling her finger around. "It wasn't as bad as I thought it was going to be. I actually like it here. The kids are great and I don't visit my parents nearly as much as I should."

Marissa nodded. "It's a beautiful town. The bars are nothing special, but the houses, the land, and the lake…it's cozy. It's the type of place to move to when you settle down." She thought for a few moments and said, "You know…I've known you, Paige, what…seven, eight years? Maybe even longer than that. This is my first time meeting your parents."

Everyone sat in contemplation for a few minutes with Shane gulping down his beer like he was in a chugging contest.

"That makes me feel as old as hell," Deana muttered. "I don't need to be reminded that I'm thirty-one and still single."

"Thirty-one and the director of your own department in a Fortune 100 company," Marissa emphasized, her eyebrows lifting dramatically. "I'm an administrative assistant. Ten years ago if you asked me where I'd be, I definitely wouldn't have told you that I'd be an administrative assistant." The buoyant mood seemed to fade from her countenance, and the corners of her mouth tugged downward.

"You were the most intelligent person I knew in college," Deana commented, setting her beer glass down. "With all of the knowledge you had, and with how smart you were, the college boys were what you invested all of your effort into. It was…"

"Perplexing," Paige supplied, nodding her head in agreement.

Deana nodded. "Marissa was the flirty one, Paige was the level-headed and creative one, Evelyn was the fashion expert, and I was the ball-buster."

Marissa nearly spit out her drink, laughing. "I can't tell you how many people came up to me and asked me if you were a lesbian."

Deana rolled her eyes. "That's just because I spoke my mind and wasn't into the whole dating scene back then."

"We had some crazy times back then," Paige murmured, stroking the rim of her beer glass with the tips of her fingers. "The parties Marissa dragged us to…"

"How she could party until three in the morning and wake up at eight and nine a.m. to go to a class is beyond me," Deana agreed.

"I shouldn't have spent so much time partying," Marissa said, folding her arms across her chest. "I should have focused more on my classes. Maybe then I would be more successful than I am now."

Before anyone could assure Marissa that she would be a huge success someday, a Kylie Minogue song came on over the speakers, and her mood switched gears. Her eyes widened and she pushed at Shane to move so she could stand. "This is my song!" she cried enthusiastically. "You guys have to dance with me."

Deana shook her head firmly. "I don't dance."

"You danced at the reception," Paige accused.

"No one's expected to look like a professional dancer at a reception," Deana explained.

Marissa, now on her feet, grabbed one of Deana's hands. Paige was still clasping her beer glass, but Marissa grabbed her free hand also. "Come on," Marissa urged, tugging Deana and Paige towards the dance floor.

Evelyn and Shane, still seated at the booth, watched the group of three in amusement.

Paige danced in a reserved manner, swaying her hips left and right and shuffling her feet, while Marissa proceeded to dance and gyrate as if she were in a dance video. Deana stood at the edge of the dance floor stiffly, resembling a statue. Marissa saw this and danced over to Deana, a wide grin on her face. She pulled Deana towards the center of the dance floor, holding firmly onto her friend's hands. In her red, knee-length, spaghetti strap dress, she looked like a tall, leggy hellion.

Deana resisted, protesting loudly over the music, "I don't dance!"

Marissa waved Deana's arms about. "Loosen up, have fun."

Paige danced and sipped her beer, noticing that Deana and Marissa were gaining an audience forming around the dance floor. She laughed and shook her head, turning around in a small circle as she danced.

Once Marissa was successful in getting Deana's feet moving on the dance floor, she headed towards Paige.

"Oh, no," Paige muttered.

Marissa grabbed Paige's free hand. "I swear, you and Deana are so damned stiff on the dance floor," she cried, dancing around her friend in a half-circle and lowering her hands from Paige's shoulders to her waist. "Loosen up, get wild with it. You're not dancing to classical music." She guided Paige's hips and moved with her.

The spectators at the edge of the dance floor gawked at the two girls dancing closely on the dance floor. Some of the men murmured amongst themselves about how hot it was to see two lesbians dancing together. The women staring at the fiasco had their noses wrinkled in disgust and tucked up into the air, whispering to each other, "Look at those two women dancing like that, that's disgusting. They're obviously crying out for attention."

Shane approached Paige and Marissa with a grin stretched across his face. "Now isn't this a pretty picture?"

Marissa moved away from Paige and draped an arm around Shane's neck. "I'm just giving my friends some dance lessons."

Paige closed her eyes and moved with the music, trying to follow Marissa's advice and loosen up her limbs. When she wasn't concerned about people gawking at her and when she wasn't analyzing every move she made, dancing felt much more natural. She swayed with a silly grin on her face, and when she opened her eyes, the group of spectators was still huddled around the small dance floor, gaping at Marissa's and Shane's hip-grinding.

Turning this way and that, Paige danced until she ended up at the edge of the dance floor staring at a familiar heap of candy apple-red hair…except now, Paige could see the man the redhead had been sitting with, dressed so casually in an olive-green button down shirt rolled up to the elbows and dark blue jeans.

The glass in Paige's hand crashed to the floor in what seemed like slow motion, thousands of shards exploding and scattering about the floor. The other dancers gasped in shock, dispersing and clearing the floor.

Chapter Four

I'm drunk right now, Paige thought to herself. *I'm drunk off of one glass of beer, because I'm seeing what can't be here.* She hadn't yet realized that she'd dropped her beer glass. Her head was swimming, drowning in memories as emotions that had been hibernating for ten years burst forth to the surface.

As the redhead's date surged forward to her aid, her vision blurred and transformed. Old images mingled with new and the setting was altogether different. "Are you all right?" he was asking her, dark brows furrowed in concern.

"Are you all right...You're young...you have your entire life ahead of you...Care to cut the rug with a shabby ole' dance chaperone...Back in my day, I had skills on the dance floor, you know..."

"My dream guy," Paige murmured dazedly as the gentleman led her to a table and sat her down. Somewhere in the depths of her subconscious, she was aware of the fact that she was shamelessly staring at him wearing a huge, silly grin on her face.

The woman with the outrageous red hair approached them, looking sickeningly cheerful. "Are you cheating on me, Ethan?" she joked, possessively snaking an arm around her date's waist and pressing a kiss to his cheek.

"I'm just making sure she's all right," Ethan answered, still looking at Paige with concern. "I think she's drunk."

"Well I'm going to pull the car around," she said, glancing at the jewel bedecked watch laced around her wrist. "We have to be up early tomorrow. I'll meet you out front."

Paige watched the woman walk away, unable to stop the disappointment from spreading like a cancer in her stomach. "Your girlfriend?"

"Diane. If you asked her, she'd tell you she was my fiancé," he told her sheepishly, bringing a hand up to rub the back of his neck. "How many drinks did you have? Are you sure you're all right? Do you think you can drive yourself home?"

Marissa rushed to Paige's side, crouching down and putting an arm around her shoulders. "Are you all right? I'm sorry I didn't get here quicker. I didn't see what happened. Are you okay? What happened?"

"You two came here together?" Ethan asked, glancing from Marissa to Paige.

"Yes," Marissa replied. Then she turned her attention back to Paige. "Did someone bump into you? Are you feeling all right? You look a little dopey."

"I saw you two dancing together. I just wasn't sure you came here together," he said, observing them with his hands shoved in the pockets of his jeans.

Rising to her full five feet and nine inches, Marissa turned to Ethan. "Thanks so much for helping her." She offered him a small smile, pushing back some of her wild hair and crossing her arms over her chest.

"No problem," he said, "but are you sure she's all right? She looks… heavily medicated."

"She probably just had a little too much to drink," Marissa guessed, looking down at Paige, who was slowly but surely coming to her senses.

Paige shook out of her daze. "I'm not drunk," she said finally. "I just…I don't know what happened. I dropped the glass-"

"You don't have to explain," Ethan interrupted, smiling down at her.

God, ten years has been kind to him, Paige thought, nearly losing herself in his slightly crooked grin. His hair was still just as dark, his face still smooth and devoid of facial hair, and his eyes were still the same electric shade of blue. He was still beautiful, and from the chivalrous behavior he'd exhibited tonight, he was still just as kind and caring as he had been ten years ago.

"I do have to get going," he was saying in an apologetic tone of voice. "I hope everything is all right, and get her home safely, all right?" He looked down at Paige. "Nice meeting you and keep out of trouble."

No, don't leave. There's so much I have to say to you. Paige watched him leave in frustration and then stared down at her hands, unbeknownst to the fact that Marissa was watching her closely.

"What the hell was that all about?" Marissa demanded with her hands on her hips. A fine sheen of sweat graced her deep brown skin and her curly dark hair billowed around her head. "You didn't even finish your first beer so you can't be drunk."

Paige didn't answer. She didn't know *how* to answer. She didn't answer the question until she was seated in the passenger seat of her own car with Marissa sitting beside her at the wheel. Shane, Evelyn, and Deana were slurring one- and two-syllable words in the backseat. "He was my teacher," she said after moments of gazing out of the car window at flitting scenery.

"Your teacher?" Marissa repeated, her jaw dropping open in shock. She laughed and shook her head.

"Yeah, my teacher."

"Your *teacher*, teacher? He doesn't look much older than we are."

"Yes, my *teacher*, teacher. He was my teacher," Paige said, wincing at the redundancy of the conversation. "He was twenty-four when I was a junior in high school. That should make him about thirty-five now."

With her fingernails drumming on the steering wheel, Marissa whistled. "Wow."

Paige took a deep breath and told Marissa about the spitballs being thrown in her hair when she attended high school, about how she'd gotten fed up and stormed out of the classroom, and about how Ethan had chased her down the hallway to make sure she was all right.

"Wow, a little Lolita action," Marissa commented.

"No, nothing like that," Paige corrected, frowning. "Anyway, the next year, my last year in high school, I hardly saw him."

"So...what happened just now, back there at the bar?"

Paige turned and looked at Marissa's profile, then returned to gazing out of the window. "I don't know what happened back there. The shock of seeing him just brought up a lot of old emotions."

"What kind of emotions?" Marissa asked, cursing under her breath as a small, red Ford Focus cut in front of her.

"I don't know. I should just forget all about it," Paige said, trailing her fingers down the window.

"Forget all about it?" Marissa parroted. "Paige, Paige, Paige."

Paige didn't say anything.

"Paige, this right here, what you just told me, this is real romance." She tapped the top of the steering wheel with the bottom of her hand. "This is what you should be writing about, not knights and princesses and secretaries and their bosses and shit."

"I'm not going to write a romance about a teacher and a student, 'Rissa, that's taboo," Paige said, rolling her eyes.

Marissa shrugged and pulled the car to a stop at a red light. "So that gorgeous guy was your teacher, huh?"

"I thought we already covered that."

"Man, if he'd been my teacher, I would have graduated with straight A's, like...top of my class."

Paige's brows drew together, and she turned to face Marissa. "You *did* graduate with straight A's, top of your class."

The light flashed green, and before pressing her foot down on the gas pedal, Marissa looked at Paige and insisted, "I would have graduated with straighter A's."

Paige spent most of Sunday morning sleeping, trying to mentally block out the sounds of Olivia screaming and running up and down the hallway like a banshee on speed.

She'd had a restless night of tossing and turning in bed, plagued by dreams of a man she knew she'd never get the chance to be with.

There were so many questions she wished she'd asked him while she'd had the chance. She wished she'd felt confident enough to tell him who she was and ask him how he'd been all this time, whether or not he still taught at the local high school, and just how serious were he and Diane?

By the time she woke up, more than half the day had passed by. Deana called her from her hotel room to tell her that she, Marissa, Shane, and Evelyn, were going to be driving back to Chicago.

"We might be up next weekend," Deana said noncommittally, her voice sounding heavy and thick with exhaustion. "And Shane said he'd call you. I hope you have fun. Treat this like a vacation, all right? And no more drinking for you."

Paige padded barefoot into an empty kitchen at two in the afternoon, dressed in a silk royal blue pajama shirt and matching pajama pants with her hair gathered in a knot at the top of her head. She rummaged through the contents of the refrigerator, scouring through leftover casseroles, jugs of V8, and various condiments. "Ugh," she muttered after opening the freezer door and discovering several bags of frozen, glassy-eyed fish.

Her father walked into the kitchen, fully dressed in slacks and a polo shirt. He had an open newspaper in his hands and he was reading the newspaper as he walked, eyes skimming the words over the rims of his spectacles. When he saw Paige, he halted his steps and smiled. "Come out of hibernation, have we?" he quipped, sitting at the small, round kitchen table with the newspaper still in his hands.

She closed the freezer door without responding to her father's attempt at humor. "There's no ice cream in the house," she muttered crabbily.

"The stores are open 'til five today. You still have a few hours if you want to get in some grocery shopping," her father replied, glancing at his watch.

"I don't want to go grocery shopping," she grumbled, claiming a seat across from her father and folding her arms across her chest.

"Are you going out with your friends today?"

"They're headed back to the city," she replied.

Her father set the newspaper on the table and looked at her. "You feeling all right?"

"No."

"Want to talk about it?"

"Not right now."

"There's something I want to ask you." He braced an elbow on the surface of the table. "It would mean a lot to me."

Her face remained expressionless.

"I want to take your mother somewhere nice for a few days," her father began. "Like a second honeymoon, you know?"

A small smile formed on Paige's lips. "That's so sweet, Dad."

"Don't say that yet," he said, glowing with cheer. "While we're gone, Olivia and Sam are going to need someone watching them. Their mother won't be back in town for several days."

The smile on Paige's face faltered and she sat back in her chair. "I don't know about that, Dad."

"You don't have an office job you have to get back to. You write," her father said. "The beauty of writing is you can do it anywhere. You can use the computer in my office, and they're darling kids. You used to look over Sam."

"I babysat her ten years ago. She's...all grown up now," Paige said, rising from her chair and proceeding to search the cabinets for the closest thing to comfort food.

"Sam and Olivia are great kids and they wouldn't give you any trouble," her father guaranteed.

An image of Olivia clanging pots and pans on the floor and running up and down the halls flashed in Paige's mind and she laughed dryly as she rummaged through cabinets.

"Please, Paige? For your mother and I? You don't know how much I'd appreciate it."

Everything in Paige screamed for her to decline, to make up an excuse as to why she couldn't possibly stay and watch the kids. They were *kids*. When she was a teenager herself, she took to babysitting the neighbor's daughter, but now that she was an adult, she felt as if she'd lost a grip on watching over children. She hadn't had constant contact with children since babysitting Samantha ten years ago. Then there was the fact that the thought of waking up to Olivia every morning for a week was about as terrifying as waking up and finding out she'd grown a second head overnight.

As much as she wanted to refuse to watch Olivia and Samantha, she couldn't refuse her father. He looked so hopeful, so cheerful about surprising her mother with a second honeymoon, and they were her parents. She owed them a lot. "Of course I'll watch the kids," she said finally.

"We're going to be leaving early in the morning," her father said, standing from his chair and tucking the newspaper under his arm. "I'll post contact numbers for us on the fridge, but don't call unless it's a dire emergency," he added with a mischievous grin.

Evelyn waved goodbye to Deana and withdrew her car keys from her purse. The air was extremely chilly, biting at the skin that was exposed due to wearing a black, knee-length skirt, black, long-sleeved blouse, and no jacket. The coat she'd brought along to Beach Park was stashed in the small blue suitcase she held in her right hand. Her heels clicked on the pavement as she strode up the walkway that led to the front porch of a white, two-story house that had cost her husband roughly six hundred thousand dollars.

In her mind, she was going over what she would tell her husband, because Paige had been right. She couldn't continue cheating on him behind his back, no matter how neglected she felt in their marriage. He might not make enough time for her in his schedule, but he was working hard, and he was a decent man. When he did have time for her, he spent it spoiling her every need, and while it wasn't often enough to please her, she supposed that cheating on him was horrible of her.

She was ashamed of her actions, unsure if she'd be able to confess them to her husband. He was a mild-mannered man; she had never witnessed any violent behavior from him in the past, but then again, she rarely saw him express anger, since...she rarely saw him. She wasn't certain as to how he was going to react to whatever she decided to tell him. She wasn't certain about a lot of things.

She definitely wasn't certain as to how she'd gotten to this point in her life, a point where she had to stand outside of the front door of her own house, thinking up a monologue to tell her husband, thinking up reasons to tell him why she'd cheated on him. All of a sudden, "You were never there," didn't seem sufficient.

Maybe I don't have to tell him tonight, she thought to herself, inserting the house key into the front door's lock. *I can wait until tomorrow, and that way, I'll have time to think about everything.* She turned the key in the lock, opened the door, extracted her keys and returned them to a pouch in her purse. The living room light was off, the corridor light was off, but the upstairs hallway light was on.

From looking at the eccentric, glass wall clock in the living room, Evelyn could see that it was nine o' clock at night. Neither she nor Eric left lights on in the house before leaving, so she deducted that Eric must be home. Still carrying her suitcase in hand, purse still slung over her shoulder, she climbed the winding stairs that led to the upstairs hall.

When she was halfway up the stairs, she thought she heard her husband laughing. *He must be watching Seinfeld reruns again,* she thought, smiling to herself. She continued walking up the stairs, conquered the last step and turned left. The master bedroom was at the end of the hall, and the bedroom door was cracked open. Reaching the door, she pushed the door open with her foot and felt her heart break in two.

Her husband was stretched out beside an Asian woman with long, glossy black hair; his own blonde hair gleamed with sweat. Sheets were pulled up to his waist, but it was obvious that both he and the woman lying beside him were naked. He was unaware of Evelyn's presence and continued stroking down the woman's flat belly, whispering dirty things into her ear and nipping her shoulder with his teeth.

The suitcase dropped to the floor with a heavy thud and it popped open, spilling designer blouses and Revlon cosmetics onto the carpeted floor. She didn't dare step over the threshold of the room in fear that she'd surge forward, grab a handful of the woman's hair, and bang her head against the bureau.

Eric's gaze lifted at the sound of the collapsing suitcase and when he saw his furious wife, an "uh-oh" look came across his face. The muscles in his jaw flexed and he lie in bed staring up at his wife while his mistress, feeling his body tense, followed his gaze. Her eyes widened slightly, but otherwise she didn't look surprised or shocked.

His mistress had known he was married, Evelyn realized, tears starting at the corners of her eyes. Voice failing her and hyperventilation seeming inevitable, she kicked her suitcase farther into the room so that she could close the door and leave the two lovers. She turned away from the door and walked to the staircase.

She was confused by her own grief and dismay. For the past two months, she'd been shacking up with her personal trainer. This was no doubt her comeuppance for her actions. The logical part of her could admit that she deserved this.

The woman in her wanted to storm back into that bedroom and give the bastard a piece of her mind, using every vulgar word she could think of. She stood at the staircase, lost in thought, wondering what her next move should be.

The bedroom door at the end of the hall swung open and Eric's frame filled it. The expression on his face wasn't one of apology. He looked to be annoyed that he'd been interrupted. "So now you know," he said, approaching her and stopping a few feet away from her.

"Yeah, now I know," she confirmed, not meeting his eyes.

He ran a hand through his short, blonde hair. "I would have preferred for you to not find out this way."

"I would have rather not found out at all," she said honestly.

"She works with me."

"I don't want to know what the fuck she does with you," she seethed in a quiet voice.

"You and I were spending less and less time together," he went on despite her request. "I was in need of companionship. What can I say?"

"You can say you're sorry," she suggested, her usually high-pitched voice now a flat monotone.

The muscles in his jaw worked. He let out a deep sigh and said, "Well, I *could* say that, but it wouldn't be true."

"And we know you have a record of being an honest man." She looked down the stairs, for a moment considering throwing herself down them. Dismissing the absurd urge, she turned to face him. "Since I've found out about you, that makes it easier for me to tell you that for the past two months I've been fucking my personal trainer within an inch of his young life."

He smirked. "Only two months? Lin and I have been at it for nearly a year now."

Anger spiked along her spine. "A year?" she demanded, her voice cracking. She clamped a hand to her own mouth to refrain from shouting belligerently at him. In her mind, she asked herself how she could have married such a bastard. She asked herself how was it possible that she hadn't realized he *was* such a bastard. Was she that naïve? How *could* she have been so naïve? Why had he even felt the need to cheat on her with another woman when she'd been in front of his nose every night when he came home? Was there something wrong with her? Maybe he found her undesirable; it was possible that he was no longer attracted to her.

I should have sensed that something was wrong, she thought to herself, standing in front of her husband and not quite knowing what to say. She knew what she *wanted* to say. She wanted to ask why he'd cheated on her, and then follow that with a barrage of cursing.

As if reading her mind, he said, "I'm a man of power, Evelyn. I'm a man of wealth. Before I had either, I thought what I wanted was a housewife kept at the home front to support my aspirations, someone to agree with everything I said, and to laugh at all of my jokes, so I felt important." He paused dramatically, rubbing the back of his neck. "When my career exploded and took off, I realized that I didn't need a cheerleader at home making me feel important, because I *was* and *am* important. What I needed wasn't a yes-man. I needed someone who was as successful as I was, a professional who could challenge me and put me in check when I needed to be. I needed someone who complements me. Lin does that.

"*You*...you don't do that. You sit around the house, and the activities that take up most of your time are watching soap operas, spending money I've earned, and going to the gym." Mentioning the gym, he gave her a look as if to scold her. "When you found about Lin and me, I was expecting some huge drama fest with you shouting and yelling at me, possibly throwing shit, I don't know, but now that I know that you've been fucking a personal trainer that *I* hired for you, you don't really have the right to go doing all of that, do you?"

Her marriage was falling apart right in front of her eyes, and she couldn't come up with anything wise or intelligent to say to counter his argument.

Still rubbing the back of his neck, he pressed on, "You know, when you get right down to the bottom line, I guess the truth of the matter is that I've grown bored of you. You've never had to work a day in your life, and even though you're a college graduate, you have the mental capacity of a child. You're not intelligent and you're not comical…well, except with your bedroom habits."

"You…*prick*," she muttered, shaking her head in disbelief.

He arched a brow quizzically. "I'm standing in front of you telling you that I've grown bored of you, that you're awful in bed, and that you're dim-witted, and that's all you have to say for yourself?"

"Did you expect me to scream at you and start a fight with you?" she questioned. "You're not important enough to me for that."

"It's what my type of woman would have done."

That statement was the straw that broke the camel's back. She raised a clenched fist and proceeded to clock him in the nose. Adrenaline rushed through her limbs, and seeing that he didn't topple to the floor immediately (which was the desired effect), she drew her arm back another time and punched him again.

She wasn't disappointed this time. He crumbled like the Berlin Wall, falling to his knees with his hands clasped over his nose. "You fucking *bitch*," he growled, his words muffled behind his hands, but his words clear nonetheless. "You fucking *bitch*, I think you broke my nose."

"You want a yes man? You want a cheerleader?" she demanded, hyped up on anger, frustration, and temporary insanity. "I'll show you a fucking yes man." She walked around his fallen body and re-entered their bedroom. Fortunate for her, her husband's mistress was still lying in bed. She stormed across the room, towards the spacious, walk-in closet. Flicking the light on, she spotted what she was looking for.

Eric stumbled into the room, and the mistress sat upright in bed. The mistress forgot the fact that she was completely naked and leapt out of bed. She walked across the room and collected her lover in a comforting embrace. "Are you all right? What did she do to you?"

Evelyn, armed with a Polaroid camera, snapped consistently, and lowered the camera when Eric whirled to glare at her. "My, my," she murmured in a voice cloaked with counterfeit sweetness. "Look who's dimwitted *now*, asshole."

Chapter Five

Paige never wanted to have children. They were as cute as buttons, but they were also loud, needy, and persistent with questions that they wouldn't remember the answers to the next day anyway. Olivia was an energetic girl who seemed to be allergic to sitting still; even her inquisitive little mind was constantly moving. If she wasn't asking Paige for help on her homework, she was asking why Paige never wore much makeup or telling Paige more about her "boyfriend," Jeremy. Samantha was basically a good kid. She was constantly on the phone, but when she wasn't, she was doing homework or helping out with Olivia.

Paige felt an entirely new respect for her parents, for *all* parents in general. Keeping up with a kid on a sugar high was no easy feat, and keeping up with *Olivia* on a sugar high was damned near impossible.

Early Monday morning, Olivia walked into Paige's room and proceeded to shake her awake. "Sam and I need a ride to school," she whispered.

Eyes narrowed into sleepy slits, Paige slung an arm over her eyes. "Isn't there a bus or something?"

"We don't ride the bus," Olivia explained.

"You're riding the bus."

"No, we *can't*," Olivia said. "Some girl picked a fight with Sam, so Sam beat her up and we can't ride the bus anymore."

"You ride the same bus as Sam?"

"No, but if you're dropping Sam off to school, you might as well drop me off," the young girl reasoned. "It's on the way."

Paige groaned and rolled over on her stomach, trying to the best of her ability to ignore the child. When she turned her head to the side and opened her eyes, Olivia was still standing there, dressed in a purple turtleneck with unicorns on it, jeans, and sneakers. She held her backpack and her lunchbox in her hands, and Paige laughed and sat up. "All right, all right," she muttered.

In the car, Samantha sat in the passenger seat, dressed in a sweater, jeans, and a sports jacket with her hair pulled back in a ponytail. Olivia sat in the back seat and inspected the contents Samantha had filled her lunchbox with the previous night. She piped up, saying, "And I get out of school at three o' clock, but Sam is staying in school until six, because she has volleyball practice after school."

Samantha rode silently, looking out of the car window. She was about as much of a morning person as Paige was.

"And we should really get some grocery shopping done," Olivia continued thoughtfully. "There's no food in the house."

Paige dropped Olivia off in front of her school, an unassuming one-story brick building with the words Beach Park Elementary above the double door entrance. Once Olivia was out of the car and inside the school building, Paige felt like putting the car in Park, stepping outside, and performing a series of cartwheels in celebration of getting rid of the kid. Instead, she pulled away from the curb and, following Samantha's solemnly-given directions, drove towards the high school.

"Are you all right?" Paige asked, touching Samantha's shoulder.

Samantha looked surprised for a few moments, looking down at Paige's hand on her shoulder. "I'm fine, just tired," she said finally.

"You look...unhappy," Paige said. "If you don't want to talk about it, that's fine, but if you *do*, just talk to me, all right?"

Smiling and nodding, the dark-haired teenager opened the car door and slid out of the passenger seat.

Paige gazed at the school building, rocked by the nostalgia that attacked her. She remembered the times she'd walked to school because whenever she rode the bus, objects were thrown at her. She remembered crouching in the teacher's parking lot when she skipped class because she'd grown tired of tolerating the jerks and class clowns.

All of a sudden, Paige couldn't get away from the school fast enough. She put the car into Drive and pressed her foot on the gas, but swiftly moved her foot to the brake when she saw that she was about to mow down a certain six-five, dark-haired teacher.

Ethan Carson closed the car door of his silver Dodge Intrepid and pressed a button on his key ring that caused the car alarm to chirp. He was dressed in dress slacks, a maroon polo shirt, and a black leather trench. He slung a leather satchel over his shoulder as he turned away from his car and walked towards the school's front entrance. He noticed the navy blue Ford Explorer parked at the curb, but the driver of the Ford Explorer must not have noticed him, because all of a sudden the car roared to life, lurching towards him and stopping with an abrupt screech.

Nothing like being scared shitless before a day in the classroom, he thought to himself, stepping farther away from the front bumper.

A brunette jumped out of the car, apologizing profusely. "I'm *so* sorry, I didn't see you there. I'm in a hurry and I wasn't paying attention like I should have-"

"Don't I know you?" he asked, approaching the distressed woman with a knowing grin on his face.

Paige panicked and a lump the size of Texas formed in her throat. *Oh my God, he recognizes me,* she thought. *He knows who I am now, he knows I had a crush on him in high school, and now he thinks I'm stalking him.*

"Um, I-I-I-" she stammered helplessly.

"You're the woman from a few nights ago, at the bar," he went on, shoving his hands in his pockets.

"Oh," she said, his words taking awhile to register to her mind. Then she said, "*Oh.* Oh, yeah, that was me. I'm sorry about that."

"No problem. I guess your girlfriend drove you home and everything turned out all right. I did wonder about you after that."

My girlfriend? He must be talking about Marissa. "Yeah, she had to drive me home. I was in a bit of a stupor. I apologize."

"Like I said, it's no problem. I was just worried. You seemed really..."

Ditzy, flighty...I seemed like I should have been riding the short yellow bus. It's okay, you can say it. "I think I had a little too much to drink," she lied, now regretting that she'd left her hair up in its usual topknot. She should have let it down, dragged a brush through it a few times, and she was wearing her silk pajamas with a coat over them. What the hell had she been thinking?

"You have to watch that liquor, it can sneak up on you," he warned, his blue eyes sparkling with mirth. "So who were you dropping off? You're not old enough to be a mother to someone who attends this school."

"Oh, umm..." *My neighbor's kid? My friend's kid? My niece, nephew...*

"A younger sister or brother?"

"Yeah," Paige said quickly, and smiled sheepishly. "Sam."

"Sam?"

"Samantha Waterford."

"Oh, *Sam*? She's on the volleyball team, isn't she?"

Was she? "I don't want to make you late for class," she said lamely.

"I don't have a class first period, so it's all right." He studied her from her floppy topknot to her puppy dog slippers. "I'm glad you and your girlfriend got home safe, and it's good that you guys are unashamed to be with each other. You know...in public, in a small town."

She didn't know what the hell he was talking about, but he looked so good, she didn't quite care. Her fingers tingled at the tips, yearning to brush some of his hair back from his forehead. "Well she's my best friend," she responded finally.

"You two's dancing really threw everyone in the place for a loop-it was amazing. I'm glad that you two are proud to show the world you're together."

We're together? Her mouth dropped open as she realized what he was saying. *He thinks I'm a fucking lesbian!*

"Keep your head up. Since you're Sam's sister, I might see you around...what was your name again?"

"Paige," she replied automatically and cursed under her breath. She hadn't meant to tell him her real first name.

He nodded his head. "Hope to see you again, Paige. I really should get inside now, but this is a small town so we'll probably be bumping into each other from time to time."

She watched him turn and walk up the long walkway to the front doors. Turning to her car, she didn't know whether she wanted to laugh or cry. Not only did he think she was Samantha's sister, when, of course, she *wasn't*, but he also thought that she was a lesbian. The situation was so bizarre it was comical, and as Paige drove home, she laughed and shook her head. She vowed to kick Marissa's ass the next time she saw her for dancing so sensually with her in front of a room full of drunkards, who were no doubt spreading word around town that she was a raging lesbian.

Instead of driving straight home, she decided to take Olivia's advice and shop for some groceries. From the moment she stepped into the moderately-sized grocery store, it seemed as if everyone visible in the store turned to look at her and all noise ceased. Then, the whispering started. It seemed that whenever she passed two women speaking with each other, their voices would drop several decibels and their eyes would follow her movements. That could have been her overactive imagination, however.

When she was finished shopping and standing in the checkout line, the cashier eyed her warily, seeming to catalogue her every move in some sector of his brain. *Instead of inspecting me so closely, he needs to be inspecting his own face,* she thought to herself, noting that acne littered his cheeks and nose. *Someone needs to tell him that Noxema and Proactive aren't four-letter words.*

She drove home and, after nearly slipping on a patch of ice scabbed over the sidewalk, toted the groceries into the house. She dropped her car keys on the kitchen table and started stocking food in the cabinets and refrigerator.

The house was quiet without the children in it. She thought she was going crazy, because for the past weekend she hadn't been able to get the sound of Olivia screaming out of her ears, but she actually missed the little girl and her older sister. The boogers had actually grown on her.

The phone on the living room lamp stand shrilled and Paige lifted it to her ear. "Hello?"

"Have you had fun and spontaneous sex with the teacher yet?" Marissa demanded.

"Call me crazy, but I don't think that's going to happen," Paige said, temporarily muting the soap opera she'd been watching.

"Don't give up hope," Marissa said cheerfully.

"No, he has a girlfriend, first off," Paige said. "*Secondly* he thinks you're *my* girlfriend."

There were phones ringing in the background, so Marissa was most likely at work. "He thinks you're my what?"

"He thinks we're lesbos," Paige explained.

"What? *Why?*"

"Because you were molesting me on the damned dance floor."

"I was teaching you how to dance."

"That's not how he sees it," Paige muttered, and told Marissa about the encounter she'd had with him a few hours ago.

Marissa laughed hysterically. "You told him Samantha was your sister? Are you crazy? That's brilliant."

"Am I crazy? That's brilliant?" Paige repeated, highly irritated. "Right now, the man who I once deemed the love of my life is under the impression that I'm my neighbor's sister and attracted to women. No, the next time I see him, *if* I see him, I'm going to tell him the truth."

"Think about this, Paige. Lesbianism is a turn on to men. It'll intrigue him, not disgust him."

"He's not a man, he's a teacher," Paige whined, slumping down farther on the couch.

"He's a *man*. There are so many possibilities here, Paige. If the chick he's with thinks you're a lesbian, she won't feel threatened. Maybe you can be friends with him while he's with her, but when they break up, snag him for yourself."

"Just wake up one day and declare that I'm no longer a lesbian."

"You *aren't* a lesbian," Marissa pointed out.

"Huh?"

"What?"

Running a hand through her hair, Paige said, "I can't pretend to be a lesbian, then all of a sudden decide that I'm not when he breaks up with whatever-her-name-is."

"Happens all the time," Marissa stated.

The thought of moonlighting as a lesbian was preposterous and outrageous. She couldn't see herself attempting to hold up such a charade. In the unlikely event that Ethan would actually dump his current girlfriend and decide he wanted to date Paige, their relationship would be based on a heap of lies, and she didn't want that. She probably wouldn't even see him again, but she decided that if she did, she was going to come clean and tell him that his assumption about Marissa and herself was incorrect.

Marissa sighed, sounding just as depressed as Paige felt. "Fine, don't follow my advice," she said. "I just want to see you happy, though. If you want the teacher, you deserve the teacher."

I do *want the teacher,* Paige thought to herself, telling Marissa, "You'd better get back to work before you no longer have a job."

Marissa laughed, but agreed with that sentiment. They said their goodbyes and Paige hung up the phone, wanting to bury her face in the couch cushion like an ostrich's head in the sand.

If Ethan Carson had to sit through another documentary on how damaging cigarette smoke was to the lungs, his head was going to explode. He sat at his desk at the front of the classroom, feigning interest in the educational video, which was more than he could say for most of the students in the room. Every few minutes, he was calling a student's name for passing a note, whispering too loudly, or attempting to catch some Z's on class time.

Being a teacher wasn't easy. You had to wake up early in the morning, discipline misfits, and have the patience of a *saint*. There were days he questioned himself on the career path he'd chosen. He could have easily become a college basketball coach, as his father had been. He would have been great at it.

His father had expected him to follow in his footsteps. Imagine the old man's surprise when Ethan approached him and told him that it was in his heart to be a teacher.

The old man had nearly keeled over, riddled with shock and disappointment. "A *teacher?*" he'd croaked in a voice that had grown nasally with age. "You're giving up 'ball for what? For the chance to babysit a bunch of suburbanite troublemakers?"

Ethan had never been more disappointed in his father than he had been at that moment; his father had spoken as if the profession of teaching was inferior to coaching college basketball. His father died without understanding why Ethan chose teaching over coaching college basketball.

Ethan wasn't sure why he, himself, had chosen teaching over coaching college basketball…probably because in junior high school, the most awkward point in his life, at a time when his parents weren't there for him because they were too busy working, teachers *were* there for him. Those teachers had been nothing short of heroes for him. They'd patiently listened to him vent after school hours and let him know that just because he was tall and gangly for his age, it didn't mean that he was odd or freakish. Surprisingly, teachers had been the first to suggest that Ethan consider participating in sports, not Ethan's father. Only after Ethan was involved did his father attempt at molding him into a splitting image of himself. Only after Ethan was assigned as point guard for his junior high's basketball team did his father set aside his busy schedule to free up some time for his son.

Well, that was the past. In the present, Ethan was one of the most popular teachers and one of the toughest coaches in Beach Park High School. He'd been teaching for nearly eleven years, and he didn't regret one minute of it. He was content with the career choice he'd made. His love life was another story.

It wasn't that he didn't enjoy spending time with Diane. She was a very elegant, well-spoken woman with steely determination. When she didn't overdo her makeup or overdress, she was a beautiful woman. In actuality, Ethan was boggled by the fact that someone as glamorous and well put-together as Diane was interested in him. Initially, he'd assumed that she was only interested in a casual bedmate. He hadn't anticipated her enthusiasm and determination to make their relationship work. He definitely hadn't expected her to fall in love with him.

Whenever he was around her, he found that more and more often, he was deliberately *trying* to find what she said funny, what she wore beautiful, and the remarks that she made intelligent. He was *trying* to love her the way she loved him, but when he pictured himself moving in with her, standing beside her at their wedding, and having children with her, it made him shudder. She wasn't the woman he wanted to spend the rest of his life with, but since he couldn't find a decent, diplomatic way to tell her that, he continued to take her on dates, whisk her around town and out of town, and allow her into his bed. It wasn't right. It was downright despicable, even, but he didn't know what else to do. Breaking up with her would break her heart, and he didn't know if he had the heart to do that.

After his seventh-and last-period class was over, he watched the last student exit the classroom and allowed his head to fall forward on his desk.

A small knock sounded on the windowpane next to the door. "Don't go getting suicidal on me," came a gruff voice. Richard McCade, known around the campus as Coach Dick (a term of endearment tagged by his students), leaned against the doorjamb with his hands shoved in the pockets of his jogging pants. His blonde hair was slicked back and he didn't look much older than Ethan was, even though he was pushing his mid-forties. He taught physical education and coached the school's varsity football team. Lately, when he wasn't teaching or coaching, it seemed that he was counseling Ethan. "You look like you're having a day from hell."

"I'm having the *month* from hell," Ethan corrected, raising his head from his desk and leaning back in his chair. Covering his face with both hands, he shook his head.

"Woman troubles again?"

"It would take a few weeks just to tell you the problems I'm having," Ethan answered. "It's…it's a mess, that's all I can say about it."

Richard sauntered into the room. "If a woman's giving you that much trouble, get rid of her."

"*Not* that simple."

"Yeah, it is," Richard insisted. "Tell her that it's not working out, or that you need space, or that your time will be limited because you're still taking classes for your Master's degree. You *are* doing that, right?"

"I don't want to *lie* to her. I'm breaking up with her and that's bad enough."

"You wouldn't be lying. You'd be stretching the truth," Richard said.

"I don't want to do that either," Ethan groaned. "I don't even want to break up with her. It's immature as hell, but I wish I could leave a message on her voicemail or something, you know? I don't want to hear her voice or see her face when…when I tell her."

Richard shook his head in sympathy. "If you don't do it soon, you'll be trailing behind her while she shops for china patterns and scouting for bridesmaid's dresses."

The very concept sent knots into Ethan's stomach. "You're right. I definitely have to end it before all of *that* goes down." He ran a hand through his dark hair. "Are you staying after school today?"

"I have to give make-up fitness exams," Richard said, suppressing a yawn. "The joys of my job. You staying after?"

"We have practice tonight, and being the coach, I have to be there."

"Go figure."

"After that, Diane and I are supposed to go out."

"You should take that opportunity to tell her it's over," Richard suggested, leaning his hip against the front of Ethan's desk.

The knots in Ethan's stomach intensified and he braced his elbows on his desk, leaning his face forward into open palms. "I can't," he said. His voice was slightly muffled by his hands.

"I don't want to *hear* you can't," Richard said, nearly as exasperated as Ethan was. "You have to nip this shit in the bud or you'll be regretting it the rest of your life."

"No...I can't tell her tonight," Ethan repeated, letting his hands slide down his cheeks and looking over his fingertips at Richard.

"Why can't you tell her tonight?" Richard demanded. "Give me a valid reason."

"Because," Ethan replied, "tonight's our six-month anniversary."

Richard was quiet a few minutes. Then he nodded and said, "Shit."

"Yeah," Ethan said, rising from his chair and stuffing his books into his satchel. "'Shit' is right." He led Richard out of the classroom and locked the door behind them. Richard stayed by his side as he walked down the hallway, down a flight of stairs, and towards the gymnasium on the main floor.

"It's been six months, wow," Richard thought aloud as they walked. "You didn't buy her anything, did you?"

"Of *course* I bought her something, Rich. It's our anniversary."

"You know you're going to break up with her, so what the hell's the point in buying her something?" Richard demanded to know.

Ethan chuckled at his friend's logic. "I wouldn't expect you to understand."

Richard chortled in surprise. "And what's that supposed to mean?"

"Just that you're going on forty-five and you're still a bachelor. More than that, you *prefer* to be a bachelor."

"Too many beautiful women in the world to just settle down with one," Richard reasoned.

"You're a teacher."

"I'm a man first, teacher second," Richard corrected. "Just because I'm a teacher doesn't make me inhuman. A man's got *needs*."

"Mental help should be scribbled in somewhere on your list of needs," Ethan joked as they entered the large gymnasium that was sectioned off by a divider.

Richard shrugged his shoulders. "Hey, I'm not offended," he said. "I know what I am and I'm proud of it. It's definitely gotten me through forty-five years without getting into a messed-up situation like the one you're in now."

Some of the basketball players trickled onto the court and Ethan turned to Richard. "I have to get to practice. I'll see you tomorrow. You can cause more damage to my self-esteem then."

A dark-haired girl in maroon, white, and gold gym shirts and a junior varsity volleyball t-shirt jogged past Ethan and Richard.

Richard whistled under his breath and Ethan nudged him in the ribs. "That's disgusting," he chastised. Then he called to the girl in the volleyball uniform, "Sam!"

Samantha Waterford turned around in mid-stride and waved at Ethan and Richard. She approached them. Her face was flushed and her hair was pulled back in a ponytail. "Hi, Mr. Carson, Mr. McCade," she greeted cheerfully.

Richard said his good-byes to Ethan, nodded towards Samantha, and turned away from them, walking towards the gym exit.

"Looks like we have to share the gym with you guys again," Samantha said, gesturing to the boys practicing lay-ups several yards away.

"Rich-Mr. McCade-has to give make-up exams in the other gym," Ethan explained. He rubbed his jaw and told her, "I got the pleasure of meeting your sister this morning."

Samantha's brows furrowed in confusion. "You did?"

"Yeah, and I can see the resemblance between you two, too." He started backing away from her, glancing at his watch. Practice was due to start any minute. "When you get home, tell her I said hi, will you?" He turned and jogged away, leaving Samantha with a stupefied expression on her face.

"The weirdest thing happened at practice," Samantha said as she climbed in the passenger seat of Paige's car.

"What happened?" Paige asked, starting the car.

"Mr. Carson-he coaches the boys' varsity basketball team-he said he met Olivia this morning," Samantha explained, pulling her seatbelt across her torso and clicking it into its proper slot. "He couldn't have though, right? You dropped off Olivia before you dropped me off."

Paige nervously tapped her fingernails on the top of the steering wheel, pulling the car away from the curb and hesitating before blurting out to Samantha, "He didn't meet Olivia this morning. He met me."

"But he said he met my sister," Samantha said with her brows furrowed in confusion.

"I…kind of told him I was your sister," Paige admitted after wincing.

Samantha looked at Paige and laughed. "Why did you do that?"

To tell the kid or to not tell the kid, Paige thought to herself, *that is the question.* She decided to tell Samantha part of the truth. "He was my teacher in high school and I didn't want him to remember who I was."

"He was your teacher when you went to high school?" Samantha released her hair from its ponytail holder and shook it out so that it fell to her shoulders. "Wow, I didn't know he was that old."

"Thanks a lot," Paige said, laughing.

"Why didn't you want him to remember who you were?" Samantha asked curiously.

Paige shrugged. "I don't know. I was a different person back then."

"So we're sisters now?"

"Temporarily, yes," Paige answered, nodding.

Samantha nodded her head cooperatively. "Cool."

After basketball practice, Ethan was usually more exhausted than his players. Nine times out of ten, his voice was hoarse from yelling and screaming at them, his shoulders tense from watching their shooting, his muscles sore and strained from showing them how they *should* be shooting.

As he unlocked the door to his apartment, he mentally pictured himself relaxing in a tub of hot water soothing every aching muscle. When he walked into the apartment, he didn't expect to see a naked redhead standing a few feet away with a wine glass in each hand.

At the sight of him, her mouth relaxed into a coquettish grin and she walked up to him, offering him one of the wine glasses. She rose on her tip-toes and whispered, "Happy anniversary," in his ear, nipping his earlobe. Settling on the balls of her feet, she turned and walked away from him, slender hips swaying.

He swallowed the lump that had formed in his throat at the sight of her and took a long swig of wine. He followed her into the living room, setting the wine glass on the top of the entertainment center and shedding his leather trench coat while she languidly positioned herself on his couch. "How'd you get into the apartment?"

"I had a copy of your apartment key made," she answered silkily, still holding her glass of wine.

He awkwardly stood next to the entertainment center, not knowing exactly what to do. He watched her writhe seductively on the couch, thinking to himself that he couldn't possibly have sex with her. He was planning on ending their relationship. To have sex with her now would be taking advantage of her, wouldn't it? On the other hand, her body was slick with either sweat or oil (he couldn't tell which). In addition to that, the round curves of her breasts and behind were slowly unraveling his resolve. "How long have you been here?"

"An hour." She stretched out on her stomach and slipped an index finger into her mouth, peering up at him. "I've been here for an hour, all by myself, nothing to do... no one to do." She pouted prettily, laying her head on the armrest of the couch.

"An hour," he repeated, trying to clear his head and think logically. That was pretty difficult to do with a naked woman lying on his couch and pouting lipstick-smeared lips at him.

Realizing that he wasn't going to be making a move towards the couch, she sat up and planted her feet on the floor. Then, she stood and walked around the glass coffee table until she was standing directly in front of him. Reaching a hand up to brush a lock of his hair back, she asked him casually, "So how was your day?"

Trying desperately to not be aware that her medium-length red hair was draped sexily over her shoulders and pink-tipped nipples were brushing against the front of his shirt, he answered, "It was fine."

"Practice?"

"Good."

"Aren't you going to touch me?"

He raised his eyes to the ceiling and prayed that something, *anything*, would interrupt them. Nothing did, and she inched closer to him, making it difficult for him to breathe. "I've got a lot of...papers to grade," he said and cleared his throat.

"It's our anniversary, Ethan," she said, her pout looking less manufactured and more genuine by the second. "I'm sure you can put it off for one night."

"I told them I'd get these quizzes back to them by tomorrow," he insisted, avoiding her probing gaze.

The corners of her mouth tilted downward and she took a step back. "So, what, our anniversary takes a backseat to a bunch of quizzes?"

"It's my job, Diane," he said, relieved that she was getting worked up. If he could get her to argue with him, then it was pretty much guaranteed he wouldn't have to be intimate with her tonight.

"Your job?" She pressed her hands on the front of his chest, slid them down to his waist, where she untucked the t-shirt he'd worn for basketball practice. With her tongue sticking between her teeth, she tilted her head to the side. Her hands were still tugging at the hem of his shirt as she said, "Your *job* is to make me happy. And you know what would make me happy right now?"

He didn't want to know what would make her happy right now. What would make *him* happy was being as far away from her as possible. "The grading," he said morosely, looking at some point over her head, anywhere but her eyes, which had sex written all over them.

She lifted the t-shirt over his head, having to rise on tip-toe to do so. Pleased at the sight of his bare chest, she tossed the shirt over her shoulder. "I want you inside of me," she told him matter-of-factly, watching him closely to see his reaction.

"I'm really burnt out from practice. Can I just have a few minutes? I could use a bath and-"

"A massage?" she interjected.

A cold shower and the sports channel, he thought, and smiled at the thought.

She mistook the smile for encouragement and stuffed her hands down the front of his sweatpants. Delighted with what her hands found there, she smirked and pressed the length of her body to his. The expression on her face told him that she wasn't going to allow him to grade papers on the night of their six-month anniversary. She wasn't going to allow him to do anything until he'd satisfied her.

A bead of sweat trickled down his forehead. His hand shot out and grabbed her wrist, and his eyes locked with hers. His deep blue eyes flashed hot with what was a combination of both passion and anger. He felt his resolve retreating and was desperately trying to hold onto it. Gently extracting her hand from his crotch, he cleared his throat and closed both of his hands over hers. "Don't you want to see what I got you?" he asked her, hoping to God she'd say yes.

"Exchanging our gifts can wait until tomorrow," she said, pulling her hands from his. "Is something wrong?"

This is it. This is the opportunity to tell her that it's over, that this relationship isn't working out, he thought to himself, turning away from her and stroking his jaw in contemplation. He tried not to think of how humiliated she would be, being dumped while standing in front of him completely naked on their six month anniversary. Throat constricted with anxiety, he turned back to face her and wished he hadn't.

She observed him silently, nervously biting on her lower lip, looking delicious as hell in her birthday suit.

He took a deep breath, not knowing what the next words out of his mouth would be. "Nothing's wrong," he said finally, wrapping his arms around her and resting his chin on the top of her head.

"Good," she told him, "because I wasn't going to accept no for an answer." She led him to the bedroom with her hips swinging sensually, and he followed her like a loyal terrier. The next few hours sped past in a sweaty blur. Ethan lie in bed on his back, staring up at the ceiling. She'd been outrageous in bed, wilder tonight than she'd ever been, but even so, she hadn't completely captivated his attention. His guilt prevented him from getting any pleasure out of Diane's body caressing his body, or her tongue lapping him up in every which way.

He was aware of the fact that she was still awake lying beside him. He wondered what she was thinking, whether or not her female intuition was causing her to sense that he was truly troubled about their relationship. With his mind replaying the events of the past two hours, he slowly sat up in bed, looking down at her. She was lying on her side with her back facing him. Her hands were folded together in front of her face as if in prayer.

With his lips pursed, he watched her for a few moments, trying to bring himself to the point of calling her name and telling her that he couldn't be in this relationship anymore. He couldn't bring himself to speak those words aloud. His throat tightened up on him and his heartbeat quickened. He lowered his head onto the pillow, staring up at the ceiling for another half an hour before tumbling into a restless sleep.

Chapter Six

"You…look like shit."

Ethan ran a hand over his face. He *felt* like shit. His eyes were heavy-lidded with fatigue. He'd spent the previous night tossing and turning; he'd hardly gotten any sleep. The guilt had kept him awake the majority of the night. He'd stared up at the ceiling, trying to plan what he could say to her to make it feel like the breakup wasn't her fault. He was sure that there was a man out there in the world for Diane who would make her happy and whom she would make ecstatic, but thinking that didn't make him feel better about what he knew he would eventually have to do.

Richard followed him to his classroom with a look of concern etched across his face. "You look like shit," he repeated, thinking Ethan hadn't heard him.

"I heard you the first time," Ethan muttered.

The hallways were empty. It was the middle of second period, and Ethan's first class of the day was third period. In the mornings, he'd often arrive to school early so he could grade papers or go over the week's schedule for the class. It was what he'd planned on doing this morning, but Diane had been demanding and insisted on him staying in bed.

He was just now getting to work in the middle of second period, and he never liked arriving this late. It threw his entire day off balance. *Which is fitting, because she throws my whole damned life off balance*, he thought to himself as he walked in silence beside Richard.

Richard stopped walking and grabbed Ethan's arm, yanking him back. "Okay I can't put up with this shit anymore," he said. "You've got to get rid of this woman. She's interfering with your job now? How long are you going to let this go on? How hard is it to break up with someone?"

"I wouldn't know. I've never had to do it," Ethan replied, starting to walk again.

"You've never had to do it?" Richard asked, his eyebrows lifting. "You're how old?"

"You know how old I am, Ri-"

"Just answer the question."

"I'm going to be thirty-five in October," Ethan answered.

"You've never dumped a woman?"

"I've never had to."

"Christ."

Ethan shrugged. "I haven't dated many women."

"Why do you think that is?"

It was a question Ethan had wondered himself. "I don't know. Dating isn't my reason for breathing. If I don't fall head over heels, I don't fall at all, and I'm fine with it."

"You worry too much about emotions and feelings, Carson."

"What *should* I be worried about?"

"I don't know. Getting *laid*. Just having someone to do things with, movies, dinner, whatever." Now it was Richard's turn to shrug. "Whatever the hell, I don't know what gets your rocks off."

Ethan laughed and shook his head, reaching his classroom and unlocking the door. "I don't date women just to sleep with 'em, Rich. Not my M.O."

"Maybe it *should* be."

"I'm a teacher."

Richard's brows drew together as he followed Ethan into the classroom. "How come whenever I advise you to do something true to your *testosteronic* nature, your excuse is always 'I'm a teacher'? Does being a teacher make you superhuman? I think at times you confuse being a teacher with being the pope."

"Is 'testosteronic' even a word?" Ethan set his satchel on the top of his desk and began removing a legal pad, a daily planner, and writing utensils from it. "But it's funny you were thinking that, because I was just thinking that at times you confuse being a teacher with being a jackass."

"I am what I am," Richard said, watching Ethan set up shop. "No, but seriously. Just because you're a teacher doesn't mean you can't drink. It doesn't mean you can't be selfish sometimes by having hot, steamy, raunchy sex with some chick whose name you barely know."

"Not my style."

"I know, and it's too bad. Because you're the one who's miserable and I'm the one who's quite happy with my sex life."

Ethan's face twisted in disgust. "Hearing about your sex life isn't on today's schedule."

"My point is, you need to be selfish for once in your life and stop using your job as a reason not to be."

"Are you listening to yourself?" Ethan asked, sitting down in his chair. "And if you're listening to yourself, does what you're saying make sense to you?"

Richard rolled his eyes and folded his arms across his chest. "You're too much of a Clark Kent, man."

"Clark Kent?"

"Never does anything wrong, always thinking of others, always trying to save someone," Richard elaborated. "The female faculty are always talking about you in the teacher's lounge. Maybe you should ask one of *them* out. A no-strings-attached kind of deal, of course. Those are the best kind."

The thought of dating someone he came into constant contact with at work appalled him. "No. After this whole deal with Diane is over, I'm just going to want to spend some time alone. I don't need you playing Chuck Woolery for me."

"'Spend some time alone'?" Richard mimicked. "Are you listening to *your*self? Does what you're saying make sense to *you*? Spending time alone means no sex."

"Sex isn't everything."

"That's what you tell hormone-raging students, Ethan, not yourself."

Ethan pinched the bridge of his nose and closed his eyes. "Rich, that's what I tell hormone-raging students *and* myself. I wouldn't tell my students something I didn't believe. That's first off. Second off, don't you have a P.E. class to be teaching somewhere? Why are you in my classroom?"

"Oh, you're kicking me out?"

The bell signaling the end of second period rang, and Ethan lifted his eyes to the clock. "I have to get ready for my first period of the day. Can you help me out?"

By the middle of fourth period, Ethan had already made several vows to himself, starting with no longer allowing any woman, including Diane, to dictate what time he would be going to work. Another vow he made to himself was that he would break up with Diane sometime today. He couldn't take another sleepless night, because, as Richard had pointed out, it was beginning to interfere with his work. During class time, when his focus should have been on the students, their questions, issues and concerns, all he could think about was what he would tell Diane. While students were raising their hands and asking him questions, he was thinking about the next time he was going to see Diane and what he would tell her.

He was sitting at his desk grading homework assignments and the students, for the most part, were working studiously on the assigned work for the day, when the classroom door opened.

Diane invited herself into the classroom, dressed to the nine as usual in beige, skin-tight pants and a fashionable, baggy sweater. Her red hair was piled on top of her head in a slick updo, and a suede jacket was slung over her shoulder. "Hey, stud," she crooned. A devilish smile lit up her face.

Several of the students in the classroom looked up from their papers and started whispering. A few of the boys whistled and hooted. It took a significant amount of effort for Ethan to stifle a groan. He wouldn't be hearing the end of this for a long time.

"Mr. Carson, you *stud*," mocked one of the class clowns in the back row.

Diane closed the door behind her and walked further into the room, steadfast until she reached Ethan's desk. When she reached his desk, she walked around until she stood beside his chair. Then, she leaned back on his desk and gave him a look. "I wasn't done with you this morning."

"Diane, I'm at work."

"I noticed." She glanced over her shoulder at the class full of sophomores. "I told myself that on the way, too, I did. I told myself that you were at work and I shouldn't bother you, that it was inappropriate, and that I *shouldn't*, but you know what? I don't care."

His cheeks flushed a bright shade of red. "I'll talk to you in the hallway," he said under his breath, standing from his chair.

With one hand, she gently pushed him back into his seat. "Don't leave the room on my account," she said, grinning naughtily.

"Diane..."

The bell signaling the end of the period rang. Most of the students rushed for the door, itching to give the two adults privacy, but a few of them lingered until Ethan gave them a look that made them scatter.

"Diane, you shouldn't have done this," he said, walking around her so that he could close the classroom door. "This is *highly* inappropriate. It makes me look unprofessional. I'm going to be hearing about this for the rest of the damned school year."

"But-"

"What the hell are you doing here?" he fumed. "You know what? Don't answer that question. I know what you're doing here. I'm going to talk with you after work, okay?"

She frowned. "What the hell is the matter with you? You were like this last night. I thought it was because you'd had a tough day at practice. So I thought I'd surprise you at work, give you a reason to smile, and you bite my head off?"

"I've been thinking about things lately."

"And?" she asked, arching a brow at him in question.

He licked his lips and shoved his hands in his pockets, moving to stand a few feet away from her. "And, I don't think we're in the same place right now."

She looked at him as if she expected him to continue the sentence. Then she shook her head and burst out laughing. "Are you kidding me?"

She's not crying; she's laughing, he thought to himself. *That's a good sign.* "Diane, listen-"

"No," she interrupted. "Are you fucking *kidding* me? You're breaking *up* with me? *You?*"

She's starting to make me feel like shit. Not a good sign. Because he didn't know what to say, he walked around his desk and seated himself. "We aren't right for each other," he said simply.

"We aren't *right* for each other?" she repeated. "That wasn't what you were saying when I was sucking your-"

"Whoa, I'll just leave you two alone," a student who'd just stepped in the door mumbled.

"Watch your language," he scolded. "You're in a school. The fact I have to *tell* you that makes it easier for me to end this. You have to leave, Diane. Now."

The tips of her ears were red. She nodded with her lips pursed tightly together. Without another word, she turned and left the classroom.

He released a sigh of relief and let his head fall on his desk.

"This is the second time this week I've found you like this," Richard said, leaning against the doorjamb. "*Now* what's wrong?"

"You didn't see the steaming redhead that just stormed out of here?" Ethan asked with his forehead still pressed on the desk's cold surface. "That was Diane. She popped in here while class was still in session. I got pissed and broke up with her."

Richard's eyes widened. "Oh, thank God. I thought that chick was a student that you tried to take advantage of, so I wasn't going to say anything about it."

Ethan turned his head to the side and glared at his colleague. "That's sick, Rich."

"Isn't it?" Richard asked.

"How many P.E. classes do you teach, exactly?" Ethan questioned suddenly. "You're always hanging around my classroom. This classroom and the gymnasium aren't anywhere near each other."

"I'd better hurry on to class then, shouldn't I?" Richard said, grinning and leaving the room.

Ethan dragged himself through the rest of the day, wishing for the life of him that he didn't have to coach basketball practice tonight. He wished he could just cancel practice and go home, claiming to be sick or something, but his team needed the practice. Lately the team hadn't been playing their best, and now that Ethan thought about it, maybe lately he hadn't been coaching his best, due to his romance issues.

His mood worsened as the day dragged on. During practice, he was extremely crabby and a bit tougher on his team. He made them run more laps than usual and practice longer than usual. There were often students who stayed after school to watch practices, and he usually let the kids watch the practices, but not tonight. He yelled at the couple of stragglers that were clowning around in the gymnasium bleachers and directed them to leave the gym.

After practice was over, he sat in the bottom row of the bleachers with his head hanging low. The volleyball team was still occupying half of the gym floor, and for a few moments he watched their practice and let himself get lost in thought.

A brunette stood at the door of one of the gym entrances. She wore jeans and a beige turtleneck and had a leather jacket draped over her forearm. He recognized her immediately and rose to his feet. Without knowing exactly what he was going to say to her, he crossed the gym and approached her. "We meet again."

Smoky green eyes slid to meet his cool blue ones, and her eyes widened in surprise. "I didn't expect to see you here," she said, sounding a bit breathless.

He looked down at her with a smile on his face. Whenever he saw her, he couldn't stop himself from smiling. *You look like the Joker, stop grinning like a dummy,* he told himself. "Are you here to pick up your sister?"

Who the hell...Oh. "Yeah, I came here to pick up Sam," she told him, nodding her head. "I see practice isn't over, though."

"They've been at it for awhile." He glanced at his watch. "They've been going about three hours. It has to end sometime soon. Until then, you can sit with me and watch."

The last thing she wanted to do was sit down with him, to be within mere inches of him, and not be able to touch him. This must have shown somewhere in her expression, because he said, "If you don't want to, I'll completely understand."

"No, no, it's not that," she said after a slight hesitation, looking up at him but not quite looking into his eyes. "I just...it's...it's been a hell of a weekend," she said finally.

He led her to where he'd been sitting in the bleachers. "Tell me about it," he agreed.

"*You've* had a weekend from hell?" she asked, sounding surprised.

"This week is turning out to be from hell, too." He shook his head. He leaned forward, braced his elbows on his knees, and glanced over his shoulder at her. She looked so calm, cool, and collected sitting beside him. There was something he wanted to ask her, but he didn't know if he should. Nah, he probably shouldn't. He didn't want to pry into her personal business. And yet... "Have you ever been with a woman who was sexy, smart, beautiful...everything you thought you wanted, but...it turned out to be something you *didn't* want?"

Switch around the gender, and yeah, I've been in that situation, Paige was thinking to herself. An image of Brandon flashed before her eyes. Sure, he hadn't been all that smart, but when she'd first met him, he'd been incredibly sexy and good-looking.

She parted her knees and braced her elbows on them, mimicking his position. "I know what that's like," she worded carefully. "You get someone who you think is perfect-or perfect for you at least-and later on you find out they were only perfect for you because you wanted so much for them to be what you wanted." She was going to continue talking, but didn't. Instead, she turned away from him and busied herself with watching the volleyball practice.

He studied her profile while she watched the practice. When he thought about those words, he realized that they were words that applied to his situation with Diane. "I know what it's like, too," he said, bowing his head again.

"The girl at the bar?" she asked him, turning back to face him.

"The girl at the bar," he confirmed.

"I'm sorry to hear that." *No I'm not, no I'm not, no I'm not.* She offered him a sympathetic smile while her heart did cartwheels.

"I'm not," he said. "I don't know what I was even *doing* in that relationship. We weren't even close to being right for each other. I guess it was just…convenient, you know? I don't go out much. I teach classes and I coach the team. I'm also going to school for my Master's degree. Those three things alone take up so much of my time. When we first met, she approached me and told me that she wanted me. That took the work out of finding someone of substance to date. I don't know," he said, all of a sudden feeling like an idiot.

She watched him as he spoke and tried not to fall for him all over again. It was difficult. He was a basketball coach and looking very much the part, dressed in a t-shirt and sweatpants tinged in the school's colors, maroon, white, and gold. His hair was matted with sweat. "We all make mistakes when it comes to relationships," she said finally. "We all date people who are wrong for us. Without dating the wrong ones, how would we be able to recognize the right one?"

Damn, she's good, he thought, his grin stretching wider.
"Good point."

"I try."

"What do you do for work? Are you a counselor or a psychiatrist?"

"No, nothing like that."

"What do you do?"

She was looking for a point in their conversation when she could slide in that she wasn't Samantha's sister and she wasn't a lesbian, but she couldn't find one. He was pouring out feelings to her, and she didn't want to interrupt that to tell him that she'd lied to him or misled him. "I'm…between work right now," she answered finally.

He nodded as if in understanding. "Maybe you should work here at the school, be a guidance counselor."

"No, thanks."

"We're not even actually looking for one," he said. "I'm just saying."

She laughed and gently nudged him. *Being with him feels so natural,* she thought. Being close to him felt good. Their conversation wasn't forced; it flowed. She didn't even feel nervous around him. Talking to him now came just as easily as it had ten years ago, and the irony wasn't lost on her, the fact that a decade ago she'd come to him for advice and now he was seeking her counsel.

Both of them were quiet for a few moments, observing the girls' volleyball team practicing bumps, sets, and spikes. Then he said, "I know I met you at the bar and everything, but I can't get rid of this feeling that I've met you before then. I should have, right? I mean, you're Sam's sister, so you'd have gone to high school here? How old are you?"

Panic unleashed within her and she said cheerfully, "Enough about me, huh? What about you? Tell me something about you." *Please tell me something about you. I don't want to have to tell you another lie.*

Looking confused, but obliging, he asked her, "What do you want to know? Pick a question, any question."

"Well…how long have you been teaching?"

"About eleven years now," he replied.

"You seem happy with it."

"Do I?" He shrugged his shoulders. "I mean, I *am* happy with it. If I wasn't, I wouldn't have been a teacher this long."

Curiosity getting the best of her, she leaned towards him and asked, "Why do you do it, you know? I mean, why do you teach?"

"Not for the money, I'll tell you that," he said, half-joking and half-serious. "I do it because when I was in school, I had teachers who were there for me, who helped me through some pretty hard times. I wanted to be that type of person for someone else, you know?"

You were and probably still are, she couldn't help but think to herself. "That's…chivalrous and amazing of you."

"I'm just passing along a gift I was given," he told her modestly. "That's how I see it, anyway. I don't look at it as I'm doing something special or anything like that."

"You're very humble."

He shrugged and decided to quote Richard, for once in his life. "I am what I am."

"You are," she agreed, sighing.

Samantha approached them, using the bottom of her maroon volleyball practice t-shirt to swipe at sweat glistening on her forehead. Her breaths were coming rapidly, but when she caught her breath, she asked Paige, "Hey, what's going on?"

"Nothing much, just thought that your practice ended at six o' clock," Paige said, tapping her watch and looking up at Samantha. "What happened to that, Sam?"

"Practice is running late, I know," she apologized sincerely, still breathing hard. "I was going to call you, but I forgot your cell phone number and even if I had remembered it, I wouldn't have had a phone to call you on. I'm sorry."

"It's all right," Paige said, smiling up at the teenager.

"You going to wait for me or do we have to go now?" Samantha asked, not yet acknowledging Ethan's presence.

Paige glanced at her watch. "I let Olivia play with a neighbor across the street. I don't want her over there too long," she said, "but I can wait a little bit longer."

Samantha grinned and started backing away from them. "Great. Thanks, Paige, I owe you." Almost as an afterthought, she turned to Ethan and said, "Hi, Mr. Carson!" She turned and ran back to where the volleyball nets were set up.

"You guys seem to really get along and love each other." Ethan turned to Paige. "You can really see the resemblance between you two."

"*About* that…" Paige began slowly, thinking about exactly what words she'd say.

"You don't have to tell me," he said. "When people tell me I look like someone, I don't agree with them either. But you two really do look alike." He rose from his seat and stretched his arms over his head.

She sensed that he was going to tell her he had to leave for some reason, and she didn't want to let him do that. There was so much she wanted to tell him and ask him. She wanted to tell him the truth, what she *should* have told him in the beginning.

"I'm going to lock up the locker room and get ready to get out of here," he told her, looking down at her, "but you should come to our game on Friday."

"Friday?"

"My team plays, along with the junior varsity basketball team," he enlightened. "You can come. Bring Samantha-it'll be great. I might even be able to spare some time during the junior varsity game to sit with you two. Sound good?" He was already backing away from her, rubbing his hands together.

She was torn between wanting to go and not wanting to go, but of course she accepted the invitation. Then she watched him jog off across the gymnasium towards the gym doors, taking her heart with him.

"What was *that* about?" Samantha asked, giving Paige a look as they both settled in their seats.

Paige tried her best to conjure up an innocent expression, but failed. "What was what about?"

"You were cozying up to Mr. Carson," Samantha accused. "You guys looked like you'd known each other for forever."

Paige shrugged and started the car. "He's an easy person to talk to."

"All of the girls at school have a crush on him," the teenager said, clicking her seatbelt into its buckle. "Even some of the female teachers. It's funny to watch, actually. And now, he's grown on you, too. Priceless."

For some reason being thrown into the same category as all of the students and teachers who had a crush on Mr. Carson irked Paige. "I don't have a crush on him," she said finally, maneuvering the car smoothly, weaving in and out of traffic. "He's just a friend."

"For *now*."

Paige laughed. "What are you doing prying in adults' business anyway?"

"You're my sister now, so it's my business," Samantha insisted.

"You're milking this for your own benefit, I think."

"You think?" Samantha countered.

Paige laughed again. "You're just as bad as Olivia."

The comment seemed to be a compliment to Samantha; she took it as such. "Where do you think she got it from?" she quipped, tilting her nose into the air.

An hour later, both Olivia and Samantha were tucked into their beds. Paige had attempted to make dinner and miserably failed. Fortunately, Samantha knew a little something about cooking and whipped up sloppy Joes for the three of them.

Paige was reclining on the couch, flipping through television channels, when her cell phone chirped. She lifted the cell phone from the coffee table to her ear. "Yeah?" she said into the phone.

Evelyn's voice came across the line. "You won't *believe* the week I've had."

"Tell me about the week you've had," Paige said, muting the television.

"I've been dealing with lawyers all week."

"Lawyers?" Paige probably sounded as dumbfounded as she felt, but she couldn't help it.

"It all started Sunday night," Evelyn explained, her voice sounding on the verge of ecstatic. "Deana dropped me off at home. I walk in the house, right? The upstairs hallway light is on, so I figure Eric is home, so I go upstairs. And he's home, but he's lying in bed with some bitch from work, right?"

Paige's eyes widened. She was alarmed by the casual manner in which Evelyn said those words.

"I leave the room, Eric comes out, and we have a talk. The way he was talking to me, he didn't regret a damned thing and he told me he'd been cheating on me for a year, right? I was shocked and upset, and I know I didn't have a right to be, because I've been cheating on him for the past few months." Evelyn paused for a breath and then drove on. "He basically tells me that I've been this worthless wife and that I'm a worthless person and that he doesn't find me sexy or pretty or intelligent or anything, and he actually had the *nerve* to say that the kind of woman that turned him on would have yelled at him or slapped him or something, right? So I *punched* him, Paige!"

"You did *what?*"

"I clocked him. Right in the fucking nose. And not once, Paige. *Twice.*" Evelyn sounded proud of herself.

"You KO'd your husband?" Paige asked, her mouth dropping open in shock.

The pride in Evelyn's voice disappeared and now she sounded somber and depressed. "You should have heard what he said to me, how he said it," she whined.

Paige had met Eric on several occasions; she couldn't imagine him being anything but cordial, if not adoring, towards his wife. For the past year, all of that had been a front? "So…what's going to happen?"

"I'm not done with the story," Evelyn said, the pride returning to her voice. "He was calling me stupid and everything, right? So after I punched him out, I went back to the bedroom, and his slut was still in the bed naked. I went to the closet, got the camera out, and by this time, Eric had come in the room. His whore ran up to him, trying to see if he was hurt or whatever, and I got pictures of them naked together. I'll be getting a divorce. And I'll be taking at least half of what he owns."

Evelyn continued talking. She talked about the plans she had for herself. Even though she was going to sue her husband for all he was worth, she wasn't going to rely on the money she received from him. She claimed that she wasn't taking Eric's money to live off of it. She was taking his money to diminish him, to punish him for the way he'd made her feel and the way he'd talked to her. No, she wasn't going to live off of the money she took from him. She was going to make a name for herself and start a career. She was going to sit down and do some thinking as to what she wanted to do with her life, what changes she wanted to make.

Paige was hearing the makings of a brand new Evelyn. This wasn't the Evelyn she'd gone to college with. Hell, this wasn't even the Evelyn from last week. She sounded older, more mature, definitely a hell of a lot more independent. Paige was thrilled to hear this new Evelyn. She was no longer the self-absorbed former cheerleader/current housewife.

When Evelyn was just about out of breath, she asked Paige, "So how have the past few days been for you?"

"Not as good as yours," Paige muttered, running a hand through her hair.

"What's wrong?" Evelyn asked, sounding concerned.

"Nothing, except for everyone in town thinking I'm a lesbian."

"*What*? Why would they think that?"

"Because of the way Marissa and I were dancing at the bar on Saturday night," Paige responded, standing up from the couch and pacing around the living room. "This is a small town and rumors travel fast."

Evelyn was trying her best to suppress a giggle. "Wow, Paige, that's..."

"That's not good," Paige finished.

"Nothing good has happened today? You're watching the kids, right?"

Paige stood at the window, pulling the curtain to the side and peering out into the front yard. "The kids are amazing," she said. "I have no problem with the kids. They're both just...I don't know, phenomenal kids. And then..." She stopped herself, laughing and letting the curtain fall in place.

"And then what?"

"No, never mind," Paige said, shaking her head and turning to press her back against the wall.

"Paige, you were going to say something, and it was going to be juicy," Evelyn guessed. "Say what you were going to say."

Paige chewed nervously on her bottom lip. "There's a guy, all right?"

"A guy? That's great!" Evelyn exclaimed, joyous for her friend. "Lord knows after Brandon you need some real romance."

"I don't know if any romance is going to be happening, since that lesbian rumor is going around," Paige said, relieved that Marissa hadn't filled Evelyn in about Ethan.

Evelyn was optimistic. "You never know. Just tell him you aren't one."

Because Paige didn't want to go into the whole scenario about the fact she'd lied to him and led him into believing she was someone that she wasn't, she merely agreed with Evelyn. "You're right, that's what I should do."

"I'm going to have to let you go. There are some loose ends I have to tie up," Evelyn said.

"Yeah, I'm sorry you had to find out about Eric that way."

"So am I, but I'm glad it's over. I know a lot of things now that I didn't know even a few days ago." Evelyn paused. "I just want to thank you for all the advice you gave me, you know? I mean Eric did cheat on me for longer, but by cheating on him, I wasn't being any better than he was."

Paige was filled with sympathy for her friend. To have had her husband bad-mouth her to her face and still come out feeling victorious, she had to be a strong woman. "Cheating on him wasn't the best thing you could have done," Paige told Evelyn, still pacing around the living room as she spoke. "But you came out a winner in this, and you came out strong. I'm very proud of you. I don't know if I would have been as smart as you were, had I been in the same situation."

Evelyn sniffled and murmured, "Thank you, Paige. You don't know how much I had to hear that, I…thank you."

Paige said her good-byes to Evelyn and settled back on the couch, drawing her knees up to her chest and wrapping her arms around them. Evelyn had been strong, had thought intelligently, and had maneuvered herself well in the situation between Eric and herself. Despite the circumstances she'd been given and had given herself, in the end she'd come out shining like a bright star, facing her responsibility and colliding with it head-on.

The only question now was, could Paige do the same by being honest with Ethan? The next time she was face to face with him, could she tell him the truth about who she really was?

Chapter Seven

Ethan stood by the entrance to the gymnasium on Friday night with his arms crossed across his chest, scanning the audience in the stands. There was no sign of Samantha and Paige in the bleachers, and he couldn't ignore the pang of disappointment that grabbed him.

Every few minutes, he kept an eye out for them, thinking that maybe they were just running late, but towards the middle of the varsity game, it was evident that they weren't showing up. That night, both the junior varsity and varsity Hornets lost to one of their biggest rivals, the Stevenson Pirates.

He spent a half an hour with his team in the locker room after the game, giving them a lecture on how losing wasn't the end of the world, even though it was frustrating. The lecture didn't help to lighten up the team's mood. They changed from their maroon basketball uniforms into their street clothes and when they exited the locker room, all of them were still seething with aggravation and disappointment.

Ethan couldn't blame them. He was disappointed in himself. He didn't blame the team's loss on his players; he blamed the loss on himself. He'd been distracted. His head hadn't been entirely on coaching; he'd been busy wishing that Samantha and Paige would arrive. He loved talking with Paige. She seemed to be a laid-back woman. If she didn't have the same taste in women as he did, or any taste in women at all, he'd probably welcome the urge to be more than just a friend to her.

He strode out of the school building with his keys jingling in his hand. The air was cold, but not as sharp and biting as it had been the night before. He raised his face to the sky as he walked, looking up at the crisp, cloudless sky.

When he brought his gaze back down, he saw that a woman with a hood draped over her hair was sitting on the rear bumper of his car.

Most of the students had already deserted the school. There were only a handful of cars in the parking lot. Ethan's back straightened and his mouth set in a firm, straight line. At first glance, he'd thought the woman was Paige, but after further inspection, he recognized the body type, spotted soft, red tendrils floating free of the hood in the night's breeze. It wasn't Paige sitting on the bumper of his car; it was Diane.

She raised her face to him as she drew her hood back. "Hi."

"Hi." He walked around her, unlocked the car door and threw his satchel and gym bag across the driver side seat and into the passenger seat. Rising back to his full height, he turned and looked back at her. "What are you doing here?"

"Trying to work things out," she replied, looking back at him over her shoulder. She drew closer to him and her hands fidgeted with each other. "I don't know what I did, but whatever it is, I want to fix it."

"You didn't *do* anything, Diane," he told her. His voice was tight with frustration. "I've been thinking about this for awhile."

Her face registered shock, and her mouth opened, closed, and opened again. "Since before our anniversary?"

He closed his eyes and broke eye contact with her, cursing under his breath.

"You've been thinking about it since before then, Ethan?" she asked, reaching up and clasping his chin in her hand. She jerked his face towards hers and she searched his eyes for her answer. She found it and released his face in an instant, taking a step back from him. "You fucked me after discovering that you didn't want to be with me?"

"I didn't want to break up with you on our anniversary," he said finally.

"But you *did* want to break up with me." She shook her head, grabbed the lapels of her mink fur coat and closed them tighter across her chest. "While I was letting myself into your apartment, stripping my clothes off for you, to *surprise* you, you were thinking up ways to end it with me? Thinking of an appropriate time to drop the bomb?"

"Diane-"

"No, Ethan, you're going to hear me out!" she shouted, her voice echoing across the parking lot. Her bottom lip trembled and she was struggling not to cry. "I loved you. We've talked about this before, how I've never loved anyone before. How could you hurt me like this, after everything we've talked about, after all we've been to each other?"

Her questions stung him, and he found his resolve cracking and breaking. She had, once upon a time, told him she'd never been in love before. She'd dated men when it was convenient for her, when she was tired of sitting around the house and when she wanted to spend nights out on the town, or in the city. She'd let rich men whisk her out of town and on expensive trips to the Bahamas, Fiji, or the Virgin Islands. Upon entering a relationship with Ethan, she'd told him that she'd never dated a man who wasn't rich. Her family was rich and expected her to marry someone wealthy.

When she'd brought Ethan home, they'd strongly disapproved of him. "Your father was John Carson, wasn't he? The college basketball coach?" Diane's father, a business owner, had asked him at a dinner table laden with exquisite cuisine. "Your father coached college basketball, and you had a chance to do that, but you declined? To *teach*? What was going through your mind when you did that?"

Ethan had found their questions to be extreme invasions of his privacy, and extremely judgmental. For most of the dinner conversation, he was either silent or answered with one or two-word responses. He'd been uncomfortable the entire time, while Diane had been at his side, giddy with happiness and bursting with energy.

After dinner, Diane's father had taken her aside and expressed his disapproval. He hadn't lowered his voice to spare Ethan or Diane's mother, had merely taken Diane a few feet away from the table. "A teacher?" he'd said. "You know you can do better than this, Diane."

"He's the one I want, Daddy," she'd told her father.

Ethan didn't know any thirty-year-old woman who called her father "daddy." It was just one more thing that made him uncomfortable sitting at her family's dinner table. He'd politely excused himself from the dinner table and from their house.

Diane had chased him out of the front doors of the house, demanding to know where he was going.

"Away," he'd told her.

She'd walked up to him with a smile on her face, and Ethan remembered thinking, *Why is she smiling? Was she sitting at the same dinner table as I was?* She'd reached up, draped her arms around his neck, and gave him a long, probing kiss.

Her parents stood at the front door, eyeing them with disgust.

Later on, Diane had tried to explain to him that her father hadn't meant to be rude. He was just looking after her best interests.

"You're thirty years old," Ethan had told her. "You're old enough to look after your own interests."

She'd laughed his comment off, as if humoring a child, and proceeded to change the subject. That had been the way of their relationship for some time. He refused to go to functions that he knew her parents would be attending.

"You're being immature, Ethan, grow up," she had told him once. "They'll get used to you."

"They shouldn't have to get *used* to me," he had countered, a breath away from calling her parents stuck-up snobs. "While my father was alive, he spent his time making me feel like shit for choosing teaching over coaching college ball. I'm not going to tolerate your parents doing the same thing."

No wonder I don't want to be with her, Ethan thought to himself now. When he took a step back and looked at their relationship objectively, he could see why he and Diane weren't meant for each other and where they failed each other. Whenever her parents had made an insulting comment towards Ethan or about Ethan, Diane always came to their defense. She tried to explain their behavior, tried to justify it. She liked to think that she was different than her parents, but in actuality, she thought a lot like them.

When she spoke about loving him, she'd make little comments like, "You're not anywhere near rich, but I still love you," as if her loving him was an act of charity. She always dressed in the latest fashions, drove into Chicago for hair appointments, and, with her father's money, bought him suits to wear to formal functions.

Ethan rubbed at his jaw and faced Diane, looking her up and down. "Diane, you don't love me," he said flatly. "You love what you can turn me into.

"What the hell are you talking about?"

"I don't know, you tell me, Diane." He took a step closer to her. "You've been buying me suits and buying me watches, taking me to all of these ridiculous kiss-ass fests. When we're watching TV, you turn the channel to ESPN2 to watch college basketball. You pull stunts the way you did earlier this week, stunts that could have gotten me into serious trouble, Diane. Seems like you're trying to make me something I'm not, something that your father will one day approve of."

Her mouth dropped open and she shook her head. "If you're accusing me of trying to make a better man out of you, then yes, I'm guilty," she cried. "You have the potential to be a great college basketball coach. I don't want you to end up in this dead-end job for the rest of your life."

"Dead-end *job*?" he repeated. His nostrils flared, and he turned away from her, not able to stand the sight of her. He clasped his hands together and cracked his knuckles. "My teaching is very important to me," he said quietly.

"I...I know that," she said, sounding nervous. She'd never seen him as angry as he was now.

"You always talk about my teaching like...like it's beneath you." When he opened his eyes and turned them to her, a fierce fury burned within them, a fury that he was keeping a tight hold on. "Do you know what it *takes* to be a teacher? Do you?"

She shook her head, her mouth pursed shut.

"It takes a great amount of tolerance," he told her through clenched teeth. "It takes a backbone made of *steel.* Because all day long, students can throw insults at you, they can disrespect you, and they can make you feel like complete *shit.* And you can't dish it back to them. You have to tolerate it. You can report their behavior, you can give them detention for it, and you can have them taken out of your classroom and placed under another teacher's guidance. Chances are, though, they'll make *that* teacher's life a living hell, too. So you can keep the kid in your class and work with him on improving his attitude, or you can pass him off to be another teacher's hell.

"Being a teacher takes the skill to guide, to be counsel to any student who might need a listening ear. You have to be patient, because some students don't learn as quickly as others. You have to be willing to commit to these children." His sentences were beginning to run together, and he felt himself losing control.

She was looking up at him and shaking her head. "You don't have to explain your job to me, Ethan," she whispered.

"Really? For some reason, I feel like I do," he said. His temples were throbbing. "I'm not what you want. What you want is some wealthy lawyer, or maybe a doctor. What you want is someone like your dear old daddy, who can buy you all of this shit you wear, and take you on expensive trips and spoil you. That isn't me, and it never will be."

Her fingers tugged at each other, and she turned her back to him.

"The only thing that gets me," he went on, "is how you can be so independent when it comes to your career in fashion, and at the same time, so dependent on your dad's money. It boggles my mind, you know?"

She didn't say anything.

"Not to say that I care, because I don't. We're done. We're through."

When she turned back to face him, he'd expected that her eyes would be filled with tears, that her face would be an expression of apology. Neither was the case. Her face was devoid of emotion. "Fine, it's over," she said. "You're right. I can buy you all of the suits, take you to all of the political and professional functions, and try to persuade you all I want to, to try and get you to try and be a better man. The truth of the matter is, if you don't want it for yourself, then there's nothing else I can do."

"I don't need to be made into a better man," he told her, impatience growing within him. "And you're right. I don't have to explain my profession to you."

"Well you need to do something," she said, sneering nastily. "Because the next woman you come across isn't going to want to settle down with a middle-class teacher with no goals for himself. What's the quote I'm looking for?" She tapped fingers against lips heavily coated in dark lipstick. She smiled. "Oh yeah...those who can't do...*teach*." Seeing she'd hit a nerve, she took a step closer to him.

He looked down at her, struggling to stay in control of the anger coiling within him.

"Your father knew it, *my* father knows it, and *I* know it. It's cute that you want to be a teacher and help out children, but when it comes to your wants and desires, and when it comes to having to support the family you're going to have, what are you going to do? Hmm?" She looked up at him, looking smug and sure of herself. "You might feel all confident now that you're dumping me, but I'll come around to visit you in ten years, twenty years. I'll be married and happy. Where will you be? Teaching and alone. Teaching and *broke*. Teaching and *sorry* for yourself."

He opened the door and lowered himself into the car. As he closed the car door, she was still talking, shouting at him that he could leave her if he wanted, but leaving her was leaving a chance at happiness. He drove out of the parking lot, annoyed at the fact that he was beginning to wonder if she was right.

Chapter Eight

For the first time in a week, on Sunday morning, Paige rested in her own bed, staring up at her own ceiling. She'd hated saying goodbye to Olivia and Samantha the previous day, hated saying goodbye to her parents, and for once in her life, had hated saying goodbye to her hometown, despite whatever rumors were flying around about her.

She was supposed to have gone to the high school basketball game on Friday night; Ethan had invited her. She had been too chickenshit to go. She knew that she wouldn't have been able to tell him the truth about who she was. She could barely act like she had common sense whenever she was around the man. She couldn't imagine sitting next to him, telling him that her name was Paige Turner, that she wasn't Samantha's sister, wasn't a lesbian, that-in fact-she was a former student of his. From what she'd seen of his personality, she doubted that he would be seriously angry with her, but it would freak him out, and that's the last thing she wanted to do.

So she'd decided not to go to the game that night and the following night, she'd been on her way back to Farmington Heights, where she moped around the house and contented herself with pigging out on Cherry Garcia ice cream to help ease her depression.

She checked her voicemail. Shane had left her several messages, telling her that they had to talk business, and there was one message where the person who'd called had hung up without saying anything. She dropped onto her bed, wanting to drown out everyone and everything in the world. She didn't want to think about writing or Shane. She didn't want to think about what she'd do with herself for the next few weeks. She didn't want to think about anything.

Her sadness and depression ran deep. She missed spending time with her mother and her father; she missed spending time with the kids; she wished she'd had the guts to tell Ethan the truth. She wished she'd never lied to him in the first place. She rewound the scene in her head, tried to explain to herself why she'd felt the urge to lie. Why couldn't she have just told him who she was? Maybe he'd have been impressed that she'd made something out of herself.

The thought that he might have welcomed her and still befriended her had he known who she really was depressed her even more. The next few days for her were hell. When she slept, she dreamt of him. When she was awake, she thought of him. On several occasions, she entertained the idea of driving back to Beach Park, storming inside of the school during one of his practices, and yanking him aside to tell him the truth, that she was Paige Turner, acclaimed author and former student, and that she wanted to be with him.

It was a ridiculous idea, really. It would throw him into shock, for sure, and he wouldn't know what to think at first. In the end, she'd only be extremely humiliated in front of a gym full of students.

Thursday afternoon, she sat in her home office, brainstorming on ideas for the next novel she wanted to write, when her doorbell shrilled throughout the entire house. Frowning because she hadn't been expecting anyone, she walked out of her office, down the hallway, and down a winding staircase to the foyer and front door. Standing on tiptoe, she looked through of the peephole and lowered back on the balls of her bare feet.

Pulling the door open, she faced an anxious-looking Brandon Davies. When he saw her, his eyes brightened and a smile appeared on his face. "Hey."

"Hey." She surveyed him, looking him up and down. "What are you doing here?"

"You don't look happy to see me." He breezed past her, a puffy sleeve of his sports coat brushing her arm.

"Considering we broke up, I don't see why I have reason to be happy to see you," she said, following him into the living room and stopping just inside the arched entrance. "Why are you here?"

"I've tried calling but you weren't home. I came to apologize," he told her, turning around to face her. "I was an idiot. I was an asshole and I know that. I'm sorry about that." He made himself comfortable on her couch and shed his jacket.

She watched his movements in amazement. "So you apologize to me, and you expect what?" she demanded of him, stalking further into the living room until she stood in front of him with her hands on her hips. "You expect me to take you back? Just like that?"

"You have to have missed me," he said confidently, stretching his arms across the back of the couch. "And I missed you. I missed you a lot, more than I thought I would. So I was *hoping* we could go back to being like we were before. You know…happy. And together."

"What reason would I have to go back to you?" she asked after a brief hesitation.

"Have you found anyone better in the time we've spent apart?" he asked smugly.

"We've spent, what, a week and a half, two weeks apart?"

"In the time we've spent apart, I've fucked two women," he boasted, standing and crossing the living room so that he stood behind her. His hands settled on her shoulders and he stroked down the length of her bare arms, admiring how great her body looked even in a plain black tank top and gray sweatpants. He lowered his head and nipped her shoulder with his teeth. "Those women didn't come close to making me feel the way you did."

She rolled her eyes and shook her head. If she went back to Brandon, she'd be stupid. She knew what kind of man he was. She knew he didn't love her, not more than he loved himself. She told herself this, but yet, feeling his lips on her bare shoulder made her weak. Her gaze wandered around the room as she tried to think about her options here.

As she thought about her options, he slid the right shoulder strap of her tank top down to reveal a milk-white shoulder. His lips caressed her skin and his arms reached across her abdomen, clutching her to him, pressing her to the length of him.

He wasn't the man she wanted; he didn't come close to measuring up to the man she truly wanted. He wasn't Mr. Right, but he *could* be a Mr. Right Now. She hated thinking of him that way, but she realized that Ethan definitely wasn't going to come calling for her anytime soon, if ever. She closed her eyes, allowing Brandon's hands to manipulate her body. While he touched her gently, stroked her arms and massaged her back, she kept her eyes closed. In her mind, it wasn't Brandon touching her.

When she opened her eyes, it wasn't Brandon she saw. It was Ethan, Ethan roughly snatching her up into his arms and carrying her up the stairs and into her bedroom, throwing her roughly on the bed and crawling in the bed after her. It was Ethan yanking the tank top up and over her head, unhooking her bra and tossing it carelessly to the floor.

A hot mouth came into contact with one of her erect nipples, and she felt teeth barely skimming over them. Brandon lifted his mouth and sat back on his heels, looking at her. He'd never seen her this hot for him, this eager for him. She looked about ready to explode, and he'd barely touched her. While he dragged her sweatpants down her legs, he kept his eyes focused on her face.

A drunken grin was plastered on her lips and she lifted her hips so that he could remove her panties. Confused as to why she'd changed her mind so quickly and why she was letting him have her, he slid the silky material down her long legs. He pulled her legs apart, expecting her to jump up and tell him that he couldn't fuck her...that she'd teased him because it was what he deserved. She did no such thing.

She couldn't catch her breath as his mouth worked wonders on her. Her eyes were still cloaked with fantasy and she was still deluding herself into believing that Ethan was the one pressing his hands to her thighs, pressing his hand on her mound and pushing fingers inside of her. She arched her back to meet his hand, delirious with passion. "Don't stop that," she whispered urgently, thinking to herself that it was wrong for her to be making love to one man and imagining it was another.

For a brief moment, she wondered if that made her a slut. Did it make her horrid? Her nipples wouldn't be as hard as they were, she wouldn't be as hot as she was if she made love to Brandon knowing it was Brandon. Picturing Ethan doing these things to her, imagining it was him that was driving her body crazy was what was sending her over the edge. Her body had never been to the point of aching for a man, not Brandon, not anyone, but it ached now. She rolled over so that she was on top of Brandon, and she grabbed his arms and held them above his head.

She drew her face down close to his, grabbed his bottom lip in between her lips, and sucked on it. Her hands trailed down from his hands to his arms, to his chest and stomach. They dipped lower, beneath his navel and waist, found what they were looking for, and guided it inside of her. She threw her head back and closed her eyes.

He raised his hands up to touch her stomach and breasts, dazed at how passionate she was. He'd never seen her like this; it was new to him. Is this how make-up sex would always be with her? If so, he'd deliberately start an argument with her a few times a day. God, she was driving him crazy. Just watching her face, her movements, was driving him nuts. He held back, trying to wait for her, but he was dangerously close to bursting.

Beads of sweat trickled down his brow as he watched her bouncing on top of him with an index finger at the corner of her mouth. Her eyes were heavy-lidded and her hair was saturated with the sweat seeping from her body. Her soft moans became louder, her bouncing harder, and she grabbed at his arms.

Holy shit, he thought, watching her, and then trying *not* to watch her. The muscles in his jaw worked and he turned his gaze over to the closet, because that was a safe place to look. He stared at the closet for a few moments, trying to think of anything else but the woman moaning crazily and bouncing on top of him. *Oh my God...oh my God...*

She leaned down, pressing fervent kisses to his mouth and his cheek, his chin and his neck, her breaths coming faster and faster. Feeling her clench around him, he pulled out of her and rolled over, emptying himself onto the sheets.

She lie on her back, staring up at the ceiling and trying to catch her breath.

He tried to catch his breath and stared at her over his shoulder. He liked to think of himself as a confident man...at times he was an arrogant asshole, even. He knew he had skills in the bedroom, had even entertained the notion that he could turn on any woman if he truly wanted to. He would like to think that she'd been so wild because she was drunk off of the lust she was feeling for him, but he had a certain measurement of common sense.

She rolled over and looked at him with sleepy eyes. "Wow," she breathed.

"Yeah, 'wow,'" he echoed, running a hand through his hair. "That was...different," he said finally.

"Yeah, it was," she admitted, rummaging around her nightstand for a hair tie. She found one and pulled her hair back into a ponytail. The pillow she wanted to lie on was soaked with sweat, so she flipped it over.

"Why was it so different?" he questioned.

"Why are you asking me?"

"Because you were..." He stopped, looking for the right words. "I don't know. You've never been like that."

She shrugged her shoulders.

"Have you fucked anyone since we broke up?"

"What does it matter to you if I did?" she demanded. "Not more than an hour ago you told me you've fucked two women."

"I'm just asking."

"No, I didn't."

"So is make-up sex with you always this good?"

She smiled up at the ceiling without replying.

It didn't take long for him to realize that she wasn't through with him. Her sexual appetite was at its peak, and whereas before they'd broken up, he'd always been the one to initiate sex, things changed. And they had. She couldn't seem to get enough of him. She was driven; she was uncontrollable, insatiable. There wasn't a room in the house where he was safe.

Marissa hung up the phone and stared at it a few moments, then glanced over her shoulder at the black-haired Italian lying in her bed. "Paige and Brandon are back together," she informed, lowering onto the pillow.

Shane's eyebrows lifted, then furrowed. "What the hell is she thinking?"

"She's *not*," she alleged firmly. "She doesn't love him and he doesn't love her, and she knows it. At this point, I guess she doesn't care."

"The teacher you told me about…isn't that the guy she wants?"

"I told you, she's not thinking. And anyway, he has a girlfriend and he thinks she's a lesbian, so she probably figures she won't have a chance with him any time soon."

Sitting up abruptly, he demanded, "He thinks what?"

She waved her hand in the air. "Long story."

"Shit," he muttered, relaxing again and sinking down into his pillow.

"She deserves better than Brandon," she said stubbornly. "Maybe I should step in-"

"And do absolutely nothing," he finished, grumbling and turning over so that his back faced her. "Meddling will only make things worse."

She pouted up at the ceiling, pulling the sheets up to her chest. "I hate seeing her like this. You should see how much Cherry Garcia ice cream she can chow down."

"I know how much Cherry Garcia she can chow down," he said, "and you're right. It's not a pretty sight, but you sticking your nose in her business could blow up in your face. You don't want that, right?"

She shook her head, even though he wasn't looking at her. "*Still.*"

He turned his head and looked over his shoulder. "Just leave things alone, all right?"

"She's my *friend*, Shane," she protested. "What am I supposed to do? Should I stand by while she fucks some dude who couldn't give two shits about her, much less *love* her? You know me, Shane. You can't possibly expect me to stand by and do nothing."

"That's exactly what I expect you to do."

She chewed on the inside of her cheek in contemplation. "Maybe I could go back to Beach Park myself, tell the teacher the truth, get him to drive up here and sweep Paige off of her feet."

"Tell me the situation again," he grumbled. "Break it down for me."

Marissa glanced at Shane's back, then turned and rose up on her elbow. "Okay. The man she wants to be with was her teacher ten years ago. She bumped into him while we were in town last weekend. He saw her and I dancing and assumed we were both lesbians. On top of that, she told him she was Samantha's sister."

"Who the fuck is Samantha?"

"A teenager staying at Paige's parents' house. You met her and her younger sister, remember?"

"All right, keep going."

"Okay, so on top of him not knowing who Paige really is, he has a girlfriend, but I guess things are a bit rocky with her, because he confided in Paige a little about his relationship. He also invited Paige to one of the high school basketball games, but she didn't show because she was too chicken, and to date, she went back to her ex, who went by her house earlier today and apologized." She took a deep breath. "That's the gist of it."

He turned his head slightly, looking at her with tired eyes. "So let me get this straight," he said, his voice gruff with sleep. "The guy you guys call 'teach' *really* used to be her teacher. She saw this guy recently. He thinks she's someone's sister when she *has* no siblings. He thinks she's a lesbian...and he doesn't know she used to be a student in his class."

"Pretty much."

His eyes widened. "Holy shit." The wheels in his mind were turning. In the new piece he'd submitted for Paige to be published, there was an entire chapter dedicated to the teacher that Marissa spoke of now.

"See?" Marissa asked. "She *needs* me to help her out, to jump in the situation."

He shook his head. "What she needs is a fucking prayer," he remarked, falling back on his pillow.

Chapter Nine

The rest of the winter melted away, made way for spring and summer, which were both slow for Paige. Summer faded into fall, which fell into winter. Winter thawed into spring and spring sprinkled into summer. A lot had changed in a year's time. Marissa and Shane were claiming that they were in love, and they were practically joined at the hip. Evelyn owned her own house and would soon be legally divorced from her husband. Deana was promoted to a VP position within her company.

The one thing that remained constant was Paige and Brandon being together. Paige didn't know why she *was* still with him, half the time. Being with him was convenient, if nothing else. He frequently filmed on location, so she usually only saw him a few times a week. Sometimes she didn't even see him that much. Once in a blue moon, he would fly her out to Los Angeles or New York City for a well-publicized movie premiere.

He did a lot of traveling, and once in awhile she would travel with him. Lately, the well from which she withdrew her creativity and ideas for novels was running as dry as the Sahara Desert, so she declared herself on hiatus. Marissa had been right; she needed to get inspired, and she set out to do just that.

She'd taken Brandon to Beach Park to meet her parents and her mother loved him on sight. Her father was cordial with Brandon, but not as sweet on him as her mother was. No matter how skilled he was at charming her parents, when it came to Paige's friends, he had no luck. Marissa and Deana were always on his case for one reason or another, and if they weren't on *his* case, they were on Paige's. Why had she taken Brandon back? Didn't she wonder what he did when he was out of town and with whom? Didn't she see that he was playing her like a fiddle? While Paige was on his arm in public venues, he ogled other women. He wasn't worth the time of day...he was conceited, arrogant, and inconsiderate of Paige's feelings. Why did she tolerate it? Their questions never stopped, possibly because half of them, Paige didn't have answers to.

She didn't know why she tolerated Brandon's shortcomings. She was a twenty-eight year old, decent looking woman, wasn't she? She had a moderately successful career, a considerable amount of book smarts, and she was easy to get along with. Wasn't she? Sure, she wasn't the most *outgoing* person in the world-far from it. She was a homebody, bordering on being a hermit. If she wasn't dating Brandon, who was one of the most outgoing people she knew, she wouldn't have any kind of social life.

She was sure that a lot of her fans thought that being an author meant a lot of parties, meant a lot of celebrity-filled events. She was sure they thought that being a romance novelist meant red carpets, fancy parties, and a completely booked schedule. For some of the big name writers, certainly, that might be true. If it weren't for Brandon's invites to award shows and whatnot, she probably would have never set foot on a red carpet.

That can't be all he's good for, she thought to herself on a warm, June day, reclining in the sun on a beach bordering Lake Michigan. She watched Brandon and Shane playing Frisbee near the water and shook her head. Olivia and Samantha were in the water, splashing at each other and laughing loudly. Off to her right, a volleyball game was in progress. Both teams were predominantly made up of men.

The beach was filled with citizens of Beach Park and some of the neighboring towns. No one wanted to be cooped up in the house when the sun was beaming down and while Lake Michigan's waters were as warm as they were going to get. The sounds of splashing water and rolling waves carried up to where Paige sat, shaded by a large, pink-and-white polka-dot umbrella that had been driven into the sand. A magazine that she'd neglected to open lie on her lap.

Samantha and Olivia were calling to her and waving their arms. One of the girls would call, "Look at me," and dunk herself underwater.

The other one would yell, "No, look at me," and attempt to outdo the first.

She tried her best to keep an eye on them both. The children's mother had declined the invitation to accompany them to the beach. Their mother was a beautiful woman, really. She always seemed to be in a hurry, though, as though there weren't enough hours in the day. The hours she worked every week were excessive, and she took a lot of business trips, two things that seemed to irk Samantha a great deal. Even so, she was too sweet of a kid to show her mother anything but support. Paige admired the girl for that.

Olivia, now nearly ten years old, was the same menace to society she'd been when Paige had first met her. She seemed to be untouched by anything negative. She was the most optimistic child Paige had ever met, and she wouldn't trade knowing the little girl for anything in the world. Watching Olivia and Samantha together made her think about her own children, made her wonder what they'd look like, what their personalities would be like.

"Come in the water with us!" Samantha shouted with her hands cupped around her mouth.

Paige shook her head and waved the magazine in the air.

"Come in the water with us!" Olivia yelled, mimicking her older sister.

Paige shook her head again.

Samantha grabbed her younger sister's hand and they both walked with difficulty out of the lake, droplets of water falling from their bodies. Samantha wore a plum-colored, one-piece swimsuit, while a multi-colored, two-piece swimsuit stuck to Olivia's little body. They tiptoed over the sand. Olivia hopped and skipped, declaring that the sand was hot. The sisters made their way to the beach towel Paige sat on. Without saying a word, each of them grabbed one of Paige's hands and started tugging to the best of her ability.

By this time, Shane and Brandon were looking over at them. They paused their game to laugh at the sight of the two girls trying to pull Paige towards the water.

Paige anchored her feet in the sand as they tugged. Her feet began dragging in the sand. "No, I don't want to get wet!" she cried.

Brandon jogged over to them, swept Paige up, and carried her to the water. She squealed in terror, looking down at the water beneath her.

"Bran, I swear to God, if you drop me..." she threatened, not bothering to finish her sentence.

A devilish grin stretched across his face as he held her body suspended over the gentle waves. "You'll what?" he asked her, tauntingly lowering her.

She arched her back and kicked her legs. "Put me the hell down, Brandon, I mean it!"

Without warning, he dropped her in the water. The water was warmer than usual, but compared to the sun's rays, it was a shockingly cool change of temperature. She sank underwater and struggled to her feet. When she resurfaced, Olivia, Samantha, Shane, and Brandon were all laughing. If the two children weren't present, she would have raised two middle fingers to Shane and Brandon, but because the kids *were* present, she settled for cursing under her breath and stomping out of the water.

As she walked, she wrung the water out of her hair.

Brandon, who'd resumed the Frisbee game with Shane, called to her, "I'm sorry baby, but I had to do it!"

"You're gonna' get it, I swear to God!" she screamed, settling back on her towel and drying the water from her legs.

She'd been sitting for no more than five minutes when a round, white ball came out of nowhere and struck her in the calf. She gasped-more out of surprise than pain-and her hand automatically reached down to massage the spot on her calf that had been hit.

"Sorry!" one of the volleyball players called to her.

She raised her gaze from her calf to the makeshift volleyball court, and spotted a tall, dark-haired figure jogging towards her to claim the ball. Her breath caught and held in her throat.

Ethan looked down at her, and his previously friendly expression transformed to one of recognition. "Aren't you-"

"Yes, I am," she replied before he could finish the sentence. "Was that your ball?"

He looked sheepish. "Sorry about that," he said, bending at the waist and lifting the ball from the sand. "We've got to stop meeting like this."

"You're telling me," she muttered, pushing damp hair back from her face and tucking it behind her ears.

"It's been...what..."

A year, six months, three days, and eleven hours, Paige thought to herself jokingly, and smiled at the fact that she'd been tempted to say that aloud. "About a year," she told him.

He nodded his head and narrowed his eyes at the bright rays from the sun. His chest was bare. He was only wearing swimming trunks, and by God if Brandon wasn't playing Frisbee with Shane a few feet away... "Who are you here with?"

"Sam, Olivia..." *My boyfriend.* "A few friends." She glanced around, searching for Shane and Brandon and praying that Brandon didn't approach them.

"I thought I saw Sam," Ethan said, bringing a hand up over his eyes to shade against the sun. He gazed towards the water where the two girls were still splashing each other. Seeing them brought a smile to his face. "You girls are inseparable, huh?"

Swallowing a lump in her throat, she nodded. "Um...yeah."

"I love seeing you all together. It's endearing to see siblings who get along so well."

She simply nodded her head again. "They're amazing kids," she said finally.

"They really are. Sam is supposed to graduate next year, right?" He stood, holding the volleyball against his hip.

"Yeah, she's stoked," she answered.

"I didn't think I was going to see you again," he said, sitting down on the towel next to her.

The volleyball players he'd been playing with started protesting and shouted for him to return with the ball. Paige wanted him to go over and resume the volleyball game so Brandon didn't see them together. Ethan looked down at the ball in his hands, looked up at Paige, and raised the ball. With a twist of his torso and release of his hands, the ball was sent flying across the sand to the makeshift volleyball court.

Oh shit, she thought miserably, not knowing how to get rid of him and not really *wanting* to get rid of him.

"So you've been doing well, huh?" he asked her, drawing his knees up and resting his elbows on them.

She nodded her head, tight-lipped. *Don't encourage conversation.* "I don't want to interrupt your game," she said lamely, gesturing towards the volleyball court. "We can talk another time."

"I haven't seen you in a year," he said. "I see *them* just about everyday. They can wait."

"I should be watching Sam and Olivia," she said, standing to her feet and brushing the sand off of her legs.

He looked up at her, at the indigo bikini that was barely covering her curves. *Christ,* he thought to himself, his eyes traveling up the length of her body. "Still with the same girlfriend?"

She shook her head. "No, umm…we're friends now. I should really get going."

He looked amused. "You're blowing me off?"

"I'm sorry," she said, looking genuinely apologetic. "I really don't want to, but if Sam or Olivia gets hurt…"

"I can help you watch them," he offered, standing as well and brushing himself off.

She bit her bottom lip anxiously, shifting from one foot to the other.

Why is she so nervous? he wondered, looking concerned for a moment.

Why does he have to look so damned good? she wondered to herself. She took a few steps back to put some space between them. "I'm going to get going. You can get back to your game," she said, her voice faltering.

"Are you all right?" he asked, taking a step towards her.

A blonde man barely taller than Paige was stepped up behind her, his hands possessively settling on her shoulders. "Anything wrong?" he asked, lowering his head to nip at her shoulder.

As soon as his hands touched her, Paige's shoulders jumped and she turned around to look at him. "No, nothing's wrong," she replied quickly, turning back to Ethan. "I was just talking to…Sam's teacher." She gestured towards Ethan.

Ethan looked confused, his gaze moving from Paige to Brandon. "Hi," he said, stepping forward and extending a hand towards Brandon. "Ethan Carson."

Brandon stared down at Ethan's hand for a few moments and slowly extended his own hand. "Hi," he returned. "Brandon Davies, daytime actor, Paige's boyfriend."

Both men appraised each other.

Shane ran up to them, a grin on his face. "Is a party going on without me?" he demanded, breathless. He was quick to size up the situation and the smile left his face in an instant.

"Shane, this is Sam's *teacher*," Paige introduced, giving Shane a pointed look.

At the word "teacher," a knowing look crept into Shane's eyes and he nodded. "Hey, man," he said, extending a hand. "Shane Luciani."

Ethan nodded. "I'm going to get back to my game," he said slowly, taking a few steps back. "Tell Sam and Olivia I said hi." He turned and broke into a slow jog towards the volleyball court.

Brandon shook his head, blowing air between his lips and chuckling. "That guy's a teacher? He must have all the little girlies at school worked up."

"Shut up, Brandon," Paige said more harshly than she'd intended. She reclaimed her seat on the large towel.

Brandon stood over her with his hands on his hips. "What the hell did I do now?" he demanded.

She shook her head. "Nothing."

Shane dragged Brandon off to continue their game of Frisbee with Brandon glancing back at Paige over his shoulder, looking confused. Paige followed him with her eyes until he was no longer glancing at her; then, she turned her eyes to the volleyball game and the dark-haired man standing off to the side, looking towards her with his arms barricaded across his chest.

His eyes locked with hers, and even from this distance, she could read what was in them. *What the hell is going on? I thought you were gay. What are you doing with a boyfriend?*

Breaking eye contact with him, she pulled the magazine she'd discarded back onto her lap and flipped through it, not really paying attention to any of the words on the pages. She could still feel the heat of his gaze on her skin. She attempted to read bits and pieces of the articles scattered across the magazine's pages.

Thoughts tumbled around in her head...thoughts about the fact that she'd been happy. *No,* she mentally corrected herself. *I'm* still *happy.*

The truth was she should have been aware of the possibility of bumping into Ethan; Beach Park was a small town. For some reason, she hadn't expected to see him again. She didn't know why; lately she'd been spending more and more time in Beach Park with her parents, Samantha and Olivia. She'd subconsciously pushed Ethan out of her mind in her mission to make a life with Brandon.

Seeing Ethan again had jolted her. She didn't know what was up or down, what was right or left. All she knew was that when Brandon introduced himself as Paige's boyfriend, the confused look on Ethan's face had just about crushed her heart. She and Brandon had weathered a year and a half together. She had somehow managed to convince herself that she was over Ethan, had neglected to think of him in several months. She liked to think that she was over the prolonged crush she'd developed on Ethan Carson, but if that were true, then why had it bothered her when Brandon had introduced himself as her boyfriend? Why hadn't she wanted Brandon to approach and interrupt them in the first place? Why did she keep visualizing the perplexed look on Ethan's face, and why did visualizing that expression make her feel so miserable?

"You feel miserable 'cause you still want him," Shane speculated, filling his mouth with a dozen peanuts. He stood with his hip leaning against the bar counter. Before Paige could protest about how happy she was with Brandon, he said, "Doesn't matter how much Brandon's changed or how much you love or *think* you love him now. As cool as Brandon is now, he's probably just not the one for you."

After dropping Samantha and Olivia off at home, she and Shane ventured to Harry's, the same bar Paige and her friends had visited one year ago. Brandon and Marissa were supposed to be joining them there, but so far neither showed.

The venue hadn't changed much; there was the same small dance floor with blazing white lights hanging over it, the same cramped booths and small tables, the same beer-belly, butt crack-exposing patrons. Despite its exaggerated casual atmosphere, there was something about the place that made a positive impression on Paige.

Shane looked at her and shook his head solemnly. "You have to decide what you want, Paige."

She offered him a half-smile. "Since when did you become the love doctor?" she joked. "Only a year ago you were declaring that you'd die a bachelor. All you were interested in was sex."

"There are only so many women you can fuck before it starts to get redundant," he told her, claiming the seat beside her and placing his hands on the countertop. "It got to a point where, yeah, fucking still felt good, but it only satisfied me temporarily, you know? Afterwards, there was still this hole in me waiting to be filled. And then..." A wistful look reached Shane's eyes, and color came to his cheeks. He turned his head, brushing the tip of his nose with his thumb.

She nodded knowingly. "And then, Marissa," she finished for him.

"And then Marissa," he agreed, looking at her and smiling. "She's unlike…anyone I've ever been with. She's *it* for me, you know? She's interesting on so many levels, it's ridiculous."

"When did you know she was it for you?" she asked, glancing over her shoulder.

"That one weekend we spent here," he answered with his eyes narrowed in concentration. "The *first* weekend we spent here, I should say."

"All the way back then you knew she was the one for you?"

He swirled the contents of his glass and said, "When the right one comes into your life, you know it. There *is* no question about it. It's just something you know. Anyway, that's what I think. Who am I but a horny-assed Italian, right?"

"No, I think you're right," she said sullenly, her eyes lowering.

"Cheer the fuck up. Your situation isn't that bad."

She arched a brow at him. "You think not?" she countered. "Either way I go, I'm screwed. I can stay with Brandon my whole life, but in the back of my mind I'll always be wondering what would have happened or could have happened had I told Ethan the truth, or I could dump Brandon, but I'd have to tell Ethan the truth."

Shane nodded in thought and laughed. "Well when you say it like that, yeah, you're in a pretty shitty situation."

"Marissa's supposed to be meeting us here, right?" she asked, suddenly desperate to talk about anything else.

He withdrew his cell phone from his pocket and glanced at the time in the LCD display. "Yeah, she got off of work about two hours ago, so she should be here any minute," he replied. "I'm going to switch gears here and change the topic if you don't mind."

"Feel free."

"We're ready to release the new book," he said without any preface to the topic. "I meant to bring your proof copy with me, but my brain's mush, you know. I didn't remember. I'll get it to you when we get back to Farmington Heights."

She nodded. "I bet the critics will love *this* one," she muttered sarcastically.

"You give them too much thought," he observed, scooping more peanuts out of the small bowl beside his beer glass. "A critic is nothing but a glorified consumer with an overrated opinion. You're never going to be able to please everyone. Some people will like your work and some people won't. If everyone liked the same things, it'd be a boring ass world, wouldn't it?"

"You always know how to make me feel better," she said, restlessly spinning around on her stool. "But glorified consumers or not, critics can make or break you."

"Just focus on the writing, will you?"

"That's the last thing I think I'm going to be able to focus on," she said honestly. "I can't think of anything to write. My motivation is just *kaput*. I don't know where it went." She was going to continue speaking, but she recognized a familiar mop of dark curls and beckoned Marissa over to join them.

Marissa was all smiles as Shane stood and embraced her.

Paige watched the two of them, trying to shoo away the envy that built up within her. They were both so certain that they were meant for each other. Neither of them seemed to have doubts about their relationship. Paige wished that she had that sense of faith when it came to Brandon, but she didn't. What she and Brandon had in no way resembled what Marissa and Shane seemed to have.

Feeling like a peeping tom, she turned her gaze elsewhere. There weren't many people dancing on the dance floor; the majority of the patrons were seated in booths or playing at one of the pool tables set up near the back of the bar. Her writer's eye appreciated the seediness of the place, the dim lighting, dull, scratched wood, and pungent odor of strong liquor mingling with cigarette smoke.

When she swung her head around to Shane and Marissa, they were both eyeing her with concern. "You all right, Paige?" Marissa asked, moving out of Shane's embrace to lean against her friend. "I heard about what happened."

"Word travels fast," Paige muttered, but accepted the hug that Marissa offered her.

"How do you get yourself into these situations, I mean really?"

"I seriously don't know. Love doesn't like me." Paige lowered her index finger into her beer, swirled the finger around idly, and stuck the finger in her mouth.

Marissa clucked her tongue. "Well if you're looking for a bright side, at least he knows you're not a lesbian now." She looked positively radiant in her candy apple red skirt, red and white blouse, and white heels.

At Marissa's remark, Shane replied, "Yeah, the man probably thinks she's *bi* now."

Marissa cut him a look over the top of Paige's head. "Could you help me out here?"

"I'm trying, I'm trying," he claimed. He proceeded to bury his nose into his drink.

"I'm all right, I really am," Paige said, standing from her stool and rubbing her hands on the thighs of her jeans. "I mean, I have Brandon and we're happy together. I don't even know why I'm worrying about anything, really."

"Speaking of Brandon, where the hell is he?" Marissa demanded, stepping back and glancing around the bar.

"He's probably back at the hotel, brushing his hair and making sure his eyebrows are perfectly lined," Shane joked. He saw the expression on Marissa's face and once again tipped his beer glass back.

"Brandon isn't *that* bad," Paige protested. Then she thought of her own words and admitted, "Yeah, maybe he is."

"He takes longer getting ready than *Marissa* does," Shane exclaimed, his eyes wide. "And Paige, you know how long Marissa takes to get ready."

A man with reddish-blonde hair seized the stool to Paige's left, but she paid him no mind. She didn't acknowledge his presence until he banged a fist on the bar counter, demanding a drink.

The bartender, who was towards the other end of the bar, slowly made his way to the newcomer. "Rich, you haven't been here in forever, man!" the bartender greeted jovially.

Both Marissa and Paige turned their heads towards the man who'd been called Rich. He noticed that their attention was on him. "I apologize for the yelling," he said, wiping a hand over his brow. "It's been a long day."

"I hear you," Paige muttered.

Rich smiled and accepted the glass of cool liquor from the bartender. "Thanks, Eddie," he said, nursing the glass of beer between two palms. The bartender started to make his way towards the other end of the bar. "Actually, I'm going to need another glass, Eddie. A friend of mine is parking his car, and his day's been just about as long as mine."

The bartender stayed, leaned over the counter and made small talk with Rich.

Marissa shook her head and retrieved the nose she'd stuck into Rich's business. Paige wheeled around to face Shane so the bartender and Rich could have a measured amount of privacy.

"Brandon should be here by now," Paige said, glancing at the silver and turquoise watch on her wrist.

"I told you, he's grooming himself," Shane told her, trying to suppress laughter. "Give him time."

Marissa nudged Shane in the ribs. "Do you ever shut up?"

He smiled at her. "You should know better."

At Paige's back, Rich suddenly bellowed. "There he goes!"

A deep, sullen voice, neither the bartender's, nor Rich's, greeted, "What's up?"

"I had a beer prepared. I knew you'd need one," Rich said.

"Thanks."

"A shocker for you, huh?" Rich turned his conversation to the bartender. "This guy right here found out today this woman that he was into, who he hasn't seen in awhile, has a boyfriend."

Paige could hear the conversation behind her, but she didn't turn to face Rich; she kept her back to him. Instead, she looked up at Marissa and Shane to see if they were listening also. They were.

The bartender scoffed. "A boyfriend? That happens to the best of us, man."

"No, no, no, but get this. She *told* him she was a lesbian."

"*Ouch.*" The bartender hid a chuckle behind the back of his hand. He busied himself with wiping the bar down.

"Yeah, *ouch*," Richard mocked, clapping his hand on the counter. "I asked my old buddy here if he'd had broccoli stuck in his teeth or something the day she told him she was a lesbo."

"First off, she didn't tell me she was a lesbian. I assumed it," the new voice said, "and second off, I had a girlfriend at the time, so whether or not she was lesbian wouldn't have even mattered. I was just surprised, that's all. You're making too big of a deal out of this."

Paige knew it was Ethan's voice speaking and she wanted to turn around to look at him, to apologize to him. More than that, she wanted to slip off the stool, tiptoe a couple of steps, and run like hell. She tucked her hair behind her ears and grabbed her glass from the bar counter.

"Maybe we should get a booth or something," Marissa whispered into Paige's ear.

Sliding off of the stool, trying to draw the least amount of attention as possible, Paige nodded. Without looking over her shoulder, she followed Shane and Marissa to a booth and slid in across from the inseparable couple. "Oh my God," she muttered, tilting her head back and pressing her hands to her temples.

"You have, like...the worst luck ever," Marissa murmured, stretching her neck to look towards the bar. "Of all places for him to go tonight...of all places for *you* to go tonight..."

Eleven o' clock rolled around and Brandon was still a no-show. Marissa and Shane were engaged in a deep conversation; they were dangerously close to rubbing their noses together and calling each other "snookie wookums." Paige excused herself and headed towards the Ladies bathroom, where she locked herself in a stall, made use of the toilet, and exited the stall. She stood at the sink washing her hands and looking at her god-awful reflection. Christ, was that her?

The reflection looking back at her looked frazzled and tired, as if she hadn't had a good night's rest in weeks. Her eyes drooped at the corners and her hair hung limply past her shoulders. Her arms, exposed in the bright blue tank top she wore, looked thin and gaunt. She leaned down and splashed some of the running water on her face. Snatching coarse napkins from the dispenser mounted on the wall, she thought to herself, *He's probably gone now. He came in to knock back a few beers and now he's gone. Stop looking so tense. Relax.* She walked out of the bathroom door, made a sharp turn, and nearly collided with a man bent over the water fountain. Eyes wide, she jerked herself back in mid-stride to prevent the collision. "Oh my God," she cried in alarm.

Ethan straightened to his full height, wiping his mouth with the back of his hand. Steely blue eyes settled on hers and a brow lifted slightly. "We've got to stop meeting like this."

"You're telling me," she muttered.

For an instant, he looked amused. Then he turned, preparing to leave her standing there. She stepped forward and grabbed his arm. He stopped walking, but didn't turn to face her. Beneath her fingers, his forearm tensed.

"I'm sorry about what happened earlier today."

"You don't owe me any explanations."

She released his arm from her grasp and clasped her hands together in front of her. "I feel like I do."

He sighed and slowly turned to face her.

"You saw me and my best friend dancing that night, and you thought...we were more than friends," she blurted, "and I tried to find a right moment to slip in that she and I were just friends, but there wasn't one. I didn't mean to lie."

A muscle in his jaw moved. Otherwise, he was still.

She felt as if she were under a microscope with his eyes on her, as if he was inspecting her every move. "I just wanted to say that I'm sorry." She blinked back tears and walked around him, striding towards where Marissa and Shane were still seated at the booth. "Let's go," she said, wiping her eyes.

Marissa and Shane looked up in surprise, as if they hadn't even noticed she'd left.

"Never mind," she mumbled and made as if to leave. A six-five, dark haired, blue-eyed barricade stood in her way.

"You didn't give me a chance to say anything," Ethan said, raking a hand over his hair.

She folded her arms across her chest.

"I was going to tell you that I wasn't angry with you," he went on, choosing his words carefully. "I was just confused, really. I didn't know what was going on. I was...surprised." *Surprised because the only reason I didn't make a move on you a year ago was because I didn't think you'd be into me.*

"I'm sorry I misled you," she apologized, debating on whether or not she should tell him the entire truth.

Leaving Shane and Marissa to stare after them, Ethan led her away from the booth and back towards the bar counter, where they staked their claim on two stools. "So you have a boyfriend."

Not anymore, she wanted to say, but that would have been another lie. Instead, she said, "Yeah."

"And I've seen him somewhere before."

"He's an actor."

"Yeah, he did mention that. Figures." He ordered two beers and slid one glass her way after the bartender delivered.

She accepted her glass and turned it around in her hands. "So teachers go to bars and drink beer nowadays?"

"This one does," he replied, a devilish sparkle gleaming in his eye. "So, this actor…is he a good guy?"

"He tries to be," she said, focusing a little too intently on the glass in her hands.

If he ever steps out of bounds with her, I'll kick his ass, he thought to himself. He had despised Brandon Davies on sight. The possessive way he'd held Paige, the look in his eyes when he'd introduced himself as her boyfriend…the guy had known what he'd been interrupting, Ethan was sure of it. And an *actor*? "How did you two meet?" he asked her curiously, running a finger along the rim of his beer glass.

"I was on a book tour and he was filming on location," she answered. "He had this big ego, and he was sure of himself when he asked me out. He thought I was just going to say 'yes' and give myself to him on a silver platter. He found out the hard way that he actually had to put in a little effort to get me."

He absent-mindedly stroked the side of his glass with his eyes focused on her. She was a beautiful woman, and laid-back, too. He liked watching her mouth when she spoke; she had some of the most expressive lips he'd ever seen. Her eyes were remarkable, also…at times they were the color of green olives, like they were now, but when her moods shifted those eyes could be as bright as emeralds. He wanted to know about her. He wanted to spend time with her and listen to her talk. *What's she doing with some arrogant ass of an actor?* he wondered, watching her take large gulps of her drink. *She should be with someone who really cares about her, someone who'd do anything for her.*

After listening to her description of Brandon for only a few moments, he had wanted to pound the man's face in. He wasn't accustomed to having jealous tendencies, but he recognized it; it's what was coursing through him as he listened to Paige talk about Brandon.

Two beers later, her words were starting to slur, and as she talked, she'd lay a hand on Ethan's arm. When she laughed, she'd lean on his shoulder, and he was able to feel her cinnamon-colored hair brushing across his neck. She was an entertaining woman when intoxicated.

She called to the bartender behind the counter, leaning over the countertop and waving her arms. Ethan laughed and pulled her back onto her stool. "I think you've had enough to drink," he advised her.

She shook her head. "No…I don't think so."

"I do think so," he argued, shaking his head when Eddie, the bartender, started to walk towards them.

"But I'm thirsty," she whined. She grabbed her glass and turned it upside down, gently shaking it. "See? My glass is empty. I need something in it…I'm thirsty."

He took the glass from her and set it down on the bar counter. "You're a horrible drunk," he told her, but couldn't help smiling.

She smiled back and raised an index finger to his jaw. "You have the prettiest eyes I've ever seen on a man," she said, and hiccupped. Her eyes widened and she covered her mouth.

Something inside him tugged, but he shoved the feeling aside. "I think it's time for you to call it a night," he said, surveying the bar and looking for the friends he'd pulled her away from. He spotted them on the dance floor, dancing closely with each other.

"'Rissa's dancing," Paige said, sliding off of her stool and following Ethan's gaze. "She's good at that."

"I remember," he said, watching Paige's two friends grinding their hips into each other on the dance floor. "We should really get you home. It's time for you to call it a night."

Her feet were moving even though she didn't want them to. She didn't know where she was attempting to walk, but she stumbled several times. Three times, she nearly fell. He caught her all three times. The last time he caught her, she remained in his arms, looking up at him with vulnerable eyes. "I'm so sorry," she whispered, attempting to stand on her own.

"You don't have to apologize," he said. He cleared his throat a few times and took a few steps back from her. He reminded himself that she had a boyfriend. Acting on any emotions or urges he had at the moment would result in nothing but pain and/or humiliation for one or both parties. Still, those beautiful, helpless eyes were undoing the very core of him.

"I should really get home," she said suddenly, brushing her hair back.

"Did you drive?"

"I drove...but Marissa and Shane wouldn't have a way to get back. They rode with me."

"Maybe we should go tell them you're ready to go home," he suggested.

"Or *maybe* I'll take Paige home," interjected Brandon's voice. He stood a few feet away from the both of them, an entire head shorter than Ethan. He gently grasped Paige's arm and pulled her away from the taller man. "What a small fucking world. This must be one small fucking town, if everywhere you go, you see the same people."

Ethan squared his jaw and told himself to relax several times before facing Brandon.

"My, my, my, Mr. Teacher...Isn't alcohol *bad* for you?" Brandon taunted, boldly looking up at Ethan with an intense fierceness to his eyes. "Isn't that what you teach the kiddies? And here you are, cozying up in a bar with my girlfriend?"

"We didn't meet up here intentionally," Ethan explained, keeping his voice level. He wanted to pound the actor's face in. He wanted to so badly that his knuckles tingled, but it wouldn't be right. He was a man with morals; he didn't go around swinging his fists at every man he happened to dislike. "I think she's drunk. She should probably get home."

She was clinging to Brandon, her head on his shoulder and her eyelids drooping. He shrugged his right shoulder a bit, trying to wake her up. "Paige, will you get *up*, dammit! You got drool on my fucking shirt!"

Anger flared up within Ethan and he fought hard to keep it in check. "Watch the way you talk to her. She's intoxicated."

"Okay why are *you* still standing in front of me?" Brandon demanded, looking around for a napkin to wipe the sleeve of his shirt with. "She just drooled on my fucking shirt. You don't know how much this shit cost me."

Marissa's heels clicked on the wood floor as she hurried over to them. "Are you guys causing a scene? What's wrong?" She saw Paige and her expression transformed from one of puzzlement to one of worry. "What's wrong with Paige?"

"She doesn't know how to hold her fucking liquor," Brandon muttered, now fanning a hand over the small wet spot on his sleeve. "She drooled on my fucking shirt."

"Where the hell have you been anyway, Brandon? We've been waiting for your ass all night." Marissa planted her hands on her hips. "You were supposed to be here, what? Two hours ago? Two *hours,* Brandon? What the hell's wrong with you?"

Ethan saw that Marissa seemed to have control of the situation. He said, "I'll leave you two to handle this."

"Where are you going, Teach?" Marissa asked, pinning him with her hazel eyes.

"You two seem to have this situation under control," he replied, grabbing a thin sports jacket from one of the stools. He pulled it across his shoulders. "I've got to get going."

"While you're going, you might as well drop Paige off," Marissa proposed. She grabbed Ethan's hand in one hand and Paige's hand in the other. Without another word, she linked their hands together and looked up at Ethan with a hint of a smile on her face.

Brandon paused in fanning his shirt to proclaim, "Paige isn't leaving with him, Marissa."

"Yes, she is," Marissa said firmly. "You're acting like a dickhead and pissing in your pants over a shirt."

"She's *my* woman."

"Your *woman* doesn't translate to being your property, Brandon." Marissa turned her attention to Ethan. "She's staying at her parents' house on Ford Avenue, do you know where that is?"

"I know the area," Ethan answered, digging hands into the pockets of his khakis and withdrawing a set of keys from one of them. He smiled at Marissa, appreciative of her take-charge attitude. He let Richard know that he was leaving and gave Brandon little more than a passing glance as he escorted Paige out of the bar with her hand tucked in his.

The drive to Paige's house started out with silence. The car radio was set at a low volume; a Lifehouse song was playing. At every red light or stop sign Ethan stopped at, he'd glance over at the sleeping woman in his passenger seat. As beautiful and as sweet as she was, she deserved a man better than Brandon. Why was she *with* him? She'd sat on that stool with him not even a half an hour ago and explained to him in plain English why she was with him, but he still didn't understand it.

She groaned, bringing a hand up to her head and opening her eyes. "My head hurts," she moaned, struggling to sit up.

"Don't sit up too fast. It'll only hurt worse," he cautioned, making a left turn and glancing at her once the turn was completed. "I've never seen anyone get drunk that quickly. Did you eat before drinking?"

She shook her head, massaging her temples with her fingers. "Why am I in your car?"

"You got drunk, your boyfriend came in, made a scene, and Marissa ruled that I should be the one to take you home."

"Oh my God. Brandon...he..."

"Yeah."

"And it was bad?" she asked in a small voice.

"He's a character."

"Shit."

He laughed. Her voice was slightly high-pitched. Hearing her curse was like hearing Minnie Mouse use vulgar language. It didn't sound anywhere near intimidating; it only sounded comical. "He was about to give you a royal beat down for drooling on his new silk shirt."

"The neon orange?" she croaked, closing her eyes.

"How'd you know?"

"When he bought it, you would have thought he was buying a Porsche with how much he carried on about it."

"Sounds like a real winner," Ethan mumbled, focusing his eyes on the road and keeping them there. If he spent too much time looking at her, they would most certainly end up in a car collision.

She shook her head and stared out of the window. "I thought he turned a new leaf. I guess that was my wishful thinking."

"Maybe he did and…he just really liked that shirt." Even to Ethan it sounded lame.

"Or maybe he's an asshole," she muttered, rubbing the back of her neck.

"You're going to have to let me know which house it is."

"We've got a few more blocks to go."

"He's very possessive of you."

The abrupt change in conversation topics threw Paige off. The alcohol still seemed to be affecting her mind. She had to think about everything he said for about thirty seconds before responding. "Marissa calls it 'Little Man Syndrome.' She says since he's so short, he's overcompensating by being such a possessive terror."

"I was wondering earlier why you're even with him if he's such a jerk."

"It's the second house on the right up here," she announced. "And to be completely honest, I don't know *why* I'm with him. He can be an asshole sometimes. I know that from first-hand experience, but…there are times when he's

this amazingly charismatic guy. There are times when..."
When it seems like he actually loves me.

He turned the car into her parents' driveway and turned off the engine. "You deserve better than that, you know," he said after a few minutes of deliberating on the words he'd use. He'd been appalled to see how Brandon had treated her, pushing her away from him for the preservation of a shirt. How a beautiful woman like her could stay with an asshole like that was beyond him.

Her head was tilted to the side and she was staring at him. "I don't know if I *do* deserve better than that." She pushed open the car door and set a foot on the ground. "Thanks for the ride." She climbed out of the car and closed the door.

He rolled down the passenger side window as she turned and started walking up the driveway. "Hey!" he called.

She turned around, silhouetted by the darkness of midnight.

"I'm going to want to be your friend. Do you think your boyfriend can handle that?"

"He's going to have to," she said after a slight hesitation. "Because I'm going to want to be friends with you too."

Chapter Ten

"You…traded phone numbers with him?"

Paige nodded, pulling her dark hair into a ponytail.

"He…told you he wants to be your friend?" Marissa demanded, following Paige around the hotel room.

"And I told him that I want to be his friend, too." Paige stood with her hands on her hips, searching for the faux alligator purse that matched the crimson, short-sleeved blouse she wore.

"And you're still with Brandon…*why*? The teacher is obviously into you."

"I can't become romantically involved with Ethan," Paige said, getting on her hands and knees and peering underneath the bed. "If I do, I have to tell him the truth."

Marissa scratched her head. The expression on her face twisted into confusion. "But you *can* be his trusted friend and still live a lie," she said slowly, not grasping the concept. "He's the love of your life and you're letting him get away."

Getting back to her feet, Paige glanced around the hotel suite's bedroom with her hand fisted under her chin. "Being in a relationship would only complicate things." She went to the bureau and began opening drawers. "Enough about me and my twisted love life. How is yours doing? You've got Shane wrapped around your finger."

A red tint touched Marissa's bronze cheeks, and she avoided her best friend's inquisitive gaze. She walked around the room, fidgeting with the knick-knacks atop the dresser and smiling to herself. "What I have with Shane, I've never had with anyone," she said finally. "It's like…I don't know. You know me. You know what I've done and who I've done it with. I'm not the purest girl you'll come across, far from it.

"I think of how I was in college, how smart I was and still *am* and how I've wasted it all of these years to party hard and go to dance clubs three nights a week...I get depressed. I do. It was a phase I should have grown out of, you know?" She paused. A dreamy look that Paige didn't recognize crept into her eyes. "I've never known love. Partying? Fun? Maybe even a one-night stand here or there. I *knew* that. I knew living it up. I didn't know anything about settling down. I thought settling down made you boring and I thought it would make life redundant. But Shane...he's a lot *like* me. He thought the way I did. He thought settling down automatically meant accepting this boring way of life. I'm not a boring person and Shane's not a boring person. Settling down together would be *far* from boring."

"I'm glad you found him," Paige said, her voice thick with emotion.

"Without you, I wouldn't have." Marissa crossed the room and threw her arms around her best friend's neck.

Paige hugged her friend back. "What you two have is special. Whenever someone mentions your name, his eyes light up. He really loves you."

Marissa pulled back and shrugged. "I kind of like him too, you know?" She paused, then said, "You've been spending a lot of time here in the past year."

"I know."

"Wonder why that is."

"Stop wondering." Paige slid the closet door open and all but screamed in delight. The deep red, faux alligator purse hung on a hook embedded in the closet door. She yanked it off of the hook and hugged it to her chest.

"Are you thinking about moving here?"

Paige faced her friend. "The thought hadn't crossed my mind," she said, shutting the closet door. "After coming here last year for my parents' vow renewal ceremony, I realized my parents wouldn't be around forever. I got to spend time with Sam and meet Olivia for the first time. They're really the most amazing kids. I just couldn't stay away. At the same time, though, I love my house in Farmington Heights."

Marissa nodded with downcast eyes.

"Why?" Paige asked, a brow lifting inquisitively.

"I don't know, it's an awesome town," Marissa said, walking over to the window and peering out of it. "Right on the beach, you know? The city is so fast, so crowded, but here it's not so crowded. It's the type of place where everywhere you go, you know someone, and...I don't know."

"You want to *move* here?" Paige shrieked incredulously. "Are you serious?"

Marissa crossed the room to make sure the bedroom door was closed, because Shane and Brandon were in the hotel suite's living room hooking up Brandon's Playstation to the television. "If I told you something, would you promise not to tell Shane?"

"'Rissa, you know-"

"No I don't, Paige. You and Shane are kind of close, so I don't know how much you tell each other." Marissa stood at the door with her hands on her hips. "Would you promise not to tell him or talk to him about it or anything?"

"Yeah, I promise," Paige said with a wave of her hand.

Marissa inched towards the bed and sat near the foot of the bed, licking her lips. "I think he's the one."

"Tell me something I don't know."

"Okay...I think I want to marry him."

Paige's mouth dropped open. She laughed and shook her head, her eyes wide with shock. "Wow."

"Yeah, wow," Marissa said, her shoulders slumping. "I mean...I *think* I want to marry him, but I'm not sure."

A knock rapped on the door and it creaked open an inch. "Are you girls decent?" Shane queried.

"No, we're butt-assed naked," Marissa called out, rolling her eyes and turning towards the door expectantly.

The door burst open and a very disappointed-looking Shane filled the doorway. "Shit, don't tease me that way," he said, entering the room. He approached Marissa and pulled her off of the bed. He nodded a greeting at Paige, who nodded back. "Your man's in there getting gray hairs trying to hook up that damned game system to the TV. You might want to help him out."

"Or I just might want to pop some popcorn and watch his agony," Paige countered.

Shane shrugged. "Or you could do that. *Whatever* you do, do *something*. You need to get out of this room, get outside. It's a beautiful day. Stop moping."

"I'm not moping. I was talking to my best friend. Can I do that?"

"No you can't, because she has a date with her man," Shane said, dragging Marissa towards the door. Before walking out of the door, he stuck his tongue out over his shoulder.

Paige resisted the urge to throw the faux alligator handbag at him. Instead, she stretched out on the bed, and without intending to, fell asleep.

"Oh my God!"

Paige bolted upright in bed with wide eyes just as the door nearly flew off of its hinges. The lights in her room were off; everything was cloaked in darkness. The only light in the room was pouring in from the hallway. All she could see was an outline in her doorway, but she knew it was Marissa. "Are you all right?" she asked, her voice groggy with sleep. "What the hell's the matter?"

The lights flicked on and the first thought that occurred to her was that Marissa looked stunning. A halter-styled black dress bathed in sparkles hugged her every curve and jewels were wrapped around her wrists and neck. Her bottom lip trembled and without another word, she took a few steps into the room and jumped into the bed with Paige.

"What the hell?" Paige asked, not knowing what to think.

"He-he-he-" Marissa stammered, tears sliding from the corners of her eyes.

"Did Shane dump you?" Paige asked, unable to imagine such a thing happening.

Marissa shook her head and buried her face in the crook of her friend's neck.

"*What*? Tell me what's going on. I can't help you unless you tell me what's going on."

Marissa sat up, pushing her wild, curly hair out of her face. "He asked me to marry him," she whispered, as if the walls had ears.

Paige gasped and brought her hands to her mouth. "That's…amazing, Marissa, that's great!" she exclaimed, smiling.

Marissa shook her head, jumping out of the bed as quickly as she'd jumped into it. "No, no, no," she protested, wiping the tears from her cheeks. "It's *not* great. I left him there at the restaurant and caught a cab here."

Paige's brows furrowed and she pressed fingers to her temples. "'Rissa…why would you do that?"

"I froze. I didn't know what to say. I didn't know what to do. We were just talking about it earlier, me and you, you know? Remember? I told you I thought I wanted to marry him, but I didn't know."

"Oh my God, 'Rissa."

"He'll probably be here any minute," Marissa said, glancing over her shoulder. She looked to be more frightened than Paige had ever seen her. "I can't see him or talk to him right now, Paige, I can't."

"You walked *out* on him after he proposed?" Paige croaked in disbelief. "He has to be crushed right now. You *have* to talk to him."

"I can't talk to him," Marissa insisted, blinking her hazel eyes furiously. "Not now. I have to…think about things, you know? I need some time."

Paige moistened her lips and looked towards the nightstand, searching for a clock. "What time is it?"

"Close to nine o' clock."

"Shit," Paige cursed, throwing the sheets aside and standing. "Brandon and I were supposed to go out tonight."

"He's playing video games and he's not responding to anything else right now," Marissa said, collapsing on the bed again and burying her face into the pillow at the head of the bed. "What do I do, Paige?"

"I can't tell you what to do. You have to do whatever's in your heart," Paige told her friend.

"Oh, that's bullshit," Marissa said, sitting up. "That's psychobabble. I need real advice, not the corny shit."

"You need to rest up and take some time to think about it logically," Paige said. "You're too emotional to be logical right now. In the meantime, Shane isn't going anywhere. If he calls you, don't avoid him. Just tell him you need some time to think about it. He can understand that."

Marissa nodded sullenly. "You're right. You're right." She wiped the remaining tears trailing down her cheeks and took a steadying breath.

"So he got on one knee, had the ring, and everything?"

"The whole nine yards," Marissa replied, laughing weakly. "It was...beautiful. And I wrecked it."

"You can't take anything you did back, so there's no point in dwelling on it," Paige pointed out, rubbing her eyes and yawning.

Marissa's mood was still solemn, but she didn't look as panicked as she had been only moments before. Her eyes were now devoid of tears, and once in awhile she managed a small smile, the way she did now. "You always know what to say, Paige. You're great at giving advice."

Paige nodded and walked her friend to the door.

Marissa stood just outside of the doorway with her back to Paige. She turned and said, "If only you could take your own advice sometimes."

Chapter Eleven

Ethan couldn't sleep. Whenever he closed his eyes, he'd see Paige. It was unnerving, actually. He wasn't used to thinking about a woman so much. None of the women he'd dated in the past had captured that much of his attention and focus, not even Diane. Here he was, not even dating Paige, and she was all he could think about. The vision of her on the beach had been stunning; it was an image that wouldn't leave his mind no matter how many times he begged it to. God, she'd been beautiful.

He liked the way she talked and he liked the way she moved-*when* she was sober. When he talked to her, he liked watching her lips form the words that she wanted to say. She had the tendency to chew on the corner of her bottom lip when she was nervous or anxious, and he doubted that she knew how gorgeous she looked when she dragged a hand through her long, luxurious hair. Whenever he thought of her, he smiled, and whenever he saw her, he smiled. Whenever he'd seen Diane, he'd felt like running the other way.

Lying in bed with the sheets pulled up to his waist, he turned and looked at the phone on his nightstand. He shook his head. It was after ten o' clock; she'd probably be in bed with her jerkoff boyfriend by now. Running a hand up and down his chest, he glanced at the phone again. The desire to hear her voice was too strong. He leaned up on braced elbows with his eyes still on the phone. Clearing his throat, he leaned over, clicked on the lamp and fumbled around the nightstand for the slip of paper he'd jotted her number on.

He grabbed the phone and with squinted eyes, he dialed the number as it appeared on the shred of paper.

The phone rang and rang. He was toying with the phone cord and considering terminating the call when a feminine voice whispered, "Hello?"

"Hi." He cleared his throat. "Hi, this is Ethan."

"Ethan?"

"I'm sorry it's so late," he started to apologize. "I wasn't going to call, but I just-"

"No, it's fine," Paige said, sounding sleepy.

"No it's not. I'm going to let you go back to sleep," he said, ruffling his hair with a hand and sitting up in bed.

"Don't worry about it. I'm not tired."

He smiled. She sounded *very* tired. "Are you sure? I thought you might have been in bed, with-"

"Oh, no," she said hurriedly and then hesitated. "Well...yeah."

"I'm going to let you go." He tried to keep the disappointment out of his voice and failed.

"No, don't. I mean...I'm glad you called."

Those words made him forget that she was lying in bed with a complete dunce. The smile returned to his mouth. He reached over and turned off the lamp. Sliding down so that his head rested against the cushion of fluffed pillows, he said, "I'm glad I called too. I just...I was lying in bed, and I just got the urge to call you. I'm sorry if I interrupted anything, I just..." *I had to hear your voice...I didn't want to go to sleep without hearing it.*

"And I wanted to thank you for driving me home," she returned, and he could hear a door opening and closing on her end. "I must have been a mess."

No, you were beautiful. You always are. He closed his eyes and took a deep breath. "No, it was nothing. I was glad to do it. You're lucky to have a friend like..." He tried to think of her name, knew he'd heard it more than once.

"Marissa," she supplied for him.

"Right. You're lucky to have a friend like her. I can tell she looks out for you."

"She *is* the best friend a girl could ever have," she agreed. "Good friends are rare, and I have four of them that are stellar. I am fortunate for that."

His hands roamed over his chest and there was something he wanted to ask, but he hesitated. "Tell me if I'm being too forward or inappropriate or anything like that, but I was wondering what you were doing tomorrow." He mouthed a quick prayer up to the ceiling.

"I didn't have anything specific planned," she told him after a moment of thought. "I was just going to hang out with the kids and-"

"In the summers, I play in a basketball league," he told her, his words running together. "Usually the players bring their girlfriends to watch, some bring their family members. I was wondering if you would mind coming and maybe afterwards we could…" *Have mind-blowing sex in my bedroom, on the living room furniture, in the shower, and on the kitchen counter.* "…Grab something to eat, or something," he said instead, smiling at the sudden thought that had occurred to him.

She told him that those plans sounded great. She asked him what time she should be ready. After hanging up the phone, he stared at it for a few minutes. He was certain he'd dreamt up the entire conversation.

The next day, Paige caught her first glimpse of Ethan while she was peering out of the living room window of her parents' house. He pulled up to her driveway in his silver Dodge Intrepid and pushed the driver's side door open. He stepped out of the car looking tall and athletic in dark blue jogging pants (that coincidentally matched her navy blue shorts), a white polo shirt, and Adidas sneakers.

She didn't feel comfortable letting him pick her up in front of the hotel where she and Brandon had shared a room the previous night. Since he'd dropped her off at her parent's house a few nights ago, it was convenient to make the short drive to her parent's house and have him pick her up there.

She let the curtains fall back into place and tugged on her ponytail nervously, telling herself that they were two friends spending a day together and hanging out. It was nothing serious. It wasn't a date or anything…it couldn't be a date, because she had a boyfriend. These were the thoughts that ran through her mind as she pulled the front door open.

Ethan's hand was raised as if prepared to knock on the door. Amusement crossed his features. "Are you psychic or something?"

"Just prepared," she responded, opening the screen door. "I didn't really know what to wear. I kept in mind it was a sporting event, and I didn't want to look too dressed up for it."

He grinned and closed the screen door behind him. "You look great." He wasn't exaggerating. She was dressed down in tight blue shorts, a plain white t-shirt, and sneakers, but she still looked good.

"Do I need a change of clothes for afterwards?"

He shook his head. "No, what you've got on is fine."

Narrowing her eyes at him, she asked, "Do *you* have a change of clothes?"

"That's different," he claimed. "I'm going to be getting sweaty and nasty. I'm going to *need* a change of clothes for you to be willing to come within a foot of me. Are you ready to go?"

She nodded and followed him out of the house. She walked down the driveway, welcoming the heat blast that rushed at her. She stopped at the passenger door of his car, looking at him over the roof of the car. The sun beamed on his hair, made it shine, and his blazing blue eyes sparkled once he turned them on her.

Once she was inside of the car, she buckled her seatbelt. He buckled in his own seatbelt and they talked as he drove. She asked him about his teaching, asked him how long he'd lived in this town.

He told her about how his father had wanted him to coach college basketball, how his father had been dismayed to hear he wanted to teach high school students and coach high school basketball. "I don't really talk about it much because it's usually the first question people ask me if they recognize me on sight: Why did you give up the opportunity to coach college basketball? Why did you give up the opportunity to play professional basketball? They just don't understand my motives for being a teacher." He shook his head, and the easygoing smile he usually wore left his face. "*No* one I came across understood. Everyone I've come into contact with thinks I should have coached college ball or played pro ball. It's not a big enough accomplishment to have become the coach of a high school's varsity basketball team my first year of teaching."

"I'm glad you became a teacher," she said softly from beside him.

He looked down at her shortly before returning his gaze to the road.

She cleared her throat. "Kids need good teachers nowadays, you know? Kids need a teacher who isn't just teaching for the paycheck."

"Do you know how much teachers get paid? I can't see many people being in this field for the paycheck."

"Teachers are underpaid," she agreed.

He shook his head and the smile appeared on his face again. "We're supposed to be enjoying this day," he chided, turning the volume on the radio up a bit. A Fall Out Boy song blasted from the speakers and he turned the volume on the radio back down.

"What, you don't like this song?" she asked, reaching forward and turning the volume of the song up. She started singing along with the song off-key.

"Oh, no, not the singing," he said, braking to stop at a red light and bringing his hands up to his ears. "Oh my God, please stop."

She punched him lightly in the arm, but obliged and stopped singing. "My singing wasn't that bad," she said, pretending to take offense. She poked out her bottom lip at him.

"Your singing's an abomination," he corrected, laughing.

"Oh, what, you think you can do better?" she questioned. "I dare you to try."

He shook his head, still laughing. "There's no way you're going to get me to sing."

"Are you chicken?"

"No, I'm not *chicken*."

"Then sing."

"I don't know the song."

She narrowed her eyes at him analytically. Then she shook her head. "You're lying."

"You *are* psychic. Or, at the very least, a mind-reader." He pulled into the parking lot of the town's leisure center. She didn't hesitate in jumping out of the car, but he stood out of the car more slowly and removed a heavy-looking tote bag from the backseat. He walked around the car and joined her side, squinting at the plain, nondescript building before them.

She tilted her head up at him. "You actually look nervous," she observed, trying her best not to look amused at his discomfort.

"The other players usually bring their girlfriends or their family or their kids or their friends," he explained, still looking ahead. "This is the first time someone will be in the audience cheering me on. I've never brought anyone here-ever. These league games are my escape."

She wondered why she'd been the first person he had invited as they entered the building. He led her to the bleachers where she'd be sitting. The gymnasium wasn't much more different than a high school gymnasium. A group of middle-aged men practiced lay-ups and passes on the gleaming wood floor and the bleachers were half-filled with spectators.

Ethan talked with her for a few moments, pointing out a few people he knew. When those few moments were over, he told her that he had to get ready for the game. She watched him jog off to greet several of the men practicing on the floor. He raised his shirt over his head and tossed it over the back of a chair at the sidelines. He'd had on a gold, navy blue, and white sleeveless basketball jersey underneath the polo shirt.

It felt ethereal to Paige, sitting up in the bleachers and watching him bend at the waist, stretch out his legs and arms. She admired what a beautiful specimen he was even from where she sat. He had a long and lean body, rippling arm muscles, and well-developed shoulders.

The bleachers began filling more rapidly. A group of women who had entered the gymnasium together took the seats above, below, and beside Paige. They were chatterboxes, talking about anything from fashion to celebrity gossip.

Paige itched to find another seat, but most of them were taken. She sat with her knees pressed together and her purse lying at her feet, trying her best not to listen to the conversations of the women practically leaning across her lap or shouting to each other from the row below her to the row above her. She was relieved when the game started, because the women hushed their chatter, too busy pointing out their boyfriends or husbands and waving to them. They reminded Paige of teenagers with the way they hooted, hollered and giggled to each other, and yet they looked to be in their late twenties and early thirties.

Paige kept her focus glued to the gymnasium floor. She watched Ethan steal the basketball from the rival team and leap into the air, twisting his torso and shooting the ball into the basketball hoop. He was amazing on the court; he was on fire. He dominated the gym floor when he played. There were several comments that traveled up and down the rows of bleachers about him, inquiries as to his identity. "Who is he?"

"Who?"

"Jersey number thirty-two?"

"That's Ethan Carson. He teaches at the local high school."

"He's awesome. Does he teach physical education?"

"No, health, but he does coach the school's varsity basketball team."

"He's gorgeous."

"And single, can you believe it?"

"If I wasn't married…"

Paige caught wind of a few of the comments and smiled.

A buzzer shrilled, signaling that it was halftime, and the players scattered off of the gym floor, joining their loved ones in the bleachers or heading towards the water fountain mounted on one of the walls near the entrance to the gym. Ethan's hands slipped beneath his jersey, and he brought the bottom of the jersey up to wipe the sweat from his forehead. He glanced towards the bleachers in Paige's direction and grinned when he saw her.

Having someone in the audience cheering you on made the entire game feel different. He'd been aware of her presence the entire time he'd spent on the court. He'd wanted to impress her, wanted to make her proud that she was here in support of him. Still wiping his forehead with the bottom of his shirt, exposing his abs to all who had their eyes on him, he made his way over to Paige and asked one of the women sitting next to her to scoot over so he could sit. "Enjoying yourself?" he asked.

She brought a hand up and swiped a bead of sweat that he'd missed. "It's an awesome game. I love it. I'm glad you invited me."

"So am I." He smiled down at her, pulling his hands from beneath his shirt and raking them over his hair. "Where are we going after this?"

Her nose wrinkled. "A shower."

His brows shot up. "On the first date?"

It's not a date, it's not a date, it's not a date, she chanted to herself, arranging a forced smile on her face. "I meant for *you*. You reek."

He laughed and shook his head. "What a tease."

She rolled her eyes and nudged his shoulder with her own.

"I have to get back to the game. I just wanted to pop on by and say hi," he said, nudging her back and standing.

As soon as he was gone, the nearby chatterboxes whirled on her and exploded with questions. Was she here with Ethan? Was she Ethan's girlfriend? Did Ethan have a girlfriend? Were teachers good in bed?

They bombarded her with questions. More than half of them, she didn't answer. It was none of their business. Seeing that they wouldn't get any more answers out of her, they turned and started whispering amongst themselves. She *must* be his girlfriend; why else would she hold back information from them? Or maybe she was just his friend, but she wanted to be more than friends with him. She wouldn't tell them any information because she wanted him all to herself. That *had* to be it; look at the man, he was beautiful.

For the remainder of the game, Paige ignored the busybodies. She clapped when Ethan's team scored and she stood and cheered when his team won. She grabbed her purse and stepped down the rows of bleachers so she could meet Ethan at the sidelines.

"Not bad," she said, tilting her face up and slinging the strap of her purse over her shoulder. She could see why his family had been disappointed that he'd decided to teach instead of play professional basketball. He was a dynamo on the basketball court, a force to be reckoned with. She didn't speak those thoughts aloud because of the conversation they'd had in the car. It seemed that everyone in his life questioned his choice to become a teacher. She didn't want to be thrown into the same category as those people.

"I have to get to the showers and change," he told her. "I'll be out as fast as I can, all right?"

She nodded and watched him jog away, dismissing the graphic visuals she had of him lathering up in a locker room shower. The spectators began vacating the bleachers and exiting through the double doors of the gymnasium.

Ten minutes later the gymnasium was nearly empty.

She almost jumped out of her skin when a hand tapped her shoulder.

"I know you, right?"

Paige turned to face a woman with platinum blonde hair, pale, nearly colorless eyes, and a wide smile. "I…I'm not sure."

"Sure I do," the woman insisted, stepping back and looking Paige up and down from head to toe. "Last year sometime, I saw you in a bar. You were dancing and you dropped a glass of beer. My boyfriend at the time helped you, made sure you were all right."

It was the redhead who'd been on Ethan's arm that night. She'd opted for a new hair hue, and for some reason, was at an event she'd probably known Ethan would be performing in. "Yeah, I think I remember you," Paige said slowly. "You had red hair then?"

The blonde nodded, extended her hand. "Diane."

"Paige."

"I know. Everyone in town's buzzing about the actor you've brought into town with you," Diane informed in hushed tones. "Brandon Davies? What a lucky woman you are."

Want him? Paige wondered. *You can take him.* "He's…definitely a character."

Diane glanced around, absent-mindedly stroking her platinum hair. "Is he here with you?"

"Oh…no," Paige replied quickly, and tried to change her tone of voice. "I mean…he's hanging out with a friend of his."

"Oh, so he didn't play in today's game?" Diane queried. "Who did you come here to see?"

Before Paige could think up a lie to tell Diane, Ethan strode up behind Paige, saying, "I told you I wouldn't take that long." His stride slowed and eventually came to a complete halt when he realized with whom Paige had been speaking. "Diane."

"Ethan." Diane's jaw squared and she arched a nearly non-existent eyebrow inquisitively. "I was just asking Paige who she'd come to see."

The air was thick with tension and Ethan itched to get Paige out of the gymnasium. "It was good seeing you again, Diane," he said, giving Paige a *Let's get the hell out of here* look.

"It was good seeing you," Paige said as courteously as she could, then followed Ethan out of the gym.

"Not as good as it was to see you," Diane muttered, watching their departure with a smirk twisted on her lips.

"And she just walked out of the restaurant? Just like that?"

Shane leaned against the bar counter. "Just like that."

Brandon blew air between his lips and shook his head. "What a bitch, man."

Shane straightened and turned to look at Brandon. Anger flared in his eyes. "Don't talk about Marissa like that. That's your first and only warning."

"Sorry, man," Brandon said, nervously downing the rest of his beer. "I'm just saying. Women can't wait to get married, can't wait for the ball and chain, for the kids, the house, and the two dogs. They bait us into wanting to settle down, and when we finally bite the bait, they embarrass us and make us feel like shit, I mean…what is that about?"

"She just wasn't expecting for me to propose," Shane explained, still feeling unnerved at Brandon's outburst. He settled onto a stool and added, "*I* wasn't expecting for me to propose. I mean I was, because I had the ring and everything, but I didn't expect myself to go through with it. Before our date, I listed the reasons why I didn't want to get married. And then I saw her. She walked in and sat down…and I just knew then and there. She was the woman I wanted to spend the rest of my life with."

Brandon shrugged noncommittally. "I don't see myself ever getting married."

Looking surprised, Shane asked, "Not even to Paige?"

"Not even to Paige." Shane made a gesture to the bartender to refill his drink. "She's a great girl and all, she really is, and by God she makes me feel like no other woman has. I just can't see myself settling down and wanting to marry her. I can't see myself settling down and marrying anyone. There are too many women on the face of this earth, you know? How can I be expected to commit myself to one? On top of that, I'm an actor, so you can imagine how many women throw themselves in my direction."

Shane reminded himself that Paige asked him to keep Brandon busy for the day. He reminded himself that he was sitting in Harry's on account of the fact that he was doing a favor to Paige by occupying Brandon's time, but the truth of the matter was that Brandon Davies was a class-A, bona fide asshole. The more time he spent with him, the more he was certain that Brandon was the most self-absorbed, conceited bastard he'd ever known. Throughout the entire day he'd made offhand comments about women. He'd spent half an hour explaining woman's "role" in life, which, according to Brandon, was to cater to men. He wasn't ashamed of hitting on women in public, or ogling them.

Shane wondered if he'd ever been that much of a jackass. Had he ever been that chauvinistic, that blatantly out of control? He prayed to God he hadn't been. Brandon repulsed him. Paige was a good judge of character most of the time. She understood human behavior enough to have made herself a successful romance novelist. He couldn't see how she could have spent a year of her life with this egotistical moron. Spending a *day* with the idiot made him want to tear out his own hair. How did she tolerate him? *Why* did she tolerate him? It just didn't add up.

He sat next to Brandon on the bar stool, wondering if Paige was home yet. He didn't want to be in the man's presence for another minute, but for another hour he put up with Brandon's monologues about the demands of the acting business and the stress it would put on a marriage.

A blonde claimed the stool on the other side of Brandon and he turned his head, letting his gaze linger on her for a few moments. She returned his appraisal, smiling slightly.

Shane rolled his eyes and took a few gulps of his drink. He had to sit down and have a talk with Paige. Allowing her to invest more time and emotion into Brandon would be a crime on Shane's part for sure. He watched the looks exchanged between Brandon and the blonde and rolled his eyes again in annoyance.

"Aren't you Brandon Davies?" the blonde dared to ask.

Brandon's brows shot up. In a hick town like this, he hadn't expected to be recognized as much as he had been. Several times today, he'd been approached by women and asked if he was *the* Brandon Davies from the soap opera "Guiding Hope." Women had slipped him their phone numbers on the backs of napkins, had given him flirtatious glances, and had brushed up against him suggestively. It pleased him to be recognized and propositioned by beautiful women who wished to gain access to the world of the red carpet by sleeping with a daytime soap star. He looked down at the blonde seated beside him, noted that she wasn't dressed like most of the women in this town had been. Her clothes were highly fashionable and her hair was professionally styled. "I'm Brandon Davies," he confirmed, swirling the contents in his beer glass. "You are?"

"Diane Patterson," she replied, tilting her head to the side and grinning.

"Hi, Diane," he greeted.

"You here with anyone?"

He looked back at Shane, who seemed glad to dismiss himself from the bar counter. He turned back to the blonde. "Not anymore."

She smiled at him. "You seeing anyone?"

He rubbed the back of his neck, chuckling dryly. "I'm dating someone," he said. "We're not committed though. It's a pretty open relationship."

As the bartender set her second drink on the counter, she nodded her head in what seemed to be understanding. "I think I may know the girl you're dating. About five-nine, brunette with long hair? Goes by the name of Paige?"

Shit, he thought, and set his glass on the counter. "You know her?"

"Saw her today as a matter-of-fact," she went on, examining her nails and looking smug.

"Yeah? Where at?"

"The leisure center."

His brows furrowed. "What the hell is a leisure center?"

"It's where city leagues gather to compete in basketball, volleyball, soccer, you know...whatever." She shrugged her shoulders.

He laughed and shook his head. "What the hell would she be doing there?"

"She was there in support of my ex, Ethan," she replied, wheeling around on her stool and standing. She grasped the drink on the counter in her hand and lifted it to her lips. She let her tongue slide around the rim before grabbing the edge of the glass's rim between her lips.

"Ethan?" he repeated, licking his lips. He remembered the man he'd met on the beach, the man who'd driven Paige home the night she'd gotten drunk. "The teacher?"

"The teacher," she confirmed. "So you know him?"

A muscle in his jaw worked. "Yeah, I know him." He swallowed a lump that had formed in his throat. He wanted to punch something, to kick something, to *hurt* something. He looked at Diane and forgot about hurting something. He wanted to fuck something. The irked expression on his face relaxed and a devious look replaced it. "So what was your name again?"

Ethan pulled into the driveway of the Turner residence and turned off the car. He was silent for a few moments before turning to face Paige.

She was staring straight ahead, seemingly lost in her own thoughts.

"I had a great time tonight," he said.

"I had a great time too," she told him without meeting his gaze. "I'm glad that I got the chance to watch you play and dinner was amazing."

Whenever he looked at her, it took a significant amount of restraint not to reach out and touch her. He fought back that urge now as he said, "I'm hoping another year doesn't pass before we get the chance to spend time together again."

She offered him a sheepish smile. "I'm sorry about that."

"An apology isn't necessary. Just don't drop off the face of the earth again."

She nodded and opened the passenger side door of the car. She made as if to stand out of the car, but his arm shot out and he grabbed onto her left arm. She shot an alarmed glance in his direction.

His eyes locked onto hers. He didn't know what his next move was. He had wanted to grab her and kiss her, but he also didn't want to come on too strongly.

Her eyes lowered from his piercing stare to the hand that was squeezing her upper arm. She was trembling slightly. His gaze was heated and passionate. All she had to do was look into his eyes to know all of the things that he wanted to do to her. There was a part of her that was ecstatic about that, but there was also a part of her that panicked. She wanted nothing more than to leap on top of him and kiss him, but anything that they started would be based on a pile of lies that seemed to be growing larger by the day. As much as she wanted to kiss him and touch him and be with him, she held back. She had to. She was deceiving him and he didn't deserve to be hurt by her web of lies.

He could plainly see that there was a battle going on behind her eyes and he wished to hell that he knew what she was thinking. The mystery was killing him. He loosened the grip that he had on her arm and let his hand roam up to her shoulder and the crook of her neck.

Her breath caught in her throat and her brows furrowed together. Her mouth opened, as if she wanted to tell him something. Maybe she wanted to tell him to stop. Maybe she wanted to tell him to keep on going. Before she had the chance to utter either command, he leaned in and kissed her.

She tensed up immediately and pulled away from him. Her eyes were wide and her mouth worked, but no words came out.

He looked confused. "I'm...sorry if I was out of line."

She blinked at him. "I have to go," she said dazedly, pushing the door open and stepping out of the car.

He watched her as she moved away from the car. He hadn't wanted to frighten her away from him and he had probably done just that. He ran a tongue across his lips and could still taste her sweetness there.

Agitated, he started the car and pulled out of the driveway.

Paige wrapped her arms around her torso as she walked towards the porch, her brain swimming with thoughts about Ethan. Just as she'd always imagined, he was a wonderful kisser. As brief as it had been, the kiss they'd shared had been the sweetest, most sensual kiss she'd ever been given. In a perfect world, she would share many more kisses with him, but that wasn't likely since she'd wigged out after this one.

She hadn't meant to pull away from him, but she was afraid of how he made her feel. She couldn't allow herself to become involved with him, not under the circumstances. If she'd been thinking straight, she would have come out with the truth then and there. He may have gotten angry with her or he may have never wanted to talk to her again, but at least he would know and everything would be out in the open. Now, she was between a rock and a hard place.

As she neared the front porch of her parents' house, she noticed a hunched figure sitting on the stoop. It took a moment for her to realize that it was Samantha. "Are you all right?" she demanded, rushing over to the teenager.

Samantha raised her head. Tear tracks marked her cheeks and her face was flushed. "I didn't know where else to go," she whispered.

Paige gathered the teenager in her arms, not knowing what to think or say. "What's wrong? Are you okay? What happened?"

Samantha shook her head. "My mom," she whispered, her bottom lip trembling. She pulled back and tucked her hair behind her ears. She sniffled and swiped at her cheeks. "She's sick. She's in the hospital."

"Oh my God, is she all right?"

"She says it's probably just stress." Samantha continued wiping at her cheeks. "She's conscious and everything. The hospital just wants to keep her because she's been having stomach pains and chest pains."

"She'll be all right, Samantha," Paige assured, sitting beside her.

"Yeah, she'll be all right, *this* time," Samantha said bitterly. "But she works all the time. Who's to say it won't happen to again? And who's to say she'll make it through the next time? She can't keep working like this. She can't keep doing these business trips all the time. She has a family she has to take care of! She can't just keep dumping us off on Aunt Lori and on other neighbors. She's our *mother*."

Paige rubbed the girl's back soothingly. "You have to talk to her about this."

"I'm just a kid. She's not going to listen to me."

"You're *her* kid, and she'll listen to you. You can't just keep all of this bottled in, Sam," Paige said, leaning her head against Samantha's.

"Your parents are so nice," Samantha whispered. "Sometimes I used to wish that my mom was like yours. She was around all of the time, you know? I have more memories of her in my childhood than of my own mom." She stared down at her tennis shoes, still sniffling.

When Paige wrote a novel, a character's mood depended on her imagination. If she wanted a character to be ecstatically happy, all it took was a few keystrokes on her computer keyboard and the character was happy. If she wanted the character to be depressed, it just took another few keystrokes. She was in control of what each character was feeling. A few keystrokes on her computer keyboard wouldn't improve Samantha's mood, wouldn't stop her tears. She wished that she could do something to alleviate the teenager's pain. "My parents were awesome," Paige agreed slowly. "They did pay a lot of attention to me when I was growing up, but I mean, they had their flaws too. There's no such thing as a perfect parent and there never will be."

"Aunt Lori doesn't have any flaws," Samantha said, still staring at her tennis shoes. "She seems like a perfect mom."

"The grass is always greener on the other side, *trust* me," Paige said, laughing. "When I used to babysit you, do you remember what clothes I used to wear?"

"Dresses," Samantha said blandly.

"Dresses with big, ugly flowers on them," Paige elaborated, stretching her arms out. "Everyone at school laughed at me for those dresses. I had to wear them, though. My dad got laid off of work and we didn't have money coming in for awhile. So we did what we could, and I had to wear those big, huge dresses. Half of the time they weren't even mine, they were my mom's."

Samantha looked at Paige.

Paige looked out over the yard, her eyes misting over with memories. "I used to hate being me," she continued, her eyes looking vacant. "I used to want to be someone else. Whenever I rode around in the car with my parents, I'd be looking inside of everyone else's car, pointing out pretty girls who, I imagined, led better lives than I did. Or I would point them out in the store and think to myself that I'd rather be her because surely her life was easier than mine. Sometimes I wished that I'd rather be the most popular girl in school, because everyone loved her. Everyone thought she was beautiful. No one thought I was beautiful except my mom and dad, and that's not enough when you're a teenager." She paused, glanced down at Samantha, and laughed uneasily.

"I never knew that's how you felt," Samantha said. "Whenever I came over your house, you seemed to be happy."

"When I was at home, I *was* happy," Paige told her. "It was when I was in school and everywhere else that I felt like shit." She clasped a hand over her mouth and profusely apologized for cursing.

"It's all right," Samantha allowed. "I've heard the word 'shit' before."

"You shouldn't use it though," Paige lectured running a hand through her hair.

Samantha sighed and stared out into the night. "I guess it all boils down to the fact that it's not easy being a teenager," she reasoned, no longer sniffling. "You and I have opposite situations. You hated being at school but loved being home, and I love being at school, but I hate coming home to an empty house with a note on the fridge saying, 'Please cook dinner for Olivia, I'm going to be late.' While our situations are different, though, they're both equally difficult."

"I've seen the way you support your mom," Paige said wistfully, "and I admired you for it, because I knew you didn't like her being away so much."

"I know she's working to make sure we have a good education, food on the table, and a nice house to live in and everything," Samantha said, "but what Olivia and I really want is our mother, you know?"

Paige nodded. "Tell her that."

Samantha shook her head and laughed. "I will." She took a deep breath, wiping the remnants of tear trails on her cheeks. "Now I feel guilty for walking out of my mom's hospital room the way I did."

"You walked all the way home?" Paige demanded, looking surprised.

"Cab."

"I'll drive you back," Paige offered, looking relieved.

"Where the fuck have you been, Paige?"

Paige entered the hotel suite after having spent an hour with Samantha and her mother. She'd been dreading having to face Brandon. Upon entry, she noticed that the lights in the front hall and the living room had been turned off. His voice had come from the living room, and she walked towards it, squinting into the dark. "Bran, is that you?"

A light flicked on and he was in the far corner, sitting in a cream-colored armchair. He dropped his hands into his lap, looking up at her expectantly. He was dressed in a black short-sleeved, collared shirt and khakis. His dark blonde hair was pushed back from his forehead. The expression on his face was stony, an expression she had never seen on his face before. "I asked you where you've been," he repeated.

"I've been out," she responded, walking further into the room. "Why the hell are you sitting in a dark room waiting for me?"

"It's after midnight."

She rolled her eyes and set her purse on the coffee table before draping herself on the couch. "I didn't know I had a curfew."

"Where the fuck were you?"

"I was *out*," she repeated.

"Out where?" he persisted.

"Am I being interrogated?" she asked, bringing an arm across her eyes.

He cleared his throat. "Paige, don't make me ask you again."

"I was out with a friend, is that all right with you? I'm tired." She sat up and yawned as if to prove her fatigue. "I think I'm going to go to bed."

"Not yet, Paige."

"What do you need, Brandon?" she asked tiredly. "Do you want to fuck? *What?* I'm not in the mood right now. I'm going to bed." She stood from the couch and turned to leave the living room.

His voice boomed throughout the living room, ringing in her ears. "I said...not...*now!*"

She whirled around, looking shocked and confused. "What the hell's the matter with you?"

He stood and swaggered over to her, looking livid. His thumbs were hooked on the belt loops of his khakis and his lips were pursed. His eyes spit fire at her. "What friend were you *out* with?"

He couldn't possibly know that she'd been out with Ethan. She hadn't seen anyone she'd recognized at the leisure center *or* the restaurant he'd taken her to afterwards. Well, except for the brief altercation she'd had with Diane, Ethan's ex, and now that Paige thought about it, Diane *had* mentioned Brandon. But what were the chances that she'd cross Brandon's path and be resentful enough to tell him that she'd seen Paige and Ethan spending time together? What motive would she have to do something like that? Jealousy? Wanting Ethan back? An image of Ethan developed inside her mind. *Oh, shit,* she thought to herself, her mouth dropping open.

He nodded his head, seeing the look in her eyes. "Yeah. You were hanging out with the pretty boy teacher, weren't you?"

"We're friends, Bran. You have a problem with that?"

"I have a big problem with that," he said through clenched teeth. "And I have a *major* problem with the fact that you're only friends with him and you feel like you can't tell me that you're going to hang out with him. What the fuck's that about?"

"I thought you'd throw a temper tantrum the way you're doing now," she tossed at him. "I'm going to bed, Bran. This is ridiculous."

When she turned, he reached out and grabbed her arm roughly, yanking her against him. "You'll leave when I tell you it's all right to leave."

She glared at him and yanked her arm out of his grip. "I'll leave right *now,*" she said, her voice just as menacing as his had been, if not more so.

He followed her into the bedroom, his anger making his movements jerky. "So...what, you're fucking this guy?" he demanded loudly, watching her undress.

She didn't answer him. She wasn't going to dignify his interrogation with responses. She walked over to the closet to remove her suitcase. As she rummaged through her suitcase for her pajamas, he loomed over her.

"I asked you a question, Paige."

"You asked me a ridiculous question."

"Tell me, right now, looking straight into my eyes, that you're not fucking the teacher."

She located her pajama pants and tugged them up her legs. A few seconds later, she found her camisole and yanked it down over her torso. "I'm not fucking the teacher," she said, facing him finally. "Now can you turn off the lights? I'm tired."

"I don't believe you." He stood with his hands on his hips.

"For God's sake, Bran!" she shouted.

"Are you cheating on me, Paige?"

"I answered your fucking question, Bran, now turn off the fucking lights!" she yelled at him.

He brought the back of his hand across her cheek. "Are you cheating on me, Paige?"

Her hand shot up to touch her stinging cheek. Tears sprung to her eyes because of the pain his slap had caused.

"Are you cheating on me?" he asked her in the same quiet voice, attempting to keep his anger in check.

"You fucking slapped me, Bran," she said, her face expressionless. "It's over. Period." She walked around the bed and her gaze anchored to the floor.

He restlessly shifted from foot to foot. "What?" he asked finally.

She knelt to the floor and snatched up a pair of neon pink thong panties. "What the hell is this?"

The color left his face and ran for cover. "What do you mean? Those are yours."

"You don't think I know my own fucking panties?" She tossed them on the bed, shaking her head. "You fucking prick." After seizing her suitcase and purse, she stormed out of the bedroom. Before she could escape the hotel suite (and Brandon's clutches), he caught up to her and snaked his arms around her waist.

"You're not leaving," he said, his voice shaking. "I thought you were cheating on me with the teacher. She told me...you were out with him. She told me that she'd seen you and I remembered on the beach, seeing you two. You were talking to him. You guys looked like you were having a pretty serious conversation. And then him driving you home. I assumed you'd slept with him."

"Bran, let me go."

"I can't. I won't, Paige."

"You're hurting me. Let me go, *now*," she demanded, struggling to break his hold over her. "I'll scream if you don't fucking let me go," she warned.

He released her so suddenly that she nearly fell. The suitcase still in hand, her purse slung over her shoulder, she dragged the door open and slammed it hard behind her. Her cheek still stung from his slap. She walked down the hall, took the elevator to the first floor, stormed out into the night and towards her car, not quite knowing where she was going to go. Marissa and Shane were staying in a room in the same hotel, but she didn't want to wake them up. Her parents were asleep, no doubt, and if she'd come to them in the middle of the night, they'd assume something was wrong. There *was* something wrong, but she didn't want them worrying about it.

She scrolled down the phone numbers she'd stored into her cell phone once she was seated in her car and came across a number that she knew she shouldn't call, especially at this time of night. She found herself punching in the number anyway and saying, "Hi...I know it's kind of late. I was wondering...is it possible that I can come over right now? I know it's late and everything, but I-yeah? Are you sure? I don't want to intrude or anything. Yeah...okay, where are you located? I think I know where it is. I should be there in about ten minutes or so. If I get lost, I'll call you back. And hey...thanks."

Chapter Twelve

As soon as Ethan opened the front door of his house, she shot into his arms and buried her face into his chest. His eyes widened in surprise. He didn't know what to make of the abrupt gesture. Not that he was complaining about it. Having a beautiful woman, especially *this* beautiful woman, jump into his arms in the middle of the night was nothing but a blessing. Still…he didn't know exactly what the hell was going on. He hurried her into the house and pressed the front door closed behind his back.

After she'd called, he'd tugged on a t-shirt and a pair of pajama pants. He'd tried to make himself look presentable, but he was sure that he looked just as he felt: tired as hell. He looked her over and saw that one of her cheeks was flushed red. It wasn't a redness that was going away. It looked to be a developing bruise. His throat constricted as she brought a hand up to her cheek and turned away from his probing gaze.

No words were spoken right away. She stood, avoiding his gaze and casually glancing around the living room of his one-story house, and he stood a few feet away from her, observing her. There was so much that he wanted to say. He wanted to comfort her, to make her feel better. He wanted to ask her who had done this to her even though he knew who'd done this to her, even though he wanted to pound that certain actor's face in. He wanted to tell her that he was glad she'd known she could call him up and come to him.

She turned around in a small circle, looking around the room in all of its bachelordom. Her eyes finally landed and settled on him. A wry smile parted her lips while her eyes threatened to rain tears. She opened her mouth to say something, to explain why she'd awakened him in the middle of the night, to explain why she'd had to come over so late in the night. She felt a certain sense of déjà vu, because after all, hadn't it been ten years ago when he'd rescued her and pulled her out of a dark hole?

Her sad eyes were the very undoing of him. He stepped forward and took her into his arms. He held her for several moments. He rested his chin on top of her head and closed his eyes. Earlier, when she'd pulled away from his kiss, he worried that he wouldn't get the chance to feel her again. Most likely, she'd rejected him because she wanted them to be friends and nothing more. If that was what she wanted, he could work with that. He would respect her wishes. So even though he wanted to feel her body along the length of his and give her the deepest kiss she'd ever felt in her life, he settled for smoothing down her hair and embracing her.

She pulled back and looked up at him, tears starting at the corners of her eyes. She turned away from him suddenly, wrapping her arms around herself in a vain attempt to keep herself together.

"Are you all right?" he asked her finally, hating to see her in so much agony.

"Are you all right...you have your entire life ahead of you...you're going to leave this school and become something awesome...you wouldn't be as special as you are..." The words he'd spoken to her ten years ago echoed in her ears now. She would have given her right arm to be able to go to bed with him now and let him hold her throughout the night, smoothing her hair back from her face and whispering to her that everything would be all right. It was what she wanted now more than anything in the world. Because of the lies she'd told him, she couldn't let him get too close to her.

I should just tell him now, she thought, closing her eyes and bringing her knuckles up to clenched teeth. The words were on the tip of her tongue. But when she looked at him and saw the cloaked desire in his eyes, she couldn't breathe life into the words that she wanted to say. All she could do was take a step forward and close the distance between them. She lifted a hand to his jaw and she caressed it, loving the feel of his skin beneath her hand. This was the man she'd dreamt about for more than a decade. This was the man that she'd loved for more than ten years, and he was standing in front of her wanting nothing more than the chance to be with her.

The emotion burning within the depths of his eyes shook her. Her own emotions were swimming to the surface and she fought to maintain control of them.

His arm snaked around her waist and he pulled her against him, creating a ripple in her resolve. "I like it when you touch me," he said, his deep voice rumbling over the tips of her ears. He lowered his head and pressed a kiss to her nose, before tilting her chin up with his free hand and claiming her lips.

She whimpered against his mouth. She didn't know what she was doing, but whatever it was, it didn't feel right. She couldn't do this. She couldn't let him kiss and touch her when he didn't even know who she was.

She couldn't...and yet she wasn't pushing him away this time. It felt too good being in his embrace. It felt too good letting him hold her. The contents of her mind probably looked like the contents of a washing machine, tumbling and tumbling until everything was jumbled together. Her mind was slowly turning to mush as he pulled back and stared down at her, as he took her hand into his and led her into the bedroom.

Without releasing her hand, he closed the door behind them and neglected to turn on any lights. "Lie down," he instructed.

She snapped her head back to look at him, shocked at his audacity.

He chuckled in the darkness, and she could hear him draw his t-shirt up over his head, saw his silhouette sling that t-shirt across the room. "Do it."

She shook her head, staying near the door. "I can't."

"Trust me, all right?" In the darkness, he moved towards the bed, but he didn't sink down onto it. He remained standing and gestured towards the bed.

She moved forward, wiping her tears away, her breathing still short and ragged. She sat on the bed at first, then stretched out on it hesitantly, feeling foolish.

"On your stomach," he commanded softly.

She rolled onto her stomach and rested her chin on her hands. She felt him sink beside her on the bed and closed her eyes. *What am I doing?* she asked herself. Maybe she should have gone to her parents' house instead. Coming to Ethan's house at this hour of the night hadn't been appropriate.

Her thoughts melted away as his hands settled on her lower back and stroked their way up to her shoulders. He proceeded to massage her shoulders in small circles that grew broader, larger. He paused, reached behind him, and grabbed a pillow from the head of the bed. "Lift your head," he whispered hoarsely to her, and slipped the pillow beneath her chin.

He was the first man to give her a massage. She'd been to spas and had paid hundreds of dollars a pop for massages, but no one had offered to give her a massage just because she looked tense. She'd given Brandon massages after a tough day of shooting or filming, but he'd never returned the favor.

Why was she even thinking of Brandon now anyway? He was a dickhead. He beat up on women who displeased him and he cheated on them. He was a bastard. She hated him.

Beneath his fingers, Ethan felt her shoulders grow more and more tense. "Stop thinking about whatever you're thinking about," he ordered.

"I can't."

"Sit up."

She rolled over and sat up, not objecting when he grabbed the bottom of her t-shirt and snatched it over her head. He threw it over his shoulder.

"Lie back down."

She turned and stretched out on her stomach, resting her cheek against the coolness of the pillow. His hands worked her shoulders, moved down to her back, and unsnapped the hooks on her bra. She closed her eyes and tried to push away the erotic images that came to mind.

"I should kill him."

Her eyes shot open and she twisted her head around to look at him.

"Lie down and don't move," he said gruffly, still kneading her back with his hands.

She lowered her head again, this time with furrowed brows.

"He did that to you, right? Slapped you? In your *face?*"

She didn't answer, didn't move. The tears started in her eyes again, small droplets wetting the pillow. She sniffled and turned her head the other way, facing a window with dark curtains over it.

"I can't believe he did that to you. He deserves a royal ass-kicking. I should have given it to him the night in the bar. I should have-"

"He thought I was cheating on him with you," she said softly.

His hands hesitated, hovering over her back. "What?"

"I don't want to talk about it right now."

"But you will."

She turned to look at him. "Diane."

"What *about* Diane?"

She shook her head and closed her eyes.

"What about Diane, Paige?"

"She told him…she told him that she saw you and I together, that we were spending the day together," she said finally, bringing a closed fist to her mouth.

"Shit." He opened his mouth to say something else, but closed it again. "Holy shit." He rose from the bed and paced the length of the room with his hands on his hips. He'd been partially at fault for harm coming to Paige. His role had been indirect at best, but the fact that he'd played any part in her getting slapped on the cheek sent guilt riding up his spine.

She stayed on the bed, sitting Indian-style with her hands in her lap. "And… after she told him that, apparently, she slept with him."

"She what?"

"Her panties were on the floor next to the bed."

"He cheated on you and then he slapped you?"

She shrugged and drew her knees up to her bare chest.

"You should go to the police."

"He would just make my life a living hell," she muttered, wrapping her arms around her knees.

"You're going to let him off the hook, just like that?" he demanded. "Are you serious?"

The media would have a field day with a story like that. Brandon Davies-famed soap actor-strikes girlfriend, romance novelist Paige Turner, in the face. She could picture it now. The tabloids would run amuck with the story, drawing up assumptions as to why Brandon would be angry enough to strike Paige in the face. No, she couldn't let that happen. The paparazzi would be camping outside of her house, outside of her parents' house. Everyone Paige knew, their lives would be turned upside down. *Her* life would be turned upside down.

"He thought I was cheating on him," she repeated, her hands fidgeting with each other.

"Christ." He ran a hand through his hair and stood with his back to the window, looking down at her. "Christ," he said again, shaking his head.

"He hasn't done it until now."

"Listen to yourself. Okay? Just listen to yourself." He grunted and pinched the bridge of his nose. "If you're not going to report him to the police, then he definitely deserves an ass-kicking."

"You're a teacher."

"So the hell what?"

Even though they were having this conversation in a dark, poorly-lit room, she snapped her bra around her torso and slid the straps up her arms until they came to rest atop her shoulders.

"You've got to be tired," he said, sounding tired himself.

"Do you have a guest room?"

"What do you need a guest room for?" he asked, walking over to the bed and sitting on the edge of it.

She shrank away from him. "I think it would be…more appropriate."

"I don't have a guest room."

"I snore in my sleep."

"I don't have a guest room."

"I hog all of the covers."

He laughed. "I'm telling you, I don't have a guest room."

She bit her lower lip and glanced over her shoulder at the door to the bedroom. "I'm a bed-wetter."

He laughed harder. "If you want that much not to sleep in the same bed with me then I can take the couch."

"It's not that I don't want-"

"I'll take the couch." He was already standing.

"I don't mind taking the couch," she started.

"You're a guest here. I'll take the couch. And I'll see you in the morning."

She watched him walk towards the door, open it, and disappear through the doorway. The tears started again, not because of Brandon and what she'd gone through with him earlier tonight, but because she wanted nothing more than Ethan lying in bed beside her and knew that she couldn't have that…she couldn't have that and be guilt-free.

She was pulled into unconsciousness and awoke to the sounds of pots and pans clanging. Reminiscent of Olivia's pan-clanging rendition of "Baby One More Time," she shot upwards into a sitting position, glancing around a room that she didn't recognize. The relief that it probably wasn't Olivia's clanging she was hearing made way for panic that she couldn't remember the previous night's events and didn't know where she was.

She rose from the bed, tiptoeing around the room and noting the many trophies set up around the room. Shiny trophies were on top of the bureau, the dresser, and the entertainment center. The taller ones had been set on the floor around the room. The past night's events came to her in a rush: Brandon smacking her, running out on him and into the arms of Ethan...Ethan.

She turned to face the door just as Ethan opened it. "You *are* psychic."

She smiled and brought a hand up to her hair. She must look like a frightening mess. She looked down and saw that she was wearing nothing but a bra and pajama pants. Wrapping her arms around herself, she turned and located her t-shirt near the window. "I forgot where I was."

"I don't think you had a good look at the room last night, since it was dark and everything."

She nodded solemnly.

"I'm making breakfast. I was just wondering how you like your coffee."

"No coffee."

"Orange juice?"

She nodded.

"A cell phone was ringing earlier. I think it came from your purse. It's in the living room." He closed the door softly.

She brought her t-shirt down over her head, her mind racing. What was she doing in this man's house? Why had she come here? She stepped out of the bedroom and padded into the living room in bare feet. Her purse had been carelessly tossed on the floor the previous night. She plopped onto the couch, withdrawing her cell phone from her purse, and looked at the phone's display. Marissa's cell phone number flashed across the display screen.

Marissa had called at nine-thirty in the morning, about a half an hour ago. Paige took a deep breath and punched in Marissa's number. Leaving her purse on the couch, she stood and walked back into the bedroom for a measured amount of privacy.

Marissa answered the phone on the second ring. "Paige?"

"You called?" Paige croaked into the phone, her voice laced with sleep.

"Where are you?" Marissa demanded. "I went to your hotel room and Brandon was drunk off his *ass*. He kept mumbling that he was sorry, he was sorry. I kept asking him where you were and he said he didn't know. What happened?"

"It's a long story," Paige muttered, sinking onto the bed and wanting to cry all over again. Her friends had told her that Brandon wasn't good enough for her. They'd asked her why she was with Brandon. Even Ethan had asked her why she was with Brandon.

"I have nothing but time."

Paige dove into the story, not leaving out one gritty detail. She told Marissa how every summer Ethan played in a city basketball league and how she'd accompanied him to one of his games. She told Marissa how they'd bumped into Diane, Ethan's ex... "The one with the big, red hair, you remember her from last year, right? The bar? Well, she apparently told Brandon that she'd seen Ethan and me together, and when I got to the hotel room, he was sitting in a dark room waiting up for me. We exchanged words, he slapped me-"

"Whoa, whoa, whoa, what?"

"He hit me." Paige brought a hand up to her face, closing her eyes as she remembered the sensation of his hand coming into contact with her cheek. "So I ...came to Ethan's house."

"You did what?"

"I'm still here."

"Do you need me to kick Brandon's ass?" Marissa asked. "I can do it, you know. He's shorter than me, isn't he?"

Paige laughed and shook her head, tears slipping from the corners of her eyes. "No...don't. It would cause a scene and I can't afford to do that. Not while..."

"I know what you mean, you don't even have to say it," Marissa said. "You need to tell the teacher the truth, Paige, you know that, right?"

Paige didn't say anything.

"Is he good in bed?"

Laughing again, Paige said, "It wasn't like that."

"You're going to tell me nothing happened?" Marissa demanded. "Come on."

"Almost, but no…I stopped it."

"Paige…I've seen the man. If you stopped him from turning you out, you're *crazy*."

Paige started speaking, but Marissa interrupted her.

"I know, I know why you can't let him turn you out," her friend said, "and it's a shame because I bet he's a tiger in bed."

The door opened and Ethan entered, carrying a tray. When he saw Paige, he smiled and set the tray on the dresser.

"I…have to go, Marissa," Paige said, her eyes locking with Ethan's. "I'll talk to you later." She clicked the cell phone off and set it beside her on the bed.

"Scrambled eggs, bacon, toast…tell me if I left anything out." He gestured to the tray.

She shook her head. "You cook, too?"

"I attempt."

"Ah." She brushed her hair back and made as if to stand.

He stopped her. "Don't." He lifted the tray back into his hands and gestured for her to scoot over. He placed the glass of orange juice on the nightstand and set the tray across her lap. After gazing at her for a few moments, he leaned down, grabbed her cell phone, and set it on the nightstand beside the glass of juice.

She poked around the contents of her plate with the fork. "You're too nice, you know that?"

"Only to people I care about."

The words touched her and she forced herself not to meet his eyes; instead, she focused on the plate of food. "No, to everyone," she said quietly, shoving eggs into her mouth.

He shrugged and turned on the television, surfing through a few channels. "A friend of mine tells me that."

"What?"

"That I'm too nice, that I have CKS."

She frowned. "CKS?"

"Clark Kent Syndrome."

She tilted her head back and laughed. "What's that?"

"He defines it as having to save everyone, always being heroic and never being selfish," he explained, settling on the Lifetime movie channel.

"I'm not big into sentimental movies," she said from the bed. "You don't have the Spice channel or the Playboy channel?"

His smile broadened as he rose from the bed. "This is going to have to suffice."

"Are you going to stay and watch this with me?" she asked him just as he was heading towards the door.

He gave her a long look. "Do you want me to?"

"I...don't want to be alone right now." She stared down at her plate. "I might get mad, start throwing things, and that wouldn't be cool since this is your house and these are your belongings."

He laughed and joined her on the bed, sitting on the edge of it.

"You can scoot over. I won't bite."

He arched a brow at her. "Not even if I want you to?"

She forced a piece of bacon down her throat and reached over to the nightstand for her glass of orange juice.

"I didn't mean to make you choke."

She took a swig of the orange juice and shook her head. "I'm not used to sexual innuendo so early in the morning."

"Sorry." He noted that her mood had definitely improved since the previous night. She was back to her usual, witty self. "Can I have some of your scrambled eggs?"

She gave him a look. "No you can't."

"I *made* you those eggs."

"And you made them for *me*," she clarified, slipping some of the scrambled eggs onto her fork and sliding the fork into her mouth, unabashedly relishing them. "And you made them well, thank you."

He rolled his eyes. "You definitely don't have CKS."

She laughed and shook her head. "Do you really want some?"

"No, I'm just playing with you." He glanced at his watch. "I have some errands that I have to run. I'm not kicking you out or anything. You can stay as long as you want. I just have to leave for a few hours."

"Fine. Leave me alone in my depressed, saddened state," she said in mock-petulance.

He stroked her cheek and stood on his feet. "If I come across Brian-"

"Brandon."

"*Whatever* his name is-I'll punch his lights out for you." He walked over to his closet and slid it open, browsing through his large supply of shirts.

"Don't go getting arrested for assault on my account," she chided.

The cell phone on the nightstand rang and Ethan looked over his shoulder. "You're in high demand, huh?"

"What can I say?" She brought the cell phone up to her ear. "Hello?" she directed to whoever was on the other line.

It was Shane. "Where the hell are you?"

"Are you and Marissa not talking?" she asked him. "I just told her, not twenty minutes ago."

"I haven't seen her. She's already gone."

"Jesus, Shane. Have you talked to her yet?"

"No, but forget that. Where are you now?"

"I'm...at the house of a friend." Her gaze snapped up to Ethan's back.

"Well we need to talk," Shane insisted. "Are you coming back to the hotel anytime soon?"

"I'm not planning on it."

"Paige what the fuck is going on?"

"I don't want to talk about it right now, Shane."

"Well you're going to talk about *something* right now," Shane said. "I spent all of yesterday with your little boyfriend, and I'm telling you, you need to get rid of him."

She smiled and forked a bite of egg into her mouth. "I do?"

"You really do. He's an asshole, Paige, and I don't know how you haven't seen it all this time. He was flirting with other women-"

"Fine, then I'll leave Brandon," she said. "He and I are over, kaput."

"He badmouths women and there was this one woman I swear he traded phone numbers with, and at one point he actually called Marissa a bitch, and...What? Are you serious?"

"Last night, Brandon and I had a talk." She didn't want to tell Shane that Brandon had hit her. He'd no doubt flip out and go looking for Brandon. It wouldn't be pretty. "He and I are over. We're through."

Shane laughed heartily. "Awesome. Great, that gets that out of the way. Then the next thing I have to get out there in the open is we need to get this book tour going, Paige. I've got the advance copy. Joan didn't even want to *touch* it. She thought it was that good."

Joan Ryan was Paige's editor. Paige sat up straighter in bed. "Joan didn't want to touch it?"

"She thought it was that great. Isn't that great?"

She hesitated, her brows furrowed in concentration. "Joan's a shark when it comes to editing. She didn't change one thing?"

"She didn't change a *thing*. I've looked over the advance copy and as far as I could see, no changes."

Something wasn't right. It was a feeling that started at the bottom of her spine and crept up to her shoulders. Joan was always finding mistakes and inaccuracies. The piece she'd let Shane turn in for her, Joan would have found *plenty* of problems with. "Are you sure?"

"Yeah. Stop sounding so damned worried," Shane ordered. "I told you, I read it and I loved it. I learned some things I never knew, yanno? I'm itching to get this out on the shelves."

"Yeah...okay," she muttered, sliding the contents of her plate around with her fork. She said her good-byes to Shane, clicked the phone off, and sat staring at it, deeply perturbed.

Shane had liked the piece she'd written-he was damned near giddy about it. Joan hadn't found anything to correct within the piece. There was something wrong here, but she couldn't figure out for the life of her what it was. *What the hell is going on?* she wondered.

Chapter Thirteen

[*Dear Diary*],

The past two months have been absolute bliss. Ethan is amazing. After seeing Brandon for the asshole he truly was, I felt that I had nowhere to turn. Marissa, Evie, and Deana all would have just told me "I told you so." So I turned to Ethan. And he was there for me. He was there for me that night, the morning after, and the weeks that followed.

Spending time with Ethan has made me think about my career. He truly loves teaching, and he's an extraordinary teacher. Writing romance novels is becoming less of a passion and more of a chore for me. I wouldn't put myself in the same league as Danielle Steele or Nora Roberts. I don't feel like I'm a master of my craft.

Realizing this, I thought long and hard. I thought about what I want to do with my life, where I want to take my career. I came to a conclusion.

The first decision I made with Samantha's assistance. I mean, look at her situation. She wants her mother home more often, but feels that if she tells her mother that, her words would go unheard. There's got to be a plethora of teenagers out there that feel the same way, and if they don't feel that way, they've got other issues going on. Let's face it: It's difficult being a teenager, more difficult than they're given credit for.

As a teenager, I had Judy Blume books to read, and at the time, those books meant so much to me. They got me through some tough times. I want to be that person for somebody else, the way that Judy Blume was that person for me, the way that Ethan is that person for a school full of children today.

Which brings me to my second decision: Ethan.

On more than one occasion, he's hinted that he wants to be more than friends, but to be more than friends with him would be a mistake. You see, Diary, I kind of...fibbed. Fibbed and misled him, if you want to get technical.

When I first bumped into him, I couldn't be honest. I couldn't tell him, "My name is Paige Turner and I used to be a student of yours." Of course I couldn't do that. If I had, all hopes of ending up underneath him, tangled in sheets would have to be thrown out of the window. Telling him that would definitely screw up any minute chance I had at ending up with him. Or so I thought.

Who knows...if I had told him the truth, we might have had past experiences we could have laughed at. Maybe he wouldn't always conjure up the image of me as a high school junior, all mousy and geeky. Maybe instead of being stuck in the past, he would have been geared for the future. Maybe he'd have been able to get past the fact that I was a former student of his. Who knows?

Now I never will know. And now I feel guilty just being friends with him. He's amazing with Samantha and Olivia, but whenever I have to remind the two of them that we're all supposed to be sisters, I feel pretty shitty. Beyond shitty, if that's even possible.

I don't want to lie anymore. I want to come clean and tell him the truth. Yet every time I look into his eyes, I don't see how I can do that. His trust in me would falter. He'd never want to talk to me again. He's the most understanding person in the world, and yet for some reason I don't think he'll understand why I did what I did, said what I said.

The book tour that kicks off tomorrow is going to give me time away from him, which will be good. I need a breather, a chance to come up for some air. I'll be so hard at work that I won't have to think about what a phony I am. I won't think about what Ethan will do when he does find out that I've been lying to him, because even though I'm a chronic procrastinator, I never delude myself. The truth always comes out in one way or another. I won't be able to lie to him for the rest of our lives.

I'm thankful for this tour. I can step away from the situation and think about it objectively. While I'm away, I can answer questions such as: When should I tell Ethan the truth? *How* will I tell Ethan the truth? What will I do if he says he never wants to see me again?

Oh, Diary…please help me. Give me strength.

Paige stopped typing and stared for a few moments at the laptop's monitor.

"Don't kill that thing," Ethan warned, striding into the living room shirtless, dressed in nothing but jogging pants. "I heard your typing all the way from the kitchen. What did that poor computer ever do to you?"

"I type fast," she threw over her shoulder, and went back to typing.

"You type *loud*," he added, disappearing back into the kitchen.

"While you're in there, could you make me a sandwich?" she shouted over her shoulder.

He poked his head into the room from around the corner of the kitchen entrance. "Do I look like my name is Jeeves?"

She bestowed a candy-sweet smile upon him over her shoulder. "Pleeeease?"

"You know how to make a sandwich."

"What happened to the good old days when you cooked for me?" she huffed, turning back to her laptop and typing away.

"Those good old days are over, and besides, you were distraught then."

She pouted at her laptop display. "I'm distraught now."

"Over what?"

"You refusing to make me a sandwich."

He rolled his eyes and turned into the kitchen. "Just for that, I'm definitely not making you anything." When he was finished with whatever he was doing, he turned off the kitchen light and re-entered the living room. He set a plate down on the coffee table next to Paige's laptop and walked over to the entertainment center. *"Running Scared* is coming on," he announced without looking back at her. He turned and rejoined her on the couch, frowning down at the coffee table. "What the hell?"

Her face was half-stuffed with a bite of sandwich. "What?" she asked, her voice muffled since her mouth was full.

"That was my sandwich."

"You set it right by my computer after I asked you for a sandwich!" she cried.

He snatched the other half up, rolling his eyes but looking amused. As the film's title sequence started, he dimmed the tall lamp beside the couch.

"I love Paul Walker," she murmured at some point during the movie.

"He's a good actor."

She snuggled up closer to him and rested her head on his chest. She felt the muscles in his chest tighten and closed her eyes, lulled to sleep by the rhythmic beating of his heart.

When he realized that she'd lost consciousness, he used the remote control to lower the volume of the television. He'd tried his damnedest to pay attention to the movie's plot, but with her head on his chest, all he'd wanted to do was gather her up, carry her to the bedroom, and have his way with her. Rubbing at his jaw, he lifted his eyes to the television screen. He tried to ignore the fact that whenever she shifted positions, she was scooting closer to him.

He'd survived two months of being her friend, of spending time with her platonically. He was aware of the fact that she shied away from answering direct questions about her past. On several occasions, he had asked her about her childhood and where she'd grown up. Her answers were vague at best. Out of the two months they'd been spending constant time together, the only solid facts he knew about her was that she was twenty-eight years old, she did freelance writing, she had two younger sisters, and when she wasn't visiting Beach Park, she lived in Farmington Heights, a suburb of Chicago. Maybe that was a slight exaggeration…he knew a lot more details than that, but he wanted to know a great deal more about her. For some reason she was withholding information from him. His guess was that there was a valid reason why she wasn't quick to give away personal information. Considering the last relationship she'd been in, he didn't find it unusual that she was guarded with information and with her emotions.

Brandon had been completely brainless in letting Paige slip away from him. How could he not be appreciative, thankful to God or whatever Creator was in existence, for the amazing woman that was right in front of his nose? She was the most remarkable woman Ethan had ever known, besides his mother. He'd known Paige was a woman to be reckoned with the day she'd nearly run him over with her Ford Explorer, the same day she'd dropped off her younger sister wearing a robe over pajamas with puppy dog slippers. She had the most eccentric personality he'd ever witnessed. She always kept him laughing and never failed to brighten up his day.

There had been times he'd come dangerously close to kissing her, times when she would find some opportunity to move away from him or turn her head and start talking about nothing in particular. Most of the time he was perfectly content with being just her friend, but there were also those days when he ached to touch her, when seeing her dressed only in a camisole and sweatpants drove him crazy. There were days when she wrinkled her nose as she was laughing, making him want to lean forward and kiss the tip of that cute, pert nose.

She shifted in his arms and tilted her head up to look at him through sleepy eyes. "Hi."

"Hi."

She lifted her head from his chest and dragged a hand through her hair, trying to suppress a yawn. Tomorrow morning, she'd be leaving Beach Park. She'd be leaving Ethan and once again, she'd be leaving her parents, Samantha, and Olivia. Her hiatus was officially over and she would be diving back into work. Her days would no longer be filled with playful pillow fights and wrestle matches or watching Ethan play basketball with the city's league.

She would hate leaving, but she would love getting back to work. She'd told Shane about the fact that she wanted to create a line of novels for adolescents. When she'd pitched the idea to him, he had loved it. He'd gone so far as to call her a genius. She had never seen him so enthusiastic about one of her ideas, and she couldn't help but admit that she was a bit enthusiastic herself. Talking to Ethan about his past, how he'd been as a teenager, looking back at her own experiences, and counseling Samantha, she was certain that creating a line of novels for teenagers was what she wanted to do. Had it not been for authors such as Judy Blume, Ann M. Martin, or Carolyn Keene, Paige didn't know where she would be. Because of those talented novelists, she'd been inspired to write novels of her own. She wanted to be that type of inspiration to someone else.

She told herself that getting back to work would be good for her, but now, as her eyes met Ethan's, something pulled at her heart.

"You have to get up early, don't you?" he asked her, getting on his feet and stretching. "You should probably go to bed."

She nodded, but she wasn't listening to what he was saying. She was remembering how it felt to be lying on his chest, remembering how it felt to have his hands massaging her shoulders and brushing her hair back. She would have to go without that feeling for the next several weeks.

He smiled and shook his head. "You can stay up if you want to, sandwich thief, but I'm going to bed."

She watched him walk around the couch and down the short hallway to his bedroom door. He turned his head and glanced at her for a few moments before opening the door and walking into the room. The door closed softly behind him.

The look he just gave me doesn't mean anything, she told herself, her hands clutching at each other. *Don't go doing something incredibly stupid. Please, don't.* Seemingly against her own will, she rose to her feet. Nervously biting her nails, she padded around the couch in bare feet, quietly walking down the hallway and stopping at Ethan's door. She quickly checked her hair and smoothed it down. Then, she proceeded to tug at the hem of her beige camisole and pull at the waistband of her pastel pajama bottoms. She was about to do something really stupid. She knew she was.

She reached out and touched the doorknob. She jerked her hand back as if she'd touched a stovetop burner. What was she doing? Did she really intend to walk into Ethan's bedroom and sleep with him? If she did, what would the next morning hold in store for them? She had to go on a book tour, a book tour he wasn't even aware about. There was a lot about her life that he didn't know, and it was her fault. Still, she didn't want to leave Beach Park without...*Without what?* she asked herself.

The door was pulled open and Ethan stood filling the doorway, dressed in a t-shirt and boxers. A surprised expression was on his face.

She started to speak, but he hushed her by bringing an index finger up to his lips. He grabbed one of her hands and pulled her into the darkness of the bedroom. He didn't bother closing the door behind them; he preferred to have the soft sliver of light shining in from the hallway so he could see the way she looked in her pajama pants and camisole. She started to speak again and he shook his head. "No," he said, his voice rough with tension and desire. "No words."

She stood in the middle of the bedroom, feeling self-conscious beneath his adoring gaze. He circled her as a lion would its prey, moistening his lips with a flick of his tongue and stopping when he was directly behind her.

"You're beautiful without even trying." He slipped one strap of her camisole down a creamy shoulder and caressed the curve of her shoulder appreciatively, letting his gaze drop down to the arc of her back. Her muscles grew taut under his fingers and she remained still, not daring to move. He gathered a handful of her cinnamon-colored hair in one hand and lifted it from the back of her neck so he could admire the nape. The back of his hand grazed the base of her neck, and something in him awakened.

Her head lolled to the side a bit and he let her hair fall so that it cascaded down her back. He delighted in tracing the lines of her body with his fingers. He was in no rush; he had all night with her, and he wanted to use it, because she would be leaving town the next morning. He didn't want her to leave town without knowing how he felt about her, how much he wanted her.

The light from the hallway spilled onto her left shoulder and made her hair shimmer. He pulled his hands away from her, stepped back from her. No, he didn't want any words. He didn't want her to say a thing, to give him some lame excuse why she didn't think he should be making love to her tonight. He wasn't going to let her wiggle out of it. He knew what he wanted: her. He also knew that she wanted him. For some reason she denied that fact to herself. If it were in his power, he wouldn't allow her to deny herself of that fact any longer.

She turned and gave him a long look over her shoulder, her lashes lowered and dark green eyes watchful of his every move. She chewed on her bottom lip anxiously as he walked up to her and took her chin in his right hand. His free hand slipped the other strap of her camisole down her shoulder, and his eyes drifted down to her shoulders momentarily before lifting to meet her eyes. Smoky embers lie within the depths of his eyes; the lack of light didn't hinder their shocking blueness. He tilted her head back and lowered his face to hers, claiming her bottom lip between his teeth. He proceeded to suck on her bottom lip, warranting a whimper from her.

She pulled her lip back and blinked at him for a few moments. Then, she stood on tiptoe and outlined his mouth with her tongue. She stepped back and smiled. "Mmm."

He grabbed one of her hands and walked backwards, leading them towards the bed. He sank onto it and sat with his knees parted so that she could stand between them.

As he snaked his arms around her waist and hugged her to him, her hands lowered to the top of his head, tangling her fingers in his mass of short curls. This was what she wanted. *He* was what she wanted. As much as she didn't want this to happen because of the complexities of the situation, she *did* want this to happen. His hands stroking her skin made her tingle to the point where she wondered how she could have lived without him for as long as she had. When his eyes were on her, looking intense and lusty, she didn't know what to do with herself. A look from him drove her crazy.

She wanted him to rip the clothes from her body and take her as quickly as possible, but he was taking his time with her. He was taking pleasure in every second of feeling the texture of her skin, of holding her in his arms, and of savoring the feel of her hands ruffle his hair. He sat with his forehead pressed to her stomach, his eyes closed, and his arms still wrapped around her. He sat that way for so long that she thought he must have fallen asleep, until he stirred and raised his face to look at her.

His eyes searched hers, tried to read them. He wanted to know what she was thinking but didn't want to ask her. He didn't want any words or any conversation. He just wanted touching…he just wanted to feel her. He just wanted her to feel him. With his fingertips pressing into her spine, he pulled her closer to him.

Her shins bumped against the side of the bed. She lifted one knee onto the bed beside him, raised the other knee and set it on the other side of him. She sat on her heels watching him shift slightly, her knees on either side of his hips.

He lie on his back and brought his hands up to her waist. He kneaded the skin at her waist with his fingers and lifted his hands higher to her arms, where the camisole straps drooped. He slid both straps down her slender arms and let the thin material bunch at her waist. She modestly brought hands up to cover her breasts. He lowered her hands back down with his eyes locked on hers. "Don't."

She nibbled at her bottom lip, breaking eye contact and looking at everything else in the room but him. He wrapped his arms around her back and pulled her down to him, then rolled the both of them over so that she was below him and he was above her. Grunting with satisfaction, he ducked his head down and firmly pressed his lips to hers. His kiss was gentle, his tongue sliding over her lips as if asking for an invitation. She granted him an invite and parted her lips.

He pulled his head back and was fascinated by the way her hair fanned out in a halo around her head. He loved having her in his bed, beneath him, loved the feel of her soft, full breasts. He stroked his thumbs over the tops of her nipples, watching her face to see her reaction. She caught her bottom lip between her teeth and closed her eyes, turning her head to the side.

He cleared his throat and touched a few tendrils of her hair, stroked the lines of her jaw, saying in a voice husky with need, "I'm going to make you feel like the most beautiful, most wanted woman in the world." He proceeded to do just that, framing her face in his large, strong hands and pressing fervent kisses to her lips, sliding his hands down to spoil the rest of her body.

He felt so good on top of her. Her skin tingled where he touched her. Her lips were plump from being kissed. She kept her eyes focused on him, on this beautiful specimen of a man braced above her. She watched him as he tugged her pajama pants and panties down her slender legs, watched him as he sat up and removed his shirt and tossed it over his shoulder. His boxers were the next to go.

Skin mingled with skin. Their bodies pressed together and just that was enough to take Paige's breath away. Her dream man was moving above her right now, was touching her in ways she'd never been touched, kissing her in places no other man had ever thought to kiss, and making her shiver in a way that was all new to her. She dared to think that she never knew what making love meant until this night. The moment he pushed himself inside of her, her perception of the world, of love, of perfection, all changed. He was perfection, he was love, and he was the world to her.

She arched her body up to his, met his hips thrust for thrust. His grunts and low groans were turning her on beyond belief. She didn't want this to end. She didn't want him to stop making love to her. She didn't want him to pull out of her, to roll over and turn his back to her.

After both of their worlds collapsed, he didn't roll over and turn his back to her. He stayed inside of her, looking down at her. He stroked her face and caressed her cheek with the palm of his hand. Then, he leaned down and kissed her mouth with an intensity that shook her. When he raised his head again and looked at her, she had a dreamy grin on her face.

Realizing she had a stupid grin on her face but not able to get rid of it, she attempted to cover her mouth with the sheets. He moved off of her and lie beside her on his back, breathing heavily. "Wow."

"Wow," she seconded, breathing just as heavy.

Several minutes passed with nothing but silence, until he rose up on one elbow and stared down at her. "What are you thinking about?"

"I'm thinking that I don't want to leave tomorrow morning," she told him honestly.

"I don't want you to leave either."

She was also thinking that she shouldn't have done this. She shouldn't have been standing in front of his bedroom door when he had opened it. She'd let herself get way too carried away with this, and now she was at a point of no return...

Not that she wanted to return to any way of life that didn't include Ethan in it. He was the most wonderful man she'd ever met in her entire life. He was caring, considerate, sensitive, athletic, hilarious and comedic, intense, and sexy as all get-out.

She rose up on her elbow and observed him as he was observing her. A fine sheen of sweat blanketed his skin and shimmered in the limited amount of light shining in from the hallway. His hair was damp with sweat. His eyes left her face to travel over her body, and in turn, she let her eyes roam over his. God, he was a beautiful man.

"What are you thinking?" she asked him.

His eyes flicked back up to hers. "I'm thinking I'm ready to go again."

Paige awoke in Ethan's embrace. It was an amazing feeling, to wake up in the arms of a wonderfully masculine man. She could feel the length of his body pressed against her back, could hear his slow breathing. She grabbed the hand that lie limply at her stomach and raised it to her lips, sucked an index finger into her mouth.

Behind her, he stirred and groaned. She released his hand and turned over in his arms so that she faced him. One of his eyes was cracked open. "Not a bad way to start the day," he said with his hand pressed at the small of her back. "Did you sleep well?"

"What little sleep I had was good," she replied, pressing a kiss to the bottom of his chin.

He angled his head so that he could peer at the clock on the nightstand. "It's only seven in the morning. You should go back to sleep."

"I can't. I'm leaving, remember?" She kissed his chin again and sat up, clutching the sheets to her breasts and rising from the bed.

He watched her go about the room collecting articles of clothing for a few moments, then closed both of his eyes.

She watched him sleep for several moments. She was conflicted. There was a part of her that was overjoyed, elated...she was now involved with a man who embodied what she felt was the perfect man. She was now involved with a man who made her happy and yet...there was a part of her that was glum and miserable. She was now involved with a man she'd lied to, who didn't have the full picture of who she was. She was involved with a man who she hadn't been completely honest with, and while she knew enough about him to love him, to *truly* love him, he didn't know enough about her to feel the same way.

She showered, dressed, and called Shane to tell him that she was ready to go to the airport. Then she returned to the bedroom for another glimpse of Ethan sleeping. She leaned against the doorjamb with her arms folded across her chest. The longer she kept the truth from him, the bigger the risk. *When I get back from the book tour,* she told herself, pushing herself from against the doorjamb, *I'm going to tell him everything. He deserves to know the truth.*

Chapter Fourteen

"All right, what we have here is a ten-city book tour. You're going to be bouncing from Orlando to Atlanta and from Atlanta to New York City. From there, you're on to Indianapolis, Chicago, San Antonio, Phoenix, Los Angeles, San Francisco, and you close out the tour with Seattle." Shane flipped between the pages in his leatherbound business planner, not the least bit disturbed by the several people who brushed against him in an attempt to squirm past him.

The airport was jam-packed with men and women dressed in expensive business suits, parents taking their children on vacations, and airport personnel. The atmosphere was hectic and noisy with the broadcasts of flights that were coming in and going out, the people who were late for their flights running throughout the airport halls, and the boisterous reunions of family and lovers alike. A couple stood at one of the gates frozen in a solid embrace as if they hadn't seen each other in ages, blocking a line of impatient people who'd just gotten off a flight that had flown in an hour late.

Paige hated airports. They were usually crowded and chaotic and she was a fan of neither crowds, nor chaos. For that matter, she didn't like flying. It bothered her to put her life into the hands of someone else. It also bothered her to be more than fifteen thousand feet off of the ground.

"Your flight's not goin' out for another hour and a half," Shane informed her as he escorted her to the designated gate with his hands jingling the change in the pockets of his dark slacks. He remained standing as she took a seat in one of the plastic chairs bolted to the floor. "You have everything together? You're sure you haven't forgotten anything?"

Just Ethan. "No, I should have everything," she responded, setting the carry-on bag she'd been holding at her feet. She'd dressed as casually as she possibly could have for the flight, in a short-sleeved, carrot-orange blouse, a pair of worn jeans, and sneakers.

"And you still haven't read the advance copy."

"I didn't really have the time."

"With how sensitive this piece was, I would have thought you'd make time to look over it and make sure everything appears as you want it to."

As far as Paige was concerned, the piece wasn't "sensitive" at all. It was mediocre, and after all, she'd known what she'd written. When she had proofed and edited it, she'd read it over and over again. She didn't need to read it another time just because the pages were bound together in book form. If both Shane and Joan approved of the book, then she approved of it. They were tough critics when it came to her work, so she trusted them completely.

He detached the palm pilot stationed at his hip. "Now, I won't be joining you in Florida or Georgia, but once you hit New York, I'm already going to be there. I'll also be seeing you in Chicago, Phoenix, and L.A. You think you can do all right without me?"

She rolled her eyes. "I'm a big girl. I can take care of myself. What could possibly go wrong in a few bookstores? I'll manage."

"Hey-Barnes & Noble isn't just a bookstore," he corrected in a serious voice. "It's a way of life."

"Mingle with a few fans, sign a few books, a few publicity photos, and it's onto the next store," she cited. "Nothing I can't handle."

Oh my God...I can't handle this.

Paige had been shocked to see how many people turned out for the first book signing in Orlando. At past book signing events, maybe twenty people had actually shown up because they knew she would be there. A few patrons who'd been wandering around the store aimlessly also decided to get an autographed copy of her novel. They'd stopped by her table, not necessarily because they were interested in reading her novel, but because she was a well-known author. She'd assumed it would be the same way this time, but she was blown away by the long line of people waiting for her to sign the inside cover of their books.

"I saw a description of the book on the Barnes & Noble website," a middle-aged woman with dark hair exclaimed. "I think it's awesome you've done this. I'm one of your biggest fans."

A short, stout woman with a hint of a moustache above her upper lip said, "I like the cover."

Paige closed the front cover and frowned in puzzlement. Shane had requested to change the cover and the title, and he had. What looked like an open diary was drawn on the front cover, and above the diary, the words: "*Open Book* by Paige Turner." Neither the cover art, nor the title, were appropriate for the piece she had submitted. She turned the book over in her hands and read the summary.

"*Open Book* chronicles the life of established romance novelist, Paige Turner. From her troubled past to the every day life she leads now, this is a success story narrating what is in the minds and hearts of a lot of adolescents and adults alike. Anyone can fulfill their dreams, no matter who they were in high school, and this is what is revealed in...*Open Book*."

The color drained from Paige's face as she turned the book over in her hands and flipped past the publishing house information page, the critical acclaim page, and the title page to the first page.

"*Dear Diary...In high school I didn't dress up in stylish clothes. My family didn't have the money to support...*"

A scream built up in her throat and she tossed the book on the table, her eyes wide.

The moustache-sporting woman cried, "Hey! Aren't you going to sign it?"

Paige snatched up the book, opened the front cover, and scribbled her signature across it with a shaking hand, on the brink of hyperventilating. Her breathing quickened and the pen she'd held in her hand clattered to the tabletop. Her heartbeat's pounding was similar to that of a jackhammer. Her eyes were unnaturally wide, beads of sweat popped along her hairline, and…it was hot in here. Had anyone turned up the heat about fifty degrees?

The people standing in line stood on tiptoe, whispering amongst themselves. What was wrong with Paige Turner? She looked as if she were about to faint. Was she all right? Why had she stopped signing books? Should someone dial up an ambulance? She wasn't looking well.

Paige closed her eyes and kept them closed for several minutes. This wasn't happening. There was no way in the world this was happening. She laughed suddenly. She was *dreaming*. Of course! That was the most plausible explanation. How come she hadn't thought of it before? If she pinched herself, she'd probably awaken and find herself on Ethan's couch, or in Ethan's bed, or in *her* bed with a box of Cherry Garcia ice cream on the nightstand.

With her eyes still closed, she reached over and grabbed a piece of skin on her arm between two fingers. She pinched herself once, peeked an eye open. Nope, there was still a long line of confused fans observing her every move. She closed her eyes again, and pinched her arm once more, as hard as she could. This time, she held the pinch for ten counts. When she opened her eyes, the environment hadn't changed. And the people were still there, growing restless.

The next person in line, a tall, slender, thirty-something blonde, stepped forward hesitantly, hugging the book in her hands to her chest. "Are you all right?"

"What?" asked the frazzled-looking author. A forced smile relaxed the features of her face and she held out a hand for the book. "I'm fine, I'm just…it's this heat, you know?"

The woman placed the book in Paige's hand. "Make it out to Eliza, please," she requested, wrinkles forming at the corners of her eyes when she grinned.

Paige nodded, her eyes roaming over the cover of the book. She flipped the book over to the back. The same summary she'd read moments before stared at her now. She turned the book over, flipped through a few pages.

Somehow, in some weird twist of fate, her diary had gotten published. But it wasn't...*possible.* It *wasn't.* How could this have happened? Paige replayed scenes in her head, conversations with Shane. Shane had retrieved the computer disk from her home office. She'd been in Beach Park. She'd told Shane which disk container to grab-God, that's what happened, wasn't it? He'd grabbed the wrong disk container.

She hurriedly scratched a signature across the inside of the front cover and waved the next fan forward, trying her best to appear calm and sane. She wasn't dreaming. This was real.

Okay, she thought to herself. *Stay calm and don't scream at the top of your lungs. Don't run around the store maniacally. Get through this book signing. Get through this, and then call Shane and let him* have *it.*

She somehow managed to survive through the rest of the entire affair. As soon it was over, she caught a cab and ordered the driver to take her to the hotel. She sat in the backseat, staring out of the window at the beautiful, towering palms. Even the picturesque scenery did nothing to improve her mood. Right now, her diary was gracing bookshelves all across America. People were going to buy it...and *read* it. People were going to be reading her *diary.*

Her diary held all of her innermost thoughts about everything and everyone: celebrities, her friends, the lovers she'd had...Brandon, Ethan...

Oh shit. Ethan. She breathed in sharply, her eyes wide.

The cell phone in her purse chirped, and she pulled it out with a trembling hand. *Oh shit, oh shit, oh shit.* "Hello?"

"I wanted to wait a bit longer to call. I didn't want to seem too eager."

Speak of the damned devil. "Ethan." She bit down on her bottom lip. "Hi."

"Hi. Where are you right now?"

"In a cab."

"Everything going well so far?"

She had to remind herself that he didn't know she was traveling around the nation on a book tour...not yet anyway. "Yeah, everything's fine," she answered. "How are you?"

"Missing you."

She winced and took a deep breath. "I'm missing you, too."

"We have some unfinished business to handle when you get back," he said, his voice lowering.

"I know."

"You sound like something's bothering you. Are you all right?"

"Yeah, I'm fine...just tired, that's all."

"I *did* keep you up all night, didn't I?"

Yes, he had. And he'd been wonderful. He had known exactly where to put his hands, his lips...He'd known exactly what he was doing. She cleared her throat. "You definitely did."

"I didn't want to interrupt anything. I just wanted to give you a quick hello."

"I'm really glad you did," she said sincerely.

"I'll call you again in a few days, maybe. Check up on you."

Don't do that. "Do that."

"'Bye, baby."

"'Bye, Ethan." She ended the call with the press of a button and sat tapping the cell phone's antennae against her bottom lip. When she thought about it, her situation wasn't as bad as she thought.

Oh, who the fuck was she kidding? Her situation was horrible.

She dialed Shane's cell phone number into her phone and lifted the phone to her ear.

Shane's greeting was, "Speak."

"Shane?"

"Paige! What's up, you're out already?"

"Shane, what the fuck is going on?" she demanded in a hushed whisper so that the cab driver couldn't hear every word of her conversation.

There was a long pause. Then, "What are you talkin' about?"

"Shane...this book. It's my diary."

"Yeah it is and it's *awesome*, Paige," he said. "It's a work of art. This angle you took...it's going to work for you, sit back and watch."

"I *can't* sit back and watch!" she cried, no longer caring what the cab driver heard. "This is my *diary*, Shane. My *diary*."

"Yeah...I got that." He laughed heartily. "You're acting like you didn't know-"

"I *didn't* know! What the hell, Shane? I told you which disk container to take from my desk-"

"Wait a minute, wait a minute, wait a minute," he interrupted. "What are you trying to say here?"

She took a deep breath. "What you submitted...isn't the piece that I meant for you to submit. It's not what I wanted published."

The cheeriness evaporated from his voice as he asked, "What?"

She covered her face with her free hand. "There were two disk containers on my desk. I told you to grab...I forget if it was right or left. But you must have grabbed the wrong one."

"You told me to grab the disk container on the right hand side of the monitor, I remember," he informed. "Are you sure you even told me the right side?"

"Yeah, I'm sure!" she exclaimed. "I pictured myself sitting at my desk-"

"Well I didn't walk around your desk. I stood at the front of your desk and grabbed the disk container on the right hand side of the monitor."

She pictured herself sitting at her desk again. "Then, shit, Shane, you grabbed the wrong fucking container! You grabbed what would have been on the left hand side if you'd been sitting behind the desk."

"Why would you assume I'd sit at your desk? All I had to do was grab a disk container!" he exclaimed, sounding just as frustrated as she felt.

"Oh my God," she moaned, closing her eyes and shaking her head. "Oh...my God."

"Okay, chill out and calm down. It's not the end of the world. What you submitted was great work."

"It's *not* work. It's a *diary. My* diary."

"I know, I know."

She was still shaking her head. "I should have followed your advice," she said, almost speaking to herself. "I should have looked it over. Who the hell doesn't look it over?"

"It's in the past. There's no point in worrying about it now."

"It's in the past, but it's about to fuck up my future," she muttered. "This...this is not good."

"All right...all right...okay, let's look at our options."

"They're printed up already, Shane."

"We could pull them off of the shelves if that's what you want."

The cab parked in front of the hotel and she dug into her purse for her wallet. She handed the Hispanic driver several bills, not even caring to count how much money she'd given him. She thrust the car door open and stepped out of the cab, slinging her purse strap over her shoulder and still holding the cell phone to her ear. "We can do that?"

"We can do that."

"Then let's do that."

"Only..."

She groaned as she strode down the sidewalk towards the hotel's revolving doors. "Only what?"

"Paige...I read it. Joan read it. We both agreed that it's a masterpiece."

"Shane, I don't *care*," she stressed, entering the hotel lobby and heading straight for the elevators.

"You *should* care, Paige. I can guarantee that the piece you meant to submit wasn't as half as great as this is. I mean...what made you write it in the first place?"

She sighed and ran a hand through her hair. "I don't know...I kind of wanted to write an autobiography to help the teenagers who might be going through similar situations that I had going on in high school. I wanted them to know that they weren't alone."

"That is exactly why I think you should keep that book on the shelves."

"I didn't edit anything out, though, Shane," she cried. "I wasn't going to include all of the details to my sex life, all of my thoughts, all of my...everything! I can't...I *can't* let that stay on the shelves. And...Ethan."

"The teacher? What about him?"

"We kind of..." she halted, not knowing exactly what words she should use.

Shane whooped with laughter. "You boinked the teacher? You hooked up with him?"

"We're involved now."

"You've got to tell him the truth, regardless of whether or not you're going to keep this book in the stores."

"I know that, but..."

"But what, Paige?"

"Nothing."

He was quiet for a few moments. "All right, all right, this is what we do. We wait."

She took the elevator up to the fourteenth floor and walked through the doors once they slid open. "We wait?" she repeated.

"To see what happens."

"You should have seen how many people were at this book signing," she said. "It was...a mob scene."

"Really?" he asked, the tone of his voice changing. He was no longer Shane, her friend. He was now Shane Luciani, successful literary agent.

"Don't even think about it, Shane."

"No, no, no, Paige." He took a second to think. "This is your first stop. You're still in Orlando, right? Of course you are. This is your first stop, your first store and it was already chaos? Do you know what that means?"

"I don't *want* to know what it means," she said stubbornly, sliding a hotel key card into the slot on her hotel room door. "I can't have people reading about the intimate details of my life. It's an *Enquirer* reporter's wet dream."

He chuckled.

"How can you laugh at a time like this?" she demanded, unlocking the hotel room door and slamming it behind her. "I am completely and utterly screwed."

He brought his laughter to an abrupt halt. "You're freaked out and you have every right to be," he told her. "And I know that telling you to relax is easier to say than do, but you've got to try and calm down. I want to see how it sells."

"Shane-"

"Give me a week."

"Shane, I-"

"Ah, ah, ah…a week," he interrupted smoothly.

She pursed her lips, pacing the length of the hotel suite's living room. "A week."

"Continue the book tour. This may be a blessing in disguise."

"A blessing my ass," she haughtily said under her breath.

"I heard that."

She collapsed on the narrow ink black couch and stared up at the ceiling.

"Marissa always says you have the worst luck," her agent said thoughtfully. "She was right. You are the unluckiest person I've ever known."

"This…is not good," she mumbled. "This…really, really is not good."

"It's all going to work out. Give it a week."

"A week," she repeated. Lasting throughout the rest of the *day* was questionable. Lasting an entire week, knowing that her fans were flipping through pages of her innermost thoughts…it made her shudder. It made her light-headed. It made her nauseous. "A week," she said again.

"Everything's going to be all right, Paige. Fucking trust me, okay?"

One Week Later…

Two teenaged girls sat in a classroom, speaking in conspiratorial whispers. One of the girls had a short, jet-black pixie haircut while the other had shoulder-length, dirty-blonde hair.

"My mother bought it for me," the girl with the pixie haircut was saying, "and I wasn't even going to read it, because she does this type of thing all the time, you know? Gets me these self-help books because she thinks I'm this suicidal mess because of the one time she caught me trying to take a knife to my wrists.

"So I wasn't even going to read it, but I did…and you know, it's not even half bad? I mean…it doesn't seem fabricated." The girl gestured as she spoke, causing the cheap bracelets on her wrists to jingle. There were three holes punctured into each of her ears and both of her eyebrows were pierced. "I don't know…just, for once, my mom bought me something that makes sense."

The blonde nodded in agreement. "I read some of it…everyone has a copy. Everyone's talking about it. I've never seen anything like it."

"Me neither," the ebony-haired girl muttered. "This much hype over a *book*?"

Ethan strode up to Melanie and Alicia, looking stern. "I hope what you're talking about concerns the assignment you've been given."

"Sorry Mr. Carson," Melanie apologized, pushing back some of her dirty blonde hair.

"Talking during class time isn't tolerated, not unless the entire class is in on the discussion," their teacher informed them.

"Sorry Mr. Carson," Alicia, the puncture-riddled girl echoed. "We were just talking about the author everyone else is talking about. You know, the one who accidentally published her diary."

"The author who *accidentally* published her diary?" Ethan echoed, shaking his head. He turned and strode back to his desk. "I don't think it's possible to accidentally get something published."

"No, seriously," another student from the back of the classroom protested. "The story is all over the place. I can't believe you haven't heard about it yet."

He leaned his hip against the front of his desk and folded his arms across his chest. "Fine, tell me the story."

"Okay," the girl with the pixie cut said. "She usually writes these steamy sex novels, right?"

"That's enough," he interrupted, uncrossing his arms and straightening his posture.

"That's not even half of it, though," the girl insisted. "She usually writes *romance* novels, I mean. And she was going to turn in one to her publisher. I don't know how, but somehow she mixed her diary up with the novel she was going to turn in. She didn't find out her diary was published until a book signing she went to…"

"In Florida," the girl's blonde friend piped in.

"You kids need to recognize that for what it is: a publicity stunt," the tall, dark-haired teacher said firmly, his eyes sweeping over the classroom. "At some point in time, she would have had to look over the final copy and even before then, chances are she would have discovered a mistake as huge as that. I mean…if the diary helps anyone or comes to their aid, then more power to that author, but let's face it. Nowadays, less and less people are reading for recreation. I'm sure the literary world just feels they need to add a little spice to get the people interested. It happens all the time in the entertainment industry."

After class, Ethan sat at his desk grading fourth period's health quizzes from the day before. Lately, it took more and more effort to *not* think about Paige. Several times a day he wondered what she was doing, where she was. He was fully aware that she didn't indulge in sharing personal information with him. He attributed that to the fact that her previous romantic experience hadn't been romantic at all. He figured that she wasn't so quick to trust another man. He was trying his best to be patient with her, but it was difficult to do that when he was aching to know more about her. He wanted to know where she'd grown up, how her childhood had been, the different jobs she'd had...he wanted to be a part of her past, present, *and* future.

On several occasions, he'd come close to grilling her about her past. She was always so damned secretive about everything. She always answered questions in the most elusive way, always skillfully changed the subject when he got too close to learning anything about her. It was frustrating. He wanted to tell her so, but he also wanted to be considerate of her feelings. Damn, it was hard being a good guy.

It was also hard avoiding Diane. Lately she'd taken up to showing up all over the place, a lot of the time in places she wouldn't be caught dead in had she not known he would be there. She was leaving him voicemail messages, apologizing for not appreciating him when she had him and telling him that she wanted to try again. He never called her back. The last thing he needed was to get involved with Diane again. He wasn't even interested in keeping a platonic relationship with her. Her behavior was psychotic.

Not wishing to encourage any thoughts about Diane, he conjured up an image of Paige lying beside him, naked and sleepy-eyed. He saw potential in her. He saw beauty in her. All he had to do was get her to open up to him.

Chapter Fifteen

Everything would be all right, he said. Fucking trust him, he said. Paige was seated on a plane, keeping her gaze directed out of the plane window. Lately, it'd seemed that her story was everywhere she turned. It was on the news. It was in the newspapers. It was in the tabloids. People everywhere were talking about it.

She had always felt that one perk to her celebrity status was that she *had* no celebrity status. She was hardly ever recognized in public. She didn't *want* to be recognized in public. She'd seen how life was for Brandon. Often when she was out on a date with him, there would be some moron snapping pictures of them or fans coming up and asking for an autograph. He'd always had frightening stories of women stalking him to his hotel rooms, his dressing rooms, and once, his condo. It wasn't the type of lifestyle Paige had wanted for herself. She liked keeping her private life *private*. What her fans needed to know of her was what she wrote in her novels, and as far as she was concerned, that was all they needed to know. They didn't need to know what her favorite type of lingerie to wear was, what she ate for breakfast, or whom she was sleeping with.

Since her diary had been published and was now gaining more press coverage than many movie star hookups were, any chances of keeping her personal life personal were nonexistent. She'd been fortunate in the fact that most of the media coverage she'd gotten hadn't included a picture of her face. They'd only included pictures of a few of her book covers.

Marissa had called Paige in a panic after seeing the story on television. "Have you confessed everything to Ethan? You *haven't*? Why not? Paige, you can't let him find out from the television or any other source but you. Oh my God,

Paige. How do you get yourself into these situations? You have like...the worst luck ever, oh my God."

Deana had called shortly after. "Congrats on all of the publicity. I haven't seen coverage like this on...any novelist, really. Everyone's buying this book. My co-workers won't shut up about it already. So, did you mention anything about me in there?"

"Paige, what the hell!" Evelyn had cried. "I saw the news, what's going *on*? I don't talk to you for a month and everything goes haywire! They say you published it on accident. Is that even possible?"

Not according to the critics, it wasn't. It was obvious that a lot of critics thought the entire incident was a stunt devised to receive publicity. One critic dared to write, "I was convinced that this entire Paige Turner affair was a publicity stunt, a plan concocted to have books almost literally flying off of the shelves. Then, I read *Open Book*, the book said to be her true diary, and now I'm convinced otherwise. No one would put themselves through such humiliation and disgrace to sell a few books. I just have one question: How does one go about publishing a book on *accident*?"

Leave it to Shane to persuade me into allowing this to go on for a week, Paige thought to herself, leaning her head back against her seat. She hated flying, but the past hour had been the only hour in which her phone hadn't been ringing. Her phone was ringing off the hook nowadays. Everyone wanted an interview or a comment for their news broadcasts. Everyone wanted to hear from the author who somehow managed to accidentally publish her diary.

She glanced over at the person seated next to her, an overweight woman with her dark, wavy hair pulled back in a sloppy ponytail. The woman returned her glance, then her eyes narrowed.

Uh-oh, Paige thought, turning to look out of the window. But it was too late.

"Aren't you..." the woman began, then shook her head. "Never mind."

Thank God.

The woman squinted her eyes and peered closer. "Aren't you Paige Turner? *Haunting Love, Heart In A Handbag,* Paige Turner?"

Paige faced the woman and nodded. "Yeah."

"You're the one in the news now."

Paige cleared her throat, feeling incredibly uncomfortable. "Yeah."

"You're probably getting asked a lot of questions by everyone," the woman said, her face laced with sympathy, "so the last thing I want to do is bother you. I do want to say, though, that I've already read *Open Book.* Finished it the first night I got it."

Paige nodded her head, wishing she were anywhere but on this plane.

"I just want to say that…I think it's amazing, you know…that you wrote and published this," the woman went on. "My childhood wasn't much different than yours. Kids always picked on me because I was heavyset. I've always been overweight, all my life." The woman was quiet a few minutes. She stopped looking Paige in the eyes as she spoke.

"Having a book like this out on the shelves…I think it's great. I don't care that it was published by mistake. It helps, you know?" The woman dabbed at her eyes with meaty fists. "Knowing that you're not alone in feeling a certain way. It helps."

Paige was speechless. She'd been set on calling Shane as soon as she'd gotten off of the plane to tell him that she wanted the remaining books pulled off of the shelves. She wanted the news coverage to stop. She wanted the madness to stop. She didn't want reporters contacting Shane, asking for an interview. Who knows how far they were from finding out her hometown, where her parents lived? It would all snowball from there. She'd spent the previous night considering all of her options, and she'd come to a definite decision. She wanted the rest of the books gone.

Meeting this woman, who'd introduced herself as Janice, was making her reconsider, and she didn't want to do that. She didn't want to reconsider. She'd done a lot of thinking the night before, and she'd been set. She didn't want to change her mind, to go through avoiding the media, to wearing baseball caps pulled down over her eyes so there was absolutely no chance of being recognized. If she went to Shane for advice, she knew he'd tell her to give it one more week. He would tell her that all of the publicity would get old and everyone would forget her name. She knew it wasn't true, because there was one thing she had to admit. She'd never heard another author's name cited so much in the news, in the newspapers, magazines, and tabloids. Never.

Don't even go there, she told herself, subconsciously biting the corner of her bottom lip. *You're not going to think of this as positive publicity. This isn't what you wanted. You've never wanted your name in the news constantly and you never wanted to be recognized in public. All you wanted was to entertain people with your writing.* She groaned inwardly and rubbed at her temples.

Her mother would tell her that hair falls out from stressing over the little things. If that were the case, then by the end of the day, Paige's head would be as bald as a baby's ass. All she could *do* was stress over this predicament.

She had to admit to herself that she felt good about helping out readers and making them feel like they weren't alone. She could even go as far as saying that it was a *good* feeling, feeling good. Janice had brought her close to the point of tears with her testimony. The thought that there were readers clear across the country who felt the same way made Paige feel uneasy about even considering taking the books off of the shelves. Could she even pull them at this point?

Damn me for letting Shane wait a week, she thought once she was off of the plane, down the ramp, and through the airport gates. If she'd pulled the books the day of her Orlando book signing, she wouldn't be going through this inner turmoil right now. There would be no question as to whether or not it was moral, pulling books that seemed to be making people feel better about themselves in a vain effort to save her image.

While Paige was getting herself lost in O'Hare airport looking for the baggage claim, her cell phone rang. Upon looking at her cell phone's caller ID display, she was able to discern that it was Ethan who was calling. She held the phone to her chest for a few moments, glancing around the airport. She was actually trembling. She didn't know whether or not Ethan knew about what was going on now. Was he calling her so he could dump her, or was he calling because he'd been thinking about her all day and wanted to hear her voice?

She wasn't taking chances. She deliberately missed the call and continued on her search for her luggage. Once she found it, she tugged it towards the exit. Originally, the plan was to have Shane pick her up since he said that he had to talk with her anyway, but Marissa volunteered to give Paige a ride home. In Marissa's mind, Marissa usually came first. This was no different.

Paige loaded her luggage into the backseat of the tan Toyota Camry and dropped into the passenger side of the car. She dusted off her khaki pants as she did so.

Marissa was dressed casually, clad in flared jeans and a tight, pink top. Her hair was held back from her face by a jeweled hairclip. She looked at her friend and compassionately shook her head. "Poor chica," she said solemnly. "How many times have I told you that you have the worst luck in the world?"

"You tell me that all the time," Paige acknowledged, clicking in her seat belt, "but for once, I actually agree with you."

Marissa pulled the car away from the curb, shaking her head. "Your *diary*...I can't even imagine how it would feel to have the whole world reading it. It's an invasion of privacy."

"Intrusive," Paige added, nodding. "And I was going to have Shane pull the rest of the books off of the shelves."

Marissa's brow lifted. "You *were* going to have him pull it? You've...what? Changed your mind?"

Paige took her time answering the question. Instead of answering directly, she told Marissa about the lady she'd met on the plane. "She was like...*crying*, Marissa," she said, still unable to believe the experience she'd had with one of her readers. "And I was near tears. I've read fan mail telling me how my work is appreciated and how I've contributed to putting the spark back into a couple's relationship, but I don't think I've ever touched a fan as much as I touched this woman."

"'That's...deep."

"Very deep."

Marissa sighed. "So basically that's your long way of saying that you're going to keep the book on the shelves."

"I'd actually feel *guilty* taking the book off the shelves."

"You have to talk to the teacher, then," Marissa stated. "You don't want him figuring out from watching TV, do you? That would be devastating for him."

Just visualizing that scenario gave Paige chills. "I know I *should* talk to him, but I just don't know how to. I don't even know if I can face him at this point."

Marissa clucked her tongue. "You're going to have to face him, chickie."

"He might already know."

"Then you still have to explain yourself. Who wouldn't understand your position? You used to be his student for Christ's sake. Who would want to admit that to a romantic interest?"

Paige pursed her lips, not responding.

"You can't seriously be thinking about just not talking to him at all," Marissa said in disbelief. "And what if he *doesn't* know yet?"

"I don't even want to talk about this right now," Paige muttered, leaning her head against the window and closing her eyes.

Marissa blew a puff of air between her lips in exasperation. "That's too damned bad, because you're *going* to talk about it."

It was what Paige loved about Marissa, but also what she hated about her, the fact that she could be the detached voice of reason. Paige knew that she couldn't just stop talking to Ethan. She wasn't cold and heartless enough to do that. Then again, she wasn't bold enough to walk straight up to his door and blurt out all of the truths she'd deprived him of.

"Honey, if nothing else, soap operas teach us that there's no point in lying," Marissa prophesized as she pulled to a stop at a red light. "The truth always comes back to bite you in the ass."

Paige more than vaguely remembered a certain best friend *encouraging* her to lie to Ethan, but she didn't vocalize those thoughts. There was no point in bringing that up. In the end, Marissa encouraging her had nothing to do with her decision to mislead Ethan. She'd cooked up the lies on her own and proceeded to keep him in the dark about who she was. She purposely held back information from him. It was deceitful and despicable. She was to blame for everything that was happening now. It was what she deserved.

And now...now she had to muster up the gumption to approach a man and confess the truth to him. Some pretty *serious* truths...truths that would most likely create a gigantic rift between the two of them. "Shit," she whispered to herself, momentarily forgetting that Marissa was sitting beside her.

The scenery flying past Paige's face became more and more familiar as they neared her house. She imagined how it would feel to collapse on her bed and drown out the world. She didn't want to hear a radio or see anything on television. Chances were that her whole dreadful story would wind up coming on "Entertainment Tonight" or "Access Hollywood."

The phone was ringing when Marissa and Paige walked into the house. Paige answered the phone in the living room while Marissa sat on the couch and made herself comfortable.

"How are you holding up?" Evelyn asked, sounding worried.

"I'm holding up fine," Paige answered, punching the Speakerphone button. She returned the receiver to its cradle. "Shane gave me a week to make up my mind, and I have. I'm going to let the book sell."

There was hesitation on the other line. "You're going to let it sell?"

"Evie, my fans are relating to me. Shane says it's the biggest masterpiece I've ever made. I mean, I'm outnumbered here."

"I would never feel comfortable with everyone reading my diary," Evelyn said after another pause. "Well…I don't even *have* a diary, but you know what I mean. If I *did* have a diary, I wouldn't want people reading it."

Marissa extracted a nail file from her purse and surveyed her hands. "Deana, Evelyn and I have all already come to the agreement that, as your friends, we shouldn't be reading your diary," she announced.

"That's noble of you guys," Paige acknowledged, sitting in the loveseat and folding her arms across her chest.

Evelyn piped up from the phone's speaker. "We came to that agreement, but if you gave us specific permission, then we thought that it would be okay."

"It would feel weird knowing you guys have read my diary," Paige admitted.

"You're letting millions of strangers read it, but you can't let your own friends read it?" Marissa demanded, temporarily forgetting about her nails.

"Whenever we had an argument, whenever we declared ourselves *not* friends, I wrote about it," Paige said defensively. "Strangers don't know me, but you guys do. I'd have to face you guys after you read it. Some of the things I wrote about you guys were pretty harsh."

"All of the more reason for us to read it." The phone's speaker carried Evelyn's voice so that it was bouncing off of the walls and creating a slight echo.

Paige sighed, wanting to change the subject. "Could we talk about anything else?"

"Sorry," Evelyn was quick to say.

Marissa shrugged her apology.

Evelyn didn't have much time to talk; she was getting ready for a date. Paige was glad that she could bounce back from a pending divorce so quickly. Evelyn seemed to be much happier being single. She hadn't really experienced much of being single; she and Eric had been together since college.

"I'm okay with everything that's going on," Evelyn told Paige and Marissa during the phone conversation. "Cheating on my husband with another man was wrong. Staying in the marriage for the sake of money and security was wrong. I'm seeing my mistakes for what they were now. I don't know, I feel like I'm finally growing up, you know?"

If Evelyn had been standing in front of Paige, Paige would have felt her friend's forehead at that moment. Evelyn was sounding more and more mature by the day.

After saying her goodbyes to Evelyn, Paige hung up the phone and turned to Marissa. "You're still angry about not being able to read the diary."

"I just don't see what the big deal is," Marissa said, shrugging her shoulders and tossing her hair. "We've been friends since when? Since forever."

Maybe I should *let her read it,* Paige thought to herself, crossing one leg over the other. *Maybe I should let them all read it. Then I should mail a copy to Ethan.* It was one easy solution to her problem with Ethan. She wouldn't even have to talk to him face to face. She could mail him a copy of the book and he'd find out the truth that way.

She couldn't even imagine Marissa's reaction to the book. No, she couldn't let her read it. She couldn't let Deana read it. She couldn't let Evelyn read it. Ethan...she would prefer that he didn't read it, either. She had to talk to him in person, in her own time.

Marissa left in a huff, but that was typical Marissa. She was emotional and hard to deal with at times. Paige wasn't offended. After having time to cool off, Marissa would calm down and call to invite her to a dance club or out for drinks.

Paige had all of two hours to relax. The sunlight outside of her bedroom window faded, making way for dusk when her cell phone chirped. She reached over to the nightstand and picked up the phone, noting that Shane's cell phone number was the number on the display screen.

"Paige, Paige, Paige," he chanted. From the background noise, it sounded like he was in his car.

"Shane, Shane, Shane," she mimicked, sitting up straighter in bed.

"What can I say? You're the talk of the town, baby. Little girls want to be you, older women are relating to you, and high schools want you to come and speak to their students at school assemblies."

Paige rolled her eyes.

"This is what you've been waiting for right here, Paige," Shane went on. "This is what every author *dreams* of. Well, maybe not every author, but the greedy ones who want fame and money...this is what *they* dream of. Your name is *everywhere*. I can't tell you how many people I had calling today wanting to interview you for their primetime shows. It's bananas, it really is."

"Right now I don't even want to talk about this, Shane, I mean really," she groaned, closing her eyes and grabbing a pillow to put over her face. "I'm not the greedy, fame-seeking type, Shane. You know me better than that."

On the other end of the line, Shane chuckled. "You're right, I do know you better than that. And okay, okay, you don't like that angle? How about *this* angle. Teenagers are reading your shit and relating to it. Parents are buying this shit for their daughters. You were a virgin until what? You were twenty-one?"

"That wasn't intentional," she said, her voice muffled by the pillow.

"Intentional or not, you're now the role model for teens everywhere."

She groaned again and rolled over. "I kind of just want all of this to die down. Isn't there any way we can do that?"

"The best PR agent on the face of the planet couldn't do that, Paige. I'll tell you why. You're a commodity right now. A *hot* commodity. You're the *it* girl right now. Know what I mean? This is one of the biggest things to happen in the literary world. The only people who get coverage like this are actors, actresses, rock stars. You've done what I've never heard of. You've crossed into that world."

"You're really excited about this, aren't you?"

"We're in the money, Paige, that's all I can say."

She didn't know if she'd ever heard him as excited as he was now. It warmed her heart that he was this exuberant, this ecstatic about their joined success. She wished that she could share his enthusiasm, but she thought differently than he did.

All of the fame and success he was speaking of now meant the end of her privacy. The stories that were being run on the entertainment news weren't accompanied by her picture, but how difficult could it be to acquire that? How long was it before they *did* have her picture and her address and were knocking on her front door? How long was it before Marissa wasn't the only friend that was pissed off at her? How long was it before Ethan caught wind of the book and found out the truth-that is, if he hadn't found out already? Her world, as she knew it, was crashing down, because she already knew the answer to those questions.

How long was it before all of that happened? At the rate her supposed success was growing, it wouldn't be long at all before all three of those events came to pass.

Chapter Sixteen

Diane couldn't believe herself. She wasn't the type of woman who got hung up over men. Men were the ones who couldn't get enough of *her*, not the other way around. She couldn't shake off what she felt for Ethan and she hated it. He was a teacher. He wasn't independently wealthy. God knows he could have been, if he'd decided to go pro or at least coach college ball, but no...he had to be stubborn. He had to be a simple teacher who earned a meager wage.

What really sickened Diane was that even though she tried to slip in encouragement to change his mind about his career path, deep down she'd known he would never change careers. He was doing what he loved. He loved teaching. He loved making a difference. He had to be the most selfless man she had ever met. He was always doing a good deed for someone, always being there for someone, always supporting someone.

She'd known he would never go pro, would never coach college ball, and she'd still stayed with the man. She'd still wanted to be with him. And now, more than a year after they'd split, she still desired him. She missed him.

It was a shame, really. After all, now she was fucking Brandon Davies, the famous daytime soap actor. Sure, he was nearly an entire foot shorter than Ethan was, but he was better suited for her than Ethan had been. She and Brandon had more in common than her and Ethan had. Not to mention that he was rich and he got along with her father a hell of a lot better than Ethan had. He was Ethan's polar opposite. Whereas Ethan was selfless, caring, and considerate, Brandon was selfish, careless, and *in*considerate. He didn't care much for talking. He only took an interest in her when she was naked, on top of him, or beneath him.

She would have thought she'd be able to get him wrapped around her finger, but somehow, he'd turned the tables on her and had her feeding right out of his hand. He wasn't amazing at all in bed. In fact, in the bedroom, all he cared about was being catered to. He didn't give a rat's ass about pleasing Diane. Whether she got her rocks off or not wasn't his concern. It irked her. She wasn't accustomed to a man not caring about what she wanted. Most men she'd dated had made it their mission to spoil her and give her everything she wanted, but that was a low priority on Brandon's list if it made the list at all.

It didn't take long for Diane to realize that Brandon was only appealing when he was portraying a character on television. He was the most unappealing man when he was just being himself. He was loud and obnoxious, he ate like a pig, and he burped and passed gas when he was in her presence.

So, why did she stay with him? If he was so horrible, so intolerable, then why didn't she leave him? That answer was easy. A childish slob he was, but even so, he was also a famous actor. He escorted her to high-profile events, the Golden Globe awards, the Daytime Emmy awards, the Oscars…she'd gotten to mingle with major celebrities.

Perfect? He was far from it. But he was rich and famous. So she did continue to stay with him. She did continue to let him fuck her whenever he saw fit, even though she desired him about as much as she desired having the chicken pox. The man she'd truly wanted, she'd let get away.

She planned on getting him back, but she had no clue as to how she was going to get Ethan back. After all, he was into Paige now.

Diane was a confident woman, but even she knew when she had valid competition. Paige was valid competition. She could tell by the way Ethan had looked at her that day in the leisure center after his basketball game. Yes, he was into Paige. So how would Diane have even the slightest chance of breaking them up?

The answer came to her at a moment when she wasn't even looking for it. She was flipping through television channels, and lo and behold, a news reporter was giving report about famed romance novelist Paige Turner, who had somehow gotten her diary published…on accident.

Diane twirled the remote control in her hand, watching the news story until it ended, at which point she turned off the television, got dressed, and drove to the closest store that sold books. She purchased *Open Book*, took it back home, and after the first few diary entries, was collapsing in laughter.

She sat Indian-style on her bed, a sly smile tugging the corners of her mouth upward. "Oh, Paiiiiiige, Paiiiiiiige, Paiiiiiiiige," she sang, shaking her head. "You've been a baaaaad, baaaaad girl, haven't you?"

Evelyn was probably a horrible friend. She, along with Marissa and Deana, had made a pact to not read Paige's diary. She'd agreed not to buy the book and yet, she couldn't pass the book section of the grocery store without stopping. She must have stood in front of the *Open Book* display rack for a full twenty minutes, debating on whether or not she should buy it.

She plucked a book from the rack and flipped through the pages idly, her heart hammering in her chest. She didn't know why she was so nervous. Even if she bought the book, even if she read it…Paige wouldn't know. Marissa wouldn't know and neither would Deana. None of them would know. She would read it and pretend that she hadn't. It was that simple.

Not giving it another thought, she dropped the book into the shopping cart. She paid for her goods, exited the store, and packed her grocery bags into the back of a brand new midnight blue BMW sports utility vehicle.

The car had arrived in her driveway a few weeks ago, courtesy of her soon-to-be ex-husband. It was his way of asking her to go easy on him in the divorce proceedings, but that wasn't going to happen. He could have left five exquisite cars parked in her driveway, but that wouldn't change how she felt about him. It definitely wouldn't change what she planned to do to him in that courtroom. He'd snubbed his nose at her, had basically told her that she was an inadequate wife. He'd made her feel horrible. He'd made her cry. He wasn't going to get away that easily. She wouldn't let him.

As she drove home, she replayed the argument she'd had with him with his mistress lying naked in their bed. The emotions she'd felt then came rushing to the surface now. Shame for her own horrible actions and selfishness, humiliation, fury. She was shaking when she pulled the car into her own driveway.

She was shaking so much that she could barely bring herself to carry the grocery bags into the house. She dropped the bags on the kitchen counter and pressed her hip against the counter's edge.

In a few months, she would be a divorcee. Having to start her life over again was overwhelming. When she'd lived with Eric, she hadn't taken care of the household chores. She and Eric had a housekeeper who came in once a week. The housekeeper cleaned the house and bought the groceries. She'd ordered out a lot, or sometimes she and Eric had a cook come in and prepare their meals. She wasn't one for cooking, cleaning, or doing laundry. In truth, she could afford a maid and a cook, but she liked doing things for herself. She was learning and she liked that, too.

He'd called her incompetent, and that wasn't far from the truth. She had been a terrible wife. She wasn't the most intelligent woman or the nicest woman. She wasn't the easiest woman to please. She was a spoiled brat. Because she didn't want to be viewed as that by anyone, including herself, she came to the conclusion that her life needed a change.

So, that's what she was doing. She was changing it. She was bettering herself. Marissa had helped her to get a job as an administrative assistant at the firm where she worked. The pay was horrible and the work load was atrocious, but it kept Evelyn busy during the day.

She was going to make Eric eat his words. She was going to show him and anyone else who thought she was a blonde ditz that she was anything but. There were three people that she knew she could always count on for support, three people who knew her and knew that she wasn't the stereotypical blonde. Soon, everyone would know that.

A smile crept onto her lips and her eyes caught the copy of *Open Book* lying at the top of one of her grocery bags. She pulled the book out, smoothed her fingers over the shiny cover, and hugged it to her chest. It was time for a little light reading.

"[Dear Diary],

Last night after studying for my American history exam, something happened that shouldn't have. I'm trying to tell myself it's because I was intoxicated. I'm trying to tell myself that it's because I was drunk and wasn't aware of my actions, but that excuse doesn't fly. I was aware of what I was doing. So was he.

Sometimes I get confused about it. I mean, we're great friends and we like being around each other, so why is it so wrong? What's so wrong about a friendship evolving to something more?

Just a few months ago I would have never been able to picture being anything but friends with him. At times, he can be chauvinistic and at all times he's arrogant. But he is beautiful, tall with beautiful dark hair and eyes, very Italian. Whenever I'm around him, I'm enjoying myself. When I've needed someone to talk to, he was there for me. Shane has always been there for me.

So why do I feel that I've done something horribly wrong just because he and I made love last night? Why do I think I'm going to get the answer from a diary who can't respond to me?

I don't know...

I left his bed this morning feeling dirty and shameful. I don't know why, but everything looked different by the light of day. Last night, everything was beautiful. Not magical, but beautiful. And he was beautiful. He'd felt wonderful. But as soon as the sun's rays hit the sheets on the bed, that wonderful feeling faded.

As far as our friendship is concerned, he's the greatest, most wonderful friend anyone could ask for, but relationship-wise we aren't meant to be together. I'm not destined to end up with Shane and he's not destined to end up with me. We were destined to be nothing but friends. That's why I felt so dirty then and that's why I'm still questioning everything now, because he and I aren't a long-term match.

I can say that with certainty, because I already know who my long-term companion is..."

Marissa closed the book gently and set it down on the coffee table. Her bottom lip trembled. It had taken all of the self-control she possessed not to tear the book apart page by page. This couldn't be her best friend's diary. These words...they weren't true. Paige and Shane had never made love when they were all going to college together. Paige would have said something about it. They'd been best friends; they'd done everything together and told each other everything.

"Oh my God," Marissa whispered, closing her eyes and clasping her hands together in her lap. When she opened her eyes, two single tears trailed down her cheeks and dropped onto her blouse.

A sleepy-eyed, shirtless Ethan answered the door only seconds after Paige had knocked. Shock registered on his face and he stepped aside so that she could enter. She watched his face closely for any signs of anger, but found none. She doubted that he knew anything about the book...he at least didn't know about her involvement in it.

"I didn't know you were coming over," he said groggily, running his hand over his hair. "I would have tried to clean the place up a bit."

"You don't have to clean up for me," she said, glancing around the living room nervously, looking anywhere but at his face.

He sensed her nervousness and gestured to the couch. "Would you like me to get you anything? Something to drink..."

"No, that's all right," she said. She sat down on the couch and placed her purse beside her.

He remained standing and folded his arms across his chest. "I can tell you're bothered by something."

She had to tell him. By some strange miracle, he hadn't put two and two together. As Marissa said, it would be best coming from her and not some news anchor on television. "I wanted to talk to you."

"Should I sit down for this?"

She nodded. "Yeah, you should."

He sat down on the other end of the couch and stretched his arm across the back of it. "Okay."

"I write."

A single brow arched. He looked as if he was waiting for her to finish the sentence. When he realized that she had finished the sentence, his brows furrowed. "Okay," he said slowly, clearly not knowing how he was supposed to respond.

"I write novels. For a living."

"That's very interesting."

"Yeah," she said, lifting a hand to the back of her neck. She was still searching for the right words. She was trying to find a satisfactory way of telling him that she was a fraud. "Lately, I've, uh...gotten a lot of exposure."

He picked up her purse and set it on the floor so that he could scoot closer to her. "That's great," he said, leaning his body into hers.

She cleared her throat and looked away from him. "It's not that great."

"You should be happy," he said, confused as to why she wasn't. The phone on the end table beside him rang and he held up an index finger. "Hello?" he said into the phone.

She wrapped her arms around her torso, trying to keep herself from shaking. If she didn't tell him the truth tonight, there was no telling what would happen. She knew that, and yet she didn't know if she was going to be able to come clean with him. She feared his reaction to what she had to say. She feared losing him.

"I don't know. I guess I'm just wondering why you're calling me," Ethan told whomever he was talking to on the phone. "You want me to what? Hello?" He stared at the phone and shook his head. He placed the phone on its base and reached for the remote control.

She glanced over her shoulder at him. "Who was that?"

"Diane. She wants me to turn to Channel 9 for some reason."

"No!" she cried, diving at him and extracting the remote control from his hand.

He looked stunned as she rose to a standing position, gripping the remote tightly in both hands. "What the hell?"

"I, um…we should go out."

"We should…go out," he repeated, one of his eyebrows lifting. "Are you drunk by any chance? I remember how you get when you-"

"I'm not drunk. I'm just a little…Could we go out somewhere? To eat or something, or-or maybe a movie." She managed a weak smile, hoping that the smile passed for being genuine.

The only genuine thing in the room at the moment was his concern for her. It was etched across his face. He looked truly worried for her well-being. "I…guess if I took a shower and got dressed, we could go somewhere," he said, speaking very slowly and surveying her.

"Okay," she said, setting the remote on the coffee table.

He stood and padded down the short hall to his bedroom.

She exhaled in relief. Diane knew about her book. That was the last thing she needed right now. She knew how fortunate she was that she'd been here when he'd gotten the call. If she hadn't been here, he would have turned on the television. He would have seen the story and he would know. She had to tell him and she had to tell him soon.

He showered and dressed in less than twenty minutes. He wore a loose, sky blue shirt and khaki slacks. Paige felt a bit dressed down in her white blouse and blue jeans, but he assured her that she was beautiful.

He escorted her out of the house and to his silver Intrepid. "So, it's after nine o' clock on a Sunday night," he mused. "Where are we going exactly?"

"Umm…" She opened her car door and folded herself into the passenger seat.

"You were going to tell me something important before Diane called me," he pointed out once they were both in the car.

A lump formed in her throat and she turned to gaze out of the window. "I can tell you after dinner."

"Is it that bad?"

You don't know the half of it, she thought. "So how have you been?"

"I've been all right," he replied, noticing that she'd dodged his question. "Some of my students are acting pretty bizarre and the ones that aren't are talking about this book non-stop."

"What book?"

He laughed and shook his head. "I talk about it all day at school. I don't even want to bring it up."

"No, come on," she pleaded, turning to look at him. "What book?"

He pulled out of the driveway with his torso twisted so he could see out of the back window. "Okay. Supposedly an author accidentally got her diary published. I keep telling the kids in my class that it's probably a publicity stunt, because it's not possible to get anything published on accident, but they swear up and down that it wasn't deliberate." He chuckled again. "A few kids want me to read it, but I'm more of a science fiction guy myself, you know?"

She nodded stiffly, staring straight ahead.

"I'm just glad these kids are reading, and they're relating to this woman. I am pleased about that." He glanced at her out of the corner of his eye. She was looking very tense. "You never told me where we're going. I'm just driving for the hell of it."

"That's okay," she said.

"That's okay?" he repeated. "Are *you* okay? You're acting a bit…"

"I just wanted to spend time with you," she said, daring to look at him. "I haven't even talked to you in-"

"I've been trying to call, but you haven't been answering your cell phone."

She nodded and looked down at her hands. "I know."

"You never called me back."

"I needed time."

"Time?"

"I'm going through some things right now," she said, "some pretty big things, and I just kind of needed time away from…this."

He pulled the car to a halt at a red light. "'This' meaning us?"

"Yeah."

"Did you get everything sorted out that you needed to?" He asked her this question already knowing the answer. If she'd sorted out everything that she needed sorted out, then she wouldn't be as tense and nervous as she was. He wished that she would just open up to him. He was nothing like her ex-boyfriend. He wouldn't judge her based on what she told him. He wanted to get to know her. That is why he spent time with her.

"I got some of it sorted out, but not all of it," she answered honestly. "I have a question and it might sound kind of silly."

"Ask me."

"Have you seen the movie *The Truth About Cats and Dogs?*"

It wasn't the question he'd been expecting. Well...he hadn't known what to expect, but that question definitely wasn't it. *"The Truth About Cats and Dogs?"*

"Yeah, it was on TV a few nights ago." She'd known that because she'd watched it in her hotel room after one of her book signings. It had probably been her third time seeing the movie.

"Janeane Garofalo and Uma Thurman?"

She nodded. "Yeah."

"I saw it three or four years ago."

"Did you like it?" she asked timidly.

He shrugged his shoulders. "It was a decent movie, not the typical kind of movie that I try to catch."

"If you were in the same situation as that guy ...if a girl had lied about something that was pretty major, what would you have done?"

He angled a look at her. She was trying to tell him something but couldn't come out with it. She was testing the waters, testing him. He nodded and turned his eyes to look out of the windshield. "I can't honestly say because I haven't been in that situation before," he said, trying to be as truthful as possible. "But I think that when you love a person, you can't help loving them. When you face something like that, it's a test of sorts. Of your faith in each other, your love, and your character. In some cases, the relationship would have to be terminated. I mean, if someone lied to me about her age and she was underage, obviously that relationship couldn't continue. It's against the law. I would try to be objective and look at the situation from all angles."

"Good answer."

"Is there something you want to tell me?" he asked after a slight hesitation.

"A little later."

He nodded and continued to drive. The next few minutes were minutes of silence. The wheels were turning in Ethan's head. Why had she asked him about that particular movie? Why would she want to know his reaction to that certain situation? Had she lied to him about something or misled him in some way? The first thought that occurred to him was that she may have somehow rekindled her relationship with Brandon and didn't know how to tell him. He couldn't think of anything else.

"Pull into this lot," she suddenly instructed, indicating the parking lot to a restaurant that was built on the sands of Lake Michigan. The restaurant boasted an entire wall of glass, showcasing an enchanting view of the lake to its diverse crowd of patrons.

Ethan pulled into a parking space and turned the car off. "I want you to know that you can talk to me about anything. You can tell me anything," he said, raising a hand to her face and running his fingers along the slope of her jaw. "I don't want you to be afraid to tell me anything. You should just come out with it and tell me. If you don't, the truth will come out somehow. It always does." He shrugged his shoulders and let his hand fall. He pushed open the driver side door and stepped out of the car.

She closed her eyes and calmed her breathing before pushing open the passenger side door. She stood out of the car and shoved her hands into the pockets of her jeans. It was breezy here, near the lake. She probably should have brought a jacket, but she hadn't planned on staying at Ethan's long. The plan had been to drop by, tell the truth, and get kicked out of his house. That had been the plan. She should have come up with a Plan B in case she didn't have the balls to tell him the truth, but that thought hadn't even crossed her mind.

As they walked to the doors of the restaurant, he reached out and grabbed her hand. He sensed that she was trying to distance herself from him. She'd been fidgety and evasive from the moment he'd opened the door and let her into his house earlier that night. The gesture of taking her hand in his was to let her know that he wasn't going to let her pull away from him. He was going to be there for her; all she had to do was open up.

A waiter seated them at a table near the wall of windows. The moon dangled over the lake and cast light over the water. Paige watched the water moving towards the shore. "I love this restaurant," she said. She hadn't even meant to say it aloud. The words were on her lips before she could think to purse her lips shut.

"So do I." He folded his hands together on the table and took a long, hard look at her.

She felt his eyes on her, but didn't turn to face him. "You are the kindest man I've ever met," she said.

"I am?" he asked, smiling.

She finally glanced at him and found herself smiling. "Yes, you are."

"Thank you for that sentiment."

She looked down at her hands. "I don't think I deserve you."

His brows shot up. "You don't?"

"No, I don't."

"I don't understand."

"You will."

A waiter approached their table. "Are you ready to order?"

Ethan's eyes were still on Paige. He gave a slight shake of his head that sent the waiter traipsing to check on another one of his tables. "Why don't you deserve me?"

"I'm trying to tell you," she told him, trying in vain to control the shakiness of her voice. "I'm trying but…I can't."

He leaned forward. "I'm a very patient man. Don't rush it."

She shook her head. "No, I-I have to tell you, before-"

"Before what?"

A girl approached their table looking very nervous. She was dressed in a waitress uniform and couldn't have been any older than seventeen years old. Her dark blonde hair was pulled up in a bun and she smiled a lot. "I'm so sorry," she apologized, "but I just had to ask. Are you… Paige Turner?"

Ethan's eyes slowly moved from Paige to the girl standing at their table. "Jessica?"

The girl looked surprised, as if she hadn't even noticed that he was sitting there. "Hi. Mr. Carson."

"Hi," he greeted slowly, his gaze shifting between the girl and Paige.

"Hi," the girl said again. Then she turned back to Paige. "Are you?"

"I, um-" Paige started, shooting a frantic glance in Ethan's direction. While holding his steady gaze, she answered the girl's question. "Yes, I'm Paige Turner."

The girl's excitement level shot up. "I have your book in the back, could I-could you...?"

Paige nodded. "Yeah, bring it by the table and I'll sign it."

The girl turned and nearly fled towards the back room of the restaurant.

Ethan's brows shot up.

"You know her?" Paige asked casually.

Their assigned waiter returned to set glasses of water in front of them. Then he scampered away again, seeing that they still weren't ready to order.

"She is a student of mine," Ethan said. "Is she friends with Sam?"

"Your guess is as good as mine," she responded, meeting his gaze.

"Paige, what is going on?"

The teenager returned with a copy of *Open Book*. She opened the book to the front cover. "Make it out to Jessica," she said, "and thank you so much. Everyone's talking about this book. Everyone at school is talking about it and my mom says everyone at her job is talking about it, too. I haven't even started reading this yet, but my friends won't shut up about it. So I know what it's about and some of the things you went through. I'm so glad that this came out, whether you meant it to or not."

"Thank you for the kind words," Paige said, offering the girl a smile.

"I had a tough time in junior high," the girl said. "I got made fun of a lot because my family didn't have that much money and my mom wasn't working at the time. I had to dress in the least expensive clothes. I didn't talk to anyone really...I was very anti-social. Things got better when I got to high school, when my mom started working, but I still kind of feel like that girl in junior high, you know?"

Paige listened to the girl and nodded her head, indicating that she was listening. "Being a kid is hard. It's something that some adults tend to forget. I haven't forgotten, so I just feel like I'm reminding everyone else."

"Thank you," the girl said as she watched the author sign the book's title page. She remembered that her health teacher was also seated at the table. "Mr. Carson, I didn't know you knew Paige Turner."

"I didn't know *you* knew her," he returned, the muscles in his jaw working.

Paige finished signing the book and closed it. She gave it to the girl, who said, "I'd better get to work before I get fired. Thanks Paige!"

"Thank you," Paige returned, and watched the girl move away from the table.

"Paige Turner? I thought your name was Paige Waterford."

"It's Paige Turner."

"Do you and Sam have different fathers, or..."

"We really should order," she hedged, lifting her menu and opening it.

He suppressed a frustrated growl and raised his own menu. He cleared his throat, letting his eyes slide over the words of the menu. His appetite wasn't raging at the moment. He didn't feel like eating. He felt like talking. He felt like getting the truth out of Paige. "Would you excuse me for a few moments?" he asked.

She nodded, not taking her eyes off the menu.

He moved his chair back and stood. He walked towards the bathrooms, which also happened to be near the back room Jessica had disappeared into. She was just walking out of a door marked "Employees Only" when he approached. She looked surprised. "I'm sorry for interrupting and I don't want to hold you up or get you in trouble," he said calmly, "but could I see the book that Paige just signed?"

The teenager nodded and crooked a finger. "Follow me."

He glanced over his shoulder to make sure they didn't have anyone's attention and proceeded to follow her into what appeared to be a storage room that kept all of the employees' belongings. It was dimly lit and he felt that it was inappropriate for him to be in a room marked "Employees Only" with one of his students.

Jessica pulled the book out of her backpack and handed it to him. "You can borrow it if you want," she allowed.

"I just want to look through it a bit. I'll give it back to you." He took the book with him to the Men's bathroom and turned it over in his hands. He read the book's summary on the back cover. It didn't take long for the metaphorical light bulb to appear above his head. This wasn't just a book. This was *the* book. The book all of his students had been talking about…the book that everyone was talking about…it had been written by Paige. He was holding Paige's diary in his hands.

This is what she wanted to tell me, he thought to himself. *She probably didn't want to tell me because she didn't want me reading it. This is what she's been hiding.* He had intended to read a few pages of the book, but he couldn't. He couldn't read any of it knowing that it was her diary. The truths he learned from her, he wanted her to tell him. He didn't want to have to read them behind her back.

He returned the book to Jessica and rejoined Paige at their table. "Sorry about that," he apologized.

"It's all right," she said. She'd taken to looking out of the glass windows and had been doing so when he'd walked up to the table.

He sat in his chair and stared at her. She was a beautiful woman; he'd known that already. Now, he knew that she was also more intelligent than he'd credited her for before tonight. She was intelligent enough to write novels for a living. *Maybe I should have read a few pages of the book,* he thought to himself now as he looked at her. *I just want a glimpse. I just want to know how she thinks and who she is.* No matter how much he wanted to know about her, though, he knew that he was making the right choice. If her diary wasn't published, if he'd just walked into her room and seen it lying on her bed, he wouldn't pick it up and read it.

She eyed him cautiously, wondering what he was thinking. "Thank you…for bringing me here," she said.

"You're welcome."

"Thank you for…everything, really."

"I haven't done anything special, Paige."

"No…you have. The night when Brandon…the night I came to your house… that meant a lot to me. It really did. I don't think I ever thanked you for that."

"You didn't deserve how he treated you. I still think I should have kicked his ass."

"I'm glad you didn't. If you got in trouble because of me…"

"That's the only thing that kept me from doing it," he said. "I knew you'd feel guilty."

She pursed her lips and folded her hands together on the table.

"Back to you not deserving me…why do you feel that is?"

"Because I'm not as angelic as I seem."

He laughed. "Who said you seem angelic?"

Her eyes widened.

"The night before you left on your trip, you did a few things that were a bit devilish, if you ask me."

She gasped and playfully slapped his arm. "Stop it, I'm being serious."

"Maybe you shouldn't be so serious," he advised.

She sighed and ran a hand through her hair. "I haven't been very… informative. When you ask me personal questions, I'm not always direct in answering. That's deliberate."

"I know."

"But you don't know why."

"Are you going to tell me?"

"Well-"

"Later," he interrupted. "I know."

She nervously fidgeted with the crimson tablecloth. "I'm sorry, I'm trying."

"Like I said, I'm a patient man," he reiterated and leaned forward to slide his index finger under her chin. He lifted her face with that finger. "Take your time. Don't rush it."

"I have no choice but to rush it," she said, her chin trembling in his hand.

"Why is that?"

She swallowed a lump that had formed in her throat and said, "Because if you don't find out the truth from me, you'll find it out from someone else."

He drew his hand back and looked at her for several moments, until she broke eye contact. When the waiter came to take their order, he ordered a steak and potatoes. She ordered a grilled chicken salad. She was close to tears. She was holding them back and he could tell that. Her behavior was frightening him and worrying him. The fact that she hadn't told him she'd written a book wasn't something that would bring her close to tears. The fact that she'd written a book wasn't such a traumatic secret. There was something else that she wasn't telling him.

They talked throughout the course of their meal. She asked him a lot of questions about his childhood, how he'd been as a child. She asked him a lot of very personal questions. She was very detail-oriented. She liked to hear the details, which Ethan found ironic because she rarely gave details about herself. He obliged her with answers. It was a good sign that she wanted to know about him. That let him know that what he felt towards her was mutual.

He told her about how shy he'd been growing up, how quiet he'd been. As judgmental and distant as his father was, he always knew that both of his parents had loved him. He always knew that his circumstances could have been worse.

It's a thought that he always kept at the back of his mind to prioritize his situations. Sure, he might be having a bad day today, but somewhere else in the world someone had just lost a loved one. In another country, there were thousands upon thousands of children starving to death. Things might be bad now, but it was just another bump in the road. Everyone had bad days. Some had worse and worst days. Pain, disappointment, it was all relative. And everyone felt it at one time or another.

Paige remarked about how considerate he was and how thoughtful, but he didn't think about it that way. He didn't see himself as being overly thoughtful just because he gave thought to other people once in awhile, and he told her so. It made her admire him all the more.

After dinner, he drove them back to his house. His phone was ringing as soon as they walked in the door. It was Diane, asking him if he'd turned to Channel 9 as she'd asked. "Something else came up," he told her. "I'm sorry, I didn't catch it. Maybe I'll catch the re-run."

"It was the news, not a TV show," she said, sounding thoroughly displeased.

"Diane…I don't want you calling me again. You've been popping up all over the place and you need to realize that it's over. It's over and *we're* over. Have a good night."

"But Ethan-"

He hung up the phone. "She doesn't know how to take no for an answer."

Paige stood in the middle of the living room with her hands clasped in front of her. "I've always liked your house."

He chuckled and disappeared into the kitchen. "It's just a simple, one-story house."

"My parents have a one-story house," Paige said. "I like simple."

"Then you'd love me," he called from the kitchen.

"I do." As soon as the words were out of her mouth, her face burned beet-red. She brought a hand up to her brow just as Ethan poked his head out of the kitchen.

"What did you say?"

She raised her eyes to meet his. "Nothing, I was-"

He finished what he was doing in the kitchen and joined her in the living room. "You said something."

"I said…"

"Yes?"

"What I said was…"

His brows rose.

She shrugged her shoulders and turned her back to him. "It's getting pretty late. I should probably get home."

"I do too."

She whirled around to face him. "What?"

He offered her a playful grin. "Nothing," he stressed, mimicking her.

She rolled her eyes, but her lips curled into a smile. "Yeah?"

He nodded and walked around the couch so that he could stand directly in front of her. "Yeah."

She reached up and wrapped her arms around his neck. "I don't deserve you."

"So you've told me."

"How can you be so…"

"Perfect?"

"I was going to say patient."

He shrugged his shoulders and reached down so that he could encircle her waist with his arms. "You're what I want."

"Don't be so sure of that," she said worriedly, the playful light in her eyes flickering.

He stroked her hair, ran his fingers across her forehead and pressed his hips into her. She smelled like lilacs. It was probably a perfume that she sprayed on or a body wash that she scrubbed into her skin. Whatever it was, he liked it. Her skin smelled like it and her hair smelled like it. He wanted to inhale that scent all night long; he wanted her to leave that scent on his pillow. He wanted to go to bed to that scent every night.

She looked up at him and he looked down at her. Both of them knew what was going to happen. She couldn't have stopped it even if she wanted to. The heat coursing through her body was too strong. The look in his eyes and pressing of his hips into hers were the very undoing of her. Her knees shook and her breathing was rapid. Her heart hammered against her chest as his face lowered towards hers.

His lips bypassed hers and instead, graced the slant of her neck. Her eyes fluttered closed and her eyelashes kissed the top of her cheeks. His hands settled onto her shoulders and he massaged them through the thin material of her blouse. His tongue flicked against the skin on her neck and he raised his head sharply to see the expression on her face.

Her eyes blinked open and she stared at him. Her lips were waiting to be kissed. Her body was waiting to be held. He trailed a finger along the collar of her blouse.

She stepped back from his touch.

"What, you're going to deny me?" he asked her incredulously.

Her mind was racing. "I'm not going to deny you," she said finally. "It's just... last time you catered to my needs and what I wanted. This time I want to cater to you. I want to give you what you want."

"All I want is you," he said, his throat thick with yearning. "That's all I want."

She pushed his chest with both hands so that he fell back onto the couch. She lowered her knees onto the couch on either side of his thighs. "Are you sure that's all you want?" She outlined his lips with her tongue, then grabbed his bottom lip between her teeth. She pulled back and looked down at him.

He grabbed her rear in his hands. "Maybe that's not all I want," he allowed, a grin stretching across his face. "You want to cater to me this time?"

She nodded, looking flustered.

"Stand up."

She followed his order without question.

"I want your shirt off and your pants off. Now."

She effortlessly pulled the white blouse over her head and discarded it. She unzipped her jeans and bent over, starting to pull them down her legs. Then she stepped out of them and kicked them to the side. She stood before him in nothing but a white, lacy bra and matching panties.

He stood up from the couch. "Undress me."

She took a step forward and grabbed the bottom of his shirt. She stood on tiptoe to yank it over the top of his head. Then, her hands were on the front of his pants. She maintained eye contact with him as she pulled his slacks down his legs. Beneath his slacks, he'd been wearing boxer briefs. She lowered those as well, slowly dragging them down his muscular thighs and calves. Her chest rose and fell quickly, her breathing near the point of hyperventilation.

"Stand up."

She stood and faced him.

He smiled. The expression on her face was priceless. She'd been serious when she said that this time, she wanted to cater to him. She was ready and willing to follow his every order. That thought alone drove him crazy. Trying to look as calm as he possibly could when his very blood was racing through his veins, he seated himself on the couch. It took him a minute to find his voice. "Come as closely as you can to me while still standing."

She inched closer to him until her toes were touching the bottom of the couch.

"Turn around," he ordered with his eyes moving down the length of her body.

Her eyebrows lifted, but she did as she was told. Her hair fell down her back and nearly touched the top of her panties. Her skin was slightly tanned from the past summer; it was smooth and unblemished.

He leaned forward to lower her panties over the curve of her rear and down her legs. "Step out of them."

She stepped out of her underwear and kicked them to the side. Then, she started to turn to face him.

He looked up at her. "Don't. Turn back around."

She turned back around. She could feel his hands grabbing her hips and lowering her onto him. Her mouth dropped open and she didn't seem to know what to do with her hands. One hand gripped the arm rest to her right and the other she placed on the couch beside Ethan's left thigh.

He watched her bounce on top of him and snaked his arms around her waist. "God..." His hands moved up her stomach to grab both of her breasts. He began thrusting into her as she slammed down on him. He wound her hair around his hand and pulled her head back, pressing hot kisses to her cheek. He moved against her, then moved with her, and damn she felt so good...he didn't want to stop. He held himself back so that he could savor this feeling, this oneness with her. "Stand up," he said in a voice so ragged that it didn't even sound like it belonged to him. She slowly stood up and turned around to face him. "Come here."

With those two words, she was riding him again, but facing him this time. He reached up to stroke her face, touching her eyebrows and cheeks, the tip of that cute nose and her beautiful, rosy lips...his fingers lingered on her lips. His fingers were soon replaced by his mouth. He sucked at her lips, penetrated her mouth with his tongue, and let his tongue wrestle with hers. He pulled back and took in her sleepy eyes and plump lips. "You like this?"

She nodded her head and circled her arms around his neck.

"Tell me."

"I like this."

"You want this?"

"I want this," she whispered, pressing her forehead to his.

"Show me you want this," he demanded. "Ride me like you want this."

She moved her body against his harder and threw her head back. She'd never felt like this. Never in her life had she been as turned on as she was right now. She felt Ethan grab one of her nipples between his teeth and she looked down to see the top of his head, his curly dark hair. It was intense, knowing that no one would ever make her feel the way that he did. "I do," she whispered, repeating her earlier sentiment.

He raised his face to her, knowing her meaning. "I do too," he whispered. His hands roamed all over her body, grazing her breasts and crawling across her stomach, tracing the arch of her back and resting on the curve of her round bottom. "I'll never want anyone else. You're the only one I'll ever want." He cradled her face in his hands and kissed her mouth as she rode him.

"You're the only one I'll ever want," she said, echoing him.

"Then trust me."

"I do."

His frustration poured out as he said, "Then talk to me."

She buried her face into his neck.

"Talk to me," he whispered more gently, nipping her shoulder with his teeth. "Please."

She raised her head from the crook of his neck and shoulder. "I thought you were a patient man."

"I thought you were catering to me tonight."

She stared into his eyes. "Ethan…"

"What?"

"Please…"

"Please what?" He trailed a finger along her collarbone. "I thought you *do*."

"I do."

"Then talk to me."

She opened her mouth as if she wanted to say something. She did want to say something. She wanted to tell him everything. Couldn't he understand that she very much wanted to tell him the truth? It was easier said than done. And this particular truth…

"Talk to me," he urged.

"I…"

"Yes?" he said with a hopeful expression on his face.

"I can't."

He looked away from her.

She stood and started collecting her clothes, trying to stop the tears. She should have never let this happen. She should have stopped this.

He watched her gather her clothes without speaking. Why was she making things so complicated? Why didn't she feel she could talk to him? Didn't she know how he felt about her? Didn't she know that he would do anything for her? What could be so horrible that she couldn't talk to him about it? "Don't."

She'd started to dress. "Don't what?"

"Don't do that." He rose and pulled her against him. He felt her tears on his chest. "And don't cry. Don't."

"I'm sorry," she mumbled through the tears, pressing her face to his chest.

"No, I'm sorry. I did tell you I'd be patient."

"You have nothing to apologize for."

"Let's go to bed." He looked down at the top of her head and caressed it.

She shook her head. "I shouldn't."

"You shouldn't?"

"Until I feel comfortable talking about everything…we shouldn't-"

"Shouldn't what? See each other?" he demanded. "Are you serious, Paige?" He felt more tears on his chest and shook his head.

She stepped back and wiped her cheeks. "It's the smart thing to do."

"The smart thing to do is fucking talk to me, Paige."

"I can't."

"You can't." He laughed dryly. "So you expect me to just stop seeing you? I refuse to do that." He pulled her back into his arms.

She avoided his eyes and shook her head.

"Let's go to bed," he said with a touch of authority in his voice. "Okay?"

She started to object, but she wanted to lie in bed with him and let him hold her. After all, chances were that this would be the last night she'd be spending in his bed beside him. Once he found out the truth, he'd want nothing to do with her.

He led her to the bedroom, where not much sleep occurred. They spent most of the night making love and exploring each other. At one point, when she was on top of him and crying, he said, "Stop it."

She'd looked surprised. "Stop what?"

"Stop making love to me as if this is our last time together." He'd sat up and pressed her head against his chest. "This isn't our last time together. Far from it."

That's what you think, she thought to herself, closing her eyes and willing herself not to cry even harder.

Chapter Seventeen

When Ethan left the house, Paige had been sleeping soundly in bed. He planned on calling her from the high school to let her know that he'd had to leave for work. He hadn't liked leaving her in bed alone, but she'd been sleeping so peacefully that he hadn't wanted to disrupt her rest. He drove to work with images of her burned into his brain. He remembered how she'd felt, how she'd looked, and how she'd smelled the previous night. He also remembered the pain in her eyes.

He parked in the teacher's parking lot and grabbed the satchel he'd thrown in the passenger seat before getting out of the car. He was still thinking about her. He'd be thinking about her all day. He couldn't wait to get back to her.

From the start, his day was strange. When he passed a few of his students in the halls between classes, some of them made passing remarks that he didn't understand. One student called, "Mr. Carson is *such* a lady's man!"

Another student held a copy of *Open Book* up and said, "I'm so jealous, man. So jealous."

When he walked into his classroom, he noticed that the words, "Mr. Carson gets all the chicks" had been scrawled across the chalkboard. For a brief moment he entertained the idea that someone must have been looking in his living room window when he and Paige were together the previous night, but that was ludicrous. He didn't know what was going on.

That is, he didn't know what was going on until he pulled aside one of the students who'd called out to him in the hallway and asked him what the comment meant.

"You don't know?" the dark-haired kid asked. "You don't know about the book?"

"What book?" Ethan demanded with furrowed brows.

"*Open Book.* By Paige Turner."

"What about it?"

The kid laughed. "Man...you're *in* it."

"I'm...what?"

The kid shook his head and slid his backpack from his shoulder. He set the backpack on the floor and unzipped it so that he could rummage through it. He finally pulled out a familiar-looking book and handed it to Mr. Carson. "Read it. You'll see the light."

Ethan's jaw set and he nodded. "I'll give this back to you."

The teenager shook his head. "Man, I can't believe you don't *know*," he said before turning and jogging to catch up with one of his friends.

As uncomfortable as Ethan was reading the book, he wanted to know why his students were calling out to him the way they were. So on his lunch break, he started reading *Open Book*. The first journal entry made his jaw drop. To the floor.

Deana was seated at her large, mahogany desk comparing reports when the door to her office burst open. Her eyes widened and her head snapped up. "Marissa? What the hell?"

Marissa stood in the doorway and she looked like a mess. Her clothes were rumpled and her hair was wild. She held a book in her hands. "Read this."

Deana's eyes widened. "You came here to give me a book?"

"No," Marissa said, shaking her head. "Not *a* book. *The* book. The one Paige wrote."

"We weren't supposed to read this, Marissa, we agreed," Deana stated, standing and raising her hands to her hips. "Paige is going to freak if she finds out you read it."

"No...*you're* going to freak when you read what she wrote about you."

One of Deana's slender brows arched. Her interest was piqued. She walked around the desk and leaned back against it. "Is it that bad?"

Marissa slapped the book against her hand. "She, um…" She tossed her hair and wiped at the tears that rolled down her cheeks.

"Marissa, are you all right?" Deana looked concerned.

"She um…fucked Shane."

Deana's mouth opened, but no words came out.

Marissa continued tapping the book against her open palm. She kept tossing her head, as if that lone action was going to stop her tears. "She umm…she fucked Shane. Shane and I…we *just* officially got engaged-again."

"Marissa, I…*wow*." Deana shook her head. "I can't believe that. I don't."

"It's all here, Deana!" Marissa screamed. "It's all right fucking here, right fucking…in this book."

Deana calmly said, "Marissa, I love you, God knows I do, but this is a place of business. Lower your voice."

Marissa started pacing the room. "In um…college. She and Shane had a small thing. She *never* told me. *Never*."

"In *college*?" Deana repeated. "I thought you meant she screwed Shane recently. College is college, Marissa."

"She's my fucking *friend*, Deana. My *best* friend, no offense. She should have told me. We told each other everything."

Deana was trying to remain calm, but her patience was wearing thin.

"Anyway, her betrayal to me was in college, but her betrayal to *you*? Muuuuch more recent." Marissa stepped to the side and dropped the book on Deana's desk. "Just some bedtime reading for you."

When Evelyn showed up to work, she'd taken the elevator directly to the floor that Marissa worked on, only to find out that she wasn't at her desk. She desperately needed to talk to her. Last night, she'd done some reading of *Open*

Book. She'd been shocked, disgusted, and a bit disappointed. She'd also been humiliated. There'd been a particular journal entry that she'd read so many times, she practically remembered it by heart.

"[Dear Diary],

Some people are blessed with good fortune. Take my friend Evie. She's got a great husband, a great life...she doesn't even have to work if she doesn't want to. She can just sit on her ass and when her husband gets home because he dotes on her. It's always been that way for her. She and Eric have been together since college. She told Marissa, Deana, and I about her life in high school and in high school she'd always had a date. She was a cheerleader for crying out loud. She is seriously the girl you love to hate.

I shouldn't say that and I know I shouldn't say that, because she's my friend. But I compare her life, which seems rosy and perfect, to my life, which isn't. She seems to take her good fortune for granted. If I had a husband like Eric, I wouldn't take him for granted. If everyone got wrapped around my finger based on my looks, I wouldn't take that for granted.

Sometimes I wish I could trade places with her for a day. Someone once asked me if I'd rather have brains or looks. I told them I'd rather have brains, but life seems a lot more fun if you're someone like Evelyn, who isn't the most scholarly person on the face of the earth. She's just the type of girl who likes to have fun and enjoy life. Maybe I should try to be more like that."

Evelyn had resented the journal entry. There were more entries that implied that she was a simpleton or selfish. She resented them all. She wondered how someone could be a close friend to her as Paige was, but yet feel so much bitterness towards her. She wouldn't be speaking to Paige anytime soon. She no longer considered Paige a friend.

Aside from what *she* was feeling, she was worried about how Marissa would feel if she knew what had been written about her. More like, she was worried about how Marissa would feel if she knew what had been written about *Shane*. Shane...and Paige...they'd fucked in college. If Evelyn knew Marissa as well as she thought she did, Marissa wouldn't take that information well, especially considering the fact that Marissa and Shane were talking about marriage.

Evelyn had talked to Paige. She knew that Paige had had a choice between pulling the books off of the shelves and keeping them on. If Paige knew what her diary consisted of, why had she kept the book on the shelves? She'd known it would make people angry, she'd known she would be airing her dirty laundry, and yet...she hadn't had them removed from stores. She'd *kept* them.

Evelyn knew that Paige felt that her book was helping people, and she could see her point, but she'd known that she would have to face the people she dealt with in day-to-day life. Did she really value helping others above keeping her skeletons in the closet? If so, then she should be commended.

Evelyn, for one, wouldn't be doing the commending. Right now, the sight of Paige would probably make her gag. Either that or it would send her into a fury. No...it would be best if she and Paige didn't talk for awhile.

Paige awakened with a long, luxurious stretch. She'd expected to see Ethan sleeping beside her, but he wasn't there. Her eyes landed on the clock on the nightstand; it was nearly lunchtime. She didn't hear a shower running across the hall or any noise from the kitchen.

It slowly dawned on her that he had to work today. This was a workday and, more importantly, a school day. So chances were, he was at the school teaching at this very moment. She settled into bed and pulled the covers up to her chin. She felt...good. For some reason, she'd expected to feel guilty and terrible after a night of lovemaking with Ethan. She did feel a trace amount of guilt, but she loved him. Knowing that he loved her comforted her. When he came home from work today, she was going to confront her fear and tell him everything.

She could hear her cell phone ringing faintly and jumped out of bed. She found her purse on the living room floor. The number in the display was Shane's. "Hi," she greeted.

"Your old high school wants to book you for an assembly," were the first words out of Shane's mouth.

"Yeah?" she asked, nervously biting the nail of her index finger.

"What should I tell them?"

"I have to think about it," she said. "I can't really think straight right now."

"Where the hell are you?" he demanded. "I've been calling your house for hours now."

"I'm not at home."

He noticed the tone in her voice. "You're at the teacher's."

"Yeah."

"You told him the truth?" Her hesitation told him all he needed to know. "Paige, I can't fucking believe you right now."

"I'm going to tell him today when he comes home from work."

"Good girl."

She could tell there was something on Shane's mind, something he wanted to say but wasn't saying. "Is everything okay?" she asked tentatively.

"Have you, uh...seen Marissa anywhere? Talked to her maybe, on the phone?"

"Not since yesterday," she said, yawning.

"Oh."

"Why, what's wrong?"

"We were supposed to go out last night, but she didn't come and she didn't call. I've been calling her since yesterday, but she's not picking up. I'm just worried."

"Have you tried her at work?"

He laughed. "I'm a creep but I don't even have that number saved in my phone."

"Here, I'll call her on three-way, all right? Hold on."
She pressed a button on her phone and then dialed in
Marissa's direct extension. She clicked back over to Shane.
"You there?" she asked as the phone started ringing.

"Yeah."

A moment later, Marissa's voice came on the line.
"Stevenson and Keates, this is Marissa, how may I help
you?"

"'Rissa, it's me," Paige said.

"And me," Shane said gruffly.

Marissa's tone remained pleasant, but there was an edge
behind it. "Oh, it's you, Paige...*and* you, Shane. What a
surprise."

"I thought we had something to do last night," Shane
said. "You didn't call or show up, so I was just
wondering...What the fuck?"

"So you had to call with Paige on the line?" Marissa
asked.

"I didn't have your work number."

"But Paige did."

"Yeah, she did."

Marissa snorted on the other line. "Since you and Paige
are so *close*, then she might as well listen in. You'd probably
tell her later on anyway. I don't think we should see each
other anymore, Shane."

"Excuse me?" he said. "I don't think I heard right."

"You heard right, Shane."

"You're fucking breaking up with me?" he shouted into
the phone.

Paige took the phone away from her ear, because
Shane's voice had pierced her ears. When she put the phone
to her ear again, Marissa and Shane were still arguing.
"'Rissa, stop yelling at Shane. You can't break up with him."

"Don't tell me what I can or can't do, bitch," Marissa
said heatedly.

Paige's eyes widened and her words got lost somewhere
in her throat.

"What the fuck are you calling Paige a bitch for?" Shane growled at Marissa. "Are you fucking dull?"

"Don't call me dull, you short-dicked bastard."

"What the fuck?" Shane shouted.

"Shane, don't call me again," Marissa said. "And Paige, don't call me again either."

"So you're through?" Shane asked her.

"Yeah, I'm fucking through," Marissa said in a low voice. "You and Paige are perfect for each other. Why the hell do you need me?"

Shane took a deep breath. "I don't know what the fuck you're talking about, Marissa. What are you talking about, me and Paige?"

"Didn't you read Paige's book, Shane? You told me you did."

"Yeah, I read it."

The color drained from Paige's face.

"If you read it, then you read the part about you and Paige," Marissa deduced. "You and Paige. Fucking. In college."

"Yeah," Shane prompted. "So?"

Marissa burst out laughing. "*So?*" she echoed.

"You're pissed about *that?*"

"What the fuck do you think?" Marissa asked him.

"But you two are best friends, so Paige would have told you about that," Shane said. "Tell her, Paige."

Paige cleared her throat. "I, umm…"

"You, umm, what, Paige?" Shane said sharply. "Tell Marissa that you told her about that."

"I didn't…tell her about that."

"Paige, stop fucking with me and tell Marissa that you told her about that."

"I can't tell her that," Paige whispered, tears starting in her eyes.

"What do you mean you can't tell her that, Paige?" he sounded livid. "You didn't tell her?"

"No, I didn't tell her."

"Paige, what the fuck!"

Marissa spoke, sounding very calm. "I'll let you two iron this out. In the meantime, I don't want either of you calling me." There was a click following her words.

Paige collapsed on the living room couch. "Oh, my God."

"'Oh my God' is right Paige, what the fuck were you thinking?"

"I...I..." Paige stammered.

"Shit, she never wants to talk to me again."

"I'm...I'm sorry."

"*Sorry?*" He could be heard slamming his fist into something. "You're *sorry*? The one woman I could see myself spending my life with just broke up with me because you didn't tell her something that you definitely should have told her."

He was right. Of course he was right. She didn't know why she hadn't told Marissa. After the fact, back in college, Paige had been ashamed of what has transpired between Shane and herself. As they grew older, Paige hadn't seen the point in bringing it up. That one decision was going to now cost her one, maybe two friendships.

"I can't believe this shit."

"I'm sorry, Shane. I'll fix it."

"You don't just 'fix' things with Marissa," he told her. "And you trying to fix things would probably just make them worse. I'll handle it."

"Shane, I-"

"I've got to go Paige. I'll talk to you later." Click.

She turned her phone off and set it on the coffee table with shaking hands. Her world as she knew it was crashing down. She stood and returned to the bedroom, where she collapsed on the bed and sank into a fitful sleep.

She didn't awaken until the front door slammed. She jerked to an upright position and sat staring at the bedroom door expectantly. Ethan filled the doorway moments later. He just stood there, looking at her.

She rose from the bed and went to wrap her arms around his neck. She noticed right away that he wasn't returning the embrace. "Did you have a bad day?" she asked him.

He paused before answering. "You could say that," he said finally.

"What's wrong?" she asked, her voice trembling because she knew what was wrong.

"My students were making comments to me in the halls today that I didn't understand," he said reaching up to pull her hands down from his neck. "I pulled one aside and asked him what the comment meant. He pulled your book from his backpack and told me I should read it."

Her cheeks grew hot and her heart beat so hard and fast that she thought it would burst right through her chest. "Oh?"

He rubbed his hands together. "Paige," he said slowly, "please tell me that you aren't a former student of mine."

She couldn't breathe. He knew. He knew everything. He'd read the book as soon as the kid had given it to him. Could this day possibly get *any* worse? "I..." Her arms dropped to her sides and she sighed in defeat. "I can't tell you that."

"Jesus fucking *Christ*, Paige!" he yelled, turning away from her and raising his hands to his hips. "How could you not tell me that?"

"How *could* I tell you that?" she returned, her voice rising.

"Something like that is important for me to know, Paige. I can't believe..." He stopped mid-sentence. "This is the secret you've been trying so hard to tell me?"

"Yeah."

"*God.*" He lifted his arms and locked his hands behind his head. "*God.* I don't believe this. I don't."

"I wanted to tell you but I thought that if I did, you would be too freaked out to date me."

He slanted a look down at her. "I may have been too freaked out to date you, yes. I've never...dated a former student. My God, I can't believe you...*God.*" He shook his head and looked away from her quickly. He couldn't even stand to look at her. Knowing the things he'd done to her and with her made him feel like a fucking pervert. There were stories about teachers being inappropriate with students and even though she was no longer a student of his, he still didn't feel right. Even if she was no longer his student, there were still memories he had of her when she *was* his student.

Of course he remembered Paige Turner. She had been an impressionable young girl, and the day she'd walked out of his classroom, he remembered that as well. She'd had an unfortunate time in high school and he'd tried his best to help her. How could he stay with her now, knowing who she'd been in high school? Knowing he had been her teacher?

He had to admit that he'd been touched that she'd thought so highly of him. He wanted to be a good teacher, wanted to be thought of as one as well. But...God, he'd made *love* to this woman. Even worse, he'd *fucked* this woman. He *loved* this woman. This wasn't something that he could just get over and accept. This...this was major. He now understood why it had taken her so long to try to tell him. Something like this could be the end of them. His students were making catcalls to him in the halls. This was serious. He would never live this down.

The both of them stood that way for several minutes. She looked at him, desperately wanting to explain, and he could barely stand the sight of her. "I...I don't even think I can talk about this right now," he said, looking down at the floor.

The tears came then. She sniffled and wiped at her nose. "But..."

"Paige," he said softly, shaking his head. Tears threatened to drop from his eyes also. "This is *very, very* serious."

"I know," she said quietly.

He dared to look at her and wished he hadn't. He hated to see her cry, hated to see her sad. "You put me in this position."

"I know."

"*God*, Paige. How could you *not* tell me?" He pounded a fist against the doorjamb.

She nearly jumped out of her skin. "If you don't want to see me anymore, I understand."

"I...I don't. I can't." The words came out of his mouth before he could even think about them, but it was how he felt. "You used to be my student. I don't feel it's appropriate. I...*God*."

She nodded. "Okay."

"I'm sorry, Paige, I just can't."

"Okay." She moved around him to walk out of the bedroom so she could collect her things from the living room.

He walked into the bedroom and shut the door. He pressed his back against the door and tried his best not to cry.

After she was dressed, she walked to the closed bedroom door and placed her hand on it. "Ethan?" she called.

He cleared his throat and wiped the tears from his eyes. "Yeah?"

She bit her lip, tasting her own tears. "I...I do."

He turned and put his hand on the door. "I...I do too. But...I can't."

"Bye, Ethan."

He swallowed before saying, "Bye, Paige."

No one was talking to Paige; no one except her fans. After finishing up her book tour, she holed herself up in the bedroom of her house and read her fan mail. She needed to believe that her book had done more good than harm. It had. She was certain it had. The letters she read from her fans moved her to tears. Then again, so did thinking about her situation.

Shane called her to give her updates about the book sales and let her know about the people who wished to interview her or talk to her. He was cold to her, though. He didn't want to talk about anything personal. They were no longer friends, it seemed; he was just her agent. It hurt her to know how much she'd hurt him, how much she'd hurt Marissa. Evelyn and Deana also weren't talking to her.

She became a recluse. She stayed in her house, called her parents to see how they were doing, called Samantha and Olivia to see how they were getting along with their mother, and that was it. That was the extent of her contact with the outside world.

She hadn't been worthy of Ethan. She hadn't deserved him. She understood that Ethan was having a hard time right now. She'd put him in a horrible position. He'd had to learn the truth from reading a book, and she hadn't encouraged him to read it; a student had. She was fortunate he hadn't shouted a string of profanity at her. Even at his most angry and frustrated, he was still considerate of her. And he still loved her.

Her self-esteem was hitting an all-time low. She'd hurt all of the people close to her. The one gift that God had given her, the one talent that she'd used to make people happy, had now hurt them and caused them pain and/or humiliation.

She made a few decisions while she was holed up in her house. Her first decision was that *Open Book* needed a sequel. *Open Book* was only half of her story. She had to set things straight with the second chapter. Her second decision was that she wasn't going to let Ethan go. It had taken her a decade to find him. She wasn't going to let him slip through her fingers. The third decision she made…was that she needed to pay her old high school a visit.

The first thing that she did was start up the computer in her home office and start typing. Her fingers flew across the keyboard as if they had a mind of their own. She didn't even have to think about what she was typing. Her story poured out, and it possessed a startling clarity that rivaled anything else she'd ever written in her life, with the mere exception of her poetry.

There were no distractions, only inspiration. She kept her radio on as she typed, her fingers keying to the rhythm of the music she listened to. She would pause only to sleep, use the bathroom, shower, and eat.

During the next few months, she completed the sequel to *Open Book* and two young adult fiction novels. She had a list of more than thirty novel ideas that she wanted to pursue.

Her name was still heavily circulated in the media. No one had seen anything like it...an author's name dominating the media for more than two months straight. There was talk of *Open Book* being transformed into a movie. Entertainment news anchors gave their opinions of who should play lead. Julia Roberts's name came up, and so did Renee Zelleweger's and Nikki Cox's. The messages that Shane left on her voice mail confirmed those rumors. Tons of entertainment executives wanted *Open Book* in the movie theaters and they were offering an obscene amount of money.

"What you should do is agree to the offer under the circumstances that you're creative director," Shane advised her. "That way, the movie is made the way you want it to be made. You could probably even get away with a bit of casting. Aside from that, I don't want you to forget that you promised to speak at your old high school. And I've been getting offers from Tina Walker of 'Primetime Live.' She wants an interview with you. I warned her you might not be up for it-"

"I'm up for it," she interrupted.

"You are?"

"Yeah. I've decided to go ahead and allow a few interviews."

"Oh...well all right, I'll set up a day and time, then. Get back to me."

"Will do."

She ended the conversation with Shane and continued typing. For the time being, she was all right with being in the doghouse with Shane, Marissa, Deana, and Evelyn. Spending time away from them was allowing her to get a lot of work done. In time, she would make other attempts at apologizing to them, but she wasn't going to break her neck telling them how sorry she was. If they weren't accepting her apologies, then she would stop making them and start doing things that would benefit her. *Starting...*

...With interviews and getting her name-and story-out there.

Chapter Eighteen

The pool hall was clouded with smoke. The small lamps hanging over the multi-colored pool tables offered minimal lighting. A Nine Inch Nails song pounded through the speakers of the joint.

Ethan stretched his torso across the pool table with his elbow bent at an angle. His brow was lined with beads of sweat, and after several moments, he finally made his shot.

Richard observed his friend with furrowed brows. "Your game is *awful* tonight, man."

"I know it is." Ethan rose to his full height and drew an arm across his forehead.

"Don't worry man, I understand."

"You understand?"

Richard scoffed as he scoped out the balls left on the table. "Of course. You recently let go of what is possibly the hottest woman to ever walk the streets of Beach Park. If I were in your shoes, my game would probably be a little off, too."

"That isn't why my game is off," Ethan insisted, twirling the pool cue between his fingers.

"Oh, it's why your game's off," Richard argued. "It's also why you've been moping around like your fucking dog died." He bent to take a shot and sent the four ball rolling into the right-hand corner pocket at the speed of light.

Ethan chalked his cue. "You know what? I'm not going to talk about this with you."

"Why not? Because I tell you shit like it is?"

"Because I'd rather not," Ethan corrected. "I'd rather just forget it ever happened, actually."

Richard shook his head in disappointment. "She was a hot number, I'll tell you that. God, what I'd do-"

"I *don't* want to hear what you'd do," Ethan broke in sharply. "She used to be my fucking student for Christ's sakes."

"You don't think teachers date former students?"

Ethan laughed dryly. "I don't want to hear this, Rich, I swear to God I don't."

"There used to be this girl," Richard started anyway, tapping the wide end of his pool cue on the floor. "She was my student maybe...I don't know...like seven, eight years ago. Saw her in a bar one night and she sat at the bar counter right next to me. Plopped her cute little ass on down. Told me that when she was in my class she used to have the hugest crush on me.

"I was shocked, because this girl was a classy one, you know? Very athletic one she was. She was quiet when she was in my class, but I'll tell you, that night we met in the bar...she wasn't quiet at all."

"That's sick, Rich," Ethan snapped.

"It's not sick, man," Richard objected. "If I'd done that to her while she was still in my class, still a teenager, then yeah, okay. That's sick. But she was a grown woman then. And I've seen how you were for this broad, this...*Paige*. That's her name, right?"

"That's her name."

"I've seen how you were for Paige. I could see the difference in you when you came to work. You were *happy*."

Ethan ran a hand through his hair, ruffling it. "How she made me feel doesn't matter. I'm not you. I can't date a former student. After I found out, when I looked at her...I saw that troubled teen, you know?"

"You have to look past that."

"I *can't*. If I could, I would, believe me. But I can't."

"Ethan, listen. You work five days a week, six when you're coaching. You go to school in the morning, stay after school for coaching, stay after school to talk about the kids with their problems, and on top of that you're going to be starting school again for your Master's soon. I mean...when are you supposed to find time to date? And where are you supposed to find the women *to* date when you're spending damn near sixty hours a week at work?" Richard missed his shot.

Ethan walked around the pool table, not really focusing on the three balls that were left. "That's no excuse."

"Do you love her?"

"Rich-"

"Do you?"

"Yeah. I do." Ethan bent at the waist and steadied the cue stick in his hand. "I really, really do."

"Love rules over all."

The cue stick shook slightly in Ethan's hand and he fought to steady it again. He wanted to believe that love ruled over all. He would give anything to feel comfortable being with Paige, but he didn't feel comfortable with her. He was disgusted with himself and all he'd done with her. "I don't know if that's true," he said, and took his shot. The seven ball disappeared into one of the side pockets.

"Do you know she's supposed to be speaking at the high school next week?"

Ethan raised his eyes to determine whether or not his friend was serious. "No, I didn't know that."

Rich looked very serious. "It's supposed to be an assembly. Don't you check your memos?"

Ethan rubbed his jaw and stood, stretching out his back. "I'll take that day off and have a sub come in."

"Are you fucking kidding me right now?"

"Rich, what do you expect from me?" Ethan asked tiredly. "I've been through some pretty amazing shit in the past two years, first with Diane, and now with this shit. Forgive me if I'm not all gung ho about seeing Paige at an assembly. I want to forget she exists. I'm going to take that day off."

"You are such a punk."

"I'm a punk now?"

"You're not facing this head-on. You're running away from it. This is bullshit. You love her and she loves you. As sappy as it is, I hate seeing you like this."

Ethan rolled his eyes and shook his head.

"Don't roll your eyes at me, Carson. Listen to me," Richard commanded in a voice that left no room for joking. "Do you know why I am the way I am? Forever a bachelor, not one for marriage and all that shit?"

"No, but I've always wondered," Ethan said, lining up another shot. If he made this one, all he had to do was sink the eight ball and the game was his.

Richard leaned his pool cue against the edge of the table and crossed his arms over his chest. "I was married, a long time ago."

"Yeah?" Ethan asked, as he sunk the shot. "I didn't know that."

"I never told you that," Richard said. "Yeah, I was once married. She was beautiful, too, and we always had fun with each other. No woman has ever been able to make me laugh as much as she did. I made her laugh, too. I loved her laugh, loved being able to make her laugh. It made me feel good, you know?" He thumbed his nose as he watched Ethan lining up the final shot.

Ethan nodded to let Richard know that he was listening.

"I mean...she's one woman I can say I loved. What she and I had ran *deep*, very deep. But...one day she was taken from me."

"She cheated on you?" Ethan asked, closing one eye and pulling his cue stick back.

"She died. Car pile up on I-94."

Ethan missed the shot. He stood and met the gaze of his friend. "I'm sorry, Rich."

"I had issues after that. I had issues with God, the 'why did you take her from me' type shit. I had issues with myself. And even you've witnessed that I had issues with women. I knew that no woman would ever compare to her, so I didn't really give them a chance. I mean, after you've tried on an Armani suit you don't really want to go back to the cheap shit, know what I mean?" He grabbed his pool cue and headed around the table. He bent at the waist and drew the cue back. "I don't know, I guess the point of me telling you this is that… Paige has to be quite a woman to make you happy. You seem to really have it for her. It's best to appreciate what you have while it's here. Because when it's not…" He shook his head and jerked the cue stick forward. The eight ball rolled into one of the corner pockets.

Ethan met his friend's eyes and nodded. "I get what you mean."

Richard walked up to him and stood for a few moments, looking at him. "Do you?"

Lori Turner had just finished taking a roast out of the oven when she heard the doorbell. She took off her oven mitts, tossed them on the counter, and smoothed her hands over the apron tied around her waist. She shuffled out of the kitchen and down the short hall to the front door. She opened the door and was greeted by a very good-looking man. *He must have the wrong house,* she thought to herself, smiling. "Hello."

The dark-haired man offered her a wide smile. "Hi. I was looking for Paige. Is she around?"

Lori's eyes widened, but she quickly got over her surprise. "Paige isn't in town."

"Oh, all right, I'm sorry for interrupting, then." Ethan turned and started down the porch steps. He thought of something and turned back to face her before she closed the door. "Is Sam around, do you know?"

"Sam?" she repeated. "I don't know, you'd have to check with her mom next door."

Confusion settled across his facial features. All he could manage to say was, "Next door?"

"Yes, Sam's our next door neighbor. You mean Samantha Waterford, right?"

He nodded. "Yeah. Um…thanks."

She started to say something, then halted herself.

"Yes?" he asked expectantly.

"Are you by any chance…the teacher?" she asked, pressing a hand to the doorjamb.

His brows arched. "I'm *a* teacher, yes," he replied.

She smiled. "Good."

He tilted his head to the side, observing the woman. Paige had told her about him. Under any other circumstances, that fact would have comforted him and made him smile.

"Do you have her cell phone number?" Paige's mother asked, eager to assist in connecting him to her daughter in any way possible.

"Yes, I have it."

"You should try calling...she always has that thing with her."

"I'll do that," he lied, and reiterated, "Thank you for all of your help."

Lori watched him walk down the steps with a soft smile on her face. No wonder her daughter was fascinated with the man. "Have a safe drive, you hear?"

He opened the door to his car and waved at her. Once he was seated in the driver side seat, his mind was racing. Samantha and Paige weren't blood sisters. They were neighbors. What the hell was going on? Had everything Paige told him been a lie? Had she *ever* told the truth?

He'd intended to talk to Paige, to work things out. He missed being with her and spending time with her. He missed having her in his arms, sitting beside him on the couch, or whispering dirty things in his ear. He missed *her*. He had intended to go against what he believed so that he could date her, but there were too many lies. There were *way* too many lies. There were so many lies that he couldn't discern the lies from the truths she'd told him.

No, he wasn't going to talk to Paige or try to work things out. And the day that she came to speak at Beach Park High? He was definitely going to take that day off.

Tina Walker was a medium-height, petite blonde who wore wired-rimmed spectacles for show. The lenses weren't prescription. Her vision was perfectly fine; she wore them because they made her look more intelligent. She was dressed smartly in a plum-purple dress suit and matching pumps. She was known in the industry for being a diva. She had to have Evian water in her dressing room at all times. If she walked into her room and saw that there weren't any bottles of Evian water in the small box fridge, chances were that someone would be fired that day.

Today was no different. She walked into work as cheerful as ever, but once she got into her dressing room and found that there was no Evian, she blew a gasket and burst into her assistant's office barking profanity and insults. "You can't even get *that* right?" she cried. "What the fuck is wrong with you? All I ask is that I have Evian water in my fucking fridge. Is that so fucking hard to grasp? Do you like working here? Do you? Too fucking bad, get the hell out, you're fired!"

She stormed into the crew's break room and sputtered. "Oh, I can't have Evian in my dressing room, but the fucking cameramen can get it in their breakroom? What the hell kind of show are we running here?" She grabbed as many bottles as she could hold and carried them to her dressing room. She kneeled and started stocking her personal fridge with Evian.

Outside of her dressing room, the crew whispered amongst themselves, warning each other that Tina was having a "bad day." Her "bad days" were notorious on set. When her fridge wasn't stocked, when her make-up artist was late, practically whenever anything went wrong, she went on a rampage. She was the star of the show; she could do that. When she snapped her fingers, she expected anyone close by to cater to her and give her what she wanted.

She walked out of her dressing room and pulled aside the nearest crew member. "Do you remember who I'm supposed to be interviewing today?"

"Um, the author…Paige Turner."

"Who the fuck is that?"

"She submitted her diary accidentally, her book is taking stores by storm…" the man read from his chart.

Tina sneered nastily. "Submitted accidentally, right...yeah, yeah, yeah I remember that one. If she submitted that diary accidentally, then my tits are natural. Do you know if she's in yet?"

"No, she hasn't shown yet."

"If she wants a fucking interview, she'd better hurry up," Tina said, starting down the corridor to get a look at the set. "We have to prep her before she goes on."

"Yes, Miss Tina."

One of the production assistants approached Tina. She was a short, plump girl with mousy brown hair and a headset perched on top of her head. "The author's here; she's in the green room. Should we send her to make-up?"

Tina rolled her eyes. "So she can look better than I do? Think again. Tell her to drag a brush through her hair or something and bring her to my dressing room so I can prep her for the questions."

Twenty minutes later, Paige and Tina were sitting in chairs that were angled towards each other. Paige picked up on Tina's bitch vibes almost as soon as she'd introduced herself. The woman had a superiority complex that was mind-boggling, because she wasn't exceptionally pretty. She wasn't exceptionally smart. She was a very average woman, all around. Paige wondered how Tina had even landed this gig.

"All right, all right," Tina called before the cameras snapped on. "Last week, Oprah's ratings topped mine. Let's make sure that it doesn't happen again, all right?" She turned to face Paige and tossed her hair over her shoulder.

As soon as the cameras started rolling, a plastic smile appeared on Tina's face. "Hello, everyone, it's another hour of 'Primetime Live.' My first guest is author, Paige Turner, who's been getting a lot of buzz recently. Paige...why don't you tell us a little about *Open Book*?"

"*Open Book* is a book that shouldn't even exist, honestly," Paige responded, glancing at the cameras only once in awhile. It was easier to focus on Tina than it was to focus on the cameras. "I wrote a romance novel that I was supposed to turn in. I had both that novel and my diary typed on disk. The wrong disk was turned in and my diary ended up being published."

"At what point did you realize that your diary was published?"

"The first stop on my book tour was in Florida. When I saw the book cover, I noticed that the cover didn't really fit the premise for the romance novel I'd written, so I read the back cover and I seriously came close to fainting."

"You had to be mortified!" Tina exclaimed, bringing a hand up to her chest.

Paige smiled and nodded. "It was...pretty humiliating. My agent told me that I could have the books pulled off of the shelves and that sounded very appealing to me."

"So...what convinced you to keep the books on the shelves?" Tina leaned closer to Paige and asked in a stage whisper, "Was it the money?"

"No, Tina, umm...actually it was a woman I met on one of my flights. She told me how much the book helped her, how she felt as if she wasn't alone in some of the things that she had gone through. At that point, I would have felt guilty taking the books off of the shelves, because I would have been doing that for selfish reasons."

Tina nodded, her eyes sliding to the teleprompter placed over Paige's shoulder. "So the content of *Open Book*...it's your diary. All of the skeletons you've had in your closet, everything wrong you've done. All of your *dirt* is in this book?" She lifted the book from the low, wooden table that stood between the two overstuffed, puke-pink chairs.

"Yeah...all of my dirt is definitely there," Paige said, dropping her eyes to her lap.

"Now...the tone in your voice changed," Tina said, sitting up a bit straighter and setting the book on the table. "Could that be because of the rumors flying around that you were recently in a relationship with the teacher you talk about in this book?"

Paige's mouth dropped open and her eyes widened. She turned towards the studio audience. Because there were microphones suspended several feet above their heads, their gasps were more defined. "I, um...you didn't prep me for that question," she said under her breath.

"I mean, Paige...the way I see it, we all know a lot of your dirt anyway, so what's the point in trying to keep anything concealed, right?" Tina's smile was sweet enough to cause cavities. She turned to her audience and asked, "We want all the juicy details, right?"

Her audience backed her up.

Paige grimaced and rubbed at the back of her neck. "That's a very sensitive topic."

"We have time," Tina said with mock-patience.

Paige uncomfortably shifted in her seat. "I, um..."

"You had a crush on your teacher when you were high school, isn't that correct?"

"I had great admiration for a particular teacher, yes," Paige clarified.

"We know how you felt. All we have to do is read the book," Tina said, grinning.

Paige indulged in a five-second fantasy of wiping the grin from Tina's face. "I developed feelings for him."

"And at *such* a young age." Tina clucked her tongue. "Now, recently, you and he were an item, weren't you?"

Paige squirmed again. "I really don't want to-"

"That's what the rumor mills are saying anyway," Tina surged on. "Word on the rumor mill is that you and this teacher became an item, but he didn't know that you used to be his student. He didn't even know that you were the renowned author, Paige Turner, did he?"

"Where did you get that information?" Paige demanded angrily.

"From reliable sources. Is the information correct?"

"I-It wasn't like...it was more like..."

"I also heard that he dumped you once he found out the truth, because he couldn't deal with dating a former student."

Paige stood from her seat. "This interview is over," she said through clenched teeth.

"So you'd rather let everyone get their information from the rumor mills?" Tina taunted, still seated in her chair. "You don't want the people to hear your version of the story?

"I..." Paige glanced at the audience again. Everyone was on the edge of their seats. They wanted to hear her story. She sighed and took her seat, folding her hands in her lap. "I, umm...I've made some mistakes in my life. Not telling him that I used to be his student was one of them. And yes, the rumors are correct. He did dump me after he found out the truth. I'm not angry or resentful for it...I deserved that."

"There you have it," Tina said, turning to face the audience. "You've gotten the story here first, on 'Primetime Live.' *Open Book* is in stores now. Go out, buy it, and thank God that your life isn't as horrific as Paige's."

"Yeah, yeah, yeah," Liza Johnson of L.A.N.Y. Entertainment said, "we all know what the book is about...what we want to know about is this teacher guy. So is there absolutely no chance of you two getting back together?"

After her interview with Liza Johnson was over, Paige had a new respect for celebrities. Everywhere they turned, there was a media enthusiast in their face asking questions and intruding on their personal lives. They took it in stride, or at least, they appeared to for the most part. She'd never seen a celebrity get as frazzled as she had the day before on Tina's show, but now she'd come to expect that same line of questioning from everyone who offered her an interview.

It didn't take long for Paige to realize that her book wasn't the only thing keeping her name in the press. It was also the scandal that had transpired between her and Ethan. Everyone wanted to know about the relationship between a teacher and his former student.

Broadcast journalists tackled the issue of how close was too close between a student and a teacher. A few talk show hosts jumped on the bandwagon, with segment titles such as "I'm Stuck Like a Leech On My Teach." A local evening news show took a poll: "Should the Teach Take Paige Back?" Eighty-eight percent of the viewers who voted said that, yes, the teacher should take Paige back.

Shane was bouncing off of the walls because of their success. *Open Book* was going to be made into a movie. No one had been cast yet, but he predicted that it would be a hit. "Just keep your name in the news, girl."

"I don't know if I can do that," Paige said. She was sitting on her living room couch with her feet propped up on the coffee table.

"What don't you know?" he asked her.

"All everyone wants to know about is Ethan and I," she said, "and I'm tired of talking about him. I'm sure that *he's* tired of me talking about him. His students see these broadcasts and they're going to keep bothering him with inappropriate comments. I'm putting him in a bad position with this."

"Talking about him is keeping people talking."

She took a deep breath and situated the phone so that it rested between her cheek and her shoulder. "I can't keep talking about him. I won't."

"All right, all right…we're fine just the way we are. We just have to find ways to get publicity, that's all."

The call waiting beep pulsed in her ear. "Hold on, Shane, I have a call on the other line."

"I'll just talk to you later, actually," he said, and hung up.

She clicked over to the other line. "Yeah?"

"Paige…got…come…something bad…Paige…"

"Who is this?" she asked, taking her feet off of the coffee table.

"My friend…Paige…oh my God…"

"Sam?" she asked into the phone. "Sam, slow down, I can only hear like, every other word you're saying."

Sam inhaled sharply and tried to calm down enough so that she could speak. "I'm…I'm sorry, Paige," she apologized. "My…my friend, Vanessa. She…she committed…she-she…" Her sobs started again, and she held the phone away from her mouth.

"Honey…" Paige spoke in a soothing voice, trying to calm the girl down. "Take a few moments to breathe. Then go ahead and tell me what's going on."

"My friend, Vanessa…but I don't understand, she wasn't sad. She didn't *seem* sad." Samantha took Paige's advice and took several deep breaths. "She was found this morning. She hung herself…in her family's garage."

Paige couldn't help the gasp that escaped from her lips. "Oh my God. *Sam.*"

"She was my best friend. How could she do this? She knew how torn up her mom would be, and they were close. She never talked to me about anything that would cause her to do this. Why would she do this?"

"Not everyone is vocal about the trauma they're going through," Paige said, her voice thick with emotion.

"She was so outgoing. She was more outgoing than I was. She was popular at school."

"Being popular isn't the same as being happy," Paige pointed out.

Sam's voice trembled as she said, "Paige, you have to come back to Beach Park. I know about you and Mr. Carson. I know what happened, everyone does actually, but…you have to. You have to." She started crying again.

"I'm going to, Sam."

"I know you're supposed to speak next Monday, but…you have to come before then."

Paige hesitated and closed her eyes. A single tear tracked down her cheek and she whispered, "I'm going to, Sam."

She took exactly ten minutes to pack. She showered and dressed in a plain black sweater and flared jeans. She pulled her hair up into a topknot and dragged her duffel bag downstairs to the front door. She wasn't looking forward to the nearly two hour drive to Beach Park in the drizzling rain that had started outside, but Sam needed her. Sam was distressed and chances were, a lot of Vanessa's other friends and family were also distraught.

Suicide was a very big issue for Paige, probably because at one point in her life, she'd considered suicide. She felt that she'd never gone through it because she was a coward. Now, as an adult, she was able to put her anxieties into perspective. What seemed so big and important to her then wasn't as important now.

Poor Vanessa, she thought to herself as she drove. She hadn't known the girl, didn't even know if she'd ever seen her, but it was tragic that such a young girl felt so estranged and pained that she would cause harm to herself to end it.

Two hours after she'd gotten into her car, she was pulling into her parents' driveway. Instead of going to the front door, though, she walked across the front yard and walked up the Waterfords' short driveway.

Samantha answered the door before Paige could even knock. "I heard you pull into Aunt Lori's driveway," she said, her voice shaking.

"Is your mom home?"

Sam shook her head. "She's at work. You can, umm...come in."

Olivia popped up beside her sister. "Paige!" she cried. "It's been forever since I've seen you!"

Paige bent at the waist to hug Olivia, who seemed to get taller every time Paige saw her. "Hi, Olivia, how have you been?"

"It's a bit soggy outside," Olivia said, pointing past Paige. "No one's happy when it's soggy outside."

"Soggy"... I have to use that in one of my books, Paige thought, smiling. She was glad that Olivia seemed unaffected by the tragedy going on. Children were fortunate in that respect. The inner workings of their minds bypassed registering trauma.

Samantha stepped aside so that Paige could enter the house. "Olivia, don't you want to finish your game?"

"I want to talk to Paige," Olivia said stubbornly, beaming up at Paige. "We haven't seen her in forever."

"We can talk in a few minutes, okay?" Paige said. "Sam and I have to talk about something right quick. Then, maybe I'll come in and play...whatever game you're playing."

"Okay," Olivia said, then skipped down the hall to her room.

Paige didn't know when she'd last been in this house. The basic layout to the house was very similar to her parents' house, but the interior decorating...was much different. It was much more modern than her mother's autumn-inspired living room. That was for sure.

Samantha took a deep breath and gestured to the gray couch, indicating that Paige should take a seat. Instead of seating herself, she paced around the room. "I didn't really think you'd come tonight," she admitted with a wry smile, "but I'm glad you did."

"You sounded very upset and you needed me," Paige said.

"Thank you so much, Paige."

"So one of your friends..."

"I found her," Samantha said, looking at some point over Paige's shoulder. She closed her eyes, then snapped them back open as if she'd seen something behind her eyelids that she'd rather not have seen. "There was a note...I didn't want to believe she'd done it, but the note was in her handwriting."

"What did the note say?" Paige asked softly.

"It said that she'd reached a point where she'd just become tired of living." Samantha hugged herself and closed her eyes again. A few moments later, she opened them and started pacing the living room. "I, umm...wow. Her parents hadn't seen it. I had to tell them. Her mom...her mom's heart broke right in front of my eyes. It was very..." She cleared her throat and closed her eyes again. "Very hard."

"It had to have been."

"She, umm...she was down to earth and sweet, you know?"

Paige didn't quite know what to say. She'd never had to comfort anyone who'd lost someone. "Come here, Sam," she said.

Samantha walked over to the couch, her sniffles becoming louder.

Paige opened her arms and Samantha fell into them, resting her head on Paige's shoulder. Paige smoothed down the girl's hair and whispered, "Shhhh, it's going to be okay."

Chapter Nineteen

The weekend moved very slowly. News of Vanessa Connelley's passing ebbed throughout the town. Samantha thought that it would be a good idea to start a support group for teenagers who were contemplating suicide and told Paige about her idea Sunday night over dinner. "My friend was obviously going through some things that she didn't feel she could talk to me about," she told Paige, "so I want to make sure that no one else at Beach Park High feels that way. Ever."

Paige admired the girl's strength. The loss of a friend had to be difficult enough to deal with; knowing that she'd taken her own life had to make it ten times harder to handle. Not only was Samantha handling it, she was also determined to prevent anyone else from feeling so alone that they'd take their own life. "I think that's a wonderful idea...you should pitch it to a counselor at the school tomorrow when you go back to school."

Samantha cleared the dinner plates from the table. "Well I wasn't planning on having a counselor head the project," she said slowly, walking over to the kitchen sink and carefully placing the dishes in them.

"It would be a good idea for a counselor to be in charge of something like that," Paige told her. "I think it's great that you want to do it yourself, but it would be best if someone who was licensed in the field of psychology was in charge."

"I wasn't planning on being in charge of it, either," Samantha said, turning her back to the sink to face Paige. "I was actually kind of thinking that maybe you would consider it."

Paige nearly spit out her orange juice. "Are you crazy?"

"I read your book, Paige," the younger girl stated. "You've thought about suicide before."

Paige pursed her lips and set her glass on the table. Wiping her hands off on a napkin, she said, "I couldn't run something that big, something that major, Sam."

"I think you could," Sam protested, returning to the table and sitting down. "Vanessa was one of the only kids I know who didn't get your book. She said that she wasn't much of a reader. I think that…if she *had* bought your book, she might still be alive today."

Paige closed her eyes and turned her head slightly. Her heart twisted at Samantha's words. "I don't know about that, Sam."

"I do," Samantha said emphatically, "and I want you to consider this."

Paige clasped her hands together and rested her elbows on the table. "Sam…I'm not licensed to do something like that. I don't know if I'd have the time to do something like that. There are a lot of factors involved with something like that."

"Like the fact that you'd have to see Mr. Carson almost every day?" Samantha challenged smartly, crossing her arms over her chest.

Paige's heart twisted again and she turned to look out of the kitchen window. "Sam…"

"Just think about it," Samantha urged, covering Paige's hands with her own.

"I will," Paige promised.

Olivia skipped into the room, oblivious to the serious matters that Paige and Samantha were discussing. The previous night, she'd delved into a lengthy oration narrating what caused the "breakup" between Jeremy and herself. "I just don't feel like I should be tied down right now," she'd said in the voice of an eleven year old, but the tone of a twenty-five year old woman who was tired of the dating world. "He and I weren't on the same path."

Paige had raised her brows in surprise. "Really?" she'd asked the little girl.

"He was too clingy," Olivia had said with a shudder of her shoulders. "I'm just a kid...I don't even think I need a boyfriend right now."

Now, Olivia walked straight to the refrigerator and started pulling out leftovers from the meal they'd all just had. "Don't mind me," she said over her shoulder.

"I should be getting home...to my parent's house," Paige said, rising from her seat. "Do you need any help with the dishes or anything?"

Samantha shook her head. "No, I'll get 'em. Just don't forget to think about... what we talked about."

"I'll think about it," Paige vowed. She grabbed her leather coat from the back of the chair and drew it across her shoulders. "You guys don't get to bed too late."

"Mom's going to be home in like twenty minutes," Olivia said, holding a casserole dish that was wider than she was. "She called a few minutes ago."

"Okay...if you need anything, you know my mom's number," Paige told them before leaving. The vow she'd made to Samantha hadn't been empty. She really did consider the proposal the teenager had given her.

Truthfully, she'd love to talk to adolescents about their problems and concerns. In the past few years, she'd discovered in herself a love for kids she didn't even know she had before returning to her hometown. She loved being around Samantha and Olivia. She loved being there for them; that was why she'd had no trouble making the two hour drive to Beach Park.

Samantha had been wise in her line of thinking. She'd known the true reason why Paige wanted to turn down the offer. There was no way Paige could work in the same building as Ethan while they were on the terms that they were on. There would be a tug at her heart every time she saw him. It wasn't an environment that she wanted to willingly put herself in.   And yet...Samantha's idea to start a support group was such an innovative, creative one. It was *needed*, especially now.

She sighed as she opened the door to her parents' house. *They should really lock their doors,* she thought to herself as she walked in and closed the door behind her. She'd spoken with her mother the previous day. She knew that Ethan had dropped by. Her mother had also told her that he was "somehow" under the impression that Paige and Samantha were sisters.

"It's probably because you and Sam look like you *could* be sisters," her mother had said with a dismissive wave of her hand. "Anyway, I set him straight on that. He left right after that."

I'm sure he did, Paige had thought to herself. He still hadn't known that she and Sam weren't sisters, so chances were he was angry all over again. She wondered why he'd even bothered to try to find her at her parents' house. What had he wanted to talk to her about? Why hadn't he just tried to call her cell phone?

She didn't spend too much time pondering about all of that. Her best bet was forgetting that he even existed. Monday morning she was supposed to be speaking to approximately one thousand high school students. The principal of the school hadn't been specific as to what she should speak about, but he had implied that he meant to have the assembly in the school's gymnasium.

Paige refused to speak in the gymnasium. "You can't fit all of the students in the school in the gym," she said. "I'd have to speak at least twice, and I don't want that. I want to make the speech once. I think it would work out much better to host the assembly outside."

The principal agreed to those terms and quickly set to overseeing matters to make sure it would be possible to host an assembly outside of the gymnasium. He decided to take advantage of the PA system that was used for school sport events. By the time everything was set up, she had five hours before she had to take a stage and speak to a thousand high school students. She still hadn't prepared a speech. *Maybe in five hours, I'll have pulled a miracle out of my ass,* she thought to herself...but she doubted it.

Ethan had planned on taking this day off. As of last Friday, he was supposed to have this Monday off. After hearing about Vanessa Connelley's suicide, he'd shown up to work early and cancelled his day off request. His students were going to need him today. One of their classmates voluntarily ended her life. He wanted to be there in case any of his students wanted to talk about how they were feeling.

As soon as the school day for him started, he realized that it was *all* students wanted to talk about. Several girls in his class started crying out of the blue, which in turn led to class discussions about teenage suicide.

Some of the students couldn't fathom why someone would want to kill themselves. Other students wanted to confess that they'd thought about suicide before.

A football jock that always sat at the back of the class and rarely spoke in class chose to speak now. "I've thought about it before," he said, not appearing to be affected when a few of his classmates twisted around in their seats to eyeball him. "Sure I have. Sometimes you're so pressured, you know? People expect you to be the perfect athlete. If you have an off game, they get on you. If you have nothing but good games, you've got colleges baiting you to come to their school. When your grades start slipping, you're pressured from the teachers, your parents. I remember once I told my dad I wanted to quit football. He gave me a black eye for that. Sure, I've thought about it at one time or another. If you think hard enough, I think most of us have."

Ethan was stunned into silence. "Well, I'm glad you didn't act on it, Brian," he said when he found his voice. His throat was constricted with emotion.

For the remainder of the morning, he talked to his students about teenage suicides in America. He dodged religious discussions about heaven and hell that the kids tried to lead him into. Teachers weren't encouraged to talk about religion in schools and he explained that to them. They were disappointed, but they understood.

Lunch came around and Ethan sat in the teacher's lounge with a hand shaded over his eyes. This was going to be a long and unbearable week. He'd known Vanessa. She wasn't a student of his this semester, but she had been a student of his last year. He remembered passing her in the hallways many times this semester. She always wore a smile on her face; she hadn't been an unpleasant or moody girl, not outwardly, anyway.

So many of his students wanted to know why she'd done it, why she'd killed herself...what was the trigger? He couldn't answer that question; he didn't know her that well. It *was* a question that ran through his mind, though. Strange, how it took someone passing away for people to realize that life was short.

Richard sauntered into the lounge dressed in one of his trademark jogging suits. He held a thermos filled with what was probably his usual protein shake. "I *just* passed by your little girlfriend," he remarked as he claimed a seat across from Ethan.

"What little girlfriend?"

"The writer."

"She's here? Now?" Ethan's back straightened slightly and he looked towards the door Richard had just walked through.

Richard held up both hands. "Calm down, boy, calm down. Yes, she's here, walking around the halls and reminiscing probably."

"I almost forgot she was speaking today."

Richard rolled his eyes. "I'm sure." He perked up slightly. "The good news is that she remembered who I was. So, if you're through with her, I was wondering if maybe-"

"Don't even think about it." The smile on Ethan's lips was lighthearted, but the look in his eyes wasn't.

Richard shrugged his shoulders. "I figured as much."

"Have you had to talk about teenage suicide today with your kids?" Ethan asked, needing a change of topic.

"That's *all* I've talked about today," Richard answered, taking a huge gulp of his shake. "I had a fitness test scheduled for today but I cancelled it out of consideration for the students. Did you know the girl?"

Ethan leaned back in his chair. "Yeah, I did. She was in one of my classes."

"How are you holding up?"

"It's…it's definitely hard. She was a good kid, you know? I'm constantly rewinding my mind, trying to remember if there was any point where it seemed like she might be dealing with some type of extreme depression, but she just seemed like a good, honest kid." Ethan shook his head. "I don't know."

Richard took a swig of his shake. "The assembly is supposed to take place after next period. I can't *wait* to hear this speech." He paused, thought about what he'd said, and decided to make a revision. "I can't wait to see your face when *you* hear this speech."

After the principal of the high school introduced her, Paige walked onto the stage clasping her speech in her hands. The words had seemed to pour from her pen. She didn't know if her hand would ever stop writing. There was so much that she wanted to say to these kids; there was so much that was on her mind.

When she stepped on stage and looked at nearly the entire body of Beach Park High school, she grew a bit apprehensive. All eyes were focused on her, waiting for her to open her mouth and speak. Everyone wanted to know what she was going to say.

She cleared her throat and looked down at the papers she'd set on the podium before her. Her script stared back at her, a bunch of elongated lines and loops. She looked up at the crowd of students again, and in one single fluid motion, she swept the pages off of the podium. They fluttered in the air with a soft rustling sound. The wind carried some of the papers yards away from the stage.

A few students hooted at this act of rebellion; some hollered.

"I had a speech written," she said, leaning forward to speak into the microphone, "because I'm not that good of a speaker. I'm about ten times better at writing than I am at public speaking." She smoothed down the blazer to her black and white pinstriped pantsuit. She glanced around at the individual faces of the audience. Almost instantaneously, she spotted Ethan sitting with a group of teachers.

He was staring back at her with an expressionless face.

She quickly took her eyes off of him and cleared her throat again. "I had a speech prepared, but I don't think I'm going to make that particular speech. Now that I think about it, it was corny, anyway. It was a bunch of the cliché bull you hear about how if you set your mind to it, you can do anything, go anywhere, be anyone. You guys are in high school, though. You should know all of that already. You shouldn't have to hear that from me.

"Another reason I'm not going to make that speech is because in it, I didn't write anything about the events that have taken place over the weekend. That's what I really want to talk to you about, because that's a huge issue.

"I hate to even have to say this word, but so everyone understands what I'm talking about, I have to. Umm...all right...suicide." She looked out over the sea of faces. "I'm sure a lot of us have thought about it at one time or another. Pressures are coming at you from every angle and you don't know how to handle it, or you have a lot of troubles in your life and you're tired of feeling sad. You're tired of the hurt.

"From what I hear, Vanessa was an amazing girl. She was constantly on the honor roll and she was on the girls' volleyball team. She had a lot of friends. From what I hear, if you were walking down the halls and saw her, you wouldn't single her out as someone who was troubled or depressed. She always smiled, always joked around, and loved making people laugh. This was a girl who should be alive right now. She should be one of the people in this audience right now.

"Why isn't she? I'm sure a lot of you are wondering why she did it. I'm sure a lot of you are wondering what was so major that she had to take her life over it. That's not a question I'm able to answer for you. The truth is…" Her voice broke and she turned her head to cough into her hand. "The truth is, I can't help Vanessa. She's not here and I can't bring her back. None of us can bring her back.

"But what I can do is try to prevent it from happening again. What I'm here to tell you is that there are people you can talk to if you're so depressed that you're contemplating suicide. It may seem like no one understands you. It might seem like you're alone, but you're not. Your parents understand more than you know. They may be your parents now, but at one time they were teenagers just like you. You don't feel you can talk to your parents because you don't get along that well with them? You have a group of counselors whose purpose is to be there for you. You have your teachers. You have your friends.

"A big reason why people don't talk about their problems is because they think that people are going to judge them. They think their friends are going to call them crazy. If they're your friends-I mean *really* your friends-they'll listen.

"I want to see a show of hands from people who have thought about suicide. Go ahead, put 'em up."

Slowly a fraction of the crowd raised their hands into the air. About a third of the students' hands were raised. The students not raising their hands looked around to see who was raising their hands. More hands lifted into the air a bit timidly.

"Don't be shy. No one's going to judge you here," Paige said, plucking the microphone from its stand and making her way down from the stage so that she was standing on the school's outdoor track. She approached the first row of stadium seats. "I'm talking about teachers, too. This isn't just about the students today. This is about everyone. Everyone who is out here right now, who thought about suicide…even if it was only for a split second, even if you didn't act on the thought, everyone who just thought about it, I want their hands up in the air now."

The row of teachers looked at each other and a few of them raised their hands. A few more student hands elevated above their heads. More than half of the audience (closer to two-thirds of the audience) had their hands raised. Paige nodded her head, making her way up one of the aisles.

"Now, you see, that's what I thought," she said, holding the microphone firmly in her hand. "I want you all to look around you at the people who have their hands in the air. I want you to look around at the people who are raising their hands. When you're feeling really down and really depressed... when you feel really alone and don't think that there's anyone who is thinking what you're thinking or feeling what you're feeling, I want you to think about the people who are raising their hands right now.

"These are the people you go to and talk to when you feel that way. These are the people who are going to help you through the tough times. I don't want to have to drive up to Beach Park again because someone tells me that another kid has committed suicide. I don't. There's no excuse for anyone to do that. There's no excuse for anyone to take their own life. You can't use the excuse that you're alone anymore. Look around. You're not alone." She stood in the middle of an aisle, meeting the eyes of the people who were sitting near her. When she was sure that her point was made, she turned on her heel and waved a commanding hand in the air. She started back towards the stage. "You may lower your hands, now."

There was a small murmur in the crowd. The murmur grew louder until Paige turned around to face them. "What?" she asked into the microphone. "What is everyone saying?"

One of the teenagers hesitantly raised a hand into the air.

Paige walked over to her and covered the microphone with her hand. "What is everyone talking about, what is everyone saying?"

"We know why Vanessa did it," the girl, who was as tall as Paige, said. She had straight, jet-black hair and deep brown eyes.

"You do?" Paige's hand remained over the microphone so that their discussion wasn't blasted over the speakers.

"She and her boyfriend broke up," the girl informed her. "He dumped her the night before because he wanted to go out with someone else."

Paige was taken aback. "Oh?" She placed a hand on the girl's shoulder. "Thank you for that." She turned and headed back up to the stage.

The murmuring died down.

"So," Paige said, setting the microphone back in its stand. "I have gotten word why Vanessa did what she did. Word is that she did what she did because her boyfriend dumped her.

"Let me tell you all something right now. In high school, chances are you start dating. You date someone, and depending on your personality, you might fantasize that this is the guy or girl you're going to marry and be with for the rest of your natural lives.

"Your romantic relationships in high school shouldn't be so intense that you're planning weddings and making a list of names for kids you don't even have yet. When you're a kid, you should enjoy being a kid. Dating in high school is for companionship. You date a guy or girl because they're fun to be around and they make you laugh all the time, not because you're in a rush to be an adult.

"I mean…okay, I'm sorry I'm bouncing all over the place here and I apologize if it sounds like I'm lecturing you guys. I don't mean for this to sound like a lecture. There's just so much I want to say to you all." She paused and looked down at the top of the podium. She had a feeling that she was about to do something incredibly stupid. The words she and Samantha had exchanged over the weekend were rushing at her and tumbling around in her head. "Could I call Principal Greer up here, please?"

The principal, seated in the front row, pointed at herself. She clearly hadn't been expecting to get called up to the stage. She smoothed down the lapels of her suit jacket and stood from her seat. She hopped up the few steps and joined Paige on the stage.

Paige turned away from the audience to look down at the middle-aged principal with skin the color of smooth caramel. "Samantha Waterford, a close friend of mine, had what I thought was an amazing idea. I know that since Vanessa...passed, the school started a support group, but Samantha's idea was to keep the support group all-year round so that if someone was feeling low and depressed, they could meet up and talk about it instead of keeping it bottled in."

Principal Greer smiled. She was a very nice looking woman with a cheerful face and expressive dark eyes. She gave her neat chignon a pat and said into the microphone, "I commend Samantha for coming up with that idea. I think we could definitely set something up."

"Her idea was also to...have me host that support group," Paige added, still looking at the principal to gauge her reaction.

Some of the students started cheering and applauding, but Principal Greer's expression was one of surprise. "I wouldn't expect you to take so much time out of your schedule, Paige. You write books, and...you don't even live in Beach Park anymore, do you?"

"The great thing about writing is you can do it anywhere," Paige said, quoting her father. "If you'd have me, I would be honored to work with the kids."

Principal Greer was at a loss for words. "We'd...we'd be ecstatic to have you."

The cheering was abrupt and explosive.

Okay, then, Paige thought to herself as she waved to the kids. *It's definitely about to get interesting.*

"...And we are told that there are no main suspects in that case," a Channel 6 news reporter was saying. "In other, more inspiring news, Paige Turner, the author known nationwide for accidentally submitting her diary to be published, is making quite a chivalrous move. She's heading a project at a north suburban high school, Beach Park High, a support group for adolescents attending the school.

"The support group will convene at Beach Park High School, but a spokesman for the school says that anyone is welcome. The idea for the group was conceived after a BPH junior committed suicide last week, and Paige Turner has volunteered to take part. For further information on that support group, you can call the number at the bottom of the screen."

Shane clicked off the television with one push of a button. "Good for you, Paige," he told himself.

He heard a distant knocking sound and stood. He walked around his desk, out of his home office, and down a short hall to the front door. The knocking persisted. "I'm coming, I'm coming, keep your panties on!" he shouted and pulled the door open.

Standing before him was Marissa, her loose, curly dark hair sprinkled with raindrops. Her bottom lip trembled, if not from sadness or nervousness, then from the cold. "Hi," she greeted simply.

His eyes softened as soon as he saw her and his hand gripped the doorknob a bit tighter. "Hi," he returned, stepping aside so she could enter. "I, umm…I wasn't really expecting you."

"I know," she said as she brushed past him with her head held high. She removed a black, knee-length trench coat from her shoulders and slung it over her arm.

He wanted to snatch her up while he had the chance. He wanted to pull her into his arms and never let go. His fingers were actually tingling; even they longed to touch her smooth, brown skin. He thumbed his nose and closed the door, standing for a few moments with his back to her. He was afraid that if he turned around and looked at her again, he'd start crying and begging.

She stood staring at his back. When she couldn't stand it anymore, she dropped her eyes to the floor. "I've been…a bit hard on you."

He resisted the urge to do a few back flips right there in his foyer. "A bit hard on me?" he asked instead.

"I didn't really know what to do or say," she said defensively. "I was…in shock. Completely in shock. I kind of felt like I was taking Paige's leftovers."

He opened the front door again. "If you're done stomping on my ego, I have work that has to get done."

She closed the distance between them. "What I meant to say was…I felt like that then. After that, I was going crazy because I'd gotten so used to being around you or having you call me. It was hard…living without you."

His lips parted. The desire to hold her close to him was still there. "Ditto."

She laughed and took a step closer to him. They were standing so close that his arm was getting wet from her rain-soaked jacket. "Don't you have more than that to say to me?" she asked him, tilting her face so that she could look up into his eyes.

"It was hard being without you, too," he said after a few moments of hesitation. "I ummm…now isn't the best time."

Her brows arched in sheer astonishment. "It's not?"

"My work is piled sky high right now."

"No," she said knowingly, backing up past his home office and towards the staircase. "This isn't the Shane I know. The Shane that I know would have already had me undressed and upstairs in his bedroom."

His eyes drifted heavenward.

She turned her head and peered over her shoulder. Without a word, she started up the stairs.

"Marissa," he called, moving towards her.

"What?" she answered over her shoulder, still proceeding up the steps.

"Don't."

Her steps slowed, but they didn't stop. Not until she reached the top of the staircase. She turned right and pushed open his bedroom door. "A naked woman sleeping in your bed," she mused to herself, closing the bedroom door and offering Shane the frostiest stare that she could muster. "Now that's the Shane that I know."

She made as if to walk past him and storm down the stairs, but he wouldn't let her. He stood in her way and didn't back down. "I didn't think you'd ever want to be with me again."

"I don't want to hear your excuses," she snapped. "Move out of my way."

"She's nothing to me. I just met her a few nights ago."

"You say that as if that's a good thing, Shane. Move the fuck out of my way." Again, she attempted to squirm past him, but he was a muscled barricade that was blocking off the top step.

He muttered something inaudible under his breath and stepped aside.

Marissa fled down the stairs, holding back a flood of tears. She yanked her coat on and pulled the door open wide.

"Wait, Marissa." He was slowly walking down the stairs with a hand extended.

She stopped but didn't turn around.

"I just want you to know...that I love you."

Her hand still on the door's edge, she told him, "You should have thought about before you brought that bitch into your house."

He watched her leave with a pain-stricken expression on his face. His heart felt like there was a stone attached to it, weighing it down. He pressed his back to the foyer wall and closed his eyes. His baby had left him again...and this time, it wasn't Paige's fault; it was his.

Chapter Twenty

It was even more difficult than Ethan had imagined it would be, passing Paige in the halls and occupying the same building that she was. She didn't even work full days, but as soon as she entered the building he could feel her. Also adding to the awkwardness was the fact that most of his students and fellow faculty knew about his involvement with her. A lot of them wanted him to take Paige back, and weren't afraid to voice that opinion to him.

He had to admit that he'd been impressed by her speech and floored by the announcement that she wished to lead a support group for adolescents. It was an idea that he'd been mulling over himself. He knew that she didn't live in Beach Park, so for her to lead the group, she'd had to move. That was something else that had amazed him. She wanted to be a part of this project so much that she would relocate just to contribute to it.

The support group's sessions were held in the school's library after school. Against his better judgment, he'd concealed himself between two rows of books and listened to what everyone, including Paige, had to say. He'd first been surprised by how many students had shown up to the group. More than fifty students were grouped around in a large circle in the middle of the library. Tables had been moved and chairs had been arranged to accommodate all of them.

He'd also been amazed by how open the kids were with Paige and the rest of the group. No one seemed to be holding back their thoughts; they spoke openly. The faces of the students were familiar to Ethan, but not the tales they were telling. The topics that were spoken about that day were vast, spanning from abuse in the family to molestation and rape. Paige was calm, cool, and collected no matter the topic that arose. If he hadn't known her, he might have mistaken her for a licensed psychologist.

He could only risk an occasional glance at her, but his heart melted every time he did chance a look at her. She'd curled her hair into ringlets, and they cascaded down her back. She sat with her chin cupped in her hand, intensely listening to whoever was speaking. Just watching her made his heart flutter.

He summoned a mental picture of Paige when she was just seventeen and compared it to what he was seeing now. To say she'd changed would have been an extreme understatement. She looked nothing like the angst-ridden teenager she'd been when she had attended BPH. Her hair was thicker, her eyes were brighter, and her lips were fuller. Her complexion was healthier and she carried herself differently. She'd done a complete one hundred eighty-degree turn from her high school years. For that, he was proud of her. For hosting this support group, he was proud of her.

He remembered watching her walking on stage last Monday. When she'd started speaking, he could tell that she was nervous, but it only took her a few moments to get comfortable speaking. Once she'd gotten comfortable, she'd commanded the stage and had the kids eating out of her palm...

...Just as they were now. He sighed and shook his head. He had to get her out of his thoughts. He had to stop thinking about her. He definitely had to stop coming to these group sessions and spying on her. He felt like a damned stalker. There was no chance for her and him. Little more than a decade ago, he had been her teacher; now, even though he wasn't *her* teacher, he still taught at the same school. The parents of his students would freak if he got back together with her. They would wonder how he behaved around their daughters, if they weren't wondering that already. That was the last thing he wanted. He drew the line when it came to his career. He didn't let anything interfere with that. Unfortunately, that included Paige.

Teenagers Against Teenage Suicide (T.A.T.S.) was under way. Paige had completely immersed herself in this project and it was showing incredible progress. During their first meeting, a lot of the kids had brilliant ideas for fundraisers and ways to get their message out. The kids were the ones to come up with the support group's name. Along with that, they suggested that they hand out temporary tattoos (tats), since their group name's abbreviation was T.A.T.S.

For some reason, Paige hadn't expected the group to be this successful. She'd expected that at the first meeting there would be five, maybe ten students who arrived, but more than fifty students showed up. Not only did a lot of them show up; a lot of them were willing to talk about very personal issues. They weren't afraid of being judged by their peers.

The students claimed that they felt safe talking about their problems because of Paige's speech. When she'd had people raise their hands, it made a lot of the kids feel as if they weren't alone. It made them feel as if there were people who felt the same way they did, in one way or another. That had been the purpose of the exercise; Paige was glad that it had worked.

The principal was so enthusiastic about the group's progress over the next several weeks that she offered Paige a permanent, full-time position as a school counselor.

"I'm sorry," Paige apologized, "but I don't have the credentials or the degree to take a position like that."

"I've sat in a few of your meetings," Principal Greer stated, "and I don't think *you* need the credentials *or* the degree. You've got enough experience to cover for both, I think."

"I wouldn't feel right accepting that position," Paige said honestly.

Principal Greer folded her hands on the top of her desk. "I'm going to be honest with you, Paige," she said slowly.

"We're in need of a guidance counselor. I've seen how you are with the kids. You're amazing. The things they talk about, and in an open space…it's very refreshing. Usually, everyone keeps everything to themselves and holds it in for so long that it takes a mental and physical toll on them. You and Samantha are preventing that. You're *great* with kids."

"Thank you Principal Greer," the young author said, tucking her hair behind both ears.

"I'm not demanding that you give me an answer now," the principal told her. "I just want you to think about it, at least."

Paige promised to consider it, but she pretty much already had her answer. She was a novelist, not a counselor. She had so many issues going on that *she* probably required the assistance of a therapist of some sort. How could she guide others when she could use a little bit of guidance herself?

The devil's advocate in her told her that she could do a lot of good working as a counselor. Talking to the students in the T.A.T.S. meetings was nearly the same thing as being a guidance counselor. The only difference was that she'd be working during daytime hours…which meant seeing more of Ethan, but she wouldn't think of that.

She'd seen him several times already and he hadn't made any effort to talk to her. He didn't even greet her when he passed by. He merely pretended as if he hadn't seen her at all and continued on his way. It was a bit unnerving. Her heart broke every time she saw him.

Open Book was still selling well in the stores. There were several other schools that wanted Paige to stop by and speak for them. Her career at the moment was straight through the roof. For her career to take off the way it had, though, she'd had to sacrifice three wonderful friends. Deana, Marissa, and Evelyn still weren't talking to her. She didn't know if they ever *would* talk to her again. She would like to continue being friends with the three of them, but if they didn't forgive her, she had enough on her plate to occupy her time.

She was currently trying to sell the house she owned in Farmington Heights and searching for a new home in Beach Park. It was the middle of winter and snow frosted the ground; she couldn't have picked a more difficult time to start looking for a house. The realtor she spoke with explained that houses were more often sold and bought in the spring and early summer.

"No one wants to lug all of their belongings in weather like this," the squeaky-voiced man informed her over the phone. "It would be a nightmare."

She considered putting all of her large possessions in storage and temporarily living in a hotel. It was quite a serious consideration. What held her back from taking action was spotting a house on the way to the high school.

Road construction had prevented her from taking the normal route to the school, so she'd had to take a few more twists and turns than usual. And there it was…one of the most beautiful houses she'd ever seen in the northern suburbs of Chicago. The house wasn't that magnificent compared to the house she currently lived in; it was actually quite simple, a white two-story with a sprawling yard, stretching driveway and three-car garage. She wouldn't value the house at more than three hundred and fifty thousand dollars, about half of what she'd paid for the house in Farmington Heights.

Funny how you always find what you want nearly as soon as you stop looking, she thought to herself, parking in front of the house and stepping out of her car. There was a For Sale sign staked in the ground at the edge of the property, facing the street. Below the words For Sale was a phone number to call for inquiries. She ducked back into her car, seeking a pen and paper. She hastily noted down the number, got back in her car, and continued on to the high school.

It was three o' clock in the afternoon, so as she was pulling into the parking lot, several cars and a line of school buses were pulling out. As students were getting into their parents' cars, they would tell their mother or father to look at the lady with her dark red hair pulled back in a single French braid. See her? That was Paige Turner, the novelist who accidentally got her diary published.

The mother or father would then hop out of the car and ask for an autograph or commend her for hosting T.A.T.S. It was a part of Paige's afternoon ritual, now. She would stand and talk to a circle of parents for fifteen minutes before actually walking into the school and heading towards the library. She would patiently talk to them and tell them how honored she was to talk to their children and listen to them.

A little more than ten years ago she would have gone to extremes to receive some of the attention she was receiving now. Her book had managed to stay at the top of the best-seller's list for more than two months. People who weren't even avid readers bought her book and related to it. She should have been on cloud nine with all of her success. She should be pleased that she was helping so many people.

And yet…there was an emptiness that dwelled within her. She'd loved and lost. She'd been surrounded by love, encompassed by it, and bathed in it, and because of her actions, love left her. Day to day she hoped that Ethan would approach her and tell her that he'd made a mistake and that he wanted to be with her. At night, she dreamed that he would knock on her door and ask to be let in.

That didn't happen. He continued to pass her without acknowledging her. It was out of character for him to pass by someone without saying hello or tipping his head towards them, so she knew that it was a conscious decision that he was making. He was choosing not to acknowledge her and knowing that hurt her.

She walked into the library and shed her black, knee-length coat. "Hi," she said in greeting to the children seated in an incomplete circle. She grabbed a chair from the closest table and closed the circle by placing her chair in an empty spot between two students. "I'm sorry I'm late. Traffic was a nightmare."

"It's okay," a petite blonde senior assured. Her name was Bianca Townsend. She'd once been the most popular girl in school. She'd once looked down her nose at everyone who dared to speak to her. Several of the smartest boys in school had volunteered to do her homework for her and tutor her. All of that had changed when her boyfriend dumped her for her best friend and then proceeded to spread word that she'd lost her virginity to him. He'd told his friends that she was an animal in bed.

"Don't let girls tell you that they don't want it just as bad as we do," her ex-boyfriend would be quoted in saying. "Bianca Townsend blows that theory straight out of the water!"

She'd gotten so depressed after finding this out that she locked herself up in her room every night and shut out the world. Her so-called friends wanted nothing else to do with her, since she was no longer Beach Park High's princess. Her image had been tainted.

She'd been in the middle of telling her story when Paige had entered. "I felt like I was no longer important," she told them with her head hung low. "I felt like no one liked me anymore, that for me to be liked, I had to be on top. I had to be popular. My own friends were talking about me behind my back...it was horrible. The most horrible thing was that I had no one I could talk to about it. I was holding it in and trying to deal with it by myself. I was driving myself crazy thinking about what people were saying about me." Tears had started cascading down her cheeks and she had to swipe them away with the backs of her hands.

There wasn't a person in the circle who hadn't heard about Bianca's fall from grace, but no one had heard her side to the story. They watched in amazement, most of the other students not knowing what to say.

"I treated people like shit before," Bianca said through her tears, "and I didn't really know how much my words might have affected someone else, you know? I never thought about it. Knowing I've made people feel the way I feel right now just makes me disgusted with myself. I want to just go around and apologize to everyone I made fun of, everyone whose feelings I might have hurt...except, I know I won't do that. If I did that now, they would think I was only doing it because of what's happened to me, because now I *have* no friends. In a way, they'd be right."

Paige leaned forward with her elbows on her knees. "Coming from someone who was made fun almost everyday in school," she'd said softly, "an apology is an apology. Don't stop yourself from apologizing because of how you *think* someone will react. So you've made mistakes. We all have. How you handle them and whether or not you learn from them are what give you strength of character."

"I just feel horrible, because I gave up my..." She hesitated and folded her hands together in her lap. She hadn't raised her head once to look at anyone in the group. She was too ashamed. "He was my first. I feel like that was the biggest mistake of all. Who you give your virginity to should be important. It's something that should be romantic, but it wasn't romantic. *He* wasn't romantic at all now that I think about it. How could I have been so stupid?"

"Bianca you weren't stupid." Paige looked around at the circle of students. "I didn't lose my virginity until my twenties, but even that was a mistake. The guy I'd given it to hadn't made me feel special. I wasn't in love with him. I *knew* I wasn't in love with him. He sure as hell wasn't in love with me. He was actually a jerk and after I dated him I didn't know *why* I'd dated him until much later. I think the reason I stayed with him for so long is probably because when I was in high school, I hadn't been able to date jerks." She paused and smiled. "Sounds stupid, huh?

"I'll explain. When I was in high school, I was basically considered a nerd, except I didn't really have the smarts that a nerd does. So I guess a more accurate term would be an outcast. When I was a sophomore, I had a crush on the quarterback of our school's football team. I just thought he was the most attractive boy I'd ever seen. And he *knew* that I liked him."

"I read about that in your book," one of the kids piped up.

Paige nodded. "Yeah, I definitely wrote about him in there. For those of you who haven't read the book, he used me. He would ask me out on a date, and I'd think it was because he liked me, but then we'd walk into a store and he's say something like, 'Wouldn't I look great in this sweater?' I would use all of my time baby-sitting for anyone who needed a baby-sitter, and I'd pick up change I found on the ground just so I could afford that sweater. And I'd give it to him. Or he'd ask if he could borrow five dollars for lunch.

"He would...kiss me when we were alone and hold my hand and everything, but once we got in school, he would ignore me. When his friends were around and I walked up to him, he acted like I was a lunatic, like he didn't know why I was talking to him."

A few of the girls shook their heads empathetically, putting themselves in Paige's shoes.

Paige looked down at her lap and chuckled to herself. "He embarrassed me, humiliated me, even, and you know what I did? I'd go home and call him and ask him why he would do it. He would tell me that he had a reputation to preserve. He would tell me that he really liked me, that he really liked spending time with me, but that if everyone at school knew about it, they would laugh at him. At both of us.

"And, I mean...I wasn't blind. I knew how I looked everyday when I went to school. I knew I didn't dress in the coolest clothes. I wasn't the prettiest girl in school or anything. So when he said that, it made sense to me. And I excused it. I didn't talk to him anymore at school and I continued to see him after school. But then, he started seeing this girl. And he'd walk around with her in school. He wasn't ashamed to be with her." She had to clear her throat. She took a steadying breath and went on. "I ended things with him and he threw out some pretty creative insults at me. He made me feel like I wasn't worth loving.

"No one and I mean no one," she said, looking directly at Bianca, "should have that power over you. No one should be able to make you feel like you're not worth loving. Losing your virginity seems like a mistake to you right now, and it might have been. But just because you made a mistake doesn't mean you have to beat yourself up for it. All you can do now is learn from it. If you went out on the streets right now and asked women whether or not their first time was magical, most of them would say that it wasn't. I know mine wasn't. But that doesn't mean you'll be unhappy for the rest of your life. That doesn't mean that you won't find someone else later on who is absolutely crazy about you." Images of Ethan crept into her mind. She subconsciously tugged on her long braid. There was a painful twang in her heart as several memories of him passed through her mind.

When she raised her eyes to look at the circle of high school students, her cheeks flushed. "I'm sorry, I was just…"

"Thinking about Mr. Carson," one of the few boys in the group spoke up.

She pressed a hand to her chest. "I try to be open and honest with you guys, but that's one topic that's off-limits."

"You really loved him, didn't you?" Bianca asked in a quiet voice, her mind temporarily distracted from thinking about her own problems.

"I, um…" Paige blew out an exasperated breath. "That topic is off-limits, I'm sorry."

"You tell us that you're here to listen to us," another girl, awkwardly tall with stringy brown hair, chimed in. "Well it works both ways."

"That's very sweet," Paige responded, "but it's inappropriate to talk about one of your teachers."

The awkwardly tall girl, whose name was Rebecca, said, "You might not be able to talk about him, but I'll tell you what I think. I think…it shouldn't matter who both of you were in the past. It shouldn't matter that he used to be your teacher. You're both consenting adults now and you love each other. I really think you do. Something like his job shouldn't get in the way of that. He might have a hard time with it, but then it's up to you to go and get him."

Paige laughed. "'Go and get him'?" she repeated, her eyes dancing with amusement. "Oh, is that what I should do?"

"It's what I would do if I were you," Rebecca admitted with a slight shrug of her shoulders. "It's the twenty-first century. Nowadays women don't have to wait around for the man to come and get her. Nowadays, women can be the aggressors."

Several yards from where the supportive circle sat, concealed behind rows and rows of bookcases, a smile stretched across Ethan's face.

Chapter Twenty-one

Marissa, Deana, and Evelyn sat at a table in Elliott's. One chair at their table stood empty. At times each woman would cast a glance at the empty chair.

"So, I've been thinking," Deana said, irked by the awkward silence amongst them. "And I'm thinking that I don't want to be angry with Paige anymore."

"We have no reason to be mad at her, really," Evelyn agreed.

"Are you two nuts?" Marissa demanded, looking at one and then the other.

"Are *you* nuts?" Deana returned boldly, staring back. "You're pissed off at her because of something that happened before you and Shane even started dating."

Marissa sulked prettily. "I'm pissed because of the fact she didn't tell me about it."

"And," Deana continued with an index finger held in the air, "you're pissed off at Shane because of something-no, some*one* he did after you went postal on his ass."

Marissa picked at her turkey sandwich, plucking off pieces of bread and popping them into her mouth. After reading what Paige had written about the escapade she'd had with Shane, it had been difficult not looking at Shane as Paige's leftovers. Her mind conjured up images of her friend and her future husband together. She'd come this close to marrying Shane without knowing something as important as that. There was that, and then there was the fact that her feelings were hurt. Someone who was a true friend would have told her about something that major. "Well, you two can make up with her if you want to, but I refuse," she said stubbornly.

"She didn't write anything that horrible about me," Evelyn said. "And what she *did* write was true. That book only covered up to the point where she and Brandon split. If it covered the point up until now, she would have also included that I've matured lately. That I've grown up and realized what a stupid woman I was, because let's face it. I was."

"I don't have a diary or a journal," Deana told them all, "but if I did, I'd probably have some choice words to call Paige after some of the arguments we've had. I can deal with her calling me bitter and saying that that's why I'm still single."

"You're going soft on me, Deana?" Marissa shrieked incredulously.

Deana rolled her eyes. "I hardly think I'm going soft. I'm just being real."

"She came within an inch of calling you butch," Marissa sneered with her upper lip curled.

Deana laughed and wiped her hands with a napkin. She'd been disappointed when she'd read a few of the things Paige had written about her. Anyone else would have been. She hadn't necessarily been angry, though. As a matter of fact, she hadn't been angry at all. Actions spoke louder than words, and when it came down to it, Deana knew that Paige loved her as a friend. There were times that neither Evelyn nor Marissa knew about, times when Deana cried on Paige's shoulder.

She'd knocked on Paige's door years before, needing someone to talk to. She'd poured her heart out, her fears that her bitterness and anger towards her father would taint her opinion of men in general and keep her from finding true love. In the past several years, she'd cried quite a few times. She didn't want to end up alone, but she didn't want to end up hurt like her mother had been by her father. It was a catch twenty-two.

Today, Deana still had that fear, but she'd had time to grow used to the resentment that she harbored towards men. She'd gotten used to the possibility of ending up alone and wasn't so fearful of it. Some people ended up alone. That was the way of the world. Not everyone had happy, fairytale lives. Not everyone found their true loves. And still the world turned. So what if she'd never experience love at its truest and purest? She had her work, she had her house, and if one day she woke up desperate to have a child, there was always artificial insemination.

Her appetite waned and she pushed her plate away from her. "Right now, I have a friend who's hurting because she lost the man she loved," she told Marissa and Evelyn. All three of them had seen the interviews between Paige and a various amount of television personalities. "She needs us right now. What kind of friends would we be if we stood by, talking about her behind her back and failing her?"

"*She* failed *me*," Marissa said, her voice taut with fury. She pushed her chair back, almost toppling it over in the process. "You may be quick to forgive and forget, but I'm not. She betrayed me. She fucked the man that I intended to *marry*. I was ready to give my life to him. I could see raising kids with him. Now, I can't see any of that. Not now, not knowing that the things he does to please me now, he may have been doing to please Paige in the past." She rose from her seat and grabbed her coat from the back of it. Her movements were jerky as she yanked the sleeves over her arms.

"Marissa, people make mistakes," Evelyn said timidly. "I know I have. We all have. Paige has been trying to apologize to us."

"Evelyn is a lot nicer than I am. Marissa, you have to snap the fuck out of whatever funk you're in." The expression on Deana's face was menacing. "Paige has been very kind to you. She's kind in general. Okay, so she and Shane got freaky back in the day. Maybe she should have told you about it. Actually, I agree with you-she *should* have told you about it. She didn't. But think about why she didn't. Maybe she knew you. Maybe she knew you'd flip out and miss out on a man who is crazy in love with you."

"I don't care why she didn't tell me. She should have told me," Marissa said, buttoning up her jacket with shaking fingers.

Deana shrugged her shoulders. "To be completely honest, I don't care what you do. You can forgive Paige, you can choose to hate her forever. I'm just going to say this.

"You have a man who would do anything for you. You loved being with him and he loved being with you. He made you laugh the way no one else has been able to before."

Marissa started to interrupt, but Deana shushed her.

"You're very fortunate, Marissa. I mean, okay, Shane has a pretty major flaw. But if you compared the list of cons to the list of pros, there's no contest." She stood from her chair and walked around the table to set a hand on Marissa's shoulder. "I'm known for bashing men quite often, and even I can say without a doubt that Shane is a good man...as far as good men go. I can also say without a doubt that I wish I was as fortunate as you are. I wish that a man could love me and look at me the way Shane looks at you. I mean, it's pretty obvious that you two are perfect for each other. Are you really going to pass up the chance at real love because of a mistake that was made when we were in college?"

Marissa swiftly brushed Deana's hand off of her shoulder and tilted her chin up. "After recent events, I'm not even sure it *was* real love," she sniffed. "I'm not sure I ever knew Shane Luciani at all." With those words, she tossed a few bills on the table and turned to make an overdramatic exit.

"I'm glad you guys came by." Paige wiped her hands on the front of her jeans. She closed the door to her hotel suite and turned to face Evelyn and Deana. "I was... surprised when you called. I didn't think you two would ever want to speak to me again."

"We couldn't stay mad at you forever," Evelyn said and threw her arms around her friend. "And anyway, everything you wrote was the truth."

"No," Paige objected right away. "Everything I wrote in that wasn't how I really feel about you. Some of those passages I wrote after-"

"We argued, I know," Evelyn finished, bowing her head. Her blonde hair was pulled into a high ponytail and she was bundled up in a faux fur coat, a beige top and black slacks.

Deana leaned against the wall and folded her arms over her breasts. "How have you been doing without us?"

"I've been...surviving, kind of," Paige answered, walking past both Deana and Evelyn into the suite's living room. "I found a buyer for my house in Farmington Heights. I'm in the process of buying a new house. Then there's the teen support group that I'm involved with. It's been kind of hard, but rewarding."

"The whole teen suicide thing," Deana said, following Paige. "I was proud of you when I heard about that."

"It's the most amazing thing I've done, I think," Paige said, her expression changing from emotional fatigue to beaming pride. "And the kids, they're wonderful. They really are. I've come to realize that I actually love kids."

Deana's brows rose. "I thought you hated kids."

"I do recall you thanking God on several occasions because you didn't have kids," Evelyn seconded, collapsing on the couch.

"That was then and this is now." Paige walked over to the window and pulled the curtain aside to watch small flakes of snow flurrying past.

"So, now you love kids," Deana said wryly.

Paige smiled and shrugged. "Now I love kids. I wish you could see them, Deana. I mean, they're funny, they're intelligent, and-and listening to their problems, trying to help them...it makes me feel good."

"I'm not in the loving children phase yet," Deana said. "I'm in the keep-kids-the-hell-away-from-me phase. I don't wanna' hear 'em, I don't wanna' see 'em, and I sure as hell don't wanna' be around 'em."

"It disgusts me when I think that I nearly bore Eric's children," Evelyn said aloud, almost to herself. "I'm glad I dodged that bullet."

"So, where's Marissa?" Paige asked, turning away from the window. "She couldn't make it?"

Deana rubbed at the back of her neck. "Um, yeah, about that..." She glanced quickly at Evelyn.

"She's umm...dealing with some...things," Evelyn offered slowly, not looking Paige in the eyes.

"Some major things," Deana added.

"She hates my guts," Paige deciphered with a hand on her hip.

Deana nodded. "Pretty much, yeah."

"I can't blame her. I should have told her."

"But you didn't because you cared about her and wanted to be happy," Evelyn put in.

Paige shrugged. "Well we see where that got me."

"I hate to say it, but Marissa is a bit retarded," Deana said. "It's going to take her more time to realize that her friendship with you is worth weathering."

"What I did was pretty horrific," Paige stated. "I don't think she's going to get over it anytime soon."

"So what if she doesn't?" Deana asked. "You've got us."

Paige gave a weak smile. "Oh, yeah. I'm definitely reassured now," she said sarcastically.

Deana rolled her eyes. "Okay, so I'm not a fashion goddess and I've never gone through a phase where I had to screw everything in sight. But Evelyn and I are still your friends, you know? You and Marissa will get through it, trust me. In the meantime, we need to discuss a certain teacher."

Paige raised both hands to her ears. "I can't hear you!" she shouted and proceeded to sing, "La, la, la, la, la..."

"Stop being such a damned baby," Deana said and walked over. She yanked Paige's hands down. "What you need to do is walk into that man's classroom wearing nothing but a trench coat. Then, you take off the coat and-"

"That's not how you get a guy like Ethan," Paige broke in. "Especially considering the situation. I used to be his student. In his classroom is the last place he'd want to see me."

"I don't give a shit." Deana threw her arms up in frustration. "I tell you, between you and Marissa, I'm going to have to fucking play matchmaker."

"What about Marissa?" Paige wondered.

Evelyn was bursting with information. "She wanted to make up with Shane," she explained, "but when she got to his house, there was a woman asleep in his bed. That, plus what he went through with you in college, has her convinced that she doesn't want to be involved with him."

"God, Shane didn't tell me about that," Paige said, looking worried. "Ouch...he almost got her back."

"Almost," Deana stressed and went to join Evelyn on the couch. "He fucked up big time. I tried to explain to her how I thought that Shane was a good guy and perfect for her, but she's as stubborn as a horse's ass."

"Colorful imagery, thank you, Deana," Paige said with mock gratitude.

"I do what I can," Deana said, crossing one crimson-panted leg over the other.

Evelyn had a silly grin on her face. "I'm just glad we're together again. Even if Marissa isn't here, I'm just glad to see you, Paige. It's definitely been too long."

There was a knock on the door and Paige arched a glance over her shoulder. She wasn't expecting anyone else and hadn't ordered out. "Hold on a second," she told Deana and Evelyn. She made her way to the door, smoothing her shirt down. When she opened the door, her jaw fell.

Marissa stood on the other side of the door with her hand shoved down jean pockets.

Deana and Evelyn came to the foyer and stopped in their tracks when they saw Marissa.

Marissa's eyes were locked with Paige's. The emotion that lie within both pairs of eyes was electric. Apologies were swapped without words. The expressions on their faces, the look in their eyes said it all. After taking a long, shaky breath, Marissa asked, "So...have room for one more?"

Paige drove to the school early Monday afternoon, a full two hours before she was scheduled to be there. The previous night, she'd had a dream about Ethan. She'd tried to keep the mental images of that dream out of her mind all day…in vain. Everywhere she turned, she could see his face. If she concentrated hard enough, she could smell him and feel his hands on her.

The morning had been rough since she couldn't stop thinking about him. She wondered if he was thinking about her as much as she was thinking about him. She hoped that he was. Today, she would do more than hope. She would ask him; she would find out.

She'd come up with a plan. The students in T.A.T.S. and Deana were right. If she loved Ethan, she couldn't give him up so easily. Who knew how long it was before he found someone else, someone who wasn't a former student of his, someone he could fall head over heels in love with?

She was a romance novelist. As a romance novelist, she knew that she should be able to think of something that would get underneath his skin. Earlier today, she had.

She pulled her Explorer into the teacher's parking lot and entered the school through the entrance near the gymnasium and the pool. She strode the halls with confidence, returned greetings when they were given, and ended up at the door of the teacher's lounge. In her hands was a thick group of papers that she had bound with two large clips. With one hand, she hugged the papers to her chest. With the other, she grabbed the doorknob and turned it.

About eleven teachers were either seated or standing in the teacher's lounge. One was crouched in front of the compact refrigerator. Ethan and Richard were seated at the same table in what looked to be a serious discussion. When the audible click of the door was heard, all eyes were on her.

One of Ethan's brows lifted and he stared at her openly, not bothering to ignore her. His lips were set in a straight line and the muscles in his jaw were working. His blue eyes turned as frosty as the weather outside of the school's walls.

Richard, in contrast, looked happy to see her. He beckoned her over to their table.

She approached their table hesitantly, not sure if she could go through with her plan. "Hi, Rich," she greeted, sounding as cheery as possible with a man spitting fire at her with his eyes.

"You'll have to excuse Carson," Richard said, hooking a thumb over his shoulder. "He's a sulker."

Ethan made as if to stand and leave. "I'll catch you later, Rich."

"Wait," Paige said, stretching an arm out towards Ethan. She snatched it back and looked down at the papers in her hands. "I came in here for you."

"We have nothing to say, Paige," he said gruffly, more so than he'd intended. He closed his eyes and cursed under his breath. There was a lot that he wanted to say to her, starting with asking her how in the hell she could hold in information so vital from him and ending with how in the hell did she expect him to get over the fact that little more than ten years ago, she'd been his student? He was distinctly aware that all of the other members of the faculty in the lounge were focused on the conversation he was having with her. He tried to make it past her, but she backed up until her back was pressed against the door.

She looked up at him. A few strands of hair were in her eyes and she brushed them back agitatedly. "You might have nothing to say, but I have a lot to say."

"This isn't the time or the place," he said stiffly, attempting to physically move her out of the way.

"Too bad," she said breathlessly. "Because I'm not leaving until I talk to you. So this is going to have to be the time and the place."

He stopped trying to make his way past her and instead turned his back to her. "Paige..." he warned, bringing a hand up to pinch the bridge of his nose.

"Don't worry. I won't lay it all out on the table here," she said. "I know you probably still can't stomach the sight of me. That's fine. I just wanted you to proofread something for me."

He turned his head slightly and angled a look at her out of the corner of his eye.

She gestured at the papers she'd left on the table. "It's a manuscript. The sequel to *Open Book*."

"I don't want to read it."

"Too bad."

"Paige-"

"I want you to proofread it," she insisted, her voice cracking. Tears threatened to sting her eyes and she brought a hand up to her mouth. She took a few moments to calm down.

He picked up the stack of papers and flipped through them. "I can't read your diary."

"You already have," she threw at his back.

He didn't say anything.

"You love me," she went on, tears starting at the corner of her eyes. "Think about what you're throwing away."

"I have!" His voice boomed and nearly shook the very walls of the small lounge. He raked a hand through his hair and squeezed his eyes closed. "Damn you, Paige. Don't you know how I feel about you? Felt about you? I can't describe the love that I felt for you in words. I can't. It's just not possible. I more than loved you. I could see spending every day of my life with you. I could see that easily. We were that compatible. I say were, Paige, because you used to be my student. I've never dated a former student before, not knowingly. And I never want to. It's not what I stand for. It's not what I believe in."

Her bottom lip quivered. Her face was abnormally pale and tears sparkled on her cheeks.

"I wish that I could change how I feel, Paige. I wish to God I could change how I feel, but I can't. When I look at you now, I see the Paige Turner that I taught in my classroom. It breaks my heart every time. I want to be with you, Paige, desperately, but I wouldn't feel right. It wouldn't feel right." He paused and added, "*We* wouldn't feel right."

She nodded, biting her bottom lip. She tossed hair out of her eyes. "I can understand that, but you're being a bit extreme ignoring me in the halls, aren't you?"

"You don't know how much it's taking out of me to have to work with you," he said in a low voice, taking a step towards her. "Every time I look at you, I remember. Everything we did together and being with you...it all comes back every time I see you. It hurts me to walk past you and to not be able to..." He broke off and shook his head.

"Just read what you have in your hands for me," she pleaded. She turned and hastily let herself out of the teacher's lounge.

Chapter Twenty-two

Ethan sat in his living room taking conservative sips of Jack Daniels. Paige's manuscript for the sequel to *Open Book*, aptly titled *Closed Book*, lie on the couch beside him. He tilted his head back and took one long gulp.

His fellow faculty had gotten on his last nerve. After the scene Paige had caused in the lounge, everyone was on him with questions and suggestions. If a poll were to be taken, the majority would be in favor of Paige getting her way. Everyone wanted to see Ethan and Paige together. Knowing that came as a shock to him. He thought that people would object to his relationship with her. He thought that parents would fear for the welfare of the daughters who were in his class if he got involved with Paige.

But no, even the parents of his students were putting in their two cents. After all, she'd declared her love for him on public television and in a published book. Her feelings for him were quite apparent; she'd left no room for doubt with her emotional outburst.

He'd told himself that he wasn't going to read the manuscript. No good could come out of that. He was trying to extract her out of his life, which was going to be difficult since he had to work with her in the same building…even more difficult if she accepted the guidance counselor job that the principal had offered her.

If she accepted that job, he didn't know what he was going to do. Not only would he have to see her in the afternoons, but he'd have to deal with passing by her a great deal more.

He couldn't feel right loving her and yet he couldn't see himself loving any other woman the way he'd loved her. People were encouraging him to take her back and yet all he was trying to do was uphold certain morals. He didn't want to read the manuscript lying next to him and understand her. He didn't want to understand her motives. He didn't want to read about why she did what she did. He knew that the manuscript contained both because that's why she'd handed it to him. She wanted him to understand. He didn't want to understand, because he knew once he understood, his heart would thaw and he would go to her.

He would go to her, collect her in his arms, and smother her with kisses. He would melt faster than a cube of ice in the Nevada desert. He would soften up and his resolve would weaken. He told himself he wouldn't read the manuscript and yet...

He lifted the stack of paper to his lap and flipped through it idly. He knew he was going to regret reading it later, but he had to read it. He had to understand her. He had to know her. He wanted to forgive her.

Closed Book started where *Open Book* had ended. It covered more on how Paige felt after Brandon broke up with her. The journal entries poured into each other, spanning from her parents' vow renewal ceremony up until much more recently. He flipped to the entry she'd written once she found out about the publication of her novel and smiled to himself. Every other word was profanity; her shock and confusion emanated off the page.

His fingers thumbed through more pages.

[Dear Diary],

I was determined to pull the book from the shelves. After all, Shane said I could. He said I could stop the circulation of the book, and I very much wanted to do that. Yes, I said, "wanted," past tense. I no longer want to stop the circulation of the books.

You're probably wondering why. It's because I met a woman on the plane. She told me how much the book helped her, how it made her feel like she wasn't alone in some of the thoughts she'd had. It melted my heart, hearing those words from her.

I haven't had to deal much with being recognized in public. In my entire writing career, I've been recognized maybe ten times. That's something that I was all right with, because I'm not one for fame or publicity. I never wanted that. All I wanted was to be happy, because happiness isn't something that I was often acquainted with as a teenager.

I've found that with Ethan and I don't want to let it go. I know that keeping the book on the shelves is a major risk. He's either going to read the truth in the book, hear it in a news report, or I'll be forced to tell him. And I don't want to, God, I don't. I want to stay blissful and happy with him for all time. He's the one, Diary. He's the one that I want to be with, the one I want to marry, the one I want to raise children with.

I dream of spending our lives together, but that's not something I want to achieve based on a lie. I have to tell him. I know I do. I don't know why I keep stalling, because it's inevitable. I'm going to have to tell him that when I was seventeen, he was my health teacher, that I loved him then, and still love him now. He may freak out and never want to see me again and I deserve that for my actions...

But I'm so afraid of losing him. I don't know what I'll do if I lose him...I can't picture living without him.

Emotion ebbed within Ethan. His heart started pounding faster as he flipped forward a few journal entries. As he read, he tried to picture Paige sitting in bed with her knees drawn up, writing.

[Dear Diary],

So, I've managed to make a complete mess of things. Ethan somehow found out the truth. He found out from someone other than me, which had to crush him. Of course, I feel horrible about it, because I should have been the one to tell him. I claim to love him, but yet I can't tell him the truth? No wonder he doesn't want to see my face ever again.

Then there's Marissa. Someone else who doesn't want to see my face again because of the book I've published. And

Deana, Evelyn, and Shane...they're all pissed off at me, and with good reason.

Maybe I shouldn't have kept Open Book *on the shelves. I should have had the copies pulled from the stores. Sure, it's doing good for some people, but it's ruining my life. I have no one to blame for that except for myself and I know that. It's just...so hard and there's no one I can talk to about it, because all of my friends want nothing to do with me.*

I feel horrible. I'm a wretched person for what I've done and I do regret what I've done. Regretting does nothing to make things right, though. Regretting doesn't fix anything. What I need to do is find a way to fix this, but I can't think of anything. I've tried apologizing. Continuously. And nothing, I've gotten no responses.

At night, I dream that Ethan comes knocking on my door wanting to take me back. He tells me that he forgives me and we hold each other all night. There's no off-the-wall, crazy, kinky sex or anything, it's all innocent. We just hold each other and fall asleep that way. We wake up that way and look at each other. We smile and tell each other how much we love each other and how we should never fight again.

But I really wake up at that point, and the bed beside me is empty. There's no one there. And I feel empty. And lonely. And I miss him. God, how I miss him.

Ethan ran a hand across his forehead and lifted his eyes from the typed words. He wiped his mouth and closed his eyes for several moments. He didn't want to read anymore. He was close to tears as it is. He flipped through a few more entries and felt hot tears shooting down his cheeks. He didn't attempt to stop them, because he knew that more were on the way.

[Dear Diary],

A friend of Samantha's has passed away of her own doing. She committed suicide and Sam is torn about it. I drove up to Beach Park tonight to console her, but I didn't really know what to say. It's hard to comfort someone who has just lost someone. I told her it would be all right when I knew it wouldn't be. How could it be all right when a teenager has just killed herself?

I felt foolish and ashamed because I know I've considered suicide before. It wasn't for long, but I've had the thought flash into my mind. I think a lot of people do consider it. Going through with it...that's another story. For someone to actually go through with it, they have to truly feel alone.

Without Ethan, without my three best friends in the world, I do feel alone, but I know if I have to talk to someone I could go to my parents and talk to them. Shane is P.O.'d at me, but if I seriously had to talk to him, he would listen.

This girl, her name was Vanessa, didn't feel like she had that option with anyone. She had some great friends, but she felt that no one would understand. And I cry for this girl that I don't know, because it hurts me that a child would think that. She was a baby, Diary...just a baby. Why did she do that? How could she possibly do something that extreme? What kind of cruel world do we live in?

I can't write much...Sam is sleeping on the couch and I don't want to leave her by herself for too long, but...what kind of cruel world do we live in where life seems so hard, we'd rather not live it?

And still flipping.

[Dear Diary],

I haven't written in the past few weeks because I've been busy, but to get you caught up with what's going on, Sam has come up with an amazing idea. She wants to start a "students against teen suicide"-type support group and she wants me to be in charge of it. At first, I declined. I couldn't see myself talking to a bunch of teenagers about why they shouldn't commit suicide, after all.

But I gave my speech last Monday, and it felt good to talk to the kids. I had everyone's attention and my point got across. I made them all realize that even when they felt more alone than ever, they really weren't, because there were people who felt the same way.

While I was up on that stage, Diary, something amazing happened to me. I came alive. Something was born inside me. There's a drive that I have, a need to help these kids, to get to know these kids.

Just two years ago if you asked me how I felt about kids, I'd probably wrinkle my nose at you…not because I disliked them, exactly, but because I hadn't had much exposure to them since I was babysitting for our neighbor twelve years ago.

But getting to know Sam all over again and meeting Olivia changed my outlook on children. Those are two amazing kids right there; they're sisters with the tightest bond I've seen between siblings. I hope they always keep that and I love them as if they were my own sisters.

As for the teen support group, I've decided to go through with it. I'm realizing that there was a reason my adolescence was so hard for me to go through. Because I've experienced so much, I can share my experiences with people and help them get through it…

[Dear Diary],

I've worked with the kids of BPH for several weeks now. I've passed Ethan a few times in the halls and he doesn't greet me. He doesn't look at me. It's as if I'm not even there.

The first time he passed me without acknowledging me, I went into the Girls' bathroom and cried. I've started to get used to it, but I just try to avoid him now. There's a twist in my heart every time I see him. I'll see him talking to Richard or a student and smiling or laughing and wish that he was smiling at me, laughing with me, talking to me.

He is such an amazing man. I admire him so much. I love him so much. Maybe I shouldn't have taken this gig, become a part of this support group. Seeing him this often is really doing a number on me. I'm seriously thinking about turning the group into the hands of someone else, but I know that the kids would hate that. They'd feel abandoned. I wouldn't want them to feel that way and I love getting to know them.

I guess all I'm wondering is: what's wrong with a teacher dating a former student? He did nothing wrong when he was my teacher way back when. He kept things very professional; he was very ethical. I admired him even more for that.

But I'm not a child anymore. I'm not his student anymore. And when he looks at me, I don't want him to see Paige Turner, the child. I want him to see Paige Turner, the woman. Sure, eleven, twelve years ago I was a teenager. Twenty years ago, so was he. But every time I look at him, I don't see a teenager.

How can I get him to see me for me? I'm a romance novelist, right? I should be able to come up with some snazzy way to entice him. "Should be" are the key words there, because I haven't been able to come up with any ideas. He seems determined to act as if he and I were never an item...which hurts, but I understand why he does it.

All I can do is be myself. All I can do is love him. And I do shout to the world that I love him. Hopefully, he loves me enough to come back to me.

The paper that Ethan looked down at was damp with his tears. Richard would probably be reaming him a new asshole about now. According to Richard, men weren't supposed to cry, but Ethan couldn't help it. The love of his life was asking that he come back to her. She wanted him back. And he wanted to go back to her.

Life was too short to be worrying about practicalities. He would never meet another woman like Paige. He would never find a love as great as the one that he already had.

Dammit, Paige, he thought, setting the papers aside. *I do love you. I probably always have.*

Deana wanted to sit in on one of the support group meetings, which Paige was pleased to hear. She and Deana drove to the school together, and she was pleased to introduce Deana to Richard.

Deana and Richard took to each other immediately and exchanged phone numbers.

Paige looked surprised. "Wow, did I just see what I thought I saw?"

"He's a funny guy," Deana said, with a wide smile on her face.

"But...he's a man," Paige said. "I thought your whole mentality was wanting to kill them on sight or rid the world of them or something."

"He's...very straightforward. The way I like them." Deana's smile grew brighter. "The takes-no-bullshit type. You know, like me."

Paige laughed and roped an arm around her friend's neck. "Definitely like you. I'm so glad you're here."

"I wish I could say the same, but knowing kids are going to be here is kind of giving me the heebie-jeebies."

"You're going to love them."

"I'm not setting my expectations that high," Deana muttered as Paige steered her into the library.

Deana's shoulders tensed as she was faced with more than thirty students. They all turned and looked at both Paige and Deana. Deana raised a hand and gave a slight wave.

The students still stared.

"Take a picture, it'll last longer," Deana snapped.

Paige laughed and found Deana a chair. "Sit," she ordered. To the rest of the group, she announced, "This is my friend, Deana. She wanted to sit in on one of our groups."

"*The* Deana?" one of the kids asked. "From the book?"

"Yeah, *the* Deana from the book," Deana replied. "I didn't know I was famous." She arched a look at Paige.

Paige shrugged her shoulders.

"Do you have any questions for me?" Deana asked, turning and eyeing everyone in the circle.

Several hands shot into the air.

"Other than asking whether I'm a dyke or not?" Deana specified.

A few of the hands lowered meekly, but two still remained in the air.

"Other than asking whether or not I hate men and want them all banished from the earth?"

The two hands remaining also lowered.

Paige stifled a laugh. "Okay, okay...let's get serious for a moment. Rebecca, last week you were talking about how you were dealing with your parents' divorce. Deana went through that when she was young. She might be a reliable source for you to talk to about that."

"I just want to know how I'm supposed to feel," Rebecca said slowly, toying with her thin, brown hair. "It's like...in the back of my mind, I know I'm not responsible. I'm not why they're getting a divorce. I just can't shake the feeling that I'm to blame. I don't even know why I feel that way, I just do. And I feel like it's up to me to make them both see the good in each other."

Paige looked at Deana expectantly.

Deana poked herself in the chest with an index finger. "You want me to talk to her?"

"You know about divorce."

"Yeah, I know about divorce," Deana confirmed, "but I don't know if I'm someone you want to be giving the kids advice."

"Tell Rebecca how you felt when your parents were going through the divorce," Paige advised. "And for Christ's sake, try to keep the vulgar language out of your description."

"Yeah, that'll happen," Deana said, snorting. She rubbed her chin. "I mean...I felt what you felt, the knowing you're not to blame but still somehow feeling responsible. I felt like I wasn't good enough, you know? I mean, they're your parents. When you're a kid, as far as you're concerned, they're supposed to always be together. I was so used to them being together. I couldn't imagine them being apart."

Rebecca nodded enthusiastically. "When they're together and they're not fighting, they're so funny and charming. It's like…why can't they be like that all the time?"

"Do you know why your parents are splitting?" Deana asked the younger girl.

"My dad cheated," Rebecca said and lowered her eyes.

"Well, that's because men are jerks," Deana said without reservation. She looked around at the boys in the room. "No offense to the male species seated in the room at the moment, but you guys are."

"Deana," Paige hissed.

Deana glanced at Paige and sighed. "Well, not all men are jerks," she corrected herself. "Some men are truly wonderful. I mean…okay just forget I said anything bad about men at all. My view of men is horrendously skewed because my dad cheated on my mother, too. So I guess my advice to you would be to not turn out like me.

"Just because your father, one man, did something horrible, doesn't mean that all men will be horrible to you. It's not an excuse for you to treat men like sh…like crap. Give men a chance. I'm not saying you should be easy, mind you," Deana said, wagging a finger, "but don't close yourself up and hide behind emotional walls."

Paige smiled at Deana. "We all like to think that our parents are going to be together forever," she told the kids sitting around in the circle, "but at times we forget that our parents are people. Sometimes people grow tired of each other, or sometimes one does the other wrong. People make mistakes. Some people who thought they were meant for each other aren't. It's something that's hard to deal with when it's thrown in your face unexpectedly, but just because your parents split doesn't mean that they don't love you. I'm willing to bet that they love you a great deal. It doesn't mean they're disappointed in you, either. Just because they don't want to be a couple anymore doesn't mean they don't want to be your parents. That will never change."

Rebecca's head dipped down until her chin touched her chest. She was hiding tears.

Paige stood and walked over to hug the girl. "You're special," she whispered, nudging the girl's chin up.

After the group's session ended and the children spilled out of the library, excitedly talking to one another, Paige slid down in her chair and pushed her hair back with both hands.

Deana blew out a breath. "Wow, that was pretty intense, huh?"

"It's like that every day at these things."

"And they offered you a full time job here? Wouldn't all of the emotional complexity make your head explode after like a week?"

Paige laughed and shook her head. "I feel exhausted emotionally, but it's also satisfying, you know?"

"It's draining," Deana mumbled, closing her eyes. "After one of those sessions, I feel like I've been awake for forty-eight hours straight. I could just curl up in bed and sleep for twelve hours."

"Well now you can see that kids aren't that bad."

"Are you kidding?" Deana cried. "They were monsters, with question after question and story after story. Once they started talking, they wouldn't shut up."

Richard sauntered into the room. "You guys sure know how to clear the joint, huh?"

Deana straightened in her chair and her fatigue washed away with the smile that appeared on her face. "What do you expect? We're pros."

"I'm not arguing that point. It's a morgue in here." He glanced around. "The work day is officially over for me. I was wondering if I could escort you two to dinner."

"No thanks, Richard," Paige said graciously, "but thank you for the offer."

Deana held up a hand. "Speak for yourself, Paige."

Paige turned to Deana in shock. "Really?"

Deana linked her arm with Richard's. "Don't wait up," she whispered over her shoulder.

Deana never ceased to amaze her. Paige started packing her notebooks and pens into a black leather satchel. When she stood and turned to leave, there was someone barricading her way. Her green eyes met sapphire blue ones and she froze mid-step.

He held her manuscript in his hands; he lowered his eyes to it and slapped it against his palm. "Hi."

"Hi." She eyed him warily, looking for traces of anger. She found none. Her eyes filled with hope, but she tried to put a leash on it.

"You're a very talented writer," he told her, quite unexpectedly.

Surprise registered on her face. She slung the strap to her satchel over her shoulder and crossed her arms over her chest. "Thank you."

He shook his head and walked around her, taking in the chairs that had been formed into a circle. "This is something great you're doing with this group."

"I'm honored to do it."

He whirled on her suddenly. "Okay, I can't do this shit."

Her brows shot up.

"I can't go into this small talk shit with you. You and I would never work."

"Okay."

He rubbed at his jaw. "What you wrote really touched me, you know? To know you've felt like that for so long and…I mean…God, Paige. You were a fucking kid in my class."

"I know," she said quietly, her head bowed. "I understand how you feel. I do."

"I…dammit…Paige…" He stood looking at her with her head cast down and he wanted to reach out and touch her. "I kept telling myself not to read that manuscript. I knew I'd end up forgiving you once I'd read it. I knew I'd end up running to you and taking you back. I didn't want to do that, mostly because being with you would be messy."

She raised her eyes. "You don't have to explain yourself to me," she said, keeping her emotions in check. "I'm all right with your decision. I don't come to this school every day to see you. I come for the kids and I'll continue to do that."

"You don't understand." He moved toward her slowly, keeping his eyes trained on her face. "I tried as hard as I could to live without you. Before I...found out, I couldn't picture my life without you in it, but for the past month I've had to deal with that and I don't like it. I need you. And you aren't a teenager, you're an adult now."

She kept her eyes lowered, even as he put a finger under her chin and tipped it up.

"I'm not saying that it'll be easy. I'm not saying that I'll just be able to jump in and start where we left off, which was pretty hot and heavy. But I do want to be with you. My beliefs about teachers dating former students...I have to cast them aside, because you're my soulmate. I truly believe that."

Her lashes lowered and she looked away from him. The words he spoke were the words she'd wanted to hear for so long. Her thinking was that this was probably another dream she was having. Any moment now, she was going to wake up and find herself alone again.

But he was standing so close to her that she could smell him and she could feel his finger on her chin. When he moved his hand to caress her cheek, she felt that too. All of the sensations were telling her that this was real, but she took her time in believing it. She didn't want another let-down.

He combed his fingers through her hair and pressed a kiss to her forehead. "I love you," he whispered. "I should have never let you go. I don't ever want to lose you."

"I don't ever want to lose you," she murmured earnestly, trying to blink the tears back so they wouldn't spill. "I thought I already had."

"Oh no, baby, no...My love for you is stronger than anything I've ever felt. Without you, I'm incomplete. That's something that this teacher had to learn." He leaned down and wrapped his arms around her.

Epilogue

"I'd like to make a toast for the bride and groom," Paige announced, standing and raising her champagne glass. A crimson bridesmaid's dress clung to her body; she'd had to hold her breath just to fit into the thing. "I've known Marissa ever since college. If you think she's wild now..."

The room erupted in laughter, and at the wedding party table, Marissa leaned into Shane and whispered something into his ear.

"No, no, but seriously," Paige said, waving a hand so that the chatter died down. "Shane and Marissa were made for each other. That was evident once you got them together in a room. The way they look at each other makes everyone envious. It's as if they constantly have this private joke that no one else knows about.

"Marissa and Shane deserve the happiness they've found in each other. They've weathered storms and stuck together through thick and thin. All of us: Shane, Marissa, Evelyn, Deana, and I, have been through...a lot. I love them all with all of my heart. I don't want to keep us here forever, so I'll just close by saying, 'Rissa, I love you, honey. I'm glad you two are together. I'm glad you're both happy. May you always be together. May you always, always, always, be happy." She lifted her champagne glass higher and tilted it.

"Cheers," everyone said in unison.

Marissa blew a kiss at Paige and grinned, a dimple deepening into her cheek.

Paige lowered into her seat.

"This wedding is beautiful," Evelyn remarked.

"Isn't it?" Paige agreed.

Once dinner was over, the deejay announced that the floor was open to anyone who wanted to dance. The wedding party's table wasn't long enough for the bridesmaids and groomsmen to sit with their dates; their dates were seated at a circular table near the wedding party's table.

Evelyn had helped craft the centerpieces at each table, beautiful glass swans filled with white rosebuds. The main colors used in the wedding's theme were red, white, and gold. The banquet hall had been decorated beautifully; Evelyn had helped with a lot of it. She loved crafting, something that she hadn't shared with her friends. She'd once wanted to either own a craft store or be an interior decorator. Eric had come along before she had the chance to establish either dream, so she'd been delighted to assist Marissa in decorating the banquet hall. The end product was breathtaking.

Paige nibbled at her food, because if she devoured the grilled chicken dish to her heart's content, the dress would probably split down the middle. She was focused on her plate when a shadow fell over her and a voice asked, "Care to cut the rug with a shabby ole' teacher? Back in the day, I used to have some pretty good skills on the dance floor, you know."

She lifted her eyes and tried to hold back a smile. "No, I didn't know that."

He took her hand in his and pulled her out of her chair. "Well, let me show you."

Marissa cupped her hands around her mouth and hooted. "You go girl!" she shouted at Paige.

Paige glanced over her shoulder and stuck out her tongue. She allowed Ethan to pull her against him and lead them into a slow two-step.

Deana and Rich danced beside them. She lifted her head from Rich's shoulder and waved at Paige. "I owe you big for introducing me to him," she said, looking the happiest and most beautiful Paige had ever seen her. Her dark hair was pulled back with a pearl hairclip and curly tendrils framed her face. She looked softer than usual, more feminine.

"You don't owe me a thing," Paige assured, shivering as Ethan's hand settled at her back.

Evelyn was the only bridesmaid to show up dateless, but she was truly happy. She was at a point where she knew she didn't need a man in her life to achieve contentment or success. Knowing that had her beaming.

Marissa took Evelyn's hand and escorted her to the dance floor.

Shane stood at the wedding party's table bellowing, "But I thought I had the first dance! What the fuck happened to that?"

Deana and Paige watched as Marissa and Evelyn stepped onto the floor. Shane soon followed, and soon they were all dancing, occasionally switching partners.

Olivia skidded onto the floor and jumped into the middle of the chaos.

Shane took the little girl's hands and danced with her.

Ethan laughed and shook his head. He turned his eyes to the woman in his arms and he rested his chin on top of her head. "I'm happy right now," he told her, holding her tighter against him.

She squeezed his hand. "So am I."

"I love you, Ms. Turner."

"And I love you, Mr. Carson."

"Don't make a habit of calling me that…it'll bring up old memories."

"And we don't want to do that," she said, pulling back slightly and looking up at him. There was a teasing glint in her eyes.

He smiled. "No, we don't."

She laid her head on his shoulder. "So, I was just wondering…"

"Yeah?"

"Say we get married."

He started laughing.

"This is hypothetical," she clarified quickly, "but say we did get married. And people asked us where we met."

His laughing only intensified.

"Seriously. What should we tell them?"

"The truth."

"Really?" She pulled back again and gave him a concerned look. "How would you word it?"

"Easy." He let a finger trail down her cheek to her chin and from there down her neck until it rested on her creamy bare shoulder. "I would tell whoever asked that I met you in my dreams."

At first she couldn't tell whether he was joking or serious, but it didn't take long for her to reach a conclusion. "You're full of shit, Carson," she muttered shortly before leaning her head against his chest.

He chuckled low, a deep rumble that made his chest vibrate beneath her cheek. "I resemble that remark."

She stood on tiptoe to kiss his nose. "I know you do."

He angled his face so that their lips met and took her breath away. Their surroundings faded, the sounds of the mingling guests faded, until they were the only ones in the room. He only saw her. And he saw *her*...not the teenager he'd known what now seemed like ages ago. When he looked at her, he saw Paige Turner, one of the most beautiful and incredible women he'd ever met in his entire life. And he vowed to never let her slip from his grasp ever again.

www.ingramcontent.com/pod-product-compliance
Lightning Source LLC
Chambersburg PA
CBHW070534260626
47161CB00002B/382